One With the Music
Cape Breton Step Dancing
Tradition and Transmission

Mats Melin

CAPE BRETON UNIVERSITY PRESS
SYDNEY, NOVA SCOTIA

Cape Breton University Press recognizes the support of the Province of Nova Scotia and the support received for its publishing program from the Canada Council for the Arts Block Grants Program. We are pleased to work in partnership with these bodies to develop and promote our cultural resources.

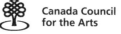 Canada Council for the Arts   Conseil des Arts du Canada

 NOVA SCOTIA

Author photo: Ingrid Melin
Cover design: Cathy MacLean Design, Chéticamp, NS
Layout: Mike Hunter, Port Hawkesbury and Sydney, NS
Copyediting: Laura Bast, Toronto, ON; Robbie McCaw, Ottawa, ON.
First printed in Canada.

Library and Archives Canada Cataloguing in Publication

Melin, Mats, author
     One with the music : Cape Breton step dance tradition and transmission / Mats Melin.

Includes bibliographical references and index.
Issued in print and electronic formats.
ISBN 978-1-77206-028-7 (paperback).--ISBN 978-1-77206-030-0 (epub).-- ISBN 978-1-77206-031-7 (kindle).--ISBN 978-1-77206-029-4 (pdf)

     1. Step dancing--Nova Scotia--Cape Breton Island. 2. Step dance music--Nova Scotia--Cape Breton Island. 3. Cape Breton Island (N.S.)-- Social life and customs. I. Title.

GV1793.M44 2015   793.3'197169   C2015-905642-X
                                                C2015-905643-8

Cape Breton University Press
1250 Grand Lake Road
Sydney, NS B1P 6L2 CA
www.cbupress.ca

Table of Contents

*To my family, my mother
and to the dance and music community of Cape Breton*

and in memory of my father, Gösta Melin (1931-2015)

Acknowledgements

The research and writing of any study could be a lonely process, but not in this case. I have had the good fortune to have had the fantastic assistance of many wonderful people over the years, particularly for this study since 1992. In totality you are all too many to mention by name but none of you are forgotten!

Travelling around Cape Breton Island over the years I have been fortunate to stay with people in the community who welcomed me into their homes, which provided friendship and a better understanding of Cape Breton life in general. In no particular order unreserved gratitude goes to: Scott Macmillan and Jennyfer Brickenden for letting me spend time in "Minnie's" house near Brook Village and in Halifax; Derrick and Melody Cameron and the Cameron family, West Mabou; Mary Janet MacDonald and family, Port Hood, for steps in the kitchen on my honeymoon, in 1995, for your continued hospitality and encouragement, and for introducing us to "Mama," the late Maggie Ann Beaton, and to your sister by adoption Minnie (MacMaster) and her wonderful family. Thanks also to: Fr. Angus Morris, Mabou, for support and hospitality over the years; Jenny and Lester Tingley, Boularderie; the Aucoin family, Sydney Mines; the Fraser family, Sydney Mines; Jean and Columba MacNeil and the Barra MacNeil's of Sydney Mines; Jan Vickers, Baddeck; the MacQuarrie family, Inverside; Margaret Gillis, Gillisdale and Halifax; Chris McDonald and Heather Sparling, Sydney; the Metcalf family, Boston; Leanne Aucoin and Jesse Lewis for great friendship and hospitality in Halifax and in Ireland; the Greenwell family, Mabou; and to Harvey Beaton and family, Dartmouth for showing me my first Cape Breton steps all those years ago.

Special thanks to all the dancers and musicians listed as primary sources in the references section, who allowed me to interview and film them and who all shared their experiences. Others were helpful in many ways for my more extensive PhD research; so, in addition, I am grateful to: Kinnon and Betty Lou Beaton, Margie Beaton, Kimberley Fraser, the late Willie Francis Fraser and his daughters Maureen and Clare, the late Jerry Holland; Mike Kennedy, Barbara Le Blanc, Kelly MacArthur, Troy MacGillivray, Burton MacIntyre, Paul

M. MacDonald, Alexander MacDonnell, Mary Elizabeth MacInnes, Joe Peter MacLean, Kelly MacLennan, Lisa Gallant MacNeil and Fr. Eugene Morris. This list could be made a mile long and please accept my apologies if you are not mentioned – you are not forgotten.

Thank you to all the staff and archivists at the Celtic Music Interpretive Centre, Judique, Kinnon Beaton and Allan Dewar in particular; and to Catherine Arseneau and all the staff at the Beaton Institute, Cape Breton University (CBU), Sydney. For the encouragement and assistance of Richard MacKinnon, Heather Sparling, Chris McDonald, Ian Brodie and Sheldon MacInnes at the Centre for Cape Breton studies, Department of History and Culture, CBU. Thanks to Rodney MacDonald and the staff and tutors at the Colaisde na Gàidhlig / The Gaelic College, St. Ann's, and to Nova Scotia Museum for the kind permission to use the maps from Michael Kennedy's invaluable report (2002).

Thank you to Celtic Colours International Festival executive director Joella Foulds, artistic Director Dawn Beaton and media and information officer Dave Mahalik of the for photography, filming and interview access.

My gratitude goes out to Dawn and Margie Beaton, Derrick Cameron, Darcy J. Campbell, Margaret Dunn, Jackie Dunn-MacIsaac, Victor Maurice Faubert, Mary Janet MacDonald and John MacLean for the use of photographs.

Thank you to Frank Rhodes, for access to his original notes and memories from his 1957 visit to Cape Breton, and Chris Metherell for the advice and help with Newcastle Notation. Thanks to Jennifer Schoonover for detailed content advice and encouragement, Colin Robertson for encouragement, Alasdair MacMhaoirn and Màiri Britton for advice in Gaelic-language matters.

Thank you to all my current and past colleagues at the Irish World Academy for their support and encouragement over the years, in particular to Aileen Dillane, Jane Edwards, Catherine Foley (my PhD supervisor), Simon Gilbertson, Sandra Joyce, Niall Keegan, Orfhlaith Ní Bhriain, Micheál Ó Súilleabháin and Colin Quigley. Also grateful thanks goes to the international office and Patricia O'Flaherty at the University of Limerick.

I am very grateful to the editor Mike Hunter and Cape Breton University Press for believing in this project and for the excellent initial editing help of Laura Bast.

Finally, I could not have done any of this if it was not for the moral and patient support of my family, my wife Emma, to my three children, Solveig, Ingrid and Magnus, Gösta and Mona Melin and to Robert and Eivor Cormack.

And finally, a huge vote of thanks goes to the Cape Breton community – thank you all for allowing me to share your wonderful music and dance culture. It "nourishes" me to this day, to use an expression I picked up somewhere along the way!

M.M.

Foreword

I no longer remember when or how I met Mats, but I do know that as long as we've been in touch, we've shared a deep interest in, and passion for, traditional Gaelic culture in Cape Breton. Mats has always supported my research and when discussing my work on *puirt-a-beul* (Gaelic "mouth music"), he told me one of the most compelling stories about the interactions between language, music, song and dance. In 1996, while performing at the first Ceòlas, a traditional music and dance festival in South Uist, he asked Gaelic singer Wilma Kennedy to sing some *puirt-a-beul* to accompany a traditional Scottish step dance at a house ceilidh. Not knowing what the affiliated Gaelic song was supposed to be, he asked her to sing a slow reel. It didn't exactly fit the dance, but they made it work. The next night, Wilma Kennedy performed a set of *puirt-a-beul* in a concert. Mats was amazed when one of the *puirt* she sang seemed to match the rhythms of the dance he had performed the previous evening. The following morning, he found Wilma and had her sing the tune while he danced. The hairs on both their necks stood on end as the tune's rhythms perfectly matched those of the dance. It turned out that Wilma's great-grand uncle had learned the *port-a-beul* (singular of *puirt-a-beul*), called "Nighean Dhòmhn'ill 'c Dhonnchaidh" ("An Tàillear Mòr" (the Big Tailor)) while working in South Uist, the place from which the dance, known as "An Latha Lùnastail" (the First of August) had come.

Aside from whatever scholarly insights this story reveals, for me it evokes Mats' deep knowledge of traditional Scottish dance; his career as a professional dancer; his extensive network with singers, musicians, and dancers on both sides of the Atlantic; his collaborative, inductive approach to learning about the dance traditions he loves; and the gleeful excitement ignited in him when all these elements come together.

As a scholar of traditional music, song and dance in Cape Breton, I've been waiting for someone to write a study of step dance for a long time. So, upon learning that Mats was planning to write this book, the first thing I thought was, thank goodness!

I was glad that the author would be Mats. There are few other scholars who are as qualified to write a book about traditional Cape

Breton step dance. After years as a professional dancer in Scotland, touring with Dannsa (the Gaelic word for "dance"), a group that researches traditional dance in Scotland in order to perform and promote it throughout the country, Mats moved to Ireland and began work with the University of Limerick's innovative and influential Irish World Academy of Music and Dance. There, he completed his MA thesis about Cape Breton step dance's connection to traditional dance in Scotland from a Scottish perspective. Several years later, he completed his PhD dissertation about how Cape Breton step dance is learned and taught, formally and informally, and how these processes have changed over the decades. It is this research that informs the book you now hold.

As part of his research, Mats came to Cape Breton on many, many occasions. He has performed in the Celtic Colours International Festival, one of the biggest Celtic festivals in the world. He's interviewed dozens of the best-known dancers. He's watched innumerable concerts and studied mounds of video footage. He's painstakingly transcribed dance steps using a special notation system (more-or-less the dance equivalent of musical notation) to facilitate analysis and to document steps for future study.

As a result of all this fieldwork, I don't think anyone in the local traditional music and dance scene is unfamiliar with Mats. In fact, he's generally held in very high regard and his knowledge is deeply respected. And that's saying something in a community with so many very articulate and knowledgeable tradition bearers. There have been many times when I've been working with local musicians and dancers, asking questions and mulling over issues, that I've been advised to ask Mats. If anyone knows, they say, he'll know.

The respect and fondness with which local dancers and musicians speak of Mats is very telling. He is not just a scholar to them; he is their friend. Friendship is a good part of what makes this book so compelling, for friendship opens doors. Through friendships, Mats has come to unique insights and understandings about how step dance has been and is transmitted today. At the core of any tradition are relationships, and without being enmeshed in those relationships, no study of traditional culture is likely to be successful. Mats' deep passion for the dance and his love for his friends and the dance community on this island are evident in the respectful way he writes about dance in Cape Breton. This is not an inaccessible, dry, scholarly dissertation about dance in Cape Breton. It is, rather, a warm, generous and thoughtful gift to the community, allowing us to benefit from Mats' profound understanding not just of Cape Breton dance, but of Scottish dance, dance scholarship and analysis more broadly.

Heather Sparling, PhD
Canada Research Chair in Musical Traditions
Cape Breton University

—

Cape Breton is a culturally rich and interesting corner of our world, thanks in no small part to the thousands of Scots who came here a long time ago. Those Scottish settlers who arrived here during the 19th century, many as casualties of the Highland Clearances, came with few material things (what choice did they have?). But what they may have lacked in terms of physical goods, they possessed an abundance of rich, cultural tradition and tangible ties to the old country: their language, their music and, of course, their dance. With few musical instruments by their side, accessible forms of cultural demonstration were fundamental, especially at a time of great upheaval. Language and dance were therefore important examples of cultural memory. Our Cape Breton ancestors were prideful people and ensured their greatest jewels were passed down with intent and honesty to the gift that was given them.

There are many dancers today that can name a long line of aunts, uncles, grandparents and great-great grand folks who had a penchant for dancing. It was said that to perform at a community picnic or perform the Scotch Four was reserved for only the best dancers. Like the priest or fiddler in the community, great esteem was reserved for a fine dancer; one that showcased impeccable timing and great rhythm in response to the tune of the fiddle or bagpipes – neat and tidy, close to the floor. Smartly dressed with a shine on the shoes, the dancers of the past also reserved reverence for the art form in their own presentation of it—a sign of respect.

We are at an interesting crossroads in the study of Cape Breton music and dance. With elders rich in the culture still at our disposal, we have the means to capture, record and document our culture as it stands now. Although we lose significant tradition bearers each year, many have made great inroads in learning direct from them. But will the next generation have a similar application and spend the time with our elders to properly grasp the language, to associate stories with the origins of those rarely heard fiddle or pipe tunes, or to understand the origins of why a square set embodied the regional qualities that it did? That will be for our descendants to ensure, despite what technology and other distractions might hold for us today.

In the past, without the modern tools to record and disseminate songs, tunes and dance steps, we rely on the aural and oral traditions passed along to us, to ensure their accuracy over time. Oh, how we could have used video capture in those days, to appreciate the finesse our older generations brought to the dance and the stylistic qualities we can only hope we are capturing today. In the absence of such technologies, it is scholars and passionate people like Mats Melin that bring attention and much needed research and collaboration to "check in" on the evolution of this physical, cultural and social expression.

Dance is a beautiful art form that we are all capable of. I hope you enjoy the journey this book takes you on, the way the history of this land and its dance has taken Mats on.

Dawn Beaton
Artistic Director, Celtic Colours International Festival

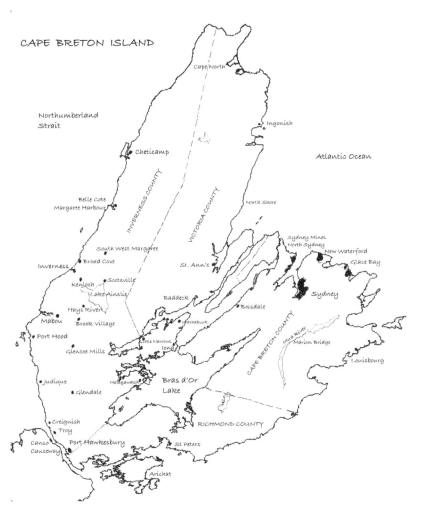

CAPE BRETON ISLAND

Cape North

Northumberland Strait

Ingonish

Cheticamp

Atlantic Ocean

INVERNESS COUNTY

VICTORIA COUNTY

Belle Cote
Margaree Harbour

North Shore

South West Margaree

Sydney Mines
North Sydney
New Waterford
Glace Bay

Broad Cove

Inverness

St. Ann's

Kenloch
Scotsville
Lake Ainslie

Sydney

Baddeck

Boisdale

Hays River

Brook Village

Washabuck

Mabou

CAPE BRETON COUNTY

Port Hood

Little Narrows
Iona

Mira River
Marion Bridge

Glencoe Mills

Louisbourg

Judique

Madagawatch

Bras d'Or Lake

Glendale

RICHMOND COUNTY

Creignish
Troy

Canso
Causeway

Port Hawkesbury

St Peters

Arichat

Map provided by Mats Melin.

Chapter 1

A Journey of Discovery: Aesthetic Qualities and Transmission Processes in Cape Breton Step Dancing

A dancer steps up onto the small wooden platform placed along the side of an outdoor marquee tent erected in the courtyard of an old barn building. It is a warm summer's evening in July, and the marquee is packed with close to a hundred people, most of whom are music and dance enthusiasts. They have travelled here to learn tunes, new fiddle techniques and to step dance. The fiddler moves to stand next to the platform as he starts playing and turns slightly to enable him to see the dancer properly. The music is a fast-paced, 4/4-time strathspey and the dancer responds to the music only a few bars into the melody. The dancer calmly holds himself erect with his arms held relaxed down by his sides. His eyes are fixed forward but at the same time he keeps an eye occasionally on the fiddler. His body hardly moves up or down but seems to float effortlessly as his feet beat out rhythms that match the melody to perfection—rhythmic patterns that respond to the essence of the tune. The atmosphere is as electric as the warm, humid air in the marquee with an added occasional whiff of the outside night air wafting in through the openings in the marquee walls. The fiddler, after about a minute or so, changes pace and enters into a reel played with a lot of groove and rhythm. The dancer follows suit and produces step after intricate step, still matching the meanderings of the melody line as if the fiddler and dancer were one. The energy between them seems to build and build, and the audience can feel, see and hear it. There is no leader or follower between the two performing bodies. They are acting as parts of one expression. The high-energy melody is coming to an end; the dancer performs a short series of movements that seem to signal "this is almost the end, I am ready to stop." The fiddler and dancer finish together. The dancer nods with a smile to the audience and steps down off the stage as the fiddler starts walking back to his seat with a wave and a smile to the crowd. The space erupts in thunderous applause and encouraging cheers for more.

Encountering Cape Breton Step Dance

This was the first time I ever saw Cape Breton step dancing performed and it had a huge impact on me. I felt immediately that this
was something I wanted to learn. It was what I had subconsciously
been searching for, for many years, but had been unable to access or
know. At that moment I also felt it would be a challenge to learn, since
percussive dance in this particular style was truly unknown to me.
The moments—really just three minutes out of my life—took place the
evening of July 6, 1992, at Sabhal Mòr Ostaig (the Gaelic university)
on the Isle of Skye, Scotland, overlooking the Sound of Sleat across
to the Moidart and Morar areas on the mainland of the Scottish west
coast. The dancer extraordinaire in question was Harvey Beaton,
the master fiddler was Buddy MacMaster, both fairly unknown to
me at the time, although this would change. The performance was
part of the kick-off concert for Scottish (but California-based) fiddler
Alasdair Fraser's new venture, a weeklong summer school in Scottish/
Cape Breton fiddle music, which emphasized Cape Breton–style step
dancing as an integral part of the soundscape and culture to be shared
and explored. Fraser's annual summer school is still running, even
though the format has changed and dance has not been featured for a
number of years. Still, the longevity of the course bears testimony to
Fraser's initial idea of fully integrating music and dance, which was
the core theme for some fifteen years.

For most participants, Scots and visitors like myself, the sound of
Cape Breton fiddle music and the style of step dancing was a novelty
at the time. Only a handful in attendance had heard or seen it before.
As a soundscape and dance style, it was different from most of the
audience's previous experience, but also very exciting. Most of us
wanted to learn the unfamiliar steps and have further opportunities
to dance this way. Some of us also wanted to someday explore Cape
Breton Island itself, just off the northern tip of Canada's easternmost
province, Nova Scotia.[1] The following four days were jam-packed with
classes and concerts, and this was to be the beginning of my twenty-
three-year journey into the aesthetic qualities of Cape Breton step
dancing, toward a deeper understanding of the verbal and non-verbal
transmission processes contained therein. That week I learned to
admire the talent and respect the humble nature of gentlemen such as
Harvey and Buddy (as I have come to know them, indeed as everyone

knows them). They were the first of many Cape Bretoners that I have since gotten to know, learn from and generally share music, dance and life experiences with. Aspects of what I have learned about Cape Breton culture, and step dancing in particular, over this period of time forms the content of this book.

Searching for a Meaningful Research Focus

This is a study focusing on how aesthetic preferences and step-dance movements are maintained, undergo change and are transmitted within the Cape Breton music and dance community. It is done with as much of an *insider* understanding as is possible for an outside observer and practitioner to appreciate. A study like this is not straightforward, and to find a focus or essence that has meaning to both the researcher and subject takes a bit of investigation. As an outsider to the Cape Breton community, a level of cultural appreciation—both general and specific to dance and music—must be achieved, and that is not without obstacles. This appreciation is in turn reflected by my personal relationship with the place, Cape Breton, itself as much as the people who live there, and it is also a reflection on my prior dance and music knowledge. One obstacle I encountered early on was the realization that to understand the place, one must appreciate the complex web of family ties (by blood or by marriage) in the community.

As a visitor with a limited window of time and opportunity, one quickly comes to recognize that only certain levels of this community web can be realized and understood on a personal level. One must also take into account historical factors of the different cultural groups—Scots, Irish, English, French Acadian, Mi'kmaq and so forth—who settled and now live side-by-side, creating a unique social environment. Also, the strong Scottish Gaelic influence on the island from a linguistic and cultural heritage point of view has to be taken into account. The Scottish Gaelic heritage and traditions feature predominantly in my research, primarily due to my previous experience with Scottish dance, which in turn led me to focus on this particular group of Cape Bretoners.[2] Before looking specifically at the aims and issues of this book, and the methods I used to gather the information, it is useful, I think, to place my own relationship with music and dance in relation to that of the Cape Breton community.

Who Am I?

I was born and grew up in Stockholm, Sweden, in the late 1960s and early 1970s, in a home environment where there was neither live music nor dancing. Swedish traditional music was featured on the radio, and traditional dance occurred occasionally in school, on television or during festive seasons such as midsummer and Christmas. It was not a prominent feature in my life but, in time, other soundscapes and cultures began to fascinate me. By the age of ten I had found an interest in all things Scottish, particularly pipe music, but I was not able to access this in person. When I was about twelve years old, I encountered Scottish country and Highland dancing by pure chance. Initially, I was taught these dance forms by an immigrant Australian Scot, Don Gilliam, whom I now know is also an authority on Swedish polska dancing. Many other teachers were to follow, some Swedish but also many visiting Scottish ones.

From then on, my interest in Scottish dance widened and deepened, and I also learned some Irish and Swedish dance. However, my main dance focus growing up was always Scottish dance, and between ages fifteen and twenty, I travelled to Scotland on numerous occasions to explore both solo and social dancing in the West Highlands and the Hebrides. I attended summer dance schools in various places around Scotland. I learned Orkney and Shetland dancing from dancers who had in turn learned from the dance researcher and English mathematician Tom Flett. I researched and learned all I could about Scottish social dances, going to rural dance halls, where the dancing did not necessarily reflect the formal class structures I encountered when learning Scottish Highland and country dancing through organization-run classes in Scotland, Sweden, and further afield in Canada and New Zealand.

As my experience of Scottish dance matured, a number of questions began formulating in my mind. Why was there was so little evidence of percussive dancing in a footwork tradition that would better reflect and interact with the music than the forms of dancing primarily promoted by dance organizations in present-day Scotland? I found a few scattered references to percussive dance in the scholarly works of Flett and Flett (1985 [1964]) and Emmerson (1972), primarily, but there was no evidence readily available of anything similar to the various forms of percussive dance found, for example, in Ireland.

As this was in the days before the Internet, finding information about Canadian or other North American percussive dance forms for comparison was difficult.

Another question I had concerned which mechanisms had shaped the development of the aesthetic preferences that formed the basis for the current styles of Highland and Scottish country dancing. I began to question some of the official explanations of the meanings of the dances, which were often shrouded in some form of mythical story, offered by manuals and the teachings of established dance organizations. Later, I also began to query the efficiencies of how aspects of Scottish dance were taught according to the rules and regulations laid down by these organizations. I often felt that what was taught lacked depth due to a methodology of teaching that favoured technique and patterns of dance rather than musicality, meaning and feeling. There were, of course, teachers who did offer a more layered approach, and I took note of their excellence in passing on movement-based knowledge.

In the late 1970s, when I started taking formal dance classes in Scottish country and Highland dancing in Sweden, we learned through a combination of verbal instruction and visually copying what the teacher was doing. I cannot recall anyone saying anything about how one should feel when doing a movement, encouraging proprioception or how to achieve a continuous flow of movement. The transmission process was firmly based on formal instruction as developed by dance organizations. Even country dancing was regulated, with the way to do the dances correctly printed in manuals, and, as indicated above, the instructional emphasis was on floor patterns and correct performance of steps.

When I first encountered Harvey Beaton in 1992 he taught in a workshop/classroom environment. The movements shown were delineated, but in a decidedly different teaching philosophy. Here, individuality and improvisation were discussed and encouraged. Not forcefully, but in a subtle way. As the students kept asking which way was the "correct" way, the answer was always that it was the timing and musicality of the dancing that mattered most. There was no standardized syllabus to follow, nor was there a competitive scenario involved in the practice. The exact position of one's foot was not emphasized. In fact, we were encouraged to find a personal way of dancing, as our own bodies dictated, while keeping to certain criteria, such as dancing lightly, keeping "close to the floor," keeping our feet fairly close together, "dancing from the knees down" and "keeping good time with the music."

It was clear that the aesthetic preferences were quite different in Cape Breton step dancing. This way of teaching initially took some getting used to—as did the notion that it was all right not to dance a predetermined routine. Improvising and adding "your own being" to the style was part of the preferred aesthetic. Now, upon reflection and recognition of the way I had been conditioned to a particular way of learning, the experience was quite inspiring. I did, however, also notice that Harvey alluded to levels of meaning in this dance form that I could only begin to guess at. It was only when I travelled to Cape Breton in the summer of 1995, to experience the dancing in its original context, that I began to appreciate that the transmission of this dance genre was happening on sensory levels I had not consciously encountered, or thought much about before. There was a verbal, but possibly even stronger non-verbal, consciousness of visual, aural and kinaesthetic, or felt, transmission processes.[3] I expect that some readers will identify and be familiar with one or the other (or possibly both) scenarios of learning, but highlighting this difference is, I think, vital to better understanding the following description on how aspects of dance transmission in Cape Breton occur.

Scope and Issues

A study of Cape Breton step-dance transmission through both a practical and an academic approach—how it is transmitted within the community, from person to person, and how it is embodied by the individual through visual, aural and kinaesthetic means—has never been done. Nor have the various Cape Breton communities' aesthetic preferences been analyzed in detail with regard to dance. By critically engaging with the subject matter, I took into account both living memory and written historical accounts, and conducted my own observations of the current dance practice and compared it to film taken in the past thirty years or so. The combined data provided me with a picture of a dance tradition that enabled me to illustrate the above focus from about 1970 to 2012, with some material dating to the early 20th century.

The featured interviews and dance commentary in Allister MacGillivray's (1988) *Cape Breton Ceilidh*, for example, allow voices in the local dance community to express what is important to them in their dance tradition. It shares memories of different ways of learning to dance, how the community's aesthetic preferences are reinforced both verbally and non-verbally. Their stories shed light on the level of importance an integrated relationship the local music tradition on their step dancing. The impact of the decline of the Gaelic language also emerges, but illustrates at the same time how the essence of that language is felt to survive within their music and dancing.

The stories told share levels of meaning that are understood locally, but which dance notation is unable to convey. This study aims to partly answer what it feels, looks and sounds like to dance "in the Cape Breton way." It conveys what aesthetic criteria are kept in mind at each performance occasion by dancer and community alike. The first academic and analytical study of Cape Breton dance concentrated on aspects of the Scots Gaelic diasporic dance tradition and was conducted by Frank Rhodes in 1957 (Rhodes 1985, 1996). Rhodes contextualized the Gaelic dance tradition in Cape Breton and gave detailed descriptions of steps and dances he had observed in the form of a word-based dance notation, recording them for posterity. Rhodes's contribution is invaluable as there is no other known notation or archival film of Cape Breton dance from that point in time. Without it, we would not now know as much as we do about certain dances and the dance tradition of late-1950s Cape Breton.

A number of other written works feature as sources on the island dance tradition in this book, but they focus primarily on the music tradition; dance plays second fiddle, as it were. My primary aim here is to highlight the local people's experience of their own dance traditions and let their words illustrate what has meaning and importance to them.

I notated numerous filmed dance sequences in the course of my studies. In part, it was to answer another question of mine, one that came out of a conversation with Harvey Beaton in one of his 1992 workshop classes. He said that most dancers improvised their dancing around a core set of steps. What this core set of steps was, Harvey did not define at the time. So, when I began looking at how dance material is transmitted, I also naturally asked what movements are transmitted. What are the most common motifs, or steps, used by Cape Breton step dancers? What do they have in common that could possibly be equated to this core set of steps? Some of my step notations will play a role in this book as they illustrate certain aesthetic points (see chapter 6), but for future reference some of them will be available online. They were already included in my PhD dissertation (Melin 2012), *Exploring the Percussive Routes and Shared Commonalities in Cape Breton Step Dancing*, which is also available online.[4]

Where I Focused My Dance Observations

To illustrate how dance is transmitted and maintained in Cape Breton, I draw from the four most common dance and music locales on the island: the home, the dance class, the community concert and the square dance. All were equally accessible to me, though it must be said that experiencing the home context is, for the outside observer and learner, the most privileged one to be part of. All these locales are inextricably interconnected, but stand out individually as providing slightly different transmission opportunities, as will be discussed in the coming chapters. Visual, aural and kinaesthetic transmission of dance knowledge occurs in all four social locales and naturally overlaps, but a different emphasis is placed on transmission processes at work in each one due to the contexts in which they occur. The recollections provided by community members often fuse one locale with another: someone may not remember whether he or she saw (and often also heard) a dancer at a concert, class or square dance. It is therefore difficult to separate one locale fully from another; indeed, it would be counterproductive to try to do so, as the overall context encompasses all the parts to form a whole. Due to this, I will use "context" to encompass both locale and the conditions in which dancing occurs. In addition, even though social and solo step dancing are interconnected, I focus mainly on the latter.

For most, but not all, of the people featured in this book, the home was the initial and most influential of the four contexts. For many of the younger dancers, as well as some of the older ones, the dance hall, the formal dance class and the local concert had equally high impacts on fostering interest in the dance genre.

Using the Body to Exemplify Experience

By reflexively referring to my own experience in these contexts I aim to further enhance the understanding of an outsider's view of them. I also try to meaningfully emphasize what was pointed out to me as essential aspects of the dance tradition by community members as they occurred in each locale.

During my first visit to Cape Breton, the importance of the transmission of dance in the home became immediately apparent. When my wife, Emma, and I arrived in Mabou in 1995 on our honeymoon, we asked some local residents where we could find information about music and dance events in the area. We were advised at a local gallery to go and see Fr. Angus Morris at the glebe house at St. Mary's Church. We followed directions and, just before lunchtime, we found him in his office. After having introduced ourselves, we told Fr. Angus what we were looking for. He smiled wryly and, with a glint in his eye, said, "Music and dance. Around here? No such thing.... Come on through to the kitchen." As we got into his kitchen, he took his fiddle out, plucked the strings to check the tuning and said, "Okay, show me what you can do." He struck up a slow tune, a strathspey, and we took turns dancing, and as he went into reel time we continued until he was satisfied. We somehow passed a test, and the rest of our visit, armed with Fr. Angus's advice and many recommendations, was filled with music and dance. Since then, I have learned that Fr. Angus and his brother, Fr. Eugene Morris, are highly regarded in Cape Breton as champions of the fiddle and step-dancing traditions respectively. That our initiation to dance in Cape Breton took place in Fr. Angus's kitchen was not strange to us, as we had encountered similar scenarios in both Scotland and Ireland. The kitchen, in Highland Gaelic society in particular, is a natural meeting point, where often a ceilidh or party is held, as described in chapter 2 (see also Melin 2006).

A few days later, when spending an evening in Port Hood in dancer Mary Janet MacDonald's kitchen, we were discussing local dancing and sharing some steps when one of her children came home. On entering the kitchen, whether detecting what the conversation was about or just by routine, he did a few dance movements in passing through. It occurred to me later that, as the kitchen was the place where you "picked up" steps, just as I was doing, this was a natural place to subconsciously reinforce your embodied knowledge.

Again, after another few days, this time in dancer Jean MacNeil's home, in Sydney Mines, I noticed a worn patch on the wooden floor in the hall, which I commented on. This was the place where her children (many of whom are members of the music and dance group the Barra MacNeils) practised their step dancing as they grew up, I was told. Jean would be in the kitchen showing them and correcting them as they took turns dancing, while the other siblings took turns on various instruments they played in the adjoining sitting room. Music and dance was a natural and everyday occurrence in the household.

Later, while staying at a bed and breakfast on a farm near Mabou, the owners were going away for the evening and left my wife and me in charge of the house, as we were the only guests that night. Upon leaving, they said, "We gather you are going to the dance tonight, but before you go, we have asked fiddler Willie Kennedy to come down and have a tune with you." At this point I did not know the significance of Willie Kennedy's position as fiddler and tradition bearer in the Cape Breton community. Not knowing him did not stop us from getting along just fine. Willie played some great sets of tunes and made us feel at ease. In between listening and chatting, my wife and I took turns step dancing. Willie, like Mary Janet and Jean, gave the familiar advice that one should dance "lightly," keep "close to the floor," "dance from the knees down" and "keep good time with the music." It was a short and small ceilidh, but a fantastic way of getting into the mood to go square dancing. Of course, the evening's little ceilidh took place in the kitchen.

The flow of energy and the passion of the dance and music was transmitted from each of these four people—Fr. Angus, Mary Janet, Jean and Willie—as they shared their dance and music knowledge, gave us a soundscape to remember and, Mary Janet and Jean in particular, shared the dance with us in close proximity, making sure we got a feel for how they move themselves while dancing.

The significance of the classroom as a transmission context, which I alluded to at the top and show in depth in chapter 3, takes us to the changing nature of passing on dance skills in more formal and verbally guided ways compared with the often non-verbal learning in the home environment. Two areas of enquiry emerge: what changes take place in how and what dance knowledge is shared in a formal teacher–learner relationship, and how does this compare to the largely private and informal learning environment in the home? Equally, what learning practices remain more or less intact and get adapted to suit this new learning context?

The two main social events where dancing is an essential component on the Cape Breton calendar are community concerts and local square dances. Chapters 4 and 5 discuss these in detail, but their cultural significance became clear to me even on my first visit to the island. Attending a lunchtime concert at Le Gabriel Lounge in Chéticamp, in August 1995, featuring fiddler Natalie MacMaster, pianist Tracey Dares and guitarist Dave MacIsaac, I saw that audience members were encouraged to give a step and join in. At one point, tables and chairs were cleared from the floor in front of the stage, as someone had requested that the musicians play for a "square" of social dances. This "square set," as it is known, was very much part of the concert; the audience took an active part in the event. At the time, this was all new to me as something similar would rarely, if ever, occur in Scotland, where I was then living. Since then, I have become accustomed to this aspect of Cape Breton concerts, whether at the Doryman Beverage Room in Chéticamp, the Red Shoe pub in Mabou, or the Celtic Music Interpretive Centre in Judique, to name but a few venues.

Proximity of audience to performers is a key component in these cultural expressions as well, though the actual distance between audience and performer may not necessarily be an important factor. Observing dancing at, for example, the Chestico Days summer festival in Port Hood, the Big Pond Festival or the Broad Cove Scottish Concert, you get the feeling that whether people are close to or far from the dance, they still take it in fully with their senses. It seems that physical distance does not impede a sense of familiarity between the audience and performers. You may stand hundreds of feet away from the stage and overhear fairly personal comments about the performers on stage: "he/she dances just like his/her father/mother," or, "I remember seeing him/her as a little boy/girl performing.... Now he/she has the family style." The audience members are not silent onlookers. Cape Bretoners are informed participants who share, discuss and reinforce their connections to those who are sharing their steps or music on stage. I have been in discussions with audience members who have pointed out dancing they admire: "Look at how he/she holds him/herself," "watch the timing of the dancer," "this one has good neat steps." The eye is critical, but I have seldom heard disparaging remarks about the dancer. The closest I have heard was: "he/she is a wonderful person, but I do not like his/her style of dancing," a comment that separates the person from his or her performance style.

At square dances, the interconnectivity in tradition maintenance is perhaps experienced the strongest by an attending outsider. For a participant and observer of Cape Breton step dance, the close proximity of dancers and musicians to each other in one place, all of different ages and genders, enables you to experience individual interpretations of the dance culture. Square dances are occasions for sharing movement and music-making together, all the while maintaining the local tradition and keeping the coherence of the community alive.

As an outsider, I have found that at square dances all my senses holistically take in all aspects of the music and dance in context, and assist me to better understand the many ongoing processes of transmission. As spontaneous home ceilidhs only occur within certain families, and not as often as they once did, I feel the square dance is now the main platform for implicit transmission processes.

Regardless of whether the hall is crowded, the dancing itself is always intimate on one level. I refer to chapter 5 for a detailed outline of the organization and nature of the dancing at a square dance, but a few comments are warranted at this point. One is always in close proximity to other dancing bodies in square sets due to the nature of the dance. Whether it be your partner, your corner partner (i.e., the woman on the man's left in the set or circle formation), the other dancers in the set during a grand chain or when all dancers form a line to step dance in the reel section, you are touching other bodies, via hand-holds, swing-holds in reel time, or taking waltz-holds in the jig figure or in the Waltz. You physically feel how the other dancers move. As dancers hold hands in circles to step in the beginning of the jig figures, you pick up the movements of the people on either side of you. You also see the other dancing bodies moving and, of course, you hear the sound of their feet (and the music). Allowing your mind and senses to open up to take in all the information around you—visual, aural and kinaesthetic modalities—will inform your own being on a much deeper level than any formal teaching ever can.

One occasion stands out in my mind: Scotsville Hall, in Scotsville, on the island, in July 2007. Well into the evening, in one of the jig figures, I began to realize that as well as being aware of my own dancing and what choices of steps I was making, consciously and subconsciously,

I could feel the other dancers around me quite strongly with all my senses. The young woman on my right danced quite vigorously, while on my left, an older partner danced in a relaxed and graceful manner; all three of us performed characteristic jig-rhythm steps, but none of us used the same combination of movements. My partner to the right's hands were moving more compared to the relatively still hands of my partner to the left. We had movements in common, but individually danced differently. I also saw dancers who were positioned one dancer over on either side, and dancers directly across from me, though I couldn't hear them as the music was too loud. I could, however, sense their movements through sight and through our hands, which were joined together. For brief moments we all danced in unison, doing the same step, but frequently there were slight differences in timing among us all as we slightly shifted our own movement choices to reflect our own reactions to the music. I sensed that the preferences in style and aesthetics allowed for these individual differences, including my own choices (see chapter 6).

Through experiences like this, my sensory modalities—sight, touch, sound—informed me of other and further possibilities of execution within the tradition. The next time I am dancing the same step, I might try one of the movements I saw or felt the previous time to see if it suits me. In the process of embodying what I have seen, heard and felt, I adjust these movements to suit my own style. I will never dance as a Cape Bretoner does. I will always dance like myself, but I am informed by the movement patterns of others. When I waltz, I experience something similar each time I waltz with a different partner: How does my partner move to the music? What can I learn from her? How can my partner's movement pattern inform my own? In the line-up in the reel-time figure in the square set, you physically step dance while holding hands with other male dancers on either side of you if you are dancing the man's part. Their movements, sensed through my hands, inform me how they interpret the music and how they perform steps that I know (or sometimes don't). Again, the individuality of their dancing creates and reveals parameters within which the genre works, and gives me ideas about how to perform the same or similar movements the next time.

Sharing Individuality and Commonalities in Cape Breton Step Dance

During a square-dance evening there is often a break from social dancing, and the fiddler strikes up a strathspey. This is the signal inviting anyone who would like to show his or her solo dance steps to all present. This is the moment when I feel that dancers are "sharing" knowledge rather than performing. If you are tuned in, in the way described above, you are doing more than simply watching the performances.

This mediated kinaesthetic knowledge has provided me with a deeper sense of observation and a greater appreciation of the minute interpretative choices or variables made within a dance. Each dancer brings something different to the floor. Many dance similar steps, but each has a slightly different take on how to execute each movement. If the music is loud, you cannot always hear their feet but you can certainly sense them hitting or touching the floor. How much effort are dancers putting into the steps? How light are they? Are the steps reflecting the tune well? How do they hold themselves? What is their exact timing of certain movements? How quick was that particular shuffle? Do they create a tension between their step rhythm and the music rhythm? Are they dancing a routine or are they dancing "off the cuff"? You see a familiar step, but it is not done in the same way that you do it. What is different? Will you try this out later to see what it is like? You see a step you don't know. What is its rhythm? You memorize the rhythm then try and work it out later, replaying the performance in your mind's eye. Certain tunes stick in your mind—what steps did a dancer do particularly well to the tune? Maybe you will try something similar if the opportunity arises.

Besides appreciating these performances through sight, touch, sound and the more elusive sense of "hearing" with your body, which is picking up sound vibrations with your whole being (see chapter 2), you also appreciate them through the sense of smell, a powerful trigger of memory. A familiar scent—the people, heat, humidity, wooden floor, dust, outside scents or chill drafts coming through an open door—helps trigger specific memories of how somebody danced and/or played. At least it does for me. Similarly, the accompanying non-music sounds—of laughter, people talking, moving about; of doors opening and shutting, chairs scraping against the floor; of the bar area—all add to the sensoriscape that solidifies your memory of a community in action. Over time, the many sensory experiences blend together, providing different sensory memories that inform your own interaction with the culture.

It is at the square dance where I feel that I have possibly learned the most about how Cape Breton dancers move, their individual movements, and what they have in common. Depending on the moment, music and people around you, you can experience something very deep—and I have. Occasionally, it seems that those present all connect on a different plane; they enter another dimension where they all share that particular moment of music and dance. Frequently, when the fiddler is "drivin'er," when the music gets that particular swing or pulse, when a particular and popular tune is played, or when the fiddler picks a good step-dancing tune, an emotional crescendo can occur and dancers will shout their excitement. Some local dancers have described this moment as spiritual (Melin 2013b). However you describe it, it certainly is a powerful moment, and it certainly creates a strong connection between all those participating.

Community-Making: Cultural Meaning and Identity through Dance

When I began to critically observe and analyze Cape Breton step dancing in its various contexts in 2006, it became clear that the transmission of dance (and music) in Cape Breton occurs in community contexts that provide meaning, identity and cultural understanding to the participant.

This community holds the repositories of symbols or mental constructs that provide individuals with the means to perceive the boundaries of a particular social group (Cohen 1985: 12-19). Intergenerational and peer-to-peer transmission processes are of equal importance in Cape Breton. On the other hand, Marie McCarthy (1999: 186) points out that in Irish traditional music, "generational transmission ... is a primary site for inducting the young into a group's musical practices and traditions." In contrast to the Cape Breton scenario, McCarthy's and Kari Veblen's (1991) studies of traditional music transmission in Ireland outline a transition of music education (and what constitutes its repertoire) from "real live" community master/apprentice transmission to a national system of music education, "whose meaning is created around standardization and evaluation by examination and competition" (McCarthy 1999: 187). Issues of increased music literacy, emigration and cultural nationalism are among the reasons stated for "transforming the way learners experienced music as community and expanding the boundaries of music learning beyond the local and the personal" (187).

Veblen and McCarthy both highlight that little has been written on the processes of traditional learning, but Veblen points to Virginia Garrison (1985) as one of the few sources. Garrison's study of the transition of Cape Breton fiddle learning, from in the home in the past to formal fiddle classes at present, shows little transitional change in teaching practices and no development of a "national" system or standardization. In fact, most of the traditional ways of teaching—by listening, observing, being shown by a relative or family member and so forth—could, to some extent, be maintained when moved into the formal teaching context, albeit in a slightly different form.

The main differences pointed out by Garrison are that, in the formal setting, a non-relative was often the teacher, which creates a distance in the teacher/student relationship; learning by note was more common; there was an increase in the number of women playing; and there was often a transition from house party to concert stage as the first performance context for young players. The study noted that in recent teaching (from the mid-1970s onward) the aural skills and learning abilities of young players were significantly reduced, and there was a fear of these diminishing further (1985: 273-89).

Both Veblen and Garrison mention many musicians who insist that no one taught them to play, seeing themselves as self-taught, having just "picked it up." Comments made by many Cape Breton dancers in MacGillivray (1988) echo those sentiments. Irish musician and composer Mícheál Ó Súilleabháin, when interviewed by Veblen (1991: 12), highlights that teaching in formal contexts brings the learning process into consciousness, while in community-based and informal learning it remains on the subconscious level. Ó Súilleabháin likened this change from informal to formal learning to an "underground river, which has always been there but is only recently appearing above ground" (12). Veblen's study points out that formal teaching of Irish traditional music in Ireland began with non-relatives, itinerant musicians, so-called dancing masters and at hedge schools (rural, oral-based) (1991: 12; see also Foley 1988, 2013). In contrast, Cape Breton dancing masters taught locally and were seemingly well known by their pupils (Rhodes 1985, 1996). When formal classes in step dance began to be organized in the 1970s, the teachers were local, had little or no formal teaching experience, and thus brought and adapted their own traditionally based transmission methods into the classroom context.

Garrison pinpoints several key phrases or notions among the fiddlers she studied that characterized successful traditional learning and that are parallel to Cape Breton dance transmission. These were self-motivation, the love of music, the music, the sense of being responsible for one's own learning, and awareness of and determination to develop one's own "natural talent." She also maintains that these characteristics did not come about automatically, but that the rich cultural environment and context in which the learners lived both encouraged and, in a sense, even urged them to be developed (1985: 276). These characteristics are key when one looks at three interconnected transmission process modes in Cape Breton step dance: aural, visual and kinaesthetic.

In this section I have alluded to how I participate, observe and use my own body and senses to analyze and make sense of what is taking place in the Cape Breton dance community. I have also highlighted some aspects of differences in formal and informal transmission processes. Therefore, it is appropriate to briefly outline some of the methods I use in acquiring dance knowledge.

The Sociality of Step Dancing

Even though my primary focus is on solo step dancing, it is important to note that percussive footwork is very much integrated in social dancing, whether in old Highland Reels in the 19th century or square sets in the 20th and 21st centuries. In Cape Breton, dance and music are social activities that are only complete when shared with family or community members. The pleasure that people take in music and dance stems not only from the immediate moment it occurs, but also from the memory of similar occasions of music- and dance-making—a kind of "embodied curiosity," as American ethnomusicologist Jeff

Titon (2008: 31) puts it. This embodied curiosity is related to what ethnomusicologist Thomas Turino refers to, in music [read also dance], as "flow" or "optimal experience," using the terms coined by Hungarian psychologist Mihaly Csikszentmihalyi (1990), as a label for a heightened state of concentration, which increases the complexity and integration of the self (1990), referring to "individuals' developing psychic wholeness through artistic experiences" (Turino 2008: 4). My own experience (see appendix 2), and that of my sources, often relates to that feeling of timelessness that occurs during a peak moment when dancing or playing music. I would argue that this "flow" is strongly related to the transmitted flow of experienced visual, aural and kinaesthetic knowledge between bodies.

The reminiscences and reflections of the Cape Breton dancers I interviewed—recounted in a separate section of this book—give us insight not only into the transmission processes of dance, but also into the complex ways dance and music in Cape Breton are experienced as both a participatory and presentational performance, to again cite Turino. As he outlines, all actors are involved in some capacity in a participatory performance of dance and music, performing different roles. There is no performer/audience dichotomy; there are only active performers and potential performers. In this book, the home, the classroom and the square-dance contexts all fit this definition. To some extent the community concerts do as well, as anyone attending could potentially be asked to perform on stage.

Turino's other category of presentational performance of dance and music is probably best illustrated at the community concerts, where we have an audience who pay to see a select group of people perform, and who have prepared themselves for this performance. In the Cape Breton context, this group can, nonetheless, be rather fluid in its composition and can on occasion involve people who initially came to watch only. I would argue that the presentational performance also occurs when individuals get up to share their steps with the assembled crowd at a square dance or at a house party. Perhaps, even, the role of a teacher in demonstrating steps to a class is a form of prepared performance. These notions are well described by Turino (2008: 23-65) and are worthy of deeper study in themselves, but it is important to note that in the Cape Breton context there is no clear-cut dichotomy between the two notions, as both often occur simultaneously to some extent. It is in these contexts of participation and presentational performance that Cape Breton dance is realized and presented to us.

Music and Dance as an Emblem for the Community

One cannot ignore that the music and dance of Cape Breton are seen as a primary emblem of ethnic or community identity, which strengthens and reaffirms the same (Feintuch 2004b: 81), and Cape Bretoners express their distinctiveness through their particular style of performance. Anderson (1991) and Bhabha and Thompson (1994) discuss the performative act of expressing a particular style, whether imagined or constructed. They describe expression through performance as a dynamic and ongoing process of negotiations of transformation taking place both within the community and when a community relates their practice to the outside world.

Anthropologists such as Boas (1974), Radcliffe-Brown (1964) and Irish ethnochoreologist Foley (2011) have pointed out that group dancing plays an important role in the processes of generating community solidarity. In the context of Cape Breton dance, participants of varied ethnic and ancestral backgrounds share the same space in performing these cultural expressions and thus help maintain and negotiate the group cohesion, identity and difference.

A similar scenario to that in Cape Breton is described in Johanne Trew's (2009: 20-39) study of the Irish heritage of the Ottawa Valley. In reference to how community knowledge shapes identity, Trew points to what Clifford Geertz (1973) calls "local knowledge"—that great quantity of information that is not stored in official documents or histories—and to Michel Foucault (1980), who refers to this knowledge as "popular knowledge." Trew shows how centralizing powers or institutions have deemed this type of knowledge less important, perhaps partly for the innocent fact that it is easier to document and transmit formal, written histories than informal, oral ones (Foucault 1980; Crampton and Elden 2007; Trew 2009: 20-39). Today, however, as many researchers are increasingly using oral histories as source material, this type of knowledge is becoming more credible.

As Barbara Rendall (1996) says in her article "A Sense of Family," living in Cape Breton is like being part of one big family—language, customs and a shared history are experienced in relative geographic isolation, with an adjoining and often depressed economy. The people are proud of their place and are loath to leave when, for example, they are compelled to do so for economic reasons. It is a place of contradictions, where passionate rivalries exist between different parts of the island, or within Sydney, where Rendall says turf wars exist due to perceived favouritism, connections and politics. A polarization also exists between urban (the Sydney area) and rural Cape Breton along similar lines. Even in dance there is a notion that Sydney people dance differently than those on the rural west side of the island, but what the differences are is not easily expressed. I have come to interpret such simply as expressions of difference in personal taste in dancing, or as Rendall puts it, "This [rivalry] hardly seems in keeping with the larger Cape Breton sense of family unity—until you realize that these complaints are just textbook cases of sibling rivalry on a bigger scale" (192). Typically, if an outside force—the provincial government in Halifax, for example—raises an issue concerning Cape Breton, the island population closes ranks.

Tune and Music Genre Repertoire

Throughout this book, it is worth keeping in mind that the connection between tunes and dance steps—in particular, the 4/4-time tunes of the strathspey and reel kind—is decided by genre. The earlier association of particular tunes with certain dance routines is largely a thing of the past. Musicians today use a wide variety of traditional Scottish tunes and Gaelic *puirt-a-beul* ("mouth music") (which would have been the staple repertoire for the old Scotch four-handed and eight-handed Reels; see chapter 2) and new and locally composed tunes. In addition to these, tunes borrowed from neighbouring traditions, such as the Irish and French, have also been incorporated into the repertoire (see, for example, Paul M. MacDonald 1999). The expansion of tune repertoire is symbiotically linked to the introduction of Quadrilles and the need for a larger repertoire, particularly of jigs, than the earlier Reel-dance tradition had previously required (see chapter 5).[5] Tunes that are used vary in length from older pipe tunes and puirt-a-beul, where each part is four bars long (AABB=16 bars), to modern tunes, where the parts are eight bars long (AABB=32 bars). Sometimes, both of these are played as ABAB. There are three- and four-part tunes, as well as tunes where the parts are of unequal length, such as "Princess Royal" (A=eight bars, B=twelve bars). The number of repeats and the order of the tunes is never set, and the musicians are free to change tune at any moment. Dancers often refer to a tune as a "round" when discussing the length of the piece of music to which they want to dance. One round of strathspey followed by two or three rounds of reels is a common length. See, for example, Graham (2006), Doherty (1996), Dunlay and Greenberg (1996) and Dunlay (2002) for further discussions on Cape Breton dance music.

Methodology

In accessing the Cape Breton dance tradition, I utilized methods from the relatively new field of "ethnochoreology," the study of ethnic dance, to guide my methodological principle of combining first-hand oral accounts, based on my own interviews or as found in written sources and historical records, to their mutual best advantage.

Ethnochoreology is the academic study of human movement systems, commonly referred to in the Western world as dance, "as a product and as social process and its relationship to the culture of which it is a part" (Foley 2013: 4). Ethnochoreology is, by de-sign, an interdisciplinary field of study drawing on research methods and concepts from many areas, including folklore, social studies and anthropology. I would refer to my own teacher Dr. Catherine Foley's (2013: 4-6) brief introduction to the field in *Step Dancing in Ireland* as a good starting point for further understanding.

Figure 1.1 – Joe Peter MacLean at Ceòlas Summer School, South Uist, Scotland, 1996. Photo by Mats Melin.

An ethnochoreological perspective allows for a more dynamic picture to emerge from my own investigation and lets, for example, first-hand acquired oral accounts to emerge clearly (i.e., allowing the Cape Breton subjects to tell their own stories, to which I add my own observations and questions). Documented records were accessed in books, periodicals and newspapers, as well as other forms of written records, such as letters, notes, emails and online sources. I acquired first-hand oral accounts, particularly for the contextual aspects and the transmission process, either directly in open-ended, face-to-face conversations and recorded interviews or by email and online video conversations.

A combination of direct observation, ethnographic writing (Denzin 1997), reflexive ethnographic writing (Davies 2008) and recording dance on video (and my own ability to learn steps and, in turn, perform them) all enabled me to notate and analyze Cape Breton step-dance movement using Labanotation (Guest 2005) and Newcastle notation (Hays et al. 2011), two separate notation systems used for dance. Labanotation, initially developed by Hungarian dance artist Rudolf Laban, is a universal movement notation system serving as a lingua franca for academic dance research; Newcastle notation was developed specifically for step dancing by clog and step dancers of the Instep Research Team in Newcastle, England.[6] Both require training to fully understand and to use, but the latter is easier to access by the layman, which was one of the reasons I decided to use it as a primary record in my research (see appendix 1).

My investigative process really started in 1992, when I met and learned from Harvey Beaton, as indicated above. It developed, expanded and is ongoing and will remain so. However, the particular focus detailed in this book crystalized during my doctoral research, from 2006 to 2012.

One dilemma that occurs when observing a living culture where there are many excellent practitioners of dance styles is: Who do you choose to study? To help solve this, in 2008 I formulated a questionnaire containing some general questions about what constitutes the aesthetic hallmarks of a good step dancer, which I distributed as widely as possible in Cape Breton through flyers, emails, Facebook messages and so forth. One of the entries asked respondents to cite examples of good male and female dancers. The returned forms showed that few people could or even would single out individuals, but I got lists of names. Some names appeared more often than others, and it allowed me to select a group of dancers—male, female and of different generations—to feature as examples of good practice in performing Cape Breton step dance over a time span ranging roughly from 1970 to the present.

I am a researcher and dance teacher in general, but also a practitioner and performer of this dance style in particular, which gives me particular advantages, I believe, in accessing and analyzing the collected information. This triple identity is very much in line with the ethos of my working environment at the Irish World Academy of Music and Dance at the University of Limerick, Ireland. I use these researching, teaching and performing identities interchangeably on a daily basis; they are mutually informative and have coloured my account in this book.

Mediations as a Participant-Observer

The research method known as participant observation is used in both ethnochoreology and ethnomusicology, among other disciplines. It refers to the observer taking on a role—as in my case, as a participating dancer or an audience member—in the social context under observation. You immerse yourself in the social setting you study; you get to know the people in a role that meanders between overt and covert observation. This way, you experience for yourself the activities you observe; you seek to discover the nature of the social reality by understanding the people's perception, understanding and interpretation—in short, the meaning—of a particular context (Spradley 1980; Emerson, Fretz, Shaw 2011: 22-29).

One must be aware of one's own subjectivities as a researcher when analyzing what is occurring, and also be aware that one's own presence may affect those that are observed in some way. A more positive note, nonetheless, is that in a close-knit community your presence at an event and what you are doing there is, to some extent, known by many in the community. You can conduct your research openly, thus minimizing ethical issues, and observations are acquired in a natural setting.

As a researcher one has to negotiate, on one hand, the source's *emic* (or insider) point of view (with its inherent "true" perspective) and, on the other, the researcher's *etic* (outsider) analysis. As Theresa Buckland (1999b, 1996), a professor of dance history and ethnography, points out, "the issue of representation in both its epistemological and political dimensions has resounded throughout theoretical literature on ethnography." Alongside Buckland, American dance scholars Deidre Sklar (1991) and Sally-Ann Ness (1992, 1996) state that the researcher is always positioned in relation to those interviewed and observed, to the fieldwork process, and to the final act of writing up the findings. It was linguist Kenneth Pike (1954) who created the distinction between emic and etic knowledge or accounts of culture and language. The ethnomusicologist Timothy Rice (2008: 54) explains that the emic/etic distinction has to do with the notion of cultural boundaries, which define "the positioning of insiders and outsiders." According to American social anthropologist Drid Williams (1991: 228), etic analysis is the search "for universal, culture-free elements of the world which transcend or in some way over-arch the diversity of local usages and references"; in opposition lies the concept of emic, consisting of "local, non-culture-free elements of the investigation." Over the years, Pike's distinction has been discussed, reinterpreted and, when used, its limitations criticized (see, e.g., Nettl 2005: 228-29).

As an outsider to the tradition, you frequently also find yourself in a teacher/learner dynamic, where the people you learn from, observe and interview naturally take on the role of teaching you something specific, like a step or aspects of their aesthetic preference. Your role and position as a researcher thus shifts again in the insider/outsider dichotomy, as now you have to interpret the information transmitted, let's say when practically learning a new dance step, and understand and embody it so you can dance it back to the "teacher" for feedback. You are now positioned in a role situated somewhere between the insider and outsider.

What I am utilizing here as a method of fieldwork is known as phenomenological hermeneutics. Rice (2008) outlines the use of this philosophical tradition as a method for ethnomusicological studies of music traditions and discusses how this method can mediate between "the knowledge of insiders to a culture and the knowledge of outsiders to that culture" (53). Rice says that phenomenological hermeneutics offers as a "productive mediation between experimental, objectivist strategies of observation, and experimental, subjective knowledge of the force of meanings and intentions" (55). The main thinkers behind this philosophy are Heidegger (1962), Gadamer (1979), Ricoeur (1981) and, to some extent, Geertz's interpretive anthropology (1973, 1985, 1988).

My mentor Catherine Foley employed this method when research-ing step dancing in north County Kerry, Ireland. Even though, being Irish, Foley is an insider, sharing Irish cultural knowledge and some knowledge of Irish dance, she was an outsider to the particular com-munity of dancers she interacted with (by geography, gender and age). Foley (2004: 51-52) describes the importance of how she represented the dancers and their dances:

> Learning, embodying, sensing, and experiencing the act of learning the dances from the dancers themselves was central to understanding the actual dances.... A *phenomenological herme-neutics* approach ... provided a framework for a more holistic un-derstanding of this declining tradition and a way of representing through the ethnographic experience, the dances as "texts," as embodiments of local knowledge, and as contextualised as "texts" within a cultural discourse; it provided a framework for embracing theory and practise; and it allowed for the interpreta-tion of the dance "texts" as both objective "text" (documented) and as subjective "textualised knowledge" (experienced).

For a deeper philosophical discussion on phenomenological hermeneutics as a research method, refer to Rice (2008).[7]

In much simpler terms, this method relates to what I interpret Cape Bretoners to mean when they tell me to make their step danc-ing "my own." When I place myself "in front of" the step dancing transmitted and performed in Cape Breton, I am no longer an insider or outsider, I dance as myself, a self formed, reconfigured and changed by all my encounters with, and interpretations and understanding of, Cape Breton step dance. This can, of course, be applied to other forms of dance and music, and so forth.

Accessing step dancing through the method of phenomenological hermeneutics greatly assisted me when practically trying out a step that I had previously observed while watching the movement patterns of another dancer. Along the same lines, the American anthropologist Adrienne Kaeppler (1967: 32) argues that to enable a researcher to no-tate a dance genre accurately, "it is helpful (indeed almost necessary) for the notator to be able to perform the movements himself in order to analyze exactly what the various parts of the body are doing and in what sequence they are done." The process becomes a kind of self check on whether what you do is similar enough to what you have previously observed. Similarly, when I focus on describing the visual, aural and kinaesthetic transmission processes, I utilize my own experience of knowing with my own body (Hahn 2007), or "embodying," Cape Breton step dance. I could thus describe my own experience in performing and learning to enhance my observations of local dancers in action and also add my own experience to their verbal descriptions of how they learned to dance.

A Some Specific Terminology Used

Dance Analysis

When analyzing movement, dance movement in this case, there are a number of areas that can be investigated by dance scholars—for example: asking questions about a culture's notion of *creativity*, or a culture's *aesthetic* values and asking what is acceptable or what is outstanding. Another investigative path that may help answer some of those questions, but which is concentrating on *the form* of a particular dance genre, or style, is *structural analysis*. Structural analysis (briefly summarized for Cape Breton step dance in appendix 1) is a way of establishing the *grammar* of dance elements (e.g., short to long movement combinations) and the rules for how these dance elements are combined into a full dance that is culturally acceptable. Dance scholars also pursue different ways of analyzing the *function* and *meaning* of dance in a culture.

Drive 'er

An important characteristic applied by Cape Breton musicians is to "drive 'er," that is, to play hard-driving dance music with a strong focus on rhythm. The distinctive Cape Breton bowing style generally involves only one stroke per beat and has an emphasis on a strong down bow while using up bows or "upstrokes which are often as powerful as downstrokes with a variety of pressures being exerted on the bow for dynamics and accents" (Graham 2006: 126). These are some of the essential components in the local fiddle style that generate drive (Doherty 1994, 1996, 2006; J. Dunn 1991; Dunlay and Greenberg 1996: 12-19; Graham 2006; Feintuch 2004b: 75-76). A step dancer is said to drive 'er when they dig deep for energy to give extra push to their movements.

Sources

I refer to the people that I acquired information from as "sources" rather than as "informants," as I feel the latter has negative connotations. I see my sources sharing their life experience and knowledge with me as analogous to a flowing river or a well or pool. Most of the people I interacted with I knew prior to this project, but I also made many new friends in the process, so I felt the word "source" was more appropriate. It is, after all, their lived experiences in making music and dance, including my own, that are to be understood, and the mutual respect involved between the actors matters. Titon (2008: 30) points out that the researcher's use of his or her own body as a tool in the research process "involv[es] reflexivity and an increase in narrative representation that is descriptive, interpretive, and evocative ... [and] sharing authority and authorship information with 'informants' (who are now considered teachers, consultants, friends, or all three)."

Tradition

Discussions about the definition of "tradition" as a concept are quite numerous.[8] The two definitions that work best for the Cape Breton case include one by Henry Glassie (2003: 192-93): "tradition is the means for deriving the future from the past and then define, tradition once again, as volitional, temporal action.... History, culture, and the human actor meet in tradition." Or, as Bert Feintuch (1993: 192) argued, "tradition is a social and academic construct standing for and resulting from an on-going process of interpreting and reinterpreting the past." Another notion worth mentioning is presented by Mike Anklewicz (2012: 97), where he states that he is more comfortable using the word "historical" rather than "traditional" "to avoid the academic and ideological burden the term 'tradition' has come to bear" when one speaks of music or dance styles of the past. Using the word "historical" allows one to discuss a plurality of styles of the past without "subscribing to a hegemonic concept of a singular 'tradition'" (86).

Transmission Processes

I align myself with American performer and ethnologist Tomie Hahn's (2007: 2) definition of transmission, in which it is seen as "a process that spans the practices of both teaching and learning ... to study transmission is to view a process that instills theory and cultural concepts of embodiment [and] ... concerns the information flow between teacher and student—the sender and receiver cycle—and embraces the personal relationships that evolve." In conjunction with "transmission," I also occasionally use the word "migration" as my own understanding and interpretation of Deidre Sklar's (2008) use of the word, to describe a two-way flow of movement information between and within bodies, from the senses to the extremities, for example.

Chapter 2

House Ceilidhs:
Transmission and Cultural Transitions in the Home

A s this book deals with sources of predominantly Scots Gaelic ancestry, the social institution of the house ceilidh is inextricably linked with learning. Between 1802 and 1840, some 20,000 mainly Gaelic-speaking Scots settled in Cape Breton; during the late 1820s and early 1830s, in fact, more Highland Scots immigrated to Cape Breton than to any other destination in British North America. This was to have a dramatic effect on the population of the island, which increased from about 2,500 in 1801 to almost 55,000 in 1851. As Hornsby (1992: 31) tells us, the ethnic composition of the island population thus changed significantly, and by 1871, "in large part, Cape Breton had become a Scottish island."[1]

It is important to note that it was common for whole family and extended kin groups to emigrate together and create specific settlement patterns in Cape Breton (Hornsby 1992). Over a number of years, Highland property owners, mostly absentee, cleared their lands of people in favour of sheep and cattle. The dislocations, many of them violent, known collectively as the Highland Clearances, forced the primarily Gaelic-speaking Highlanders into towns and villages in search of employment; thousands chose or were forced to emigrate. Occasionally, sympathetic landowners paid the overseas passage for some who opted to leave together for (primarily) North America and Australia. A pattern of chain migration developed, where those who left first would encourage other kin and friends to follow. Their descriptions of New World life played an important part in the direction of the emigration flow. The pull from family and kin, and the importance of keeping together, is described by Hornsby (46):

> Such family ties were noted by Clan Ranald's factor [agent] in South Uist when he was preparing for the emigration of many of the estate's tenants. "The people from this country will all go to Cape Breton, and no where else if they can help it." The pull of

family and friends was often so strong that even those emigrants carried beyond Cape Breton by ships returning to Halifax or Saint John, New Brunswick, struggled back to the Island to settle with relatives.

Old World Traditions in the New

The rural society of the Cape Breton Gaels was less stratified than the society they had left in the Highlands and islands of Scotland. A greater individual independence was found in this new environ-

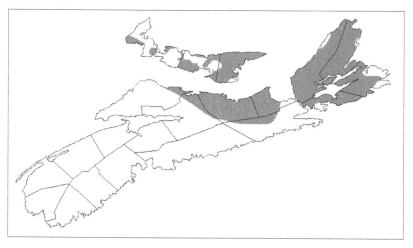

Figure 2.1 – Gaelic Settlement in Nova Scotia and Prince Edward Island. Mike Kennedy (2002) and Nova Scotia Archives, Museums and Libraries, Communities, Culture and Heritage (2002). Reproduced with kind permission.

ment, removed from the feudal system they had left behind. Even so, the relationship between "frontland" and "backland" farmers in Cape Breton (frontland constituting the superior plots, largely taken by early émigrés) was very similar to that of the tenant farmers and cottars in their ancestral areas in Scotland.

Family connections were maintained in the New World as well. Whole families (core and kin), and even whole townships, settled together on the island creating highly distinctive clusters. Hornsby gives a good example of this: Roman Catholic families from Morar and Moidart formed a series of related kin groups in Gillisdale,

Southwest Margaree, in the 1820s (1998: 76). For example, "Big" John Alex Gillis's grandfather, Alexander Gillis, who was a native of Morar and who had been taught a number of solo dances by an itinerant tailor and dance teacher named Donald Beaton, was one of the original settlers of this area, arriving in 1826 (Rhodes 1996: 189; MacGillivray 1988: 60). I visited John Alex Gillis's daughter, Margaret Gillis, in their family home in Gillisdale, in 2007, where she recalled dancing of the older style and where Gaelic cultural values were still evident in recollections of her life.

Gaelic language and culture were quite successfully maintained in this environment of transferred kin groups from Scotland, even though English was the language of business, education and government. Gaelic was used at home, on the farm, frequently in the local store and, from 1892, in the Sydney-based *Mac-Talla* newspaper and at church. The lack of immigration of other ethnic groups to the same places and the relative isolation of these rural areas were other contributing factors to the maintenance of localized customs, folklore and the regional dialects of Gaelic (Hornsby 1989: 76).[2] Besides language and its dialects, other practices such as weaving, spinning, "waulking" (fulling) the cloth, dying, rug hooking and quilting were kept alive. As was the practice in Scotland, work activities were often accompanied by songs, which kept Old World stories alive, but also generated new material in Cape Breton about the immigrants' new conditions and their journey there. Theirs was largely an oral culture.

Charles Dunn (1991) and Campbell and MacLean (1974), for example, state that in the Gaelic parts of Scotland in the 1830s, only one-fifth of family heads were literate. At the time, if formal education was supported at all in this context, it was provided in English. Right through the 19th century, and well into the 20th, Gaelic remained the everyday spoken language, in particular in the remote areas of Victoria and Inverness counties. Gaelic was stronger in the predominantly Roman Catholic areas, where the faith tradition was generally oral, as opposed to the Presbyterians, who relied on the written word of the mainly English-language bibles then available (Campbell and MacLean 1974). In 1851, 58 per cent of Cape Breton's total population was Roman Catholic. Gaelic was, however, the language at home for many Protestant families too, particularly along the north shore and in Richmond County (Morgan 2008: 172-75).[3] For nearly all of the next 150 years, Cape Breton Gaels passed on their social practices, stories, music, song and dance through the medium of Gaelic. The main occasion for the oral transmission of all these cultural practices was the home ceilidh.

The Importance of the House Ceilidh for Oral, Aural and Kinaesthetic Transmission

Until fairly recently in Cape Breton (to the post–Second World War years), the house ceilidh was still the primary context for passing on traditions, cultural practices and beliefs. Werner Kissling (1943: 87), the German ethnologist, describes a Hebridean house ceilidh he attended, a gathering from sundown to the early morning where stories and news were exchanged and discussions and singing (and music and dance) took place.[4] The powerful memories of the singers, poets and storytellers were put to the test at these ceilidhs. As Thomas McKean (1998) puts it, the *taigh cèilidh*, or house ceilidh, was the key to preserving many Gaelic vernacular traditions, as was the similar institution of the house dances in Ireland as described by Foley (1988). The particular house (or even houses) in which the community met to share the type of knowledge outlined above was a place for entertainment and learning—for sharing knowledge—and those present were encouraged to participate and experience the whole range of cultural expressions.

Ceilidhs were and are spontaneous affairs, involving family, close relations, neighbours and sometimes visitors from far afield, depending on the circumstances. Furthermore, John Shaw (1992-93: 38) states: "the ceilidh house ... serve[s] to maintain the integrity of Gaeldom's oral and musical culture by creating a social occasion which sustained the ties between the interdependent elements of the tradition." I'd like to add that the home ceilidh also serves to maintain the coherence of dancing skills, but this element of the tradition is often excluded from discussion. These gatherings were informal and most often normal household chores and the mending of tools and equipment would continue throughout the evening, but full attention would ensue if serious storytelling began or if dance and/or music took over (Thomson 1983: 281; Melin 2006).

The custom of the ceilidh house travelled with the emigrants to the Canadian provinces of Québec, Nova Scotia, Newfoundland and

Labrador, and Prince Edward Island, according to McKean (1998: 247). A comprehensive description of the *taigh cèilidh* traditions taking place among the Hebridean Gaelic immigrants in the Eastern Townships of Québec can be found in Margaret Bennett's book, *Oatmeal and Catechism* (1998: 145-61), and as they occurred in Codroy Valley in Newfoundland in the 1970s, in her *The Last Stronghold* (1989: 55-81). In particular, in *Tales Until Dawn,* MacNeil and Shaw (1987: 23-37) describe storytelling and the function of the ceilidh house in 20th-century Cape Breton in some detail.[5] Shaw (1992-93) also recalls the debates taking place about correct Gaelic-language usage, the sharing of song and poetry, song lines, accompanying stories associated with instrumental tunes and "correct" ways of dancing. In my own participation in and observations of both Cape Breton and Scotland over the last twenty years, I have taken part in many dance-related ceilidh-time discussions. When dancers come together, a healthy discussion almost always ensues on dance-related topics: aesthetic preferences in movement, rhythm, musicality and stylistic features of certain dancers and preferred ideas of good or correct dancing (Melin 2006, 2013b). The house ceilidh was the lifeblood of a Gaelic-speaking community, but as McKean (1998: 247-48) importantly points out, some building blocks of community identity are often obscured in accounts of house ceilidhs that concentrate on storytelling and singing. Exchanging views through debate, stories, anecdotes, news and such, as well as storytelling and singing, help relieve the many interpersonal pressures and frictions that build up in small, self-contained communities that depend on mutual cooperation for their survival. Thus, storytelling and singing form only part of a bigger function of the ceilidh.

Figure 2.2 – Harvey Beaton and Buddy MacMaster playing at a house ceilidh in Inverness, Scotland (1995). Photo by Mats Melin.

Michael Kennedy's (2002) report on Nova Scotian Gaelic culture highlights two vital points about the ceilidh-house transmission: Nova Scotian Gaelic culture is maintained, transmitted and retained primarily through memory, and that what Kennedy calls the common stock of Gaelic-culture values was passed on without the support of a stabilizing professional or institutional culture; thus,

> in spite of its relative vigour, the Nova Scotian Gaelic community did not recreate an elite Gaelic culture or a Gaelic institutional infrastructure. As in Scotland, Gaelic survived almost exclusively as an informally transmitted folk culture in rural communities ... [and the] Gaels nevertheless proved astonishingly adept at maintaining and passing on their culture with the less formal means [sic] available to them. Gaels from all levels of society and from every region of the Gàidhealtachd were well educated in the common stock of their culture. They appreciated the same masterworks of the same great poets, shared much of the same vast stock of traditional songs and tales, discussed the same lore, preserved the same rich historical and genealogical records, played the same type of music, and danced the same dances. Alongside this common stock of cultural expression, there was also a large store of local tradition and a vital institution of regional and *individual creativity* (p. 120; emphasis added).

In other words, the more organic ways of transmitting and maintaining core cultural knowledge and stories, songs, tunes and dance movement, for example, was continued predominantly through the Scots Gaelic community-based ceilidh tradition.

Over time, house ceilidhs in Cape Breton became better known as "kitchen rackets" or, simply, house parties. The intimacy of the occasion remained nonetheless the same. The importance of the house party's function as a learning environment (i.e., a primary source of news and gossip) has been diminished with the advent of modern communication technologies, such as the telephone, radio, TV and now the Internet. Today, the frequency of impromptu house parties has decreased according to some island residents, who lament this but see it as a sign of changing times.

The Importance of Family

The home and the house ceilidh are the site of many dancers' first contact with dance and music. Indeed, a good indication of how central the home has always been for the traditions of Cape Breton is that more than fifty of the fiddlers profiled in MacGillivray's (1997), *The Cape Breton Fiddler*, mention a family influence on their playing. The most musical households commonly became the focal point for the local community. His study features examples of mothers, other family members, visitors, friends or strangers "jigging" tunes,[6] playing an instrument and also dancing, enforcing the interconnectivity between the sound and movement modes of expression (see the biographical portraits for Mary Janet MacDonald, Minnie MacMaster, Mac Morin, Melody Cameron and Rodney MacDonald in chapter 9). House ceilidhs become a gathering place for the local community. All present become part of the family context but continue to reinforce the same cultural expressions, with the added individuality and slightly different "same" performance of each participant. What I mean here is that a dancer performing a repertoire of steps many times will always do so slightly differently each time; these performances are in turn compared to other similar performances of other community members over time. Thus, the cultural expressions they have in common (the smallest core components of their dance movements, referred to as "motifs" or "cells" in this book) further act to strengthen the cultural knowledge of the individual, family and community, but at the same time indicating individual creativity. The music and dance occur in an intimate context, where people are passing on and learning skills in close proximity to each other. This is the context that piper John MacLean (2010) laments having been diminished when recalling his own experience growing up in Washabuck with Sunday-afternoon kitchen parties at his parents' house.

Indeed, the home context is so important that Cape Breton author Frank Macdonald (2005) incorporates similar situations for his novel, *A Forest for Calum*, which aptly features his characters describing, for example, regular occasions of storytelling and gossip among the men, fortified with drink, in the kitchen or barn in post–Second World War Cape Breton, which naturally progress to tunes on the fiddle, step dancing and songs in Gaelic.[7] What is of real interest is Macdonald's perceptive descriptions of how his fictional character Roddie Gillies observes and comments on the dancing of Angus John Rory:

> Fat and half drunk, his [Angus John Rory's] feet shuffled under him in confusion at first, but then began to make sense. His belly bounced all out of tune but the rest of his body was still, barely a tremor in his shoulders or a quiver in his arms. He danced only with his feet, and I thought there must have been a time when Angus John Rory was as graceful as the tune he was dancing to. Duncan and John Alec and I clapped time for him and Johnny Rosin reached down to draw more from his fiddle. Angus was no match for the challenge. (p. 44)

It is Macdonald's description of the minute details and his eye for describing what is—and what graceful skills once were—in Angus John Rory's dancing, and how the fiddler digs deep to find energy in the tune and how the dancer matches it (as long as he can bear up), that makes this a great illustration.

To help illustrate the cultural transmission flow for music, song and language, the chart below, based on Shaw's (1992-93: 39) *taigh cèilidh* chart, has been modified to include step dancing's place in the Gaelic Cape Breton context:[8]

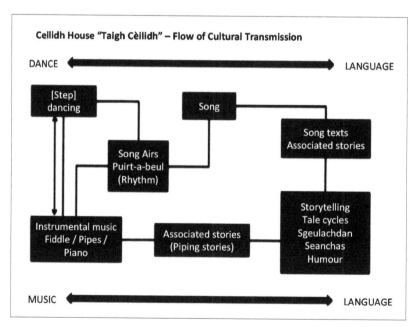

Figure 2.3 – Flow chart: Aural and visual learning links in Gaelic culture.

Before we go into further detail at how dance is passed on from person to person in Cape Breton through visual, aural and kinaesthetic transmission, it is pertinent to look at what the core Gaelic dance repertoire once consisted of and what still remains in active use.

The Core Gaelic Dance Repertoire: Reels and Games

In the historical research available to us (Flett and Flett 1985 [1964]; Rhodes 1996), dancing in the early-immigrant Scots Gaelic settlements consisted of four-handed Reels, eight-handed Reels, solo dances that are named (such as the Flowers of Edinburgh, which is also a song) and improvised step dancing that used the motifs found in the dancing of the aforementioned Reels. In addition, a few old Gaelic dance games that were reported to Rhodes (1996) by his sources in 1957 seem to correspond to the same dance games researched in the Highlands and the Western Isles (Flett and Flett 1953-54). Rhodes names some of the dances: Marbhadh na Beiste Duibhe (The Killing of the Otter), Cailleach an Dudain (The Old Woman of the Mill-Dust) and Tri "Croidhan" Caorach (Three Sheep's Trotters), as remembered by the centenarian Mary Sarah MacDonald, whose grandmother came from Barra in the Western Isles (Rhodes 1996: 189). These dances were performed to *puirt-a-beul*[9] and some, like the Reel Ruidhleadh nan Coileach Dhubha (Reel of the Black Cocks), were danced to tunes of the same name. The structure of these dances varied, but the Reels generally had alternating parts of steps performed on the spot, a position-changing figure and/or an instance of swinging the partner.[10] Both children and adults were known to have danced them. Today, a few versions of the Single Four or Scotch Four are danced around Cape Breton at festivals and concerts. The role of the Reel has shifted from being possibly the most significant social dance in Scots Gaelic communities to being largely a performance dance, but it holds the same level of relevance in the minds of the dancing community.

Visiting Cape Breton in 1957, Rhodes (1985 [1964]) described several Reel dances brought to the island from Scotland: the four-handed Reel, known in Gaelic as *ruidhleadh ceathrar* ("Foursome Reel") or *ruidhleadh beag* ("small Reel"), and the eight-handed or "big" Reel, which was known as *ruidhleadh mòr*. These dances showed close affinity to the circular reels that he and the Fletts (1985 [1964], 1996) found during their research in the Hebrides and the West Highlands in the late 1940s and 1950s. Indeed, one of the earliest references to a reel being danced in the Maritimes is from the reminiscences of an early settler among the Glenaladale pioneers, quoted in a 1931 edition of *The Dalhousie Review*, who refers to settlers who sailed from Moidart to Prince Edward Island. Upon safely landing, "they formed themselves into sets on the shore and danced a Scotch Reel to the music provided by Ronald MacDonald the piper" (quoted in Charles Dunn 1991: 55). The Reels "consist of setting steps danced on the spot alternated with a simple circling figure, the setting steps being performed with the dancers either in a straight line or in a square formation" (Rhodes 1985 [1964]: 270). The setting steps consisted of toe and heel beats, continuously marking the rhythm. While in the past a walking step, or a chassé, would have been used for moving through the figure of the Reel, from the 1950s onward, the same stepping used on the spot was also used to travel through the figure of the Scotch Four.[11] These Reels had local variations, most likely due to the geographic origin of the settlers.

The eight-handed Reel was also known as the "wild eight" because of its boisterous nature. It was a performed to a circular "Reel of Tulloch," the dance consisting of an alternating pattern of stepping on the spot and swinging partners, involving a progression of the dancers around the circle (Rhodes 1985 [1964]: 271). In some districts, local priests discouraged this dance and as a result it was discontinued in its original form. When restrictions were lifted, the dance evolved into a new type of eight-handed Reel that was not fixed but varied from place to place and from one occasion to another (271).

It is worth noting that the characteristic figure of eight pattern,[12] today associated primarily with the Highland Reel in Highland Games dancing, does not form part of the original Reel patterns found by Rhodes and the Fletts in either Cape Breton or the West Highlands and Isles. This indicates that this pattern was likely unknown in those Scottish districts at the time of emigration (Rhodes 1985 [1964]: 271). Reel dancing in Cape Breton was quite formal, however. Piper MacLean (2010) says, "I know that my grandparents' generation in the 1900s was much more formal. They preferred the Scotch Four above all else and they observed strict decorum—even in the kitchen."

The two-part tempo structure of the Reel causes a build-up of an-ticipation. It starts in strathspey 4/4 time, and commonly one or two strathspey tunes are played twice through before the music switches to reel time. The reel is often the highlight of the dance. There is no set length of time for the dance; the number of repeats is governed by an interaction between the dancers and the musicians. Sometimes, however, the number of repeats is decided beforehand in a performance context.

Step dancing today is seen both as part of social dancing and as an aspect of dancing you share, as a solo dancer, with your community.[13] Formal competitions never seem to have formed a huge part of the tradition. Nevertheless, a few recollections in MacGillivray (1988) mention dancers being "champions" and having won medals at competitions in the early 19th century.

Far more important than competition was the informal skills testing that occurred between the men, such as in the dance Smàladh na Coinnle, (Smooring [Snuffing] the Candle).[14] This feat requires the dancer to step dance round a lighted candle placed on the floor. The candle is either snuffed by clicking the heels just above the flame or by flicking the tip off the wick with the feet without extinguishing the flame (Rhodes 1985 [1964]: 273). Rhodes (1996: 192) also describes a version of Smàladh na Coinnle where "three candles were placed in a row on the floor and the best dancers tried to flick off the wicks without putting out the candles" and "dancers would sometimes step dance on tables with glasses full of whisky on them." However, it was said that anyone who could step to the strathspey tune "Tullochgorm" need not be tested; they were sure to be good dancers. The Cape Breton bard Dougall MacLennan (Dùghall Iain Ruaidh) mentions this feat in a poem: "Dhannsadh iad air ùrlar clàraich, 'S smàladh iad le 'n sàil a' choinneal" (They could dance on the board floor, snuffing out the candle with their heels) (MacNeil and Shaw 1987: 477). My friend the dancer Frank McConnell observed something along similar lines at a family event in Mabou Hall in 1996: a bottle of beer was surreptitiously brought into the hall, placed on the stage floor and danced around with not a drop spilled (McConnell 2004).

Another skills test was, according to Rhodes (1996: 192), held at the end of an evening when the "two best dancers were to 'dance it out,' taking turns to dance as many complete steps as possible on a block of wood 18 inches high and 12 inches in diameter." Hugh MacKenzie, from Sydney, whose family originally came from Barra, recounted another test of skills: the Dannsaidh na Biodag (Dirk or Dagger Dance). No one had actually seen the dance in 1957, but people recalled a dance where a dirk was stuck in the ground, point upward, and danced around without the dancer looking down; or it was held and then thrown on the ground and picked up again while dancing. The tunes for the dance were either "Thompson's Dirk" or "MacAllister's Dirk" (Rhodes 1996).

There was also, particularly within certain families, a tradition of named solo dances, such as Dannsa nan Flurs (Flowers of Edinburgh), which all had a set structure and repeat pattern of dance movements. These dances will be mentioned further in chapter 3.

Of these dances, only improvised step dancing and the occasional displays of the Reel the Scotch Four remain in active use. The repertoire has, however, been enhanced by the introduction of square-set dancing, as will be discussed in detail in chapter 5.

Visual Transmission

In her article *Building a Dance in the Human Brain: Insights from Expert and Novice Dancers,* Emily S. Cross (2010: 186) writes that a wealth of behavioural research "suggest[s] that the quickest and most accurate learning results from observing and simultaneously reproducing another individual's movements." The study of human movement has become a topic of increasing relevance over the last decade, bringing dance into the focus of the cognitive sciences. To an observer of the Cape Breton dance culture, where visual learning is common and, in many cases, often the only perceived way of learning, the recent discovery and subsequent studies of "mirror" neurons in the human brain is of special interest.

> Of particular interest to neuroscientists is the remarkable plasticity of the human brain to integrate different types of physical and perceptual experiences to learn new movements. Such abilities are quite pronounced in dancers.... Neuroscientists have recently observed that it is the extraordinary plasticity of seemingly disparate cortical regions and subcortical nuclei within the brain that gives rise to such movements. This network of brain regions works together when we observe someone else performing an action and then learn how to perform it ourselves. (Cross 2010: 177)

These studies show the same sets of the brain's mirror neurons firing when a subject performs an action as when observing another person perform the same action. This system is broadly referred to as an action-observation network (Cross 2010: 177-78). Cruse and Schilling add that "observing a dance is activating the same neuronal circuits I would use to dance myself – I am dancing along in my head: perceiving is a way of re-enacting the watched dance" (2010: 53). Furthermore, Thomas Schack (2010) states that dancers use mental representations "as a foundation to identify possible and functionally relevant sensory inputs" and, as identification is often achieved in a short time under a great amount of pressure, these mental representations must be readily available. Schack points out that these mental representations "[include] storing the perceptual-cognitive outcomes of learning processes as items [here representations of dance movements] in long-term memory" (2010: 12-13).

Moreover, cognitive building blocks are how movement effects are anticipated by a dancer; understanding the architecture of dance is part of the process of acquiring the skills to perform and control movement (Schack 2010: 14). Schack further states that basic action concepts, the levels of mental and sensorimotor representation and control, "are created through the cognitive chunking of body postures and movement events concerning common functions in realizing action goals," and, he continues, "to perform particular dance movements with high accuracy, dancers need sophisticated cognitive representations of goal postures, their functional meaning and the related perceptual events in their own body" (16-17). These sophisticated cognitive representations of "goal postures" could be equated to the concept of emic knowledge for the individual dancer, but with all the sensorimotor information included.

To summarize the science, the dancer stores mental representations of movements in his or her long-term memory "as a network of sensorimotor information" (Bläsing 2010: 84), which enables rapid realizations of action goals. These concepts could be linked to Blom and Chaplin's (1988: 13-15) discussions about kinaesthetic memory and their notion of a "creative consciousness" (11), where the performer becomes one with the movement and music.

Aural Transmission

Aural learning is often mentioned in discussions of learning music, songs (tune and lyrics) and stories in Cape Breton (see, e.g., Doherty 1996, Graham 2006, Shaw 1992-93, Kennedy 2002, Garrison 1985). Virginia Garrison (1985) explores how traditional Cape Breton fiddling is transmitted. She found that

> almost all fiddlers interviewed expressed their strong desire as youngsters to learn to play the fiddle. A number of factors which seemed to kindle this desire to learn included ... the mother's influence as a singer of Gaelic songs and by "jigging" fiddle tunes. (180)

Almost 80 per cent of the fiddlers Garrison interviewed reported that, as beginner fiddle players, they were totally dependent on their aural skills for learning. Many occasions to develop their aural skills presented themselves to these young musicians: they listened to relatives and non-relatives sing Gaelic songs or nonsense syllables in vocal renditions of fiddle tunes, a practice known in Cape Breton as "jigging" or "making 'mouth music'" (185).

Kennedy (2002) in particular summarizes the strong but conservative nature of the oral tradition in Gaelic society (Scottish and Irish). The conservative nature of the oral tradition does allow for a certain level of personal interpretation. Aural learning is at the heart of the interconnected transmission environment in the context of the home or ceilidh house. Garrison (1985: 277) gives instructions on this form of learning: listen to tunes played at house parties and dances, "pick up" the tunes from there, listen to the radio and to recordings of master Cape Breton fiddlers and play along with these tunes. According to Garrison, "the aesthetic gratification of the music and the sense of achievement in learning tunes by ear on one's own" (277) are two of the major motivators in this kind of learning. Kennedy (2002: 195) mentions the "remarkable ear for music as well as quick and retentive memories" of Cape Breton musicians and presents accounts of fiddlers who are able to recall tunes "correctly and completely," with added local Gaelic style and appropriate ornamentation after only hearing a tune once. It is not uncommon for Cape Breton dance fiddlers to have up to 1,000 tunes readily available to play from memory.

Aural learning is less emphasized when it comes to learning movement. A dancer immersed in a diverse blend of sounds must make sense of the complexity of the combination of music and movement. In their charting of interconnected skills involved in learning dance, Adshead et al. (1982: 54) point out that aural elements include sound, the spoken word and music, and that clusters of these three elements occur simultaneously with visual stimuli while a dancer performs movements. Walter Ong (1967: 128) suggests that sound and vision have different orientating effects: "Sound situates man in the middle of actuality and in simultaneity, whereas vision situates man in front of things and in sequentiality." Another way of saying this is that we view something from the sidelines, or from the front, while we are immersed in the sound. Thus sound helps to make the body aware of the physical space around it and also helps the dancer orient himself or herself in time (e.g., in a piece of music), in what Hahn (2007: 115) calls a "dynamic immersive space." Sound helps us answer questions about the space or room itself—for example, what instruments are creating the music and all other ambient sounds, such as foot tapping and the general noise of bodies moving through space that help us trace the order of events.

Hahn discusses our capacity to hear with our whole body: humans can pick up sound vibrations that are out of conscious hearing range; in other words, our senses process and absorb vibrations but we do not "hear" them. Sound can also travel long distances, through materials and around corners. We can hear things even though what causes the sound is out of sight. Sound can be evasive, and we can feel sound waves with our whole body. Our associations and experiences of different types of sound help us to make meaning and orient ourselves in the world.

> While some sounds summon innate responses, others are learned cultural constructions that help us orient ourselves in a more abstract, social way. We learn to attend to specific aspects of sound—quality, dynamics, intensity and rhythm—to acquire meaning about our sonic, musical, environment. (115)

We learn to make sense of the "many layers of complexity" of sound and to filter some sounds out through "selective attention" (115). In other words, we learn to recognize those sounds that are of more importance to the task at hand. Acculturated knowledge of movement and sound correlation helps us move our bodies in a particular way to music. Aural learning happens in conjunction with visual and kinaesthetic modes, but some of the sonic skills that Hahn describes are of real interest to this book. According to Hahn, we learn to associate previous sounds with current ones.

It should be noted that the advances in neuroscience have fairly recently established that, in addition to mirror neurons interacting to visual stimuli, they (audiovisual mirror neurons) also do so to sound, resulting in similar responses by our bodies, as described earlier (see Kohler et al. 2002; Keysers et al. 2003; and Keysers and Gazzola 2014).

Dance transmission also involves mnemonic verbal cues given to a dancer as movement and rhythm cues, as encouragement, criticism, corrections, praise and so forth. These mnemonic verbal cues can help us answer questions about the culture being studied and, in relation to Cape Breton, by giving us clues to what movements are regarded as core, as they have been given verbal signifiers, such as the "hop step," or what qualities are considered important, such as "lightness" or "neatness."

Spoken encouragement or explanations of how to place one's feet, hold one's body, comments regarding the local aesthetic preferences and so forth, are reinforced this way. The musician and step dancer Joël Chiasson says that when he received gentle comments, they acted as positive reinforcement: "Every time I received a positive comment from another dancer or musician, I thought to myself, I need to keep working on that aspect of my dancing as it is a step in the right direction" (Chiasson 2009). I discuss some of the verbal keywords that the community shares when talking about their aesthetic and stylistic preferences in chapter 6.

American ethnomusicologist and dance ethnologist Adrienne Kaeppler (1972) outlines poetry as a mnemonic device in Hawaiian dance; similarly, the British ethnomusicologist David Hughes (2000) analyzes a number of acoustic-iconic mnemonic systems in Japan, Korea and Africa; and the Irish ethnochoreologist Catherine Foley (1988) provides examples of mnemonics, such as "tip down" and "batter down" used in step dancing in County Kerry, Ireland (see also 2012, 2013). Heather Sparling (1999, 2014) suggests that Scots Gaelic *puirt-a-beul* in Cape Breton is a mnemonic device for learning melody (tune) and for rhythm cues for step dancing. Finally, Martin Stokes (2004: 68) directs us to combined aural and visual processes, "visual or aural cues in transmission: interlocking, phrase marking, call and response, droning, simultaneous group improvisations, varied repetitions, etc. What is heard implies forms and processes of embodied social interaction."

Kinaesthetic Transmission and Proprioceptive Awareness

Kinaesthetic transfer of knowledge is a key component in shaping the aesthetic, stylistic and movement preferences of step dancing in Cape Breton. What we are looking at here is the bringing out of somatic, or felt, dimensions of movement—in other words, proprioceptive or kinaesthetic awareness. Kinaesthesia as a sensorium is, in the Western perspective, an overlooked aspect of embodied knowledge. As Deidre Sklar points out, other cultural epistemologies offer other "sensory profiles" compared to those commonly valued in Western culture. Japanese culture, embodied through dance movement and body-to-body transmission, as described by Hahn's (2007) ethnographic records, is one such example; another is the emphasis of auditory and proprioceptive, rather than visual, values in African dance forms (Sklar 2008: 88).

Proprioception is sometimes referred to as a "sixth sense" to include the body's sensation of itself and its actions with the classical five senses. The term "proprioception" comes from the Latin (*proprius* "own" + reception), meaning in this case an awareness of the position of one's body, and is often used interchangeably by dancers with the terms "kinaesthesia," "muscle memory" (sense) or, simply, one's sense of movement. There are slightly different nuances between these terms, but they all refer to physically feeling one's own body in motion on an overarching but deep level, which integrates balance, flow and fine and gross motor skills. Proprioception and kinaesthesia are "intimately tied to our feeling of muscle tone, [and] perceptions of effort and balance" (Batson 2008: 1), as used in the following discussion.[15]

Sklar (2008) deliberates on theorizing kinaesthesia in detail in her essay "Remembering Kinesthesia: An Inquiry into Embodied Cultural Knowledge," which I will turn to here in detail. One problem with theorizing human movement, Sklar explains, is whether to treat it as visual or kinaesthetic phenomena. She discusses the difference in visual and somatic (kinaesthetic) modalities, between observing and doing (proprioception), where dance involves both modalities. Even though the doer primarily "uses" felt or kinaesthetic modalities and the observer primarily "sees," both modalities are mutually informing, according to Sklar (88). Maybe the gap between the two is much narrower if one considers the findings of recent research within the cognitive sciences about mirror neuron circuits—these circuits allow the observer to "dance" in his or her own head, albeit on an individual level of dance competence. Sklar refers to a number of writers to clarify the complex relationship between observing and proprioception: the philosopher Edward Casey (1987) separates "body memory" (remembering) from "memory of the body" (recollecting). The former term refers to felt sensations in the body, the latter to "representations of the body as an object of awareness" (Sklar 2008: 88). Through body memory, the past is enacted in the present. Sklar continues,

> Therefore, regarding body memory, Casey suggests, "we should speak of immanence rather than 'intersection' ... immanence of the past in the present and the present in the past." The present and the past cannot be fully identical, Casey concludes, since we would then no longer be dealing with memory. (p. 88)

When we deal with movement it is, without deviating too much, perhaps of interest to take into account the concept of "gesture" as discussed in detail in Noland and Ness's (2008) collection of essays, *Migrations of Gesture*, where various forms of understanding the concept, including phenomenological and semiotic ones, suggest that our perception of ourselves being human is itself partly created through gestural routines. Building on Adorno's (1996 [1951]) deliberations that "both instrumental and communicative gestures encode, express and perpetuate the values of specific historical and cultural formations," Noland and Ness (2008: ix) summarize that:

> He [Adorno] also knows that gestures offer opportunities for kinaesthetic experience; they "innervate" or stimulate, the nerves of a bodily part, and thus allow the body to achieve a certain awareness and knowledge of itself through movement. [B]y retrieving gestures from the past, or by borrowing gestures from another culture, subjects can actually produce new innervations, discover new sensations to feel. (p. ix-x)

In Cape Breton Island, one should take into account that the population currently consists of descendants of groups of people who, to follow Noland and Ness's and Adorno's line of thinking, had initially differing identities manifested through their gestures. Presently, one should nonetheless possibly consider it natural that groups with different geographical and cultural backgrounds, having lived side-by-side over many generations, will have influenced each other's movements and gestures. As I see it, it would also then be natural that this awareness of embodied movement and borrowing of gestures from our neighbours would filter into the domain of dance. An indication of this would be when a step, for example, is said to have been introduced from the Ottawa Valley-style of step dancing into Cape Breton step dancing. Having said that, there is a notion with some people in the community that dancers of, say, Acadian heritage dance a little differently than those of a Scots Gaelic background. Whether this perception of difference is fully real or partly imagined is another study, but it is worth keeping in mind that how we move and gesture on a daily basis, as well as how we dance, does have encoded data on certain levels about our identities.

An integral aspect of any movement (and gesture) is also the amount of internal energy applied to the motion and how that feels inside the body, and also how this may differ in different social contexts as they are transmitted and changed. Thus Sklar (2008: 103) suggests that "a concept of gesture requires not only association with movement's kinetic qualities of vitality but also an accounting of the way the sensations of kinetic vitality are socially structured, transformed and mediated." Sklar takes into consideration the migration of gestural schema during the interplay between everyday life and cultural expressions (such as dance), and their change over time. I read this: we can detect movements/gestures from daily life in the performance of dance by an individual, for instance, and how these are modified as time passes. This concept of gestural schema also allows for personal interpretation of gesture. When we indicate that a certain individual has particular stylistic traits to their dancing, it is personal interpretation that is visible. Sklar (2008: 102) further indicates that transmission processes have recently speeded up, and this speeding up has had an impact on the amount and level of information that can be absorbed while learning new dances.

Anthropologist Anya Peterson Royce discusses this interplay between everyday life and cultural expressions when studying the Isthmus Zapotec cultural practices, and the role of the ethnographer embodying these practices in order to gain understanding. Royce (2008: 2) writes that the ethnographer's use of embodied practice in studying cultural expressions "will allow us to understand how and why certain aesthetic preferences govern practice." Both the members of the Isthmus Zapotec society and Royce use their "habitus" or, to use Mauss's (1979) term, the "technique du corps," to accommodate themselves to what Royce calls the "aesthetic of the ordinary" (2008: 1). She examines the challenges of describing and learning movement by the ethnographer, not only in especially codified cultural practices but also in the multitude of gestures that occur in everyday life. Daily gestures are codified in a different way than artistic ones, such as dance, but are equally recognized and evaluated by the people of a particular culture. Growing up in a culture, these learning and embodying processes happen naturally as part of daily life. It is the embodied artistic expressions of a culture's core values such as balance, transformation and continuity that the outsider tries to understand: "The elements are passed from one generation to another through apprenticeship in some cases, and through socialization where people learn from modeling the behavior of their elders and from explicit teaching and criticism" (25).

What Royce suggests is that everyday gestures, thoughts and activities, including intentional cultural expression such as music and dance, are reflected, embodied and, indeed, embedded in the fabric of the life of a particular culture (see also Royce 2004).

The outsider, however, faces many challenges in embodying and understanding these processes. Timothy Rice's (2008) notion of experiencing the culture through phenomenological hermeneutics is relevant here. It is important to note that the process of understanding should not be seen as a universal body experience, but must be seen in relation to each individual's unique experience with the culture, language and so forth in question. It is a matter of understanding and valuing aesthetics, taking in the culture in question through all one's senses as an individual and becoming comfortable in performing them. Royce aptly refers to this using Desjarlais' (1992: 65) term "aesthetics of experience," which means "the tacit, cultural forms, values, and sensibilities" (Royce 2004: 5).

Sklar (2008: 102) in turn considers gesture "in terms of kinetic layerings ... of elaborated embodied schema." She asks us to consider how we receive gestures/movement through multiple modes, as "spatial change, rhythmic pattern, intensity" (103), and, I would argue, auditory input. Psychological anthropologist Thomas Csordas's (1993) explanation of phenomenologists' "lived experience" is again in line with Rice's (2008) outline of phenomenological hermeneutics; according to Csordas, "lived experience" is "never merely individual and subjective but develops as relational and cultural constructions in social space" (Sklar 2008: 92), and one that allows for agency, individuality and somatic awareness by all those involved. Sklar refers further to Csordas:

> Distinguishing between "the body" as a biological and material and "embodiment" as an "indeterminate methodological field defined by perceptual experience and the mode of presence and engagement in the world," Csordas coins the term "somatic modes of attention" to refer to "culturally elaborated ways of attending to and with one's body in surroundings that include the embodied presence of others." (Csordas 1993: 138)

She has applied Csordas's phrase "a somatic mode of attention" to a method of attending to one's own and others' movement with proprioceptive awareness. She summarizes her concept of gesture in this way:

> From the perspective of movement and embodiment ... the organic foundation of gestures refers, in Merleau-Ponty's words, to the "I can" of embodiment, including especially the *innate capacity for translating vitality across sensory modalities.* The concept of embodiment, as Csordas points out, refuses the separation of a material body from either the "can do" of embodied human potential or the social habitus of being-in-the-world. (Sklar 2008: 103)

Japanese cultural concepts and their various forms of dance are far removed from Cape Breton step dancing, but aspects of Tomie Hahn's ethnographic study of the process of transmission and embodiment of Japanese dance, *nihon buyo,* helps to shed light on similar processes in Cape Breton. Hahn (2007: 1) strongly believes that observing the way dance is transmitted reveals "a great deal about that culture as well as the individual dancers practising the tradition." Refinement of the senses (visual, oral, aural and tactile or kinaesthetic) as vehicles of transmission and immersion in the cultural expressions and the embodying of these cultural expressions that occur over long periods of time are among the key concepts in Hahn's study. He notes that "not only do the senses orient us in a real, physical way, they enable us to construct parameters of existence—that which defines the body, self, social group, or world" (3).

"Picking it Up": Visual, Aural and Kinaesthetic Transmission

Most dance learning involves observing, copying and embodying movements, but in the Cape Breton context strictly verbal commands, such as "step shuffle hop," commonly given by a "teacher," are often either missing or are secondary to more general, encouraging comments from those present.[16] The transmission process outlined here is not exclusive to the home environment by any means, but would have occurred in many other local contexts such as picnics, school dances and weddings. Of course, there is naturally a crossover between these different contexts of transmission. Since the 1970s, concerts and square dances in the local parish halls have become of greater importance to the transmission of dance than in the years prior to the 1970s.

There is, however, a slight difference in the priority of modes of transmission (visual, aural and kinaesthetic) in each context. As we will see in the different recollections of learning to dance, there is an indication that different sensoria act as the primary mode of transmission. Many of the interviews in MacGillivray argue that the act of observing is one of the first steps in learning the dance in Cape Breton. Indeed, although the emphasis of Frank Rhodes's (2011) research is not on transmission, his field notes from 1957 indicate that some of his sources learned their dancing at home, and some of these people also appear in MacGillivray's (1988) study. Learning from a parent, predominantly your mother and other family, was very common. MacGillivray's interviewees indicate that you watched and then practised what you saw; you "just picked it up." In many cases the dancers add that they were never formally taught. But, as will be discussed later, these statements should be seen as an indication of the informality of the transmission process rather than taken at face value. Dancers observed one another at house parties and public dances. They watched out for the "good" dancers and tried to remember their steps when practising later. For example, Harvey Beaton says he learned by frequently watching others dance, in addition to learning from his mother, Marie, at home and Minnie MacMaster in class. Willie Fraser, of Deepdale, said he remembered how Kate MacLellan, from Dunvegan, would be sitting in a chair and show him how to step dance (MacGillivray 1988: 56).

Harvey Beaton illustrates the importance of aural awareness of music and the relationship of movement: as a youngster, he practised steps in the parlour and was corrected by his mother, who was in the kitchen, but could hear that "his step did not sound right." Similarly, Mac Morin recalls that his mother taught him and his brothers "the backstep" at home and that she took great care that they got the "hop" absolutely right in time with the music. It had to sound right to feel right and reach a certain "comfort level" before other movements were added to the motif or step (Morin 2008). He remembers starting to learn to dance at home:

> It was the rhythms that attracted me. I remember hearing my mother dance in the kitchen without music, and the sound of her steps attracted me. That's not to say I hadn't heard the music up until that point.... There was music on all the time. It all happened around the same time.... I recall seeing a dancer and realizing that was what my mom was doing all the time at home to the music she and dad had on all the time.... I do remember her taking me by the hands as I was learning a step or as I would show her some of mine ... and I do also recall sitting at the supper table dancing seated while we ate (and being told to wait 'til we were done eating).... My mom had a great eye for steps, for what worked and what was more traditional and for what "looked" the best.... I truly believe she had a knack for discerning what was best in Cape Breton step dancing without knowing how perceptive her eye was.... That's definitely where I got my own "sight" in the matter.... For a while, it was dancing to the fridge for the milk, dancing waiting for the toast to pop, all these spare moments being forced to wait for silly things and filling them up with rhythms I had heard. Were these rhythms I had unknow-

ingly picked up from the music I was hearing? No doubt. But the understanding of those rhythms, I believe, [was] also shaped unknowingly. It wasn't a conscious effort.... Whether it was a combination of home/community/air/genes—who knows? It is hard to describe other than that it just happened or clicked and felt right. (Morin 2010)

Morin is describing a combination of aurally and visually based learning.

Similarly, in my own experience, the constant reinforcement of sounds in conjunction with visual stimuli inform one's own dancing: hearing different people dance; wearing different footwear; dancing predominantly on wooden floors; hearing how hard, or light, a foot touches the ground; visually and aurally taking in whether a person is using the heel or the ball of the foot for a specific movement; seeing personal differences of the same type of movement and learning to associate a particular image with a particular sound; repeatedly seeing many different people dancing to the music of many different musicians and making different but informed choices of movement; seeing how they match different types of movement to the different melody strains and characteristics and modes of the local tunes repertoire. These aural and visual associations inform one's own movement repertoire in the process of embodiment. Thus, the many movement options that become available to one over time open up possibilities for improvisation. The ability to put a personal stamp on the dancing continually develops. In this intimate context, where one is in close proximity to other people, one feels the movement of the floor when a dancer is in action, which in turn enhances

Figure 2.4 – Mary Graham dancing at a house ceilidh. Photo by Victor Maurice Faubert.

52

the kinaesthetic understanding of what is occurring. Add all the other visual, aural and kinaesthetic stimuli to this context, and a deeper understanding of the local soundscape, and what I call "gesturescape" is formed.

Piper and dancer Alex Angus MacIsaac's (1908-1960) recollections of an aural- and visual-learning home environment were recalled through his daughter, Diane (MacIsaac) Miller, in 1987. She says that her father mentioned what he called "family time" or "party time" at home. Somebody would be playing the violin and others would step dance spontaneously. Dancing was just something picked up as a family; both Alex Angus's father and mother were known to step dance. Music was played all the time and at all hours of the day. "They never had to worry about what they were going to do for entertainment; they made their own" (MacGillivray 1988: 102). In turn, Diane says she watched her father dance when she was about four years old, and was then encouraged to come forth and try some steps herself. Diane particularly recalls her father having "unique anklework—twists with the ankle and different steps like that. He was a smooth-to-the-floor dancer [and] neat as pin in his dance" (102).

The late step dancer Aggie MacLennan was born in Washabuck, in 1923 (she died in 2010), and was the daughter of "Red" Rory MacLean, a noted fiddler and step dancer. Aggie describes growing up in an environment where there was always music in the house, and she cites this environment, rather than any sort of formal teaching, as responsible for her learning to play music and dance:

> We did not hear of learning to dance in my day. When the music started, we got up and we were dancing. We were shy them years, not out in the open like today. We were behind the doors, thinking we were excellent. (MacNeil 1999: 15)

Aggie and her siblings predominantly learned their tunes and steps in the kitchen or the front room; however, they also picked up their skills at square dances held in the community schoolhouses. There she observed, for example, the MacKinnon boys from Cains Mountain, and she would say to herself: "I must see if I can do that when I go home. I remember how he did it." The MacKinnon boys were self-taught as well. Aggie describes her learning process "as the true way to learn to dance ... it just came from the heart. If it's in you, it comes out of you" (15).

Aggie's husband, Neil MacLennan, did not learn just by "picking it up"; he remembers the advice he got from Angus "Mossy" MacKinnon from Black Point in the 1940s:

> He showed me how to hold myself. Look at the hole in the wall, keep it eye level. On about a 10" x 10" [25 x 25 cm] square, stay there. Don't lift your feet too high, just barely off the floor. Never put your heel past your toe; stay in close. You put your heel past your toe, you're losing too much time coming back. That's making you ugly. And don't go wide, just barely move and stay on the 10 by 10. And not swinging hands, just hold on by your sides. (MacNeil 1999: 15)

In the case of the MacLennans, we see two different perspectives on learning. One is just "picking it up" while the other is receiving verbal advice. It is nonetheless too simplistic to single out one transmission process in isolation. The recollections of most of my Cape Breton sources describe a scenario of several transmission processes at work simultaneously. People who claim they learned by "just picking it up" could well be using this statement to indicate the informal nature of the transmission process they experienced. Jackie Dunn-MacIsaac, for example, indicates that some level of actual and directed showing of basic movements is a valuable part of dance learning:

> I don't think anyone could "pick it up" without already dancing at least one or two steps or being shown at least one or two steps already. I am thinking those people mean, after they knew the general mechanics of the steps, they then could "pick up steps" from other dancers by watching them, which completely makes sense. Since all steps are made up of specific movements/foot placements and certain repetitive rhythmic patterns, of course familiar patterns/movements can be picked up from new steps (whether taught [broken down] or learned by watching) because some of the steps are already internalized.... My mother taught me most of my steps and I guess I grew into dancing watching her teaching so after I knew a few steps I could watch others and remember steps that I could do later on without having someone actually teach them to me. When I say my mom taught [me] dancing, it was in no way strict teaching ... she would just dance for me and have me watch and then try the step. As a child sometimes I would get it right away and other times I would need her

to break the step down in a hard spot for me to get it. She would
… suggest foot placement or try not to do "this" or "that" to keep
it traditional. (Dunn-MacIsaac 2010c)

Similarly, Jackie's mother, Margaret Dunn, told me that her
grandfather, John MacMaster, encouraged her to dance and would
give her pointers, as did Margaret's father, John Willie MacEachern.
John Willie would even tell her if she was doing something in her
dancing that he did not like or that he felt she should not do (Dunn
2007). Margaret distinctly remembers Harvey Beaton's mother, Marie,
teaching her steps. Margaret said Marie lived in her home for a while,
and once homework was finished in the evening, John Willie would
take out his fiddle and she and Marie would dance and Marie would
show her steps:

> Because my father was a fiddler we always had lots of company
> and I got to see other people dance as well. After learning the
> basic steps it was easier to learn from people by watching. My
> father was able to see if I didn't have steps quite right and would
> tell me so. (Dunn 2012)

In addition to this informal learning at home, Margaret watched
many dancers. Her mother would take her along when her father
played local concerts around southern Inverness County, and there
she would pick up things that she applied to her already-acquired
dance knowledge. Music and dance was a big part of their lives, as it
was for so many others at the time (Dunn 2012; and Dunn-MacIsaac
2012a, 2012b).

Minnie MacMaster offers a vivid glimpse into an equally immersive transmission environment where visual, aural and kinaesthetic
sensoria are interacting:

> My first steps were taught to me by my mother [Maggie Ann
> Beaton]. She was a very neat and close to the floor dancer and her
> joy was in teaching her children some basic steps. She would get
> us "warmed up" by sitting on one of the hard wood chairs in our
> cosy kitchen, closing her eyes and jigging some great strathspey
> and reels, and the beat of her feet along with her jigging would
> get your energy up and you just wanted to dance, dance, dance.
> Back in her day there were no names for steps, but she started us
> off with a basic strathspey step and added a few variations and

she then would take us to the hop step and the back step and a few more simple steps to go along with that. She would often take us by the hands and dance along with us and while I never realized at the time, that was her way of getting the beat and the step into our minds and souls, and it worked! (M. MacMaster 2010)

Minnie's adopted younger sister, Mary Janet MacDonald, also recalls their mother kinaesthetically passing on rhythm to her:

I do remember vividly being always held in Mama's lap while she jigged the tunes—hearing the beauty of her voice and the timing in her feet as she jigged the tunes—and [she] would sometimes dance while sitting down ... all the while me sitting on her lap—perhaps there was a transition of rhythm there? (M. J. MacDonald 2010)

Within bodies, and from body to body, the sights, sounds and proprioceptive feel of the dance migrated, was and is reconfigured by each individual, at the same time shaped by the family and surrounding community aesthetic preferences. These preferences, however, change over time, and I would like to illustrate this by taking a closer look at how movement may be influenced by language rhythm.

Linguistic Transitions—Some Issues around Gaelic- and English-Language Pulse

The particular rhythm provided by the sound of feet as they move is deeply connected to the inherent rhythms of step-dance music. In Cape Breton, there is an ongoing discussion of whether or not a Gaelic sound, or "flavour," is a defining factor in the local fiddle style. Until the early decades of the 20th century, learning among Cape Breton Gaels through the medium of Gaelic was regarded as the key transmission method in the informal setting of the home or ceilidh house.[17]

Two of the main ideas in this area of research are: (a) the difference in language rhythm between Gaelic and English, and (b) that the rhythm of the predominantly dance-orientated tunes played is directly tied to the Gaelic songs associated with the tunes. This research corresponds with wider discussions about the notion of "correct" playing (see, e.g., Graham 2006: 114-19) and the ability of performers to "embody" specific rhythm characteristics (see chapter 6). According to some, there is a particular rhythm characteristic clearly embedded in the Gaelic language and, according to one view, particularly so as expressed through *puirt-a-beul*, and this has translated into the Cape Breton–style music (Doherty 1996: 177; C. Dunn 1991: 16; Garrison 1985: 185; Kennedy 2002: 194-95, 205-207; Sparling 2000: 225-26, 2014; Shaw 1992-93: 44).

Kathleen Lambert (1985) conducted a study of storytelling and song in Ranafast, County Donegal, Ireland, in which she describes local speech rhythms, particularly the significance awarded to vowel lengths and the concept of asking for a song as *abair amhrán* or to "say a song." This term refers to the singers' ability to tell the story properly. The Donegal area's close linguistic and cultural ties with Gaelic Scotland are highlighted as a connection point between Scottish and Irish cultures in general, but in particular as expressed in the similarities between the Donegal-area's music and dance style and that of western Scotland's.

The point I want to highlight here is that, on a certain level of understanding, a good knowledge must be had of both text (content) and rhythm (melody, speech) in relation to text/song/music as transmitted through a particular language. In addition, I query below if it is the same for the dance/music relationship. As Shaw (1992-93: 39-40) points out, some ethnomusicologists such as Finnegan (1992) and Nettl (1964) have observed that some societies see the concepts of text and music as inseparable, and Shaw places the Gaelic culture among these. The point Shaw is making, quoting Sorley MacLean (MacGill-eain 1985: 106) as an example, is that even though technical ability to play a tune from the Gaelic tune repertoire, or the ability to mimic the sounds of their song repertoire, goes a long way, it cannot replace the understanding of them without having the Gaelic language (Shaw 1992-93: 39-40).

The view on this particular topic is polarized. For some this means that, by extension, Gaelic–Cape Breton music (and song) cannot be fully understood or reproduced without having the ability to speak the language. Others take a different view and state that the music has absorbed this Gaelic rhythm and thus can be picked up through the music alone by anyone with a good musical ear, as it has retained the core of the "dirt" or "flavour" (Doherty 1996: 176, 307; Garrison 1985:

234-35; Kennedy 2002: 207; Sparling 2000: 259).[18]

A third point would be that change is inevitable in a living tradition, whether a Gaelic one or not, due to the continual changes made by those performing the music. Maybe the core issue regarding the rhythmic influences on music and dance is rather one concerning the overarching speech rhythm in the Gaelic-speaking environment being diminished in favour of one in English. Following the arguments above, one may ask if a Gaelic-language environment, in contrast to an English-language environment, has had different influences on how rhythm is aurally transmitted or understood. Do we actually hear rhythm differently if it is sung or discussed in one language or the other, or played on an instrument?

The Gaelic speech rhythm, combined with the particular use of vowel lengths in Gaelic songs (particularly in *puirt-a-beul*), is a strong point of connection to the vernacular fiddle style of the older generation of Gaelic-speaking fiddlers (Kennedy 2002; Graham 2006; Doherty 1996). One may illustrate the difference in language rhythm between Gaelic and English by using the song/tune "Mairi's Wedding" and Uist-born John Roderick Bannerman's original Gaelic words for the song. In addition, I add Kennedy's (2002: 205) comparison of the English version to "Mhòrag bheag nighean Mhurchaidh an t-saor" (Little Morag, Daughter of Murdock, the Carpenter), highlighting the stress patterns in each case:[19]

– = stressed, **v** = unstressed

S i mo ghaol-sa Màiri Bhàn
–   v   –   v –   v –

Step we gaily on we go
–   **v** – **v**– **v** –

Mhórag bheag nighean Mhurchaidh an t-saor
– v   –   v v   – v v   v –

Gaelic scholar Michael Newton (2009) discusses various aspects of song, music and dance in Gaelic Scotland in his book *Warriors of the Word*, and the difference between Gaelic and English languages in relation to song, he writes:

The Gaelic language has a number of features which complicate the relationship between melody and words but which make a close correspondence all the more powerful and integral to the native speaker. Unlike English, the length of vowels are important in Gaelic: they can be short or long (according to the amount of time that they are held) and their lengths are phonemically significant.... This vowel system, along with regular initial-syllable stress and other features, causes speech utterances to conform to particular rhythmic patterns which are usually observed when the song is sung. It is the long notes (long vowel and diphthongs) which receive melodic ornamentation. (249)

Perhaps what needs to be taken into account here is the difference between rhythm/beat and pulse. A rhythm is generally more regular, while the internal pulse of a song or melody provides it with "feeling," as it is often described, which ties in with Newton's points above. Gaelic scholar and piper Alasdair MacMhaoirn (2014) of Rogart, Sutherland, says in a conversation that "by singing the tune [in Gaelic] the pulses have to come out right because the language steers the timing and this in turn gives the tune its feeling or, as is often said, puts the song in it." MacMhaoirn added that, in his mind, he "imagine[s] that a good dancer can put the song into dance the same way, while a not-so-good dancer may be very rhythmical but somehow missing the song or feeling." So, I would suggest that when Cape Bretoners speak about the importance of keeping time to the music when dancing, they may subconsciously refer to a deeper overarching sense of pulse that fits the local aesthetic preference applied to language, music and dance. (See the discussion on timing in chapter 6.)

Let's take another example, this time from Brittany, as regards the connection of Breton dance and language. In the circular dance *dañs dro plin'*, studied by Jean-Michel Guilcher (1995 [1963]), the emphasis in the main step is reversed from when it is danced to a Breton-language *kan ha diskan* to a French-language call-and-response song. The Breton-language song would have the rhythm emphasis on counts 1 and 3, while the French would have it on counts 2 and 4, and this is manifested in the step used for the same dance depending on which language the song is being danced to. Similarly, Dickson (2006) discusses the connection between words and bagpipe music in South Uist, Scotland. Glenuig piper Allan MacDonald additionally investigates the relationship between pibroch and Gaelic song and its implications on the performance style of the pibroch ùrlar (1995). Furthermore, Sparling's (2000) research outlines the paradoxical place held by *puirt-a-beul* in Cape Breton, and, in her dissertation (2005), *Song Genres, Cultural Capital and Social Distinctions in Gaelic Cape Breton*, she uses Bourdieusian theory of cultural capital to illustrate how Cape Bretoners place themselves socially by valuing or devaluing *puirt-a-beul*. Finally, both Graham (2006) and Doherty (1996) suggest that a "Gaelic flavour" is, to a certain extent, incorporated in the local music today, and that the notion of any change in the music is coming internally, from within the musicians, rather than predominantly from external language-related changes. Doherty (176) states:

> The rhythms of the Gaelic language had already become ingrained in the musical sound before there was a threat to the continuation of the language. Thus demise of the language did not necessarily impinge upon the musical style. What I am suggesting is that many of the characteristics of the language had already become established and accepted in purely musical terms.

At the heart of this debate, perhaps, is the question of the relevance of the Gaelic language itself in Cape Breton today, an issue recently analyzed by Emily McEwan-Fujita (2013) in *Gaelic Revitalization Efforts in Nova Scotia: Reversing Language Shift in the 21st Century*.

However, no one to my knowledge has addressed the issue of how movement or dance may inform the music and song genres of the culture or if language rhythm/pulse may have an impact on the dance. If the decline of the Gaelic language has not caused significant change to the fiddle style, as Doherty suggests, would not the same apply to the dance rhythms related to the musical style? If the links between Gaelic tunes and *puirt-a-beul* are still marginally maintained, even though specific linguistic references are perhaps not understood by the majority of dancers, would not step rhythms carry an inherently understood function, which then exist independently of the Gaelic language?

I agree with Jennifer Schoonover's (2015) suggestion that the step dancing in Cape Breton is Gaelicized due to the fact that the anacrusis[20] often encountered in aspects of some percussive step-dance styles (in England and Ireland,[21] to name but two) gets absorbed onto the end of the step in the current Cape Breton step-dance tradition. Cape Breton steps are now taught as starting on the first count of the music, which is how Scottish Gaelic is accented, Schoonover points out. This notion needs to be investigated further, as most steps in Dannsa nan Flurs (Flowers of Edinburgh)[22] can be seen, as in Rhodes's (1996) description, as starting with anacrusis, but analysis of the motifs depends on the way one assigns counts to the movements and where one acknowledges the start and end of a motif sequence. Not only should a possible bias of the researcher's notation and perception of the counting of the motif be taken into account, but also the possibility of different and mixed cultural origins of these particular named dances. It should be noted that Rhodes's descriptions of steps for the Fling and the Seann Triubhas start on the downbeat, while steps danced to "Over the Hills and Far Away" and in Dannsa nan Flurs precede the downbeat, displaying anacrusis. Could it be that these different types of dances reflect different dialects of step dancing? Perhaps some of this dance material originated outside of the Gaelic-speaking areas of Scotland before migrating to Cape Breton where the notation Rhodes recorded for posterity in 1957 still carries these possible signifiers of pulse difference. At present, we can only speculate on these matters.

The process of change for both music/dance rhythm and tune/step presentation is generally a slow one. There are, however, signs that increased contact with music and dance styles from outside Cape Breton have had an impact on the current style. From the point of view of fiddle music, I would refer to Graham's (2006: 132-36) outline of other changes, such as: artists from other musical genres—from Philip Glass to the Clancy Brothers—influencing particular players as examples; interaction with other musicians when travelling abroad; the influence of Irish music on the repertoire and the composition of new tunes. I refer also to Doherty's (1996: 176) remarks suggesting that even though the changes in the music occur at the same time as the decline of the Gaelic language in the local community, these changes are "being instigated from within the music itself."

From a dance point of view, I would offer, as an example of the outside influence of other forms of music and dance on Cape Breton music and dance, the fairly recent inclusion of "five-count" rhythms in certain steps that some claim was not present in days gone by and which one can hear in certain tunes.[23] Are these recent rhythm combinations that dancers choose to incorporate in their performances an effort to reflect the good relationship with the music to which they are dancing? Or are they external influences that fit these tunes? When the older music/dance/language relationship gets disassociated over time, and the inherent links between them are weakened, maybe other internal music and dance changes take place. I would suggest that this is where music and dance may be seen as separate. In recent years, I have observed that some younger musicians favour the stage-performance aspect of the tradition to that of playing predominantly for dancing. There is, however, also a recent resurgence of Gaelic-language interest among younger people in some parts of Cape Breton. Among them, there is a possibility that the relationship between the rhythm/pulse of the language and the rhythm of the music itself will be strengthened, and that some people will actively work to further strengthen the connections. However, it is also possible that the changes to the music and dance in general have become so ingrained that the Gaelic language no longer has the power to invoke a significant rhythmic influence at this stage. A lot of questions are raised in this book; not all of them will be answered. In the comments below, referring mainly to learning before the mid-1990s, it is clear that in learning specific movements it is the music, with its inherent language rhythms and internal changes, that dictates the making of a new "step."

All this being said, there is still, conceivably, an influence of the Gaelic language on music and dancing that is more conscious than we think. Glenn Graham's (2006: 63) recent research cites premier dance fiddler Kinnon Beaton's opinion that a combination of piping, language and dancing has had an effect on fiddle playing in Cape Breton, and that these links should not be underestimated. There are young players (dancers) in the community who have been exposed to the Gaelic language, according to Graham, and

> while it might be [more] desirable to be able to speak Gaelic, it is still possible with something less than fluency to obtain sufficient experience of the language to gain a feeling for its distinctive equivalent violin sounds. For it is the cultivation of an intuitive recognition of the language's rhythms and accents combined with digital ornamentation and bowing applications that help to create a Gaelic sound in the fiddle, not the ability to speak it. (p. 64)

It is certainly the rhythm inherent in the music, or conjured up in one's mind by the music (genre-tune knowledge), that also plays a part in the combination of familiar elements, cells and motifs into new steps. Mac Morin says, the "only way I would compose [a step] is if I were inspired to compose [it] by the music or with just a rhythm." He adds,

I enjoy that aspect of Cape Breton dancing, because it is very rhythmical. Of course it has to fit the music you can't compose— I say "compose"—you can't make a step solely based on rhythm because it has to fit somewhere, you have to be able to dance it ... I would take a rhythm that I have in my head, if this was the way I was making a step at the time, I would put some tunes on and see if it would work and then I would change it. Sure, it would work better with some tunes, but for the most part you can dance any step to any tune. You could get a general feel, that would work or that wouldn't work. So, I guess, thirty-five per cent of the time I would be making a step to music first. That would inspire me to make a step, but a lot of times I would wake up with a step in my head, which happened a lot. It is so funny, because Willie Fraser, he got the dreams and the steps, like I never dreamt of step danc-

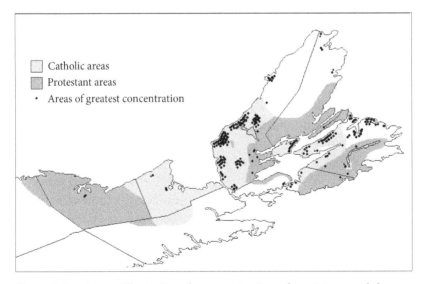

Figure 2.5 – A map illustrating the concentration of musicians and dancers in both Catholic- and Protestant-Gaelic settlement areas. Reproduced from Kennedy (2002), NSARM.

ing, but I was inspired a lot waking up. I would get out of bed and do a step in my room at home or away in a hotel. (Morin 2008)

It is worth noting that other sounds than just the sound of the music and the dance play a part in creating the soundscape; the surrounding sounds of the people interacting and so forth are important too. As Melody Cameron (2011) puts it, "You hear the music, the beats, like rhythms, of the feet on the floor and the hoots and hollers in the hall."

The above discussion and the questions asked indicate that a separate study regarding links between the rhythm and pulse of the Gaelic language and dancing needs to be undertaken in greater detail. To summarize this section, I would argue that if the prominent language (speech) rhythm in use is Gaelic, the resulting rhythm and pulse in music, song and dance would be different if the prominent language is English. That the language connection is important in the music can easily be illustrated by the often-used phrase that a particular fiddler "has the Gaelic in the music" as being the highest of compliments (Shaw 1992-93: 41; Doherty 1996: 305; Graham 2006: 61-72). I find it hard to think that some of the older rhythms from a once-dominant Gaelic soundscape would not migrate to, and be absorbed by, the preferred music and movement aesthetics in Cape Breton.

The Place of Dance in the Family and Community

The place of dance and the role of the individual dancer in relation to family and community, and the role of movement playing a vital part in the transmission of knowledge is often overlooked in the discussions of handing down the local heritage of music. The emphasis is predominantly on the ways and on the repertoire. One reason the role of the dancer is overlooked might be that most musicians in Cape Breton also step dance, and some are regarded as dancers and regularly share their steps publicly—that is, it is possible that the link between movement and music-making has often been taken for granted or not considered by the observers of the language/music link. On the basis of the accumulated data in this investigation, I would postulate that those who also hold the dance/movement repertoire have an added layer of embodied proprioceptive or kinaesthetic knowledge. This layer is integral and should be taken into account when analyzing the traditional aural and visual transmission processes. The biographies in this book concentrate on individuals who are known for their ability to dance. It is nonetheless important to hear some observations on the role of dance from a musician's point of view. In many ways, piper John MacLean's (2010) recollections of growing up in Washabuck sum up a holistic Gaelic household environment where the interconnectedness of the various cultural strands was taken for granted.[24] It was, however, an environment in transition. In relation to dancing, he recalls,

> Dancing was as natural as walking, and was taught in the homes. Square sets took place indoors and outdoors. Often (as in the case of my mother and father), an outdoor platform for round and square dancing was built on the family farm for weddings and special occasions.

All of the step dancing and square dancing in MacLean's community of MacAdams Lake was done to the pipes, and they held on to older ideals of life in general. One reason for this, as MacLean puts it, is that they were isolated. In fact, MacLean's grandfather still called Uist *an t-seann dùthaich* (the old country). Neither his maternal grandfather nor his great uncle, both pipers, could read music, and the repertoire of rare tunes they passed down to John do not appear in pipe-music collections. They learned mainly from their parents, who sang in Gaelic, and from a very old man who worked on their farm who had been born in South Uist. John makes a point of indicating that his paternal grandfather, Johnny "Red" Rory MacLean, and his father, Johnny "Washabuck" MacLean, were both well-respected step dancers as well as noted fiddlers.[25] MacGillivray (1997: 140) notes that his father could "accurately execute some ancient and difficult steps passed on to him through the family of Dan MacKinnon of Washabuck." The household was always full of music.

The MacLeans of Washabuck were, and still are, well known for having a particularly lively musical style, especially suited for step dancing, which can still be heard in the playing of people like Michael Anthony MacLean, Joe MacLean, their sister Theresa Morrison, Carl MacKenzie and the MacNeil family of Sydney Mines. His aunt, Aggie MacLennan, described above, was a noted step dancer. John's own music, however, became a hybrid. His parents felt Gaelic would be a disadvantage to him because their generation felt that "an 'accent'

Figure 2.6 – Sunday afternoon ceilidh at the MacLean farmstead in Washabuck in the late 1940s or early 1950s. Johnny "Red" Rory MacLean is step dancing to the fiddle playing of his cousin Michael Anthony MacLean. The man sitting in the background is Michael Dan MacLean (Mickey "Red" Rory), Johnny's brother. The man sitting in the foreground is Angus MacDonald, a relation by marriage. The house is Johnny MacLean's childhood home on the original homestead of the settlers from Barra. Johnny's father, Red Rory (Ruruaidh Dearg ic Domnull), is in the portrait on the wall as a young man. He was also a great dancer. He kept his dance slippers under his chair and pulled them out as soon as Johnny came home, as he was also a noted fiddler. Photo by John MacLean and used with kind permission.

from the country marked a person as ignorant and poor" (MacLean 2012). Because of this, they did not encourage Gaelic to their children. Likewise, they automatically assumed that the correct way of piping was that taught in the army and that which was common in Ontario, for example—military style. So, John pushed the local music style of his childhood into the background for many years in favour of modern style competitive piping, which in turn removed his music-making from dancing. Since the 1990s, however, he began reclaiming his family style of music-making "in the 'Scotch' style," which actually never disappeared completely and for which he is now known. It is important to understand, John concludes,

Figure 2.7 – Melody Cameron step dancing to a puirt-a-beul *sung by Joy Dunlop, Strathspey Place, Mabou, July 24, 2011. Photo by V. M. Faubert, used with kind permission.*

that many Cape Bretoners, like Harvey Beaton and myself, were raised by people who saw themselves in terms of their Hebridean roots *first*, even before being Canadian.... They only saw themselves as "Scotch" people and nothing else. In the case of the Curries and MacLeans, living in isolation, there was no outside blood from the time of the emigration to my generation—not even a mixing of religion, until I married a Morrison—whose people came from Harris in 1820 (MacLean 2012).

Due to the decline in the number of Gaelic speakers, its function in transmitting tunes and its use as a tool for teaching step dancing have also diminished. In the first half of the 20th century, Gaelic-language songs were still sung at home by women doing their daily chores or in jigging, as mentioned earlier.

In July 2009, I observed John MacLean play the pipes for Harvey Beaton's step dancing at the annual Ceòlas Summer School in South Uist. St. Peter's Hall in Daliburgh was packed with locals (many of whom are Gaelic speakers) and visitors attending the "Piping Ceilidh." Watching John playing, seated on a chair on the dance floor in front of the small stage, he played tunes from his family repertoire clearly recognized by the locals present, judging by their approving nods and the favourable comments overheard about his playing. When Harvey took the floor, there was a noticeable rise in the energy of John's playing and a wonderful interplay of a musician responding to the dancer's feet and a dancer's interpretation of the piper's tunes began. In my opinion, the equal importance of both performers was clear for all to see, hear and feel—the strong rhythms of the pipe music emphasized by the dancer. The two showed their excellence in harmony with each other, providing a strong statement that this is music for dancing and that the two should not be seen as separate.

Memorization and the Importance of Repertoire

The time factor in learning processes is important. I feel that our current world constantly emphasizes the speed of learning as opposed to taking time to learn something thoroughly. This is a generalization, but the time factor is a topic sometimes highlighted in discussions with my academic peers when we discuss what we value among "tradition bearers." A tradition bearer has taken a lifetime of experience to produce what we cherish them for, but it is felt that perhaps the younger generation is trying to fast track themselves to the same level of competence. Their ability to embody their dancing or music is applauded as is often the extent of their repertoire of steps or tunes. In addition, we applaud their ability to interpret their music or the ability to fit appropriate movement to a particular tune. Even though many current and young exponents are excellent performers, a particularly deep quality recognized in the performance of musicians and dancers of the past is lacking. Of course those deeper qualities that we say we appreciate come with experience, but is there a current need to speed up the learning process of getting to excellence that was not required in the past? Over the years I have observed, in workshop situations in particular, a notion with some people that you can learn all you need over a few days, at which point you are ready to perform it and pass it on in turn! To me, this is ignorant of the processes of learning and the time it takes to embody a certain skill set and to hone and master it with confidence. I feel further research is required in addition to my own observations and thoughts on this topic. It may well be that the speeding up of learning processes might alter the level of depth of the understanding of what we do.

I thus highlight *time* as a key component in all Cape Breton music and dance learning, and also the predominance of learning over long periods of time in the home environment. Even though, initially, learning in the home is possibly less commonplace today, it is important to note that in the past most youngsters served an informal apprenticeship in the home, soaking up the finer nuances of culture by watching, listening and kinaesthetically absorbing movement over a long period of time. Similar transmission processes occur in public spaces, but are later remembered at home, where the memories are strengthened through repetition, as indicated in a number of the recollections quoted above. All participants, actively or passively, are involved in sharing knowledge, albeit subconsciously; over time, a huge knowledge base of different cultural expressions can be embodied in this local environment. These processes of learning are seldom recalled in the written accounts we can access (though MacGillivray 1988 is an example of one) as far as what specific tunes or movements were learned. In addition, movements are also hard to describe as little terminology exists to verbalize what specific movements were learned. What I have observed, however, is the detailed knowledge displayed by performers and the detailed discussions on performance taking place in Cape Breton, which indicate an immersive and ex-

tensive level of understanding of the relationship between tunes, movements and memorized material. It is the little things, such as if a dancer does a particular movement that fits well with a particular tune, or that certain tunes trigger certain motifs when a particular dancer is in action, that may be remarked on in discussion.

A good example is highlighted by Kennedy (2002) and Shaw (1992-93) when they examine the skill of memorizing

Figure 2.8 – Step dancing at a house party in Mabou. Fr. Eugene Morris, August 9, 2008. Photo by Victor Maurice Faubert, used with kind permission.

large amounts of songs and stories by ear. Kennedy states, and my own experience corroborates, that certain fiddlers are known to have a repertoire of 500 to 1,000 tunes, and sometimes even more, readily available if the circumstances and company of other fiddlers are right (Kennedy 2002: 121). The unspoken rule for fiddlers playing at square dances is never to repeat a tune in an evening; I have experienced close to a forty-five-minute set of reels played without a single tune being repeated (at the West Mabou Dance in July 1996, for example). Having a large tune repertoire is the norm rather than the exception. In other words, very high standards of "correct" expression are set within this music tradition.

The ability to embody music is also reflected in the movement repertoire. The embodiment and memorization of many possible movement variations based on the essential (or core) movement repertoire of the local dance genre go hand in hand with the readily available, substantial tune repertoire. A dancer is commended for the ability to match fitting movements with a particular tune. Even though, in theory, any reel step can be danced to any reel, certain movements lend themselves better to certain tunes or tune types. I have observed certain movements being favoured by a good number of dancers to minor (or major) tunes. Subsequently, when trying it out

Figure 2.9 – Square set at a house party, no date. Photo courtesy D. Cameron.

myself, I have felt this work for me as well. Nobody, however, told me to match these movements with these tune types. I got to understand this by watching and listening, on multiple occasions over the years, and then, based on my observations, a kinaesthetic awareness made me realize what movements fit well for me with these different tunes types as I dance it myself.

It is worth noting that a large repertoire allows for considerable individual creativity and interpretation in music, and the same knowledge in a dancer helps them understand which movements fit best where. Furthermore, the movement repertoire seems to have expanded in recent years, alongside an expanding tune repertoire (though not expanding to the same extent), which, for example, incorporates new rhythm combinations (Doherty 2006; Graham 2004, 2006; Dorchak 2006, 2010). Is it perhaps the case in the Cape Breton community that music memory and movement memory work hand in hand to enable their performance ease of both? The great majority of Cape Breton dancers are also musicians at some level; they embody knowledge of both disciplines, and thus each aspect complements the other. I will discuss these notions of interpretation, creativity and (expanding) movement (motif) repertoire further in chapter 6.

The home environment was, at least until the 1970s and 1980s, and, in some families, still is, central to the transmission of knowledge and cultural values.[26] Aural, visual and kinaesthetic transmission processes combine in the intimate home environment and intensify exposure to the dance genre. All the actors involved produce variations around a core body of movement repertoire—that is, the most common motifs (steps) used—to a familiar soundscape. This learning environment provided good conditions for embodying this dance genre according to local aesthetic and stylistic preferences. Certain rhythmic sound combinations, repeated time and again, in conjunction with the corresponding visual stimuli of certain movement patterns reinforced by kinaesthetic transfer from body to body, are the transmission processes at work. Aural, visual and kinaesthetic reinforcement of rhythm and movement patterns was at the core of the learning, with some keywords (encouraging lightness, for example) thrown in by the elders. Copying direct visual and aural cues and working steps out for yourself, sometimes by holding onto another dancer or older relation, are the most common transfer methods at work, according to the recollections.

Some still take the natural inclusion of dance in the home environment for granted, even though it is much less common. Melody Cameron's sister Kelly (MacLennan) serves as a good example of this: she home-schools her children and takes them to dances, concerts and other events to give them further exposure. Another good recent illustration of the importance of the home environment to contemporary dancers is Mary Janet MacDonald's youngest son, Mitch. When he became a semi-finalist in the 2008 reality TV show *Canadian Idol*, the producers recorded a short clip to introduce him to the national viewers. This TV clip contained scenes from a house ceilidh in the MacDonald family home, in Port Hood, Cape Breton, complete with fiddle music and step dancing provided by family members and close relatives, to show Mitch's roots.[27] In recent years, Féis Mhàbu members Derrick and Melody Cameron have organized house ceilidhs in their West Mabou home, inviting young local musicians to meet the older generation of tradition bearers. This initiative can be seen as a step to boost the transmission processes in the home, a context that is becoming less common in most Cape Breton households.

Chapter 3

Informal Dance Transmission in the Classroom

Observing Dance Teaching in "Third Places"

Three of the contexts in this study—the classroom, the concert and the square dance (see chapters 4 and 5 for a discussion of the latter two)—fall under what sociologist Ray Oldenburg terms "third places." A third place is "a setting beyond home and work (the first and second place, respectively) in which people relax in good company and do so on a regular basis" (Oldenburg 2000: 2). Oldenburg also says third places are those where the *real thing* takes place—that is, real community interaction—and is expected to take place on an ongoing basis, unlike many modern urban "community" buildings, cafés and the like, which are constructed with the idea that people should gather there but often remain underused, just buildings (2000: 2-4). As places of community interaction and, by extension, places of transmission, the locales in Cape Breton where formal classes, dances and community concerts take place fit Oldenburg's definition of meaningful third places. The home and the people we live with are central to most people; for many, the workplace is where we spend most of our time. Third places can be seen as the places where community life is anchored, where broader and more creative interaction is facilitated and fostered. One aspect of the meaning of a third place that Oldenburg singles out is that it can be seen as a home away from home, where one can be spiritually regenerated or feel rooted in that place (Oldenburg 1989).

Formal classes in step dance can take place in a number of locations; once they were commonly held in the home of the teacher, while since the 1970s they have been commonly held in local parish halls or schools or community/sports centres. All these places are associated with other community gatherings that are strong focal points in Cape

Breton community life, and therefore the location of the class has many associated meanings.

"Dance classes" here refer mainly to classes that span a number of weeks, usually eight or more, and that local teachers teach to the local community. The study also took into account the intensive summertime dance courses that locals and visitors attend.

When conducting my research observations of Cape Bretoners teaching classes, I took the role of learner and observer rather than of a teacher. My observations were mainly conducted at summer courses and workshops in Scotland from 1992 onward, as well as at the Gaelic College (1995-1996) in St. Ann's, Cape Breton, and at various summertime workshops in Cape Breton from 1995 to the present. My experience as a teacher in many different types of teaching contexts (community halls, church halls, schools, sports halls, festival workshops, etc.) was an advantage as I was familiar with different types of floors and room environments. You may be teaching on a sprung wooden floor in an old hall with good acoustics or in a modern gymnasium on a hard floor with a lot of echo in the room. To some extent, different contexts influence how you can pitch your teaching, for example. Having this personal teaching experience was also an advantageous reference point when analyzing my research interviews with Cape Bretoners (2006-2012) recalling their teaching experience from the 1970s onward.

Early Records of Dance Classes in Cape Breton

Before surveying class-based dance instruction in Cape Breton since the 1970s, it is important to be aware that dance classes have been part of the cultural life of Cape Breton since the early days of immigration. For example, French dancing masters were active in Louisbourg as early as the mid-18th century (Donovan 2002). Most of the written references available to us, nonetheless, are about immigrants from Scotland. Studying the entries in MacDougall's (1922) *History of Inverness County, Nova Scotia*, it seems that from the early 1800s it was predominantly men who set up dancing "schools," often in their own homes, and that it was predominantly women who taught dance, presumably also in the home (Rhodes 1985, 1996; MacGillivray 1988; Gibson 2005).[1] For instance, Mary "Jack" Gillis refers to "dancing masters" who came from Scotland and taught step dancing all year round, such as "Big" John ("the dancer") Alex Gillis's father, Allan Gillis, who was a dancing master in Southwest Margaree, Inverness County. Allan taught in his home for free and enjoyed dancing to fiddler Angus Allan Gillis, who was also a good step dancer (Mac-Gillivray 1988: 66). Margaret Gillis adds that her great-grandfather (Allan's father) was Alexander Gillis (Mac Iain ic Alasdair), who had been a dancing master in Scotland before emigrating in 1826. These dancing skills were passed down through generations (60). Other names mentioned in relation to teaching in Cape Breton the 1800s are: Alexander MacDonnell in Kiltarlity, the Kennedys in Broad Cove, and Angus Beaton in Southwest Margaree and Inverness Town (Mac-Dougall 1922; MacGillivray 1988: 60, 66; Rhodes 1996: 190). According to Rhodes (1985: 274), the dancing schools disappeared around the time square dances, Quadrilles, Lancers and Saratoga Lancers were introduced to the island, around 1890-1900.

As was the practice in Scotland and in Ireland, dancing masters would travel from community to community, staying with friends or relatives. The late James D. Gillis said in a 1945 CBC Radio interview that

> the dancing master would set up a school in a community or area. The school would involve mostly young people and the training would extend over two or three days. In the beginning, graceful and simple moves would be introduced. This was followed over the next few days with more intricate dance steps. (quoted in Shears 2008: 76)

This account does not indicate if the dancing master stayed in the area for a longer period or if there was a series of repeated classes, which was the case in Scotland, where teachers could stay in an area for up to fourteen weeks, teaching in a different place each day of the week (Flett and Flett 1985 [1964]: 1-30).[2] Dance lessons in Cape Breton took place in the home, the schoolhouse or, in the case of Angus Beaton's class in Southwest Margaree, on a wooden bridge (Rhodes 1996: 190). Angus Beaton (1823-1899), son of Mary (MacDonald) Beaton (1795-1880), also taught dancing in his home in the community of Mabou Coal Mines. Angus was sometimes paid for his classes in firewood, cut by the young men of the area who attended the classes (MacGillivray 1988: 30).

Frank Rhodes (1996) notes some of the named solo dances that the dancing masters brought to Cape Breton Island from Scotland in 1957. The main solo dances taught were the Fling (not called the "Highland Fling," as it is in Scotland, according to Rhodes's sources), the Swords, Seann Triubhas, Flowers of Edinburgh (Dannsa nan Flurs), Jacky Tar, Duke of Fife, The Girl I Left Behind Me, Tullochgorm, Irish Washerwoman and Princess Royal, all ten originally having twelve steps each. Each "step" consisted of a circle movement during the "A" part of the tune and of stepping on the spot during the "B" part, as detailed below. Ronald Kennedy of Broad Cove learned the first seven dances as a young boy, watching his father teach them in classes held in the district until about 1900. The dance titles came from John Gillis and his daughter, Margaret Gillis, of Gillisdale, Southwest Margaree. Fiddle was the preferred instrument to accompany these dances, according to Rhodes; he does not mention the use of the pipes.

Detailed descriptions of a selection of these dances can be found in Rhodes (1996: 194-211), and they provide a glimpse of the remembered dance repertoire in 1957. These solo dances had a fixed sequence of steps, each with a particular tune attached to it. They all had the characteristics of a Reel in the first part of the tune, in which the dancer performed six travelling steps, dancing in a circle clockwise, ending with two bars of stepping on the spot. The travelling steps were often softer steps, which Rhodes identifies as chassés, but the dancer could mark out extra beats during the circular Reel according to some of Rhodes's sources. I noted that Margaret Gillis added these extra beats in an effortless manner, almost subconsciously, when showing me chassé steps when she danced for me in her family home in Gillisdale in 2007. These steps were alternated with particular percussive steps danced to the second part of the tune. The stepping was not always continuous stepping, but was characterized by a special movement followed by a percussive finish to the second part of the tune. Another interesting characteristic of these dances is that the second part was only danced starting with one foot and not repeated starting with the other foot, as is common with almost all solo dances found in Scotland (Rhodes 1996: 191). This last characteristic may have changed over time; in 2007, Margaret Gillis indicated that each step in the Flowers of Edinburgh should be danced off both the right and the left foot (M. Gillis 2007).

Rhodes found in 1957 that only certain families had kept these solo dances alive, passing them on from generation to generation. The aforementioned families, the Beatons of Southwest Margaree and the Kennedys of Broad Cove, were on Rhodes's list, as were the MacMillans of Creignish, to name a few.

In John Gibson's (2005) study of piping in Cape Breton, he also refers frequently to fiddle playing and dancing. With regard to the families mentioned above, among others, he brings up the interesting point that the named dances may have been perceived differently compared with extempore continuous step dancing. Gibson suggests:

> The old social stratification of Gaelic society in Scotland survived in Cape Breton and, what's more, may have been mirrored in cultural graduations. These graduations may only have differed inasmuch as some contained some formality in approach and presentation. Into this category I am inclined to put the dancing and the dances taught in the dancing schools that existed for most of the nineteenth century but had practically disappeared from living memory by 1994. (264)

Gibson also refers to an 1896 series of articles in the Antigonish newspaper *The Casket* about the dancing of a sword dance, Gille Chaluim, and how one Angus (Bàn) MacDougall is said to have danced the Sword Dance or Highland Fling in a forest clearing to the piping of Allan MacCormack (MacCormack 1998). The passage for Gibson suggests that the "formality in approach and presentation" of these dances was somehow recognized and may well refer to their structured repeat patterns, as discussed above, and, as such, that they were signified with a specific name and also linked to a specific tune. In contrast, the extempore continuous step dancing may have been thought of as something more closely related to the stepping occurring in the Reels. Why the latter has survived and become the predominant step dance form in use in Cape Breton, while the former has almost disappeared completely, is still to be determined.

What is clear, according to Rhodes (1996), is that structured and named solo dances were for close-up interaction at close-knit gatherings or house ceilidhs. They were meant to be heard as well as seen: hard shoes were worn and arm movements were not used—according to Rhodes's sources, the arms were held downward, by the sides, and the body was held upright (190). These observations were confirmed to me when Margaret Gillis danced the Flowers of Edinburgh. I saw, heard and felt her dancing as I was seated in close proximity to her in her kitchen. I heard and felt her feet beating out the steps clearly on the linoleum-covered wooden floor as well as the sound bouncing back to me from the wooden walls.

The number of people who knew these solo dances began to decline in the years between the two world wars and continued to decline rapidly afterward. Rhodes appears to have caught some of the last active glimpses of this particular aspect of the Cape Breton dance tradition. Rhodes (1985, 1996) seems to agree with Gibson (2005) that the named solo dances of the 19th century were singled out alongside improvised step dancing. Rhodes's descriptions make it clear that the nature of these named solo dances is closer to the current style (but not necessarily in their structure) of step dancing than to modern versions of solo Highland Games dances appearing in Cape Breton and mainland North America in the 20th century. Kennedy also agrees with the notion that a varying degree of formality occurred within the master schools of the 19th century, and that step dancing and the structured "Highland dances," as Kennedy (2002) refers to them, were taught interchangeably. This more formal teaching occurred alongside the informal transmission of dance (and music) knowledge in the homes of Gaels (Kennedy 2002: 211). It is also important to differentiate these structured solo dances from those Highland dances of a competitive nature that had filtered into Cape Breton by the end of the 19th century and early into the 20th, directly or indirectly from Scotland, and which have undergone a considerable transformation in their style, particularly in the latter half of the 20th century. As indicated by Rhodes, the popularity of the named solo-dance tradition, which seems to have been passed on by certain families or individuals in a more "formal" fashion, waned during the 19th century in favour of extempore step dancing.

Formal Classes in Step Dancing from the 1970s Onward

Even though some of the early settlers in Cape Breton held dance classes, we know very little in detail of how these classes were conducted or taught and, as such, they remain a topic for further investigation.

However, during the resurgence of local interest in fiddle music in the mid-1970s a number of community step-dance classes were started up, encouraged in part by local priests and musicians.

Among the generation of teachers (1970s to mid-1980s) MacGillivray (1988) covers are: Fr. Eugene Morris teaching in a number of places, including North Sydney; Minnie MacMaster and Geraldine MacIsaac teaching in the Glendale and Creignish area; Margaret Dunn in Antigonish; and Mary Janet MacDonald teaching in Port Hawkesbury and Chéticamp. Jean MacNeil held classes in the North Sydney and Sydney Mines area. Harvey Beaton recalls taking eight weeks of classes in the Creignish Hall from Minnie MacMaster, and later some lessons at her house (MacGillivray 1988: 32-33). At a workshop in Whycocomagh, in about 1979, a number of teachers—Eugene Morris, Betty Matheson, Patsy Graham, Sister Dolina Beaton, Minnie MacMaster, Margaret Dunn and Margaret Gillis—came together to share their knowledge (33). Harvey Beaton was in the next generation of teachers, starting out in 1977 with a class in Port Hastings. Similarly, Kay Handrahan started teaching in New Waterford at about the same time. Margaret MacLellan Gillis and Betty Matheson both learned from Fr. Eugene and then started their own classes in North Sydney and Dominion, respectively.

These early teachers share many commonalities, key among them is that none learned to dance in a formal, class context. They all emerged from the home and community transmission context and had to figure out how best to pass on their skills in a class setting, as will be outlined below. The next generation of teachers came out of a mixed environment of learning both at home and in a class. Dance classes in the 1970s started out small, but as demand increased, more classes were organized. For some, like Mary Janet MacDonald, classes became part of life, in between daytime work and managing a large family (seven children). She taught in Port Hawkesbury, Judique, Port Hood, Mabou, Whycocomagh, Orangedale, Margaree and Chéticamp. Some classes, like the one held in a gymnasium in Chéticamp, had fifty to seventy people. The Port Hood class, for example, ran for ten weeks, in both autumn and spring, for years. Mary Janet MacDonald recalls the Mabou class:

> that very first class, Joey Beaton asked me to come to Mabou and he'd gather a bunch of kids together. "We've got to get this

going again." And having never been taught in a formal sense, [I] didn't have a clue what I was doing. How to break them [the steps] down and everything.... I had to learn how to teach or learn to know what it was I was doing. But I will absolutely tell you this, that as you brought the dancing to ... the wider world then—like you moved out of your comfort zone—you went to Scotland and then went to California and then ... Seattle and Utah and Chicago, those places, all of a sudden people start questioning what you're doing. They want to find out, they want to get inside it and they're coming from all these other kinds of backgrounds and examining and everything else; because of that, I changed how I do things in my dancing. Where once I was totally spontaneous, all of a sudden I know that I changed the way I do things, so that it would be more correct. Now, what I mean by that is when I would get up to step dance, I don't know if I would start with my left foot or my right foot. It didn't matter. Would I start at the beginning of a phrase or in the middle of a phrase? Or would I do three steps instead of four? Would I do them all evenly? I don't know and I don't think ... that was not something that was taught, it wasn't structured like that ... that when I danced before, I never thought about what I did. Did I start with the first beat with my left foot and do everything even? No, I know I didn't. (M. J. MacDonald 2007)

This recollection is representative of those who started to teach in the 1970s. Over time, the formality and the notion of teaching "correctly" entered the equation, and the notion of structures became important. As Mary Janet further explains:

Now I will teach ... start every sequence of steps with your left foot and that will keep everybody on the right/correct foot, whatever. Did I do that [back then]? Absolutely not! ... I taught a lot of, a lot, a lot, a lot of people in those early days. Goodness knows what I taught them. (M. J. MacDonald 2007)

Even though these structures become important in teaching the genre, people like Mary Janet who learned in an informal setting still revert back to the informal when they dance socially or at home:

I revert back to that when I'm dancing, in a square set, whatever. But if I get up to solo, because people [encourage you], sometimes you want to, because the music moves you, [but I'm] not in my comfort zone.... I would do the exact same thing on the stage as I would in the hall. It would be totally spontaneous; [I] wouldn't know what step I was going to do next, the same as the fiddler doesn't know what tune he's going to play next.... I really, really like to be in the house and dancing, just getting up and doing a few steps. Not a bit long, not a whole strathspey, a full reel, whatever. I just "God that's a good tune, I'm going to get up and do a few steps." That, I think, is what it was meant to be. (M. J. MacDonald 2007)

Some structures did, however, always exist; both MacMaster and MacDonald recall their mother, Maggie Ann Beaton, telling them that the dancing should be balanced. A step done on the one foot should be repeated on the other. Leaving out a repeat would take something out of a "good" step.

Transmission Processes in the Classroom

Over the years, I have observed a number of Cape Bretoners teaching in various contexts, and they all use themselves as visual examples and emphasize the rhythm of the steps when passing on their skills. They tend to organize their class in a circle around them, or have the class form rows and they dance in front of them. Teachers commonly dance with accompanying music to show the relationship between the music and the dance, but they do not always verbalize this relationship, perhaps because it seems obvious.[3] If available, they use live music for accompaniment, or even play themselves. Recorded music is also common, and some have had special recordings made by local musicians with the music slowed down to assist learning. For instance, when Margaret Dunn started teaching, Buddy MacMaster kindly recorded some music for her at a slower tempo (Dunn 2007). Some break down steps to individual movements in a way that makes sense to them, according to how they learned the steps themselves; from an emic perspective, in other words. Leanne Aucoin, for example, recalls learning from Jean MacNeil, who would break down the steps slowly for the class (Aucoin 2008). MacNeil would first face her students and then turn around to give them an opportunity to copy the steps from the back. This way of teaching can be seen in her instructional video (J. MacNeil 2005). Other teachers just dance the movements many times over and leave the students to pick up the steps at their own pace. If asked, they may isolate a small segment and repeat it. Some teachers, however, are unable to break down their steps into smaller segments; they pass on what they themselves either picked up or made up. In other words, there is no standard way of teaching but, rather, many individual takes on how to break down and transmit the required movements.

These different ways of teaching can lead to some criticism from outsiders to the tradition about how the genre is taught. Students who come from a different cultural background or are used to different styles of teaching have been known to voice displeasure at the segmentation and lack of methodology in Cape Bretoners' teachings. Over the years, when attending workshops and summer schools, predominantly in Scotland, such as Ceòlas in South Uist, I have overheard comments along the lines of "He/she just shows us the steps but does not break things down slowly"; or "They are not consistent with how they teach the steps." People make similar comments about fiddlers sharing their style of playing: "He/she is just playing the tune, not teaching it to us" (Melin 2013b). I feel these concerns arise because there are two fundamentally different approaches to teaching and learning at work here. Keep in mind that those making these comments generally come from a very different learning environment, which creates a different set of resulting skills expectations than that of the teachers. When you have learned without consciously being taught, though, you have been part of a different kind of transmission process altogether. Those who complain have not necessarily been part of a slow, constant transmission process. Like me, many acquired their technical skills in formal classes and workshops, but some are not as able to adjust, or even appreciate, other forms of transmission. Instances of such complaints are relatively few, mind you, but they illustrate a difference between the older transmission modes of Cape Breton and the new ones. The frustration expressed by some outside learners may indicate that the detail needed to teach step dancing in Cape Breton is quite specific to the needs of that particular place, and maintains elements of the implicit visual, aural and kinaesthetic transmission processes that are understood locally. These implicit transmission processes are likely the same ones through which the dance teachers originally acquired their own dancing skills.

Transmission in the classroom involves a mixture of visual and aural cues. I found that in my first classes learning Cape Breton step dance I initially accessed the movements visually. It is the distance between the learners, positioned in a circle or in a row facing the teacher, that created and prioritized a visual learning environment for me. This is corroborated in my recollections of discussions following these first workshops in Scotland and, later, in Cape Breton. One would say things along the lines of "Did you see how he did the end of that step?" and the answer could be "No, not clearly, we should ask him to show us again." Both statements indicate something visual in the words "see" and "show" (Melin 2006).

When prompted to listen, we did, as a class, and would tune our ears to the rhythm of the teacher's feet, but initially the aural input was, at least on a conscious level, secondary to the visual for me and for a number of my contemporary learners (Melin 2006). It is important to remember that each individual learns in a different way. Perhaps my experience reflects my own previous learning experiences of Highland dancing, for instance, where the emphasis was on the visual presentation of where the feet were to be placed. Over time, however, I have adjusted my learning to prioritize the aural. I took to heart the comments of Cape Breton dancers that I should listen to the rhythm of the feet, and also, more importantly, listen for the rhythm of the music or the pulse and character of a particular melody and match my footwork accordingly. Now, I tend to shut my eyes, listen to the rhythm of the feet, get a feel for that rhythm, and then look at the visual presentation of the step to get the shape and order of the movements. I have found that I learn a new step quicker this way, but that experience is subjective.

One reason I observe that the visual takes precedence in a class situation is the combined sounds of all learners trying to copy the teacher, each with a different ability initially, which often creates an out-of-sync soundscape. If the teacher is showing a step while the class is standing still, then of course one can see and hear the step; but, when everybody dances at the same time, one might not be able to isolate the sound of the teacher among the sounds of the class footwork. My observations seem to indicate that the emphasis may thus fall on the visual as a safer way of keeping track of what to do, and thus push the sound to a secondary input. The quality of the sound received is also an important factor. The type of room the class takes place in affects how we hear things. A well-sprung wooden floor often has good acoustic qualities, which helps aural learning, while a modern concrete sports building with a hard floor, and possibly poor acoustics, provides an echo that may hamper aural learning. The number of students in the group, their individual abilities and speed of learning also affect a formal teaching environment from both visual and aural perspectives. For example, a teacher has to divide a large group into small sections and work simultaneously on different steps, and possibly at different levels and speeds with each group in turn, which may create a muddled soundscape in the room. In my experience visual learning tends to be prioritized. All these aspects of the learning environment affect the transmission processes to some degree.

Kinaesthetic learning, on the other hand, tends to require a close proximity between the teacher and the learner. This often means that the focus of the teacher goes from the general class to a specific individual. Many teachers will on occasion join hands with a student at some point and dance with them. Minnie MacMaster describes such a kinaesthetic flow from her to the students in a teaching situation:

> When you [are] teaching dancing to others, you want them to have as much fun in dancing as you have had. Some students are easier to teach than others and you try to find ways of getting them to understand the timing and the "feel of the steps." Many times when I taught dancing, I used to take each student and hold hands with them and teach them in that way.... It would seem that when holding hands with me, they could feel the music and the timing more clearly than when they danced on their own.... In the end, they would learn the step and be more confident in how they presented it. My feeling was that they could feel that beat through my hands.... It sort of made more sense to them.... It made them feel both the beat of the music and the beat of the step. (M. MacMaster 2010)

Jackie Dunn-MacIsaac told me in an email conversation of how her mother, Margaret, sometimes used to teach her students by holding their hands as well, "to help them 'feel' the beat of her step as she taught it." Jackie says, "I believe it is like a rhythmic guide to hold someone's hands. Even if the person isn't getting every move of the step, the flow of the music, and the movement of the steps gives them the end goal of what it should feel like" (Dunn-MacIsaac 2010c).

I have, over the years, observed and experienced that Cape Breton dance teachers give students a lot of individual attention and, if need be, spend time showing and explaining movements to each individual in turn in a group class.

The local style of dance music naturally has a big impact on the transmission of suitable rhythm, timing and melodies appropriate for step dancing. In class, however, it is not always possible to have a fiddler playing. Live musicians playing for a regular class does happen, of course, and if the teacher is also a competent dance fiddler she may accompany her own class. My sources did indicate that it was common to use taped music in class in the 1970s and 80s, and some, like Margaret Dunn, had cassette tapes made for them which included tracks with tunes slowed down to assist their teaching. In recent years, CDs and iPods are frequently used as music media for classes as desired by a particular teacher. At the summertime dance courses taught at the Gaelic College at St. Ann's, I observed in the mid-1990s that both recorded and live music were used. Having a musician playing for your classes is the norm at weeklong summer courses in Scotland, for instance, depending on the budget.

Teaching Routines

To assist memory and make the teaching process easier, it is quite common to teach a "routine" or a set order of steps in classes and workshops. This is, however, not a standard technique and not necessarily used by all who teach. I recall Harvey Beaton, teaching at the weeklong summer schools in Scotland in the early 1990s, telling the class that he would ease their learning by teaching a routine. As it turned out, it was not always easy for him to remember the order in which he taught the steps; it became clear that dancing a set routine was not necessarily the norm for him. Harvey ended up writing down the step combinations and short routines he taught the group to assist his own memory. Indeed, although I have observed Harvey dance countless times over the years, I have never seen him dance his steps in the same order twice. This illustrates something that most of the dancers who grew up learning at home and perhaps only later in a class situation have pointed out to me: there is quite a difference between getting up to perform a few steps and teaching the dance genre. None of the sources in this study makes an issue of teaching a routine. The routine is only part of the means to an end, which assists you in assimilating a motif repertoire. So, even if routines are used as a means of passing on movement material, the dancer's personal style is commonly more fluid and improvised. As Alexander MacDonnell remarked in class at Ceòlas in the late 1990s, "I can teach you the steps but you need to make them your own" (Melin 2006). I discuss the issue of performing a set routine or improvising to the music further in chapter 6.

My own experience was that learning a routine was primarily a visual experience that was soon combined with rhythm patterns that I picked up aurally. This helped me memorize movement sequences and, by dancing the routine many times over, I was able to transition from one motif to the next and, in time, develop a flow of movements to music. At this point in my learning experience, I never danced to a single track or selection of tunes but constantly varied the music. At some point, while dancing one of these routines, I started straying away from the set pattern and other motifs started naturally to replace parts of the routine. Upon reflection, I think that this is a natural progression, to deviate from the rehearsed routine, and is due to a combination of having acquired a better understanding of how motifs can be combined in different ways and aurally picking up motif rhythms in the music. In other words, the music started suggesting to me—on a subconscious level—suitable rhythm patterns, which triggered movement memories that were then naturally realized while dancing. It "felt right" when I danced, and I now see that on some level I had achieved kinaesthetic appropriation of the dance genre. Another realization was that I felt I could allow myself to improvise my dancing, without feeling that I was straying from what I had been taught by a Cape Breton dancer. Following Alexander MacDonnell's advice above, I took full ownership of my dancing, making the dance my own and choices of steps mine as I danced.

Another means of assisting the formal teaching of a group is to name movements and steps. However, not all dance teachers have names for the steps they teach and end up simply showing the movements, which then negates the need for an extensive terminology of movement. When formal step-dance teaching started in the 1970s, very few names for steps and movements were in the sources, so some started making up names to suit their needs. Indeed, of the various movements and steps in current use in Cape Breton, few have established names.

Naming Steps

Few names for common motifs or steps are in general use in Cape Breton. The few that are mentioned on any regular basis are the hop, or the hop step; the backstep, for common reel motifs; and the shuffle, or even Mabou shuffle, for the most common jig motif. In three stepdancing films produced in Cape Breton in the past twenty-odd years, both Mary Janet MacDonald and Jean MacNeil name all the steps they teach.[4] It should be noted that, for the most part, MacDonald and MacNeil do not use the same names for the same steps or parts thereof, but both use the names "backstep" and "the hop" for the same motifs. The individual teaching style and terminology of each teacher is retained in these instructional videos.

Naming steps seems to be a fairly recent practice and appears to have come about with the onset of formal teaching in the 1970s. Commenting on this practice in a personal correspondence, Frank Rhodes (2011) wrote that

> while the step dances had names, I was not told of any names of any individual steps or movements. I presume that there were none, since at that time Margaret Gillis could only remember 10 of the 12 steps of Flowers of Edinburgh and it appeared that she had no names or mnemonics to help her recollect the others. For my own notes I used names for movements corresponding to similar ones in the Hebridean dances.

So, naming steps seems to have evolved out of a necessity to distinguish motif combinations and to enable quicker recall. The "train step," the "spider step," "Donald Beaton's step" and the "twin step" are but a few of many names that dancers and dance teachers use today. Cheryl MacQuarrie (2007) told me that she names steps after the person from whom she learned them. I do the same, as I feel it honours the source of the step.

Individual movements may be defined according to their type, whether it is a step or a hop or known within the tradition, or known by the dancer as a shuffle, for instance; again, the terminology is not standardized. Depending on the teacher, tap or beat and stamp, tramp or heavy beat may refer to the same type of movement. It also seems, generally—and perhaps naturally so—that the piece of terminology that is used by the teacher is what you end up using yourself. I have also noted that no one seems to be concerned with the variety of terms in use, as long as the students end up dancing the movement in the preferred fashion.

Naming movements seems not to have been common in Scots Gaelic either, at least not according to current memories. In the Gaelic version of Calum Macleod's (1969: 19) book *Sgialachdan à Albainn Nuaidh* (Scottish Gaelic Stories from Nova Scotia), some step names in Gaelic are given: *ceum-siùbhla* [*sic*] (*ceum-siùbhal*: travelling step); *ceum-coisiche* (walking step); *leum-trasd* (crossing jump); *siabadh-trasd* (quick sweeping step); *aiseag-trasd* (shuttling traverse step); *ceum-baideanach* (sole step); *fosgladh* (opening step); *cuartag* (circle step); *ceum-cùil* (back step); *gearradh-àrd* (high cutting); *gearradh-dùbailte* (double cutting); *seatadh* (setting) and *bruichcath* (fluttering whirling).[5] However, I feel that the source of these names is doubtful and must be investigated further. I question whether they are names MacLeod picked up in Nova Scotia, or whether they come from another source. The first eight names are identical to and appear in the same order as in English-born dancing master Francis Peacock's dance manual, published in Aberdeen, Scotland (1805: 91-97). Note that MacLeod does not cite Peacock as his source, which I suspect it was, and, what's more, the source of Peacock's step names is debatable (Melin 2014).[6] There is a strong indication that, at least in the Gaelic-speaking learning environment of the home and ceilidh house, specific terms and names for movements were not necessary. Conversations with Gaelic speakers Mike Kennedy (2010) and Goiridh Dòmhnallach (2010) both indicate this, as do Shaw (1992-1993) and Dickson (2006: 211-26), the latter when analyzing the transmission of piping in South Uist. Dickson writes, in relation to the lack of modern Gaelic piping terminology:

> ...a comprehensive musical vocabulary has not survived in mod-ern Gaelic as much it has in, say, English, Italian or Chinese, whose literate traditions have preserved a wealth of technical terms and fostered an aesthetic based on critical discourse, notational analysis and philosophical reflection (220).... There is little basis for verbal critical analysis among the Gaelic folk because ... the musical information conveyed by an evaluative

vocabulary—words like "rhythm," "pitch," "grace note" and "quaver"—are assumed in the aural transmission of the music, making their verbalisation in many cases redundant. Naturally this means that such terms in modern Gaelic are quite rare. (222)

I feel this would be similar in dancing, where it is easier to show a dance movement than to verbalize it, just as Dickson's examples of pipers exemplified a particular feature in their playing rather than verbalizing it. "Articulate analysis in such [English] words as 'doubling' and 'timing' is inherent in the transmissive process" (223). As discussed above, a modern (English) vocabulary only became necessary when formal classes began in the 1970s, which created the need to verbalize movements to better facilitate the teaching of step dance.

The problem with verbalizing movement probably also accounts for the lack of written notation in use by Cape Breton step dance teachers. I have only come across a few dancers, such as Jackie Dunn-MacIsaac and Brandi McCarthy, that use personal systems for writing down steps, but which act more like reminders to themselves than something used actively as a teaching tool. In addition, I have only found one or two examples of local newspaper articles on dance describing steps such as an "Introduction to Traditional Step Dancing: A Quick Lesson for Children and Adults" (Rankin 1996: 5). Far more effective as a transmission tool has been the instructional videos, and later DVDs, made by Mary Janet MacDonald (1992, 2002) and Jean McNeil (2005) for example as already mentioned. To date the only published Cape Breton step dance notations are those by Frank Rhodes (1985, 1996), Simonne Voyer (2003) and Melin (2013a).

Informal versus Formal Learning

In reference to South Uist piping, Dickson (2006: 224) describes a dichotomy between natural "ear-learned" piping, with the emphasis on rhythm, and literate learning, with an emphasis on technique. My own step-dance research indicates a similar dichotomy. A number of Cape Bretoners I have met over the years explained their own dancing ability by stating that they were not taught formally; some seemed to frame this as an excuse, implying that their dancing was inferior to those having learnt in a class, while others used it to indicate that their style was highly individualized. I found the latter group more common than the former. More importantly, it should be noted that they were verbalizing the notion of a difference between formal and informal transmission.

There are both pros and cons with the formal teaching of any art form. In my experience, some things are gained while others are lost, starting with a negative aspect of formal teaching, as when the students in turn start teaching and it becomes clear that they have not fully understood the important relationship between music and dance, for example (Melin 2006). This problem is possibly more common in short courses and courses taught outside of Cape Breton, but it is nonetheless a relevant issue and one that the sources to this investigation mention. When you come from a close-knit transmission environment, where the wider cultural rules are subconsciously understood, it can be difficult to watch your dance tradition being passed on without all aspects of the inherent culture fully appreciated, or even understood. This illustrates aspects of the difference in learning in the home environment, in addition to other influences, to predominantly learning only in the classroom. It also illustrates the importance of exposure to different transmission processes in different contexts (home, classroom, concert, community dance, etc.) over extended periods of time. Compare this with learning much dance material in a workshop over a short period of time and then not having access to the dance genre on a regular basis. It would potentially allow for discrepancies in the understanding of the genre as a whole to occur.

A teacher once said to me that something is both gained and lost in the process of formally teaching dance. You might teach workshops and classes in many far-flung places but, upon returning to those places later, encounter something different being danced. Some of the students might have started teaching in their own right, but they are perhaps not suited to do so—they may not have grasped the core concepts. They call it Cape Breton step dancing, but what you see them dancing is not what you taught them; it can be very frustrating. Still, the dance genre has been taken up by people who would not otherwise have had access to it in far-flung places. The introduction to, and change within, the dance genre in Scotland, for instance, has been documented by me elsewhere (Melin 2005). A positive here is that many Scots have become aware of the cultural links between Cape Breton and Scotland and have injected something new into the traditional Scottish soundscape, so that what in chapter 2 I called "gesturescape" is formed. Many dancers in Scotland have not only explored percussive dance for the first time (whatever their level of understanding and competence in performing it), but have also taken a deeper interest in the music/dance relationship, with some even taking up learning to play the fiddle as a result.

Cultural transitions come at a price, as highlighted in the earlier discussion on the decline of the Gaelic language and the influence an English-speaking environment has had on Gaelic culture in Cape Breton. Some thus lament the change from the informal to formal transmission processes:

> Today, the entire culture is diminished. With the loss of the Gaelic/agricultural lifestyle, the family-based traditions are being lost. Music and dance is not necessarily passed on in the household—people go for lessons. The analytical/workshop approach has no cultural context. In my family, musicians and dancers learned by watching and listening to family and neighbours—then you practised until you got it. Dancers especially were always watching for a new step and appreciated the difficulty level in others. There was no differentiation of male or female. In my case, my father and his brothers and sisters learned from their parents [among them Johnny "Washabukt" MacLean and Aggie MacLennan]—taking a lesson or class was an alien notion to them because they were surrounded by a living tradition. They didn't need a "feis"—every Sunday afternoon turned into a feis in their own houses! [This is] exemplified in the photo (above) ... of my father dancing in his parlor. Today, sadly, this cultural context has been largely lost. (MacLean 2010)

Gender Shift in the Learning Environment

It is worth noting that there has been a shift in the gender of those who are passing on the tradition at home and teaching classes to the public. As outlined at the beginning of this chapter, it was mainly, but not exclusively, women who passed on dancing skills at home while men, particularly in the 19th century, were mainly remembered as dance teachers, setting up dance schools in the community. Over time and today, women outnumber men as both teachers and students. That many women were encouraged locally, often by the parish priest, to set up dance classes in the 1970s contributed to this shift. Fiddler and dancer Dawn Beaton comments on the shift from men to predominantly women dancing publicly:

> Certainly, this model of the past has changed, and quite drastically. Dancers are almost typically female although some of the best dancers are still men. There are fewer and perhaps not as drastically, some fewer males going into fiddle although it's a bit more 50-50 in fiddle where girls tend to outnumber boys in step dance class[es]. Probably a more poignant question would be to ask those who taught dance 40 years ago how many males were in their class. My guess would be not too many. I think most of the males didn't take classes and naturally assumed their style and steps over many years. Some would be taught informally by perhaps a relative or family member, and the rest would be picked up from watching others, perhaps at a square dance, but to see them in a class would be unlikely. For the most part, this still holds true today, but it would be more accepted to have a male take lessons. (D. Beaton 2010)

Summary of Class Transmission

Even though those who took up public teaching transferred many of the aspects of home transmission to the classroom, some shifts in the process can be noted. In the classroom context, where a group of people copy a teacher's moves, the visual aspect becomes more important. The many different dancers in a class depend upon the guidance of a single person. The aural soundscape is equally dictated by the leading percussive sound source as provided by the teacher and imitated by the students, rather than being exposed to many different guiding sounds in the home environment. Also, in addition to the aesthetic keywords and phrases commonly heard in informal settings—such as "light on your feet" or "close to the floor"—the formal environment has the added benefit of terminology for the movements to assist the teaching. It is important to note that, outside the class situation, many dance students are continuously and naturally influenced by the community at public performances and square dances. Still, the initial source for learning is often no longer the home.

In a formal classroom, song, *puirt-a-beul* and "diddling" as accompaniments to dancing is, to my knowledge, not common, while recorded music, or an accompanying musician who can provide music at different speeds to enable comfortable transmission, has taken their place.[7] From what I have seen, aspects of kinaesthetic transfer remain but are pushed into the background. The biggest change is that the teaching becomes structured. Movements are often taught in a specific order and routine step combinations are put together to enable students to better memorize them. There is often less emphasis on students combining the movements themselves and, significantly, observing others' choices and then basing their own choices of what to visually, aurally and kinaesthetically embody. Still, many teachers do encourage their students to improvise around the core material they have imported. There is, by default, a structured approach to the transmission in a formal classroom context, often simply because it is the most straightforward way to control a larger group of learners at any one time. Over time, however, this form of transmission has become the learning norm, and the informal learning at home gets pushed into the background. I am aware of some families still passing on dancing informally, but nowhere near as many as once were. The reason for this is not just the emergence of formal teaching, but is also due to major social change in Cape Breton since the 1970s, with outmigration due to lack of employment locally being one aspect of this.

Figure 3.1 – Mary Janet MacDonald teaching at the Ceòlas Summer School, South Uist, Scotland, July 1995. Photo by Mats Melin.

Chapter 4

Transmission Processes at Concerts

Social Gatherings in Cape Breton

We now turn our attention from the smaller settings of dance classes to larger, often community-wide social events. Before village festivals and concerts emerged in the 1950s as the main gatherings on the Cape Breton community calendar, other types of social gatherings, all of which featured music and dance, took place. These were occasional but year-round schoolhouse dances, and the many seasonal parish picnics, frolics, box and pie socials, and weddings. The frequency of these depended on the needs of family, kin and the larger community. Dancing was essential to socializing at all these events.

Public halls only began to be built in Cape Breton during the early years of the 20th century; during the 19th century, barns and schoolrooms were the only public places for indoor dancing. Outdoor dancing was common, though, especially among younger people (Rhodes 1985: 270). Wooden bridges were particularly popular as dance locations, according to Kennedy (2002: 215), "from the early days of settlement in Nova Scotia of travellers stopping horse and buggy to take advantage of the acoustic possibilities presented by a wooden bridge or of lumbermen step dancing on stumps after felling a tree." As is the case even today, dancers rarely let a good opportunity pass to share their steps, regardless of context or footwear.

Schoolhouse Dances

Before the construction of public halls, dances were regularly held in the many small wooden schoolhouses. The dances were typically contained in a small room, with a lantern in the corner and a fiddler or piper seated in a chair in another, the company present dancing four-hand and eight-hand Reels and, later, square sets, interspersed with solo step dancing. Dances helped to raise funds for teachers' salaries and the upkeep of the school building (LeBlanc and Sadowsky 1986; Rhodes 1985; MacGillivray 1988: 46 and 71).

Parish Picnics

In the summer, kinship and community groups within a parish boundary would organize picnics, where large, open-air dance floors would be built for a day or two of merrymaking. The first record of a parish picnic was held in 1897 in Mabou. From then until the mid-1900s, the parish picnic was one of the main public events at which dancing played an important role. These picnics were held to raise money for the parish, and often began with a church service in the morning, followed by an afternoon and evening of fun. In the 1920s and 1930s, some picnics, such as in Inverness, were organized by the town fire department (*Inverness Oran*, October 12, 1978). LeBlanc and Sadowsky (1986: 30) tell us that

> games of chance, contests, sporting events, meals, music, song and dance could be enjoyed by all. The main eye catcher was the dance platform made of wood set up on the picnic grounds. The fiddler, seated in the corner of the platform, would accompany the square dancers. Sometimes a separate fee of ten cents would be charged per couple per dance and would be paid as the dancers got onto the stage. Other times a general picnic admission covered the dancing fee.

In an article from 1977, *Inverness Oran* columnist Willie "the Piper" Gillis remembered the last picnic held on the picnic grounds below the railway track in the Inverness of his childhood. These community picnics were social adventures and involved the men in the area preparing the field for sports events such as running, and for piping competitions and dancing:

> It was a warm evening of the 30th of June 1913. Every able-bodied man was putting the finishing touches to the dance stages. Of course there was a stage for the step-dancers, also. There was a band shell for Highland dancing in front of Matt Ferguson's store.... The sounds of laughter could be heard everywhere and the skirl of the pipes could be heard in every corner of the field. (*Inverness Oran* 1977)

Frolics

The frolic, or in Gaelic *froilig/ean*, is essentially a form of a bee, as in a quilting bee, where people gather together to help each other accomplish a task, while having fun at the same time. The same notion holds in the Acadian community, where it is known as a *foulerie*. Milling cloth (in Scotland called "waulking" and in Gaelic *luadh*), spinning, barn-raising, woodcutting, stump-pulling and haymaking were all occasions where the hardworking community pooled their resources of tools, skills and manpower and helped to support each other in a long day's work. Clearing forests and cutting wood were known as "chopping frolics" and sometimes specifically as "stump-pulling frolics." Sparling (2005, 2014) details that song accompanied some of the activities, especially the milling frolics. At the end of the day, feasting, music and dance commenced. According to Shears (2008: 81), pipers played for Scotch Fours and fiddlers for square sets, and sometimes they teamed up, as is described as having taken place in Meat Cove, at the northern tip of Cape Breton. Graham (2006: 45) says that women came together for spinning and when the men joined them in the evening after chopping wood, the dance would commence, often lasting until the early hours in the morning. In Prince Edward Island, Macqueen (1929) recorded that the Reels and step dancing that followed a milling frolic were accompanied by *puirt-a-beul* or jigging if instruments were lacking.[1] In Scotland, milling and milling songs were primarily practised by women; in Canada, men were involved as far back as the 1830s in Gaelic communities in Québec and in Cape Breton around the turn of the 20th century (Sparling 2005: 225). There are recollections of wintertime frolics and Sparling suggests that harsh Canadian winters sometimes prevented outdoor activities, allowing men to take part, as milling frolics are often held indoors (225). Today, milling frolics continue to be held as community gatherings, re-enacted to share waulking songs in Gaelic at local festivals and as summertime tourist attractions.

Box or Pie Socials

The box social tradition appeared as a social event for young people in Victorian England, Canada and the United States in the late 19th and early 20th centuries. A generic description of a box social is "a social event at which boxes of food are auctioned to male bidders, who win the privilege of eating and dancing with the woman who prepared the box lunch."[2] The box or pie social also fills the function of a fundraising activity for the local community, as indicated by Dick (2008: 153-54) when he describes them occurring in the Abernethy district in Saskatchewan around the turn of the 19th century. According to LeBlanc and Sadowsky (1986), the box or pie social is unique to Scots Gaelic communities in Inverness County. How this custom was introduced and became popular in Scots Gaelic Cape Breton communities I have not been able to ascertain. There is, however, a clue in Margaret Bennett's description of Hebridean Gaels in Québec's Eastern Townships. She writes,

> Several celebrations that originate in shared experiences in the New World have come to be regarded as part of local tradition. They include … the Box Socials, the Leap Year Dance, the annual church picnic. Though they may not occur in Scotland, they are all regarded as characterising the activities of a "typically Scottish" society. (2005: 129)

This is now almost an event of the past, but a rare recent example is the annual Old Time Box Social and Square Dance held in West Lake Ainslie Hall each July (*Inverness Oran* 2008). LeBlanc and Sadowsky (1986: 29) describe the format of a box or pie social dance event:

> They would usually be held in schoolhouses several times a year. To prepare for these *dances*, the girls in the area would decorate boxes within which they would put sandwiches, cookies, cakes, and candy. During the evening, the dancing would stop and the boxes would be auctioned off to the highest bidder. The identities of the box owners was [*sic*] supposed to be unknown. A girl who had a steady boyfriend would give him a description of a box. In general, other boys present at the dance would attempt to outbid the boyfriend, thus forcing the price of the box to increase. The usual going price was two dollars. On occasion, the prices went as high as forty dollars. The highest bidder obtained the box and the owner of the box was required to share the contents with the winner. The format for pie socials was the same, but the women brought pies instead of boxes.

A fundraising aspect was not included in the description by LeBlanc and Sadowsky. It is, however, quite clear that the bidding for boxes (and their accompanying girls) during the evening would have added to the excitement of the dance.

Weddings

Few dances in Scots Gaelic culture seem to have a ceremonial function; the majority are celebratory in nature. As was the custom in the Scottish Highlands and islands (and this was also the case in Orkney and Shetland dancing—see, for example, Flett and Flett 1985 [1964]), the four-handed Reel, or Scotch Four, was danced as a Wedding Reel in Cape Breton. The Reel was incorporated among the other wedding rituals in Gaelic society, and served to welcome the newlywed couple, in their new social roles, back into the community. Upon returning home after the church ceremony, the wedding party would dance the Wedding Reel or Ruidhleadh nan Caraid (The Married Couple's Reel). Bride and groom, and commonly the best man and maid of honour, would dance this first Reel (Rhodes 1985: 275). Sometimes the parents of the married couple would make up another formation, and later all present would be dancing. According to Kennedy (2002: 220), a good performance of step dancing was expected—"so much so, that it has been noted that on certain occasions poor dancers were replaced for the ceremony by more skilful ones." In the days before the public halls were constructed, the wedding feast was held in the home of the bride or groom. The general dancing of Reels and, in later years, sets commenced after the meal and would continue through the night. Accounts show that up until the 1930s, wedding dances could last for days or even a week. Outdoor dance platforms were constructed, or the home kitchen was the place for dancing (LeBlanc and Sadowsky 1986: 30). In the last few decades, wedding celebrations have generally been held in public halls, with dancing confined to one evening. Other 19th-century festivities that called for music and dance were Christmas, New Year's Day and Halloween (MacGregor 1828: 73).

Modern Community Events: Concerts and Festivals

Around the 1950s, picnics died out and in their stead came village festivals and concerts, which are to this day held during the summer months. These concerts feature music, song and dance performances on a raised stage throughout the day, often followed by a square dance in the evening. Some concerts, like the oldest of them all in Cape

Breton, the Broad Cove Scottish Concert—initiated on August 7, 1957, to celebrate the 100th anniversary of St. Margaret of Scotland Church in Broad Cove—also include Mass celebrated in the early stages of the day's program. The concert is still held annually on the parish grounds, on a stage erected near the entrance to the church. Over the years the number of people attending has grown into the thousands. Other popular annual contemporary concerts are Glendale, Kintyre Farm Concert, Iona Highland Village Day, Big Pond and Judique on the Floor, to name a few.

Several weeklong festivals, such as Chestico Days in Port Hood, the summer festivals in Margaree or Chéticamp and the Inverness Gathering, are held annually. Most have kept many of the features of the parish picnics of old, but few have kept the dance platforms. The Chestico Days festival includes a parade with step and square dancers performing on the backs of pick-up trucks, and a one-day step-dancing festival, started in 1983.

The Community Concerts as a Transmission Context

Most community concerts in Cape Breton take place annually and are outdoor, summertime affairs held, for example, at a farm or on local parish grounds, with varied historical reasons for particular locations. These concerts tend to start around midday and continue until about early evening, and prove a great opportunity for the local community to mix with people from near and far who venture out for the day. It was, and for many of the older generation still is, an occasion to dress smartly. The accounts of bygone days indicate that, for dancing at annual summer picnics and frolics and, in later years, the emerging summer festivals, dress code and shoes were important. Attending the house ceilidh also meant dressing smartly; this trend continued when dancing moved from the home to the schoolhouse and public hall. Piper John MacLean (2010) recalls his home environment in Washabuck: "If there was dancing, it was a social occasion for the sexes to mingle and the decorum was quite formal—including the notion of getting cleaned up and wearing good clothes." In fact, when it came to attending the annual picnics in the early 20th century, "the young men and women would save up their money for the whole year in order to attend, so they could buy new clothes and shoes to look smart when attending" (*Inverness Oran* 1977). Port Hawkesbury step dancer John D. MacIntyre recalls walking up to fifteen miles to a parish concert:

> You would have your nice shoes for dancing at the next concert; so, what you did when you got in the dark was to walk barefoot all the way home! These were patent leather shoes with a kind of paper sole—$1.98; but $1.98 was hard to get then. The road home was all potholes—no pavement. If you hit your toes, they would be all bleeding, but it was better than having your shoes all gone.... We were always looking for the softest shoes we could get.... All those step dancers who were competing in Antigonish—like Dan Hayes—could not make noise with their feet; the judges had to see the steps, not hear them! The judges wanted to see how light they were on their feet, so you would want to get bedroom slippers with patent leather soles. The dancer almost *had* to have them for competition, and clickers were not allowed except for clog dancing and tap. (MacGillivray 1988: 100)

Note that this excerpt mentions the important dichotomy between those who prioritize the visual aspects of step dancing and those who prefer it to be based on the sounds the feet make when dancing.

The annual concert is an occasion to meet family, friends and acquaintances from farther away and, of course, to enjoy a mix of local and regional talent in music, song and dance. In the last decade or so, visitors from off the island and abroad will also take a spot and perform during the day's stage entertainment. From a dance perspective, the program now features Scottish Highland and country dancing and other forms of step dance from communities such as Prince Edward Island and the Ottawa Valley. Performers from the "Boston States" (New England), Scotland and Ireland have also participated over the years.

The Transmission Process at Concerts

As the distance between onlooker and performer is generally greater in a concert than in other transmission contexts, the predominant transmission at concerts happens visually. John MacIntyre, for example, learned steps by watching others dance: "I came home and took Alex Angus' steps with me in my head; then I would turn the mirror down and work on them" (MacGillivray 1988: 100). In the following correspondence, Minnie MacMaster (2010) describes how she also learned by watching others.

I loved to step dance, and from my mother's basic steps I so enjoyed being able to put steps together that I considered mine. I was fortunate enough to get asked to some of the concerts and parties in our area and those helped me to learn more steps and enjoy the music even more. You would see a favourite dancer getting up to dance ... you're hearing the fiddler play some great melodies and you're just eating up what the dancer is doing with his or her feet—you're loving every second of it. For the next few days those tunes and that dancer is going through your mind and you mentally go over the steps they were dancing ... and all of a sudden you realize that the step you were just doing is probably not really the same as done by the person you saw dancing ... so you get all excited and think to yourself, "Oh, that is an interesting twist—that is different—that goes really well with that melody." And you realize that you have something different that you sort of claim as your own!

Margaret (MacEachern) Dunn (2010) recounts two anecdotes in a similar vein:

We were at a concert in Johnstown, and my father [fiddler and dancer John Willie MacEachern] and I were picked out of the audience [by the local priest]. He played for almost all the step dancers that night. There was this one guy who danced ahead of me and I picked up a step from him (by watching) and did it during my own solo. My mother later said to me, "You did a new step tonight." She did not connect it to the gentleman who danced before me....

The second one that I remember was when the late Father Angus Alex MacDonnell was doing the step dancing school in Antigonish and we were deciding what steps to teach at the next class. "Let's do this one," he said, as he demonstrated the step for me. "That's a nice one," I said, "show it to me again." "What do you mean?" he said, "I got it from you!" It was one of those "ankle over" steps. "I learned it from you watching you dance one night in Glenville," he replied. It was interesting that this "ankle over" step of mine now had a completely new variation, and we taught both of them. It is interesting how steps are learned by watching and when worked out later, from memory, turn out to be slightly different and equally as good.

In contrast, Joël Chiasson (2010) and Rodney MacDonald (2009) combine observation of live dancing with the study of recorded material to learn new steps. Chiasson recalls:

Most of what I have learned was without formal teaching. It was picked up by mimicking what I would see at concerts, sometimes on television and/or recorded video. After watching *very* carefully over and over, I was able to re-enact what I was seeing in front of me. Once I was able to recreate the movements of a step, then came my understanding of the music; most importantly the difference between a strathspey and a reel for a step-dance solo setting. Then came the more relaxed, at times transcendental, side of the dancing. Only once the steps in my repertoire had been mastered was I able to actually interpret what I was hearing.

Melody Cameron (2011) stresses the many different aspects involved in learning step dancing visually:

You see the steps ... you see how they are delivered by different dancers. [You observe] their body language, if it is a dancer. Or even the fiddler on the stage, you see their body language. You see the piano player's body language, and how they are [all] relating to the music.... [You see] smiles on people's faces.

Mary Janet MacDonald's (2010) memory of when she was very young provides a good example of a combination of visual and kinaesthetic transmission:

The only way to learn new steps (for me) was to stand on the floor at a concert, standing very close to the eye level of the stage. I can visualize myself with my chin on the stage and watching the men I loved to see dancing—Willie Fraser, Thomas MacDonnell (to name a couple)—and trying to absorb a new step. I definitely remember feeling the rhythm in the wood of the stage and if that caused the rhythm to enter my soul, I believe it. I would go home then and re-create the step as close as I could get it, until I would go back to the next concert.

To Be Seen or To Be Heard?

Whether a dancer should be seen as well as heard or only seen seems to be a matter of personal preference or, in later decades, of fads and trends. Dancers performing at concerts or on festival stages in the summer generally wear hard-soled leather shoes; some wear taps.

Not surprisingly, the popularity of wearing "clickers" or taps, particularly if performing or sharing your steps on stage, coincides with the introduction of the amplification of step-dance music. If you wanted your footwork to be heard, clickers was the best way. Margaret (MacEachern) Dunn says that Fr. Angus MacDonnell introduced her to taps. While some dancers preferred small flat clickers on the toes and heels, Fr. Angus wore "staccato taps" with a loose piece on his dancing shoes. Margaret says she has danced with and without taps, and often used them for teaching but, regardless, the way she danced did not change (Dunn 2007; MacGillivray 1988: 53-54). Gussie MacLellan indicated that both he and his father used small taps when they danced (see MacGillivray 1988: 117). Indeed, Mary Janet MacDonald (2007) wore taps until she got invited to teach step dancing at a festival in the Isle of Barra, Scotland, in 1983, and Fr. John Angus Rankin advised her to take them off and dance "the right way" if she was going to influence people.

Peggy Lamey of Sydney, daughter of famed fiddler William (Bill) Lamey, shared in an email conversation with me that she was taught the Scottish strathspey and reel as a "soft shoe" dance—a dance performed without tap shoes—and one that needs to be performed with "grace and pep," she clarified. It seems that the Lamey family preferred the natural sound of feet or shoes without taps contacting the floor when dancing. One hears a deeper resonating sound, reflecting bodyweight and control of the dancer's motions. Tap shoes are more rigid in construction and metal taps produce a much sharper sound when striking the floor, a sound that is harder to control. Peggy said that the timing must be very distinct, and she continues,

> I never wore tap shoes, I would have been disowned! ... I wanted *so* much to wear the taps because when I was on a stage, I felt the audience couldn't hear me—but Dad just said to me, "They're not supposed to hear you. They're supposed to watch you." (Lamey 2008)

So, in her father's opinion, the visual aspect of the dancing took precedence over the aural. As Peggy became more adept at dancing, she describes how, while performing, she found that out the reason soft shoes were preferred in her family over tap shoes.

> The strathspey steps involve a lot of ankle movement and the hard leather tap shoe restricted and prevented me from executing steps in the manner that they are meant to be, so the rest of my body became more rigid and un-relaxed. All of a sudden, it didn't matter that the audience heard me. I knew that I didn't execute my steps the way I wanted to and I wasn't having as much fun—and it showed in my performance. That was the end of my taps.... The reel also has much ankle movement, but the important reason a soft shoe is preferred is because it lets the sound of the dancers' bodyweight be heard in their steps (like a thud when they hit the floor), adding to the peppier music. Don't forget, this type of dancing originated in the home; there were no dance halls, microphones or tap shoes. The sound of a person dancing in a house is very different than when they dance in a hall or on a stage. (2008)

The key points Peggy suggests are that one must enjoy one's own performance; in other words, enable oneself to perform at one's best as the enjoyment will come across to those watching, and that the soundscape of the feet belongs better in the intimate locale of the home and is perhaps of secondary importance.

Melody (Warner) Cameron and Kelly (Warner) MacLennan's grandfather, Norman Warner, indicated in 1987 that there had been a change in the 1960s and 1970s in favour of hearing the dancers rather than visually appreciating their musicality and dexterity (see MacGillivray 1988: 160). The Warner Sisters, Melody and Kelly's stage name, can be seen both on YouTube clips and in photographs from the 1980s wearing taps.

Depending on the volume of the amplified music and on whether dancers wear taps, it is not always possible to hear dancers' feet when they perform on a concert stage (as most of the time their feet are not amplified). It also depends on how the spectator is positioned in relation to best viewing and aural reception. In my own experience, one is sometimes able to hear the dancers' feet "in one's own head" when seeing a dancer on a concert stage even though their feet cannot be heard; it's a kind of aural mimicry of the feet's movements, conjured up internally as an audio experience or even an audio memory.

Today, dancers' preferences and performance types decide whether taps are worn or not. Some dancers only use taps when they perform with amplified music, for example.

Summary of Observations of Transmission Processes at Concerts

Visual transmission seems to be the dominant form in a concert context, where images of movements are memorized and recalled at a later stage, when they are recreated and practised. Often small and personal variations occur during this process, which add diversity within the dance genre. Aural transmission may be of secondary importance, apart from when shoes with taps are used, and when sound is prioritized in the performance. Kinaesthetic transfer continues to inform steps when of remembering one's own movements, watching a dancer's performance of steps, and feeling another dancer move while dancing together. It is also important to note that it is not only the movement of the dancer that is observed in this context. The body

Figure 4.1 – Harvey Beaton and fiddler Glenn Graham, Broad Cove, July 2008. Photo by M. Melin.

Figure 4.2 – Rodney MacDonald dancing to fiddlers Kinnon and Andrea Beaton, with Betty Beaton on piano. Strathspey Place, Mabou, July 1, 2010. Photo by V. M. Faubert.

Figure 4.3 – Jenny MacKenzie is dancing to Nuallan at Colaisde na Gàidhlig during Celtic Colours (2014). Photo by Mats Melin.

movements of the accompanying musicians (fiddlers and pianists) who perform in close proximity to the dancers are subconsciously observed as well and add to the visual effects and soundscapes of the concert locale. The dancer also senses the movements of the musicians who, in turn, feel the music through their fingering, bowing and foot-tapping, among other types of movement.

Fihure 4.4 – Mary Janet MacDonald and children dancing at Broad Cove (1995). Photo by Mats Melin.

Chapter 5

"Pickin' it up" at the Square Dance

After the home/class context, the square dance is the most important context for transmission processes. Square dances are held in
public spaces and are, since the demise of the Scotch Reel, the primary
social dance context. Square sets are sometimes danced at home, at
house ceilidhs or at parties, but are predominantly enjoyed in local
parish halls and other suitable venues around the island. Arguably the
biggest impact on the traditional Cape Breton dance scene as a whole
is the introduction of square dances to the island from mainland
Canada and the U.S. beginning near the end of the 19th century. They
were brought in by Cape Bretoners returning or visiting home from
working away and also spread by the means of instruction booklets,
such as *Dick's Quadrille Call-Book and Ball-Room Prompter* (1878)
that could be ordered by mail—as will be detailed below—coinciding
with the construction of the first parish halls around the island. The
Cape Breton Square Set, as the dance came to be known, is the end
product of a long process of what Peter Manuel calls "creolizing"—
primarily a linguistic term "denot[ing] the process by which speakers
of two or more distinct tongues, who meet on neutral territory that
is the homeland of neither, create a pidgin lingua franca, which then
becomes a first language for subsequent generations," but the term is
also applied to cultural processes such as dance (2009: 32). Manuel,
studying Caribbean contradance, reminds us that the creolization
process, when applied to culture, is sometimes criticized "for its
tendency to imply that the two or more entities—whether musical
styles ... languages—that meet and blend are somehow pure," but
stresses "the importance of remembering that the formative elements
of creolization may themselves be creolized rather than primordially
pure entities" (32). There is no pure start nor end cultural product but
only stages of constant processes of change. I would argue that this is
exactly the case in the development of the various localized versions of
Cape Breton square sets, where a hybridization of incoming material

(Quadrilles) meets localized ideas of dance patterns (Reels) and has created a mosaic of differently named square sets that involves different combinations of dance figures associated with each set.

A Brief History of the Square Dance in Cape Breton

A separate study of the square-dancing scene is needed in order to reveal further detail about the phases of change it has undergone since the introduction of Quadrilles to Cape Breton, around 1900, but I will make a few historical comments here. A Quadrille is a dance for four couples, each couple positioned along one side of a square, forming a set. It consists of a series of figures, generally five to seven, arranged in a suitable order, each often with a contrasting musical tempo from a pool of figures devised by various dancing masters.[1] The dance type developed in France and was in turn a development from the cotillion, an earlier social dance in square formation. Ellis Rogers (2002: 4) observed that, "together with the Waltz, Quadrilles reigned supreme in the ballrooms of Western Europe throughout the 19th century." The Quadrille was introduced into Britain in about 1810, and spread fairly quickly round the country and into Ireland and beyond (Rogers 2008 [2003]). By the 1830s, Quadrilles were a prominent feature in fashionable society events in Canadian colonial capitals, such as Halifax and Charlottetown, Prince Edward Island, but they did not reach far beyond these urban areas, according to Kennedy (2002: 221).

John MacGregor (1828: 67, 261) described country dances and general merrymaking at picnics and assemblies in both summer and winter in Charlottetown in the 1820s. These urban social gatherings were said to be similar to those held in Québec and Halifax, which indicates that the Quadrille had not yet arrived as a social dance (67). According to Kennedy (2002: 221), Quadrilles and Lancers (Quadrilles for eight or sixteen pairs) did not spread to Cape Breton's rural *Gàidhealtachd* (Gaelic-speaking areas) from the urban centres, *but* were instead introduced "by returning émigrés showing off the latest fashions from Boston" in the early 1900s. The Quadrille, as a dance in vogue, "was one of many new imports from the United States, including waltzes and foxtrots." During the same period, the shift in socializing, concerts, music and dancing began, first from the home to schoolhouses and then to the public halls. This change of context led to the demise of Scotch Fours and eight-handed Reels—the latter, as mentioned elsewhere, was also under scrutiny by the church.

As the century progressed, the old dance forms were ousted by the square sets—apart from the occasional dancing of Scotch Fours—as both social and ceremonial dance. The Scotch Four and the Wedding Reel were common until post–Second World War, but frequently the Scotch Four was danced as an occasional display dance. Scotch Fours have today lost their original social function, as described in chapter 2. Rhodes (1985: 274) highlights another change that came about between 1900 and 1930, which was the introduction of admission fees to attend square dances at the local halls. Also according to Rhodes, dancers were charged a small fee for each square set they wanted to dance (274). The style of dancing changed, too, from percussive foot-work, as in the Reels, to the use of sedate walking steps, which was the fashion of the Quadrille, and of waltzing and polka steps. There is no record of what music was played initially for these new dances when they arrived, but the changes outlined above allowed elements and steps of the older dances to be introduced into Quadrilles over time.

As was the case in Scotland and Ireland, the music used for the Quadrille figures was modified locally over time. In Cape Breton, jigs and reels came to be favoured. The local Scots repertoire of jigs was relatively small, so, to meet the demand of the new dance form, jigs were imported from the Irish tradition and a considerable number of local compositions came to augment the local repertoire (Doherty 1996; Graham 2006). As reels had been one of the core tune types for Reel dancing, the style of playing them remained relatively unchanged. So, if the style of playing remained closer to the older forms, then this indicates that the Quadrille was being Gaelicized, particularly in Inverness County. Here, in particular, the Quadrille was beginning to be referred to as a square set and, with modifications to suit the local music, these sets were effectively and deeply absorbed into the local dance tradition. Even though the style of music took on a local flavour, only certain areas, such as Inverness County, embraced the transition of percussive footwork into the sets. The east side of the island gener-ally retained the walking through the figures, while both jig and reel figures on the west side began to incorporate step dancing at least by the 1940s (Kennedy 2002: 222; Graham 2006: 189).

This public locale of the square dance—what Oldenburg (1989) would call a "third place," or a place of meaningful community interaction—is today perhaps the primary place for transmission and reinforcement of the step-dance genre after the class context. At "family dances" (i.e., alcohol is not served) in particular, all generations mingle in the same place. It is here that young and old observe each other dance and interact with the music, as was once common in many homes before the public halls were built.

Extensively, the square dance is today where the community consolidates or expresses its identity. This reinforcement of identity is best illustrated by questions like "Where do you belong?" or "Who do you belong to?" querying where you come from, common to social interaction in Atlantic Canada. The phrases used are directly related to the way you ask the same question in Scots Gaelic: *Co leis thu?* or *Co a th'ann?* (the first one meaning "Who do you belong to?" while the second one literally means "Who is there/exists?"). As an outsider to the community, I have often been asked these questions at a Cape Breton square dance as a community member tries to place me, but the question is commonly asked of anybody who is not well known. Summer visitors, young and old, with Cape Breton family connections are another group that is queried like this. It is a constant process of reaffirming who belongs where, and who is related to whom. In an environment where people's identity is based on their family background (including often the geographical background and/or place of origin) and is of a high level of importance, cultural expressions such as music and dance through particular stylistic markers help reaffirm and, to a certain degree, strengthen the community identity, or as Feintuch puts it, "there's no question but that the music is a primary emblem of identity here, and its performance is almost certainly *the* primary enactment of that identity" (2004: 81).

Meaning and Place of the Dance Halls

The context and place that perhaps best represent the meaning music and dance have for the local community are the local parish and fire halls, where often weekly summertime square dances are held. These halls have counterparts in other local bars, restaurants and music venues such as the Doryman (Chéticamp), the Normaway Inn (Margaree), the Red Shoe Pub (Mabou), the Celtic Music Interpretive Centre (Judique) and the recently closed Rollie's Wharf (North Sydney), to name but a few, where music and dance interact on a regular basis. Emily Addison's (2001) study of dance halls in Inverness County aptly sums up the significance of these places for the local music and dance community: they are, she writes, "unique cultural institutions, icons, places and landscape features. As such, they pull together communities and serve as teaching grounds for cultural practices among many other functions" (2001: i). Addison's study is a geography of sense of place, and she notes that local attendees (the community) are often deeply aware not only of the buildings themselves (when they were built, changes to them over the years, good or not-so-good floors for dancing, etc.) but also of the meaning and associations the halls have for the people connected with them. According to Addison (97), the halls in Inverness County, for example, create an extremely powerful sense of community because they are associated with a sense of sharing and shaping of identity as they provide a prime setting for social interaction. Addison's findings about people's associations of certain fiddlers with certain halls are of particular interest. These fiddlers (mainly men that were interviewed in the study) would play those halls every week for the summer season. Today, in contrast, halls switch fiddlers and accompanists every week. The attendees—the dancers and spectators alike—and the way everyone interacts, dances and talks, which brings these halls alive and in the local consciousness, are all highlighted as very important aspects of community life in Addison's study. In fact, the halls are important for holding the community together, to the point where the hall (e.g., the one in West Mabou, where the year-round weekly Saturday night dance is a prominent fixture on the community calendar[2]) is that community's focal point (98-99).

Even though much of the social interaction is an incidental result of gathering at these halls, most people—from Inverness County and beyond—go to the halls primarily to dance. I have many times ended up in discussions with people in Scotland, England, Ireland or Sweden who have visited Cape Breton, for whom attending a dance (either by chance or by design) stood out as a highlight experience of Cape Breton community. The common comment was about the high-energy community interaction taking place through the dancing (Melin 2013b). Addison does not discuss dance transmission in detail, but she points out that another primary function bestowed on the halls is that they are the places where the "culture is shared and transferred between individuals" (2001: 102). Unlike house parties and private social gatherings such as weddings, everyone can, in theory, access these "third place" halls for dances, concerts, ceilidhs or other public community events. I have observed and heard members of the older generation say that they take younger ones "under their wing" or help introduce them to the dancing and culture (Melin 2013b). Square dances are well advertised in local papers (e.g., *Inverness Oran* and *Cape Breton Post*) and on local radio, and more recently via Facebook announcements, but also by word of mouth. Posters in local cafés and stores, for example, play an important role in spreading the word about these dances to people both in and outside the local community. I would argue that, for the visitor to Cape Breton, a combination of tourist brochures (and online information) and word of mouth in the community (e.g., from your accommodation host or your friendly shop/café/restaurant assistant) would be the main source of inspiration to attend an evening dance. Such has been my experience (Melin 2013b). Some of Addison's (2001: 102) sources make it clear that they feel people go to the dance with an aim to learn how to dance square sets, pick up some new steps, enjoy the music and get ideas on how to play the fiddle for dancing. In these last respects the dancing in the halls is another venue for informal transmission processes.

In 2010, weekly square dances were held in West Mabou (as mentioned earlier) and in Cedars Hall, Sydney, throughout the year. During the summer months, a mixture of weekly family and adult square dances were held in Glencoe Mills, Brook Village, Scotsville, Southwest Margaree and Margaree. In addition to the weekly dances, local papers and online guides advertised many other dances held in Baddeck, Belle Cote, Big Bras d'Or, Big Pond, Boisdale, Creignish, Christmas Island, Glencoe Mills (as well as regular weekly Thursday-night dances), Glendale, Grand Narrows, Inverness, Judique, Mabou, Marion Bridge, Middle River, New Waterford, Scotsville, St. Ann's, Strathlorne, Sydney, Washabuck and Westmount, not to mention impromptu dance sessions in pubs and public ceilidhs. In recent years, the Celtic Music Interpretive Centre in Judique has provided further opportunities to both square and step dance at their weekly lunchtime music sessions and at other specific music events that regularly feature community dancing.

The Organization of a Square Set in the Dance Hall

Three interacting sets of dancing occur in the public halls during an evening of square dancing. Two of these are the square sets and the solo dancing, and the third is the occasional inclusion of a couples' waltz. An example of the characteristics of a certain square dance, the current version of the Mabou Set, arguably the most common version of the Square Set in Cape Breton today, is briefly described below. In other parts of the island, other types of sets are still danced but maybe less regularly than they used to be. In 2002, Jørn Borggreen (2012 [2002]), a Danish dance enthusiast, published a collection of sixteen local versions of distinctly different square sets from various parts of west and north Cape Breton, with a set from Boston added in a later edition. Few other printed sources of local sets are currently available but an important publication in the 1990s was *No Less No More—Just Four On The Floor: A Guide to Teaching Traditional Cape Breton Square Sets for Public Schools* (M. J. MacDonald et al. 1994).

Figure 5.1 – West Mabou Hall, July 2008. Photo by Mats Melin.

The Mabou Set has changed in recent years, from earlier versions of the dance, and it reveals the types of conditions under which transmission processes occur. The Mabou Set is no longer danced by only four couples, as were the Quadrilles of old, but in large circles, which may split into smaller circles if they get too unwieldy. The first figure consists of the original first and last parts, the middle parts having been eliminated as these figures require four couples. Since I first attended a dance, in 1995, the second figure has lost one middle part—the right-hand and the left-hand wheel by the women in the centre—as it is difficult to dance this particular part when there are more than four couples in the set. After two jig figures, one reel figure has been lost altogether; probably the most popular figure at present is the current third and last reel figure. The jig parts are sometimes danced for longer, with more repeats of the movements to make up for the loss of parts. Having said that, since about 2007 or 2008 I have noted that at times the jig figures (in the Mabou Set) are danced for a shorter length of time, while the reel part is kept going for longer, a sort of highlight of the dance. Comments made to me by musicians accompanying the dancing have corroborated this observation (Melin 2013b). I have also observed that some couples will sometimes join in only after the reel is played, indicating that the jig figures may be merely a lead-in or warm-up to the final figure. The reel could also be seen as of higher importance as it is generally danced for much longer than the jig figures, and it incorporates a greater share of step dancing than do the jigs.

Each performance of a square set is thus flexible in length, both in how long parts are danced and how many times they are repeated, thus changing the length of each figure. The amount of step dancing included in the set is also flexible as it depends on who is dancing, the composition of people interacting in the particular set, the mood of the crowd in general, the time of night, and the level of interaction with the music. The Mabou Set is commonly repeated five to seven times during an evening's square dancing. In its current, simplified state, this set has become very inclusive in nature, and many summertime tourists and visitors returning home flock to the most popular halls, such as Glencoe Mills Hall, to partake. Observing the dances since 1995, and speaking to regular attendees, it seems that visitors may boost attendance at the summertime dances by 50-60 per cent or more (Melin 2013b). In 2015 there have been several special events, notably at West Mabou and Glencoe, to boost numbers of attendees, and there is also a square set project underway to revitalize many of the local square set variations.

The aural, visual and kinaesthetic transmission modes all interact here, but the priorities in the transmission processes in the social dancing differ from those in the solo dancing (solo step dancing does not always take place at a square dance, but when it happens during the evening it depends on a number of circumstances, as is outlined later). This investigation concentrates on the transmission processes occurring during the solo dance section of the evening. The transmission processes taking place during the social square dancing cannot be ignored, as the same actors are involved in both aspects.

Solo Step Dancing in a Social Setting

Usually about three hours into the dance the fiddler will strike up a strathspey, followed by reels, to indicate a break in social dancing. This commonly featured gap in the square dancing is where individuals are called on to share their steps. I use the term "share" as I think these

Figure 5.2 – Square set at Southwest Margaree Hall: long exposure shows movement as a blur, July 2007. Photo by Mats Melin.

short performances convey a higher cultural meaning to the community than just simply being a display of good dancing. Whether this occurs or not depends on who is present and whether anyone present is deemed likely to take to the floor. Occasionally a waltz might be played if this is felt to be the better option by the fiddler. My understanding is that the fiddler picks up on the general mood of the dance crowd in an almost organic fashion and decides whether or not step dancers will likely take to the floor, or if a waltz might suit better (Melin 2013b). Commonly, though, solo dancing does occur with a range of young and old, locals and visitors. Occasionally, however, I have observed that when nobody has gotten up, for whatever reason, the musician soon stops playing strathspeys and reels and reverts to jigs to signal the start of a new Square Set. One could therefore surmise that if the conditions on that particular evening are not right, this display of solo dance simply will not occur.

There are seldom any announcements or introductions at a square dance. The crowd takes its cue from the music provided. There is no set order as to who gets up for solo step dancing, but rather a spontaneous impetus that brings dancers to the floor. Spontaneous should possibly be within quotation marks; dancers will often get up only after a little encouragement from fellow spectators. I would never get up myself to dance at this point unless a local encouraged me to do so.

As the solo dancers take to the floor, one after the other (though occasionally siblings get up together), the floor generally clears and, depending on the hall layout, the crowd sits or stands along the top (in front of the musicians) and sides of the hall, and together on the dance floor, creating a smaller empty space for the solo dancers to perform in. From an observation of each dancer in turn, a broad spectrum of individual styles and aesthetic preferences emerges. Depending on the age and location, different approaches to the genre can be detected. Predominantly, however, the use of the essential or core movements of the genre is reinforced. Each dancer's prowess, timing and interaction with the music, choice of movements and style can be absorbed. Additionally, the characteristics of each individual are equally strengthened in the consciousness of the onlookers.

Furthermore one can observe, or subconsciously be aware of, the onlookers, how they interact with each other and, through their body language, with the dancer on the floor. The onlookers are not silent. They talk, discuss and engage in what is going on. Their body language also shows signs of engagement. With small, approving nods or disapproving shakes of the head, hand gestures, feet tapping in time with the music, eyes following the movements, and approving smiles, they indicate their preferences. If a dancer performs a movement combination appreciated by the observers, they will show their appreciation with applause. A number of factors can trigger this, but a few that I have detected are: difficult motif sequences that are well coordinated with the music, steps well performed within the local aesthetic preferences, and a motif that connotes an older repertoire. Particularly popular are motif sequences that are seen as the performing dancers' trademarks or motifs associated by some with their family or the area they come from. For example, Willie Fraser, Mary Janet MacDonald and Rodney

MacDonald, to name but a minute selection of dancers, will be recognized and applauded for performing a particular trademark step or older motif they are known and appreciated for. With other dancers, as Sandy Beaton (Beaton, Beaton and MacDonald 2008) highlighted in conversation, appreciation is shown because sometimes "the dancer is trying so hard to do the steps justice that you feel like applauding," and thus the audience shows appreciation of how well the dancer fits the step with the music, or just appreciation of the effort.

Another important characteristic of the square dance is that individuals who get up to share their steps are appreciated for who they are and for their contribution through dance to the culture as a whole. Only by seeing the same dancer perform several times over the years, and taking in the reaction of the onlookers, have I been able to understand the nature of this appreciation. From years of exposure to each other, the regular dancers have become acutely aware of each other's repertoire, preferred motifs and individual stylistic traits. If a performance is really good it is sometimes commented on, as illustrated by John Robert Gillis (2009), to whom someone once remarked to him, after he came off the floor, that the fiddler had "played just the right tunes for [him]." In observing one another over the years, the community spectators come to have an appreciation for a particular

Figures 5.3, 5.4 – Dancers "sharing" their steps at a square dance at West Mabou Hall. Peter Parker, April 25, 2015. Photo by Margie Beaton; Melody Cameron, June 30, 2005. Photo by Victor Maurice Faubert.

aesthetic and, therefore, appreciate it when visitors fit within this when performing their genre. They also simply appreciate good dancing, such as when a completely different style of step dance (e.g., Ottawa Valley or Irish) is performed by a visitor. It used to be the case that only certain people got up to share their steps, but now many local and visiting dancers take to the floor. However, some local dancers comment that many "new" movements are creeping in that would not have been generally accepted some years back, suggesting perhaps that they are still not by some. Some feel that younger dancers in particular are performing increasingly involved and complicated steps that are not in keeping with good practice.

On the other hand, in addition to their dancing skills, outsiders are sometimes appreciated for the fact that they bring something new and a variation to the familiar Cape Breton expressions. A local dancer at a West Mabou dance once told me that "the visitors bring something different in! The local dancers we see all the time" (Melin 2006). The deep familiarity with the genre is probably the reason why people seldom, if ever, verbalize the crowd's reactions. The unvoiced aesthetic preferences common in Scots Gaelic society, mentioned elsewhere in chapter 6, still seem to prevail.

As the above observations indicate, the visual aspect of transmission is the predominant one, as the onlookers are generally some dis-

Figure 5.5 – West Mabou Square Dance April 25, 2015. Photo by M. Beaton.

tance away. The music is too loud for anyone to hear the feet touch the floor, and so aural and kinaesthetic transmission occurs less markedly than when the same dancers are seen performing in other contexts, or when one is dancing next to them in the square sets, where one can both feel their movements and hear their feet.

Reinforced Transmission During Square Dancing

Besides observing these dancers sharing their steps, one can join in the social dancing and dance with and/or next to them. Because of the close proximity during square dancing, it is no longer the visual transmission that is predominant. Here, based on my own experience, I feel that the various transmission processes interconnect, and the visual, aural and kinaesthetic modes interact closely and on equal levels.

I have observed people passing on their choice of movement at particular moments in square sets by holding hands or waltzing together, for example, rather than by observing and listening. Jackie Dunn-MacIsaac (2010c) adds her thoughts to this particular context of the genre:

> An extension on that [closeness that enables certain modes of transmission] is the body link between dancers when holding hands.... Sometimes when they first hold hands in the sets they may be doing their own step and [then] may automatically start doing the step the person beside them is doing to be in sync—probably again because our brains are wired for things to be organized, and dancing another beat or step [while] holding onto someone else doing another rhythm could feel awkward ... you have competing rhythms. Same thing when dancers meet in the grand chain: sometimes they will start doing the same step, and it feels great to be moving exactly the same to the music holding hands.

According to Jackie's observation, you observe and hear your fellow dancers' steps being danced, and you feel aspects of how they perform them, through contact and by feeling their bodies move next to your own. My own experiences have informed me of the different ways each person I have danced with or next to moves. I can vividly remember how a dancer moves, particularly when performing a certain movement, and I will then try to mimic it and make it my own when I dance it, but my memory of seeing it danced by another dancer remains. Likewise, remembering the sound of somebody's feet striking a particular surface, let's say sprung wooden floorboards, remains in my memory. Was the sound light and crisp or forceful and deep? And so forth. Step dancing with somebody while holding his or her hands is, for me, the strongest recollection. Here I have felt how somebody else moves, with what quality they strike the floor, for example, and to a certain degree how they channel their movement's proprioceptive qualities. My interpretation of these sensory inputs does help to inform my own dancing at a later stage. My understanding of the different movement combinations arises from a symbiotic relationship among my memory, my own dancing and the experience described above, of the transmission to me of others' performances. Also, recalling what you see, hear and feel in the sets informs your appreciation of individual dancers' sharing of their steps, both at the square dances and in the other contexts where encountered.

The music also cues the exhilarating energy one gets from a particular flow of movement. Minnie MacMaster (2010) describes this aspect of aural transmission:

> Back when I was growing up and dancing all the time—this would be from the age of about ten to the age of twenty-two or -three—before I got married and started a family—I was married in 1965 at the age of 23—it was like each time I heard the sound of the fiddle, a jolt of power went through my body and I just could [not] control myself. You just have to dance to it. It makes me feel so full of energy and the more [you] would hear your favourite tunes the bigger the jolt you got. A certain tune would be played that you have visions of certain steps that you want to put with the rhythm of that tune.... You have a craving to make the steps and the turns in the tune match perfectly. It's like you want to be the drummer or the percussion rhythm for those tunes, but you are doing it with your feet. That is one of the most exciting and powerful feelings you will ever experience as a dancer.... It's ... wonderful to get that overwhelming feeling when you see and hear a fiddler and dancer display their amazing gifts.

This crucial connection between the dancer and the music expressed above is vital to the understanding of Cape Breton step dancing and can be observed in all community locales where it occurs.

Concluding Note on Transmission Processes

In many respects, one could say that the dance-hall context, combined with that of the dance class, has taken over the function of home learning. At present, it is predominantly at the square dance that variety in style, motif, rhythm and aesthetic preferences, to name only some aspects, are actively transmitted. Even though some learning still occurs at home, it is to a much lesser extent than in days past. The informal context of casual aesthetic comments and pointers, combined with visual, aural and kinaesthetic modes of transmission processes in the home, has largely been replaced by the formal, more visual and aurally dominated teaching environment. Learning at home and in the classroom, with their particular modes of transmission processes, however, was reinforced with the dancing seen at community locales such as concerts and halls.

Figure 5.6 – Joël Chaisson, Judique Community Centre, August 9, 2008.
Figure 5.7 – Rodney MacDonald, Cedars Hall, Sydney, October 2, 2012. Photos by Victor Maurice Faubert.

Chapter 6

Lightly Dancing Close to the Floor: Characteristics of Cape Breton Step Dancing

Naming Regional Styles of Step Dancing

As global appreciation of step dancing, here used as a general term to describe forms of most often percussive footwork, has increased, the need to differentiate various regional styles of percussive step dance and, on a general level, any human-based movement systems,[1] it has become necessary to label styles. The words "genre" and "style" are often used interchangeably when discussing dance and, depending on how you look at a particular way of dancing, both could be correct. I use "genre" when we discuss percussive step dancing as an over-arching vernacular form of dance, while I use "style" to single out a particular regional variant of the same. Some, however, argue that when a style, because of its distinctiveness, has been labelled, it should be referred to as a genre (Melin 2013b).

The "close to the floor" styles of Canadian step dancing have, as Colin Quigley (2008: 35) puts it, gone from "shared [genre] vernacular to regional styles," even if two different styles share movement components. In this book, I will refer to the smallest movement motifs in dance analysis as "kinemic cells," consisting of 2-3 beats, or as "kinetic elements," consisting of single beats (see appendix 1); bigger combinations of 3+ beats are called "motifs." Motifs are generally simply referred to as "steps" in Cape Breton; they may be regarded regionally as distinctly different in their use. Canadian close-to-the-floor styles can be found in mainland Nova Scotia, Prince Edward Island, Newfoundland and Labrador, New Brunswick, Québec and Ontario. Some would include aspects of Ottawa Valley style in this list as well.[2] Some are today recognized by geographic terms such as "Ottawa Valley step dancing," "Québécois step dancing" or, as in this study, "Cape Breton step dancing." Further afield, the overarching label "close to the floor," as applied to this style, is shared with several other percussive dance styles, including Irish *sean nós* and forms of step dancing found in County Kerry, Ireland (see Foley 1988), certain types of English step dancing, and forms of American clog dancing (Appalachian, Buck and Wing, Flatfooting, etc.). When, exactly, the term "close to the floor" started to be used in Cape Breton in relation to the local style of step dancing I have not been able to establish, but the term features frequently in MacGillivray's (1988) *A Cape Breton Ceilidh*.

The need to add a regional identifier to the name of local step-dance styles is a relatively new phenomenon, and seems only to have emerged for music in the 1970s and for dance in the 1980s, as indicated by Quigley (2008). Step-dancer Harvey Beaton (2007) found it difficult to pinpoint the specific time he became aware of the term "Cape Breton step dancing" being used, but said that it was possibly with the increase in formal teaching and workshop demand abroad. He said growing up it was simply called "dancing." According to Judy MacKenzie, who lived as a child in Cape Breton but now resides in Boston where she teaches step dancing, the steps were known as "Scotch steps" when she was growing up (Schoonover 2015).

With the European-rooted dominant languages in Canada being English and French, it may not be strange that the humanly organized movement system, to use the neutral ethnochoreological term for our subject matter, is referred to as "dance" and percussive "step dance" in this particular case. It is important to remember that the Western world's concept of dance is not universal, nor is the meaning of the word (Royce 2002: 9). Dance often includes the notion of "music, dance, games, instruments, festivals, and so on within one word [and this] is not all that uncommon" (9). According to *The Chambers Dictionary*, the word "dance" has its etymological origin in Europe in the Old High German (ca. 500-1050 CE) word *dansón*, meaning "to stretch" or "to drag," and has evolved through the Old French (ca. 14th century) *danser, dancer* and the Middle English (late 12th to late 15th century) *dauncen, daunsen* (s. v. "dance," *Chambers Dictionary*, 1993). The term "dance,"[3] it is worth noting, entered Scots Gaelic as *dannsadh* or, in modern Gaelic, *danns*, and, in Irish Gaelic, *damhsa*. In Scots and Irish Gaelic, there are several words in use for dance; as an imported Germanic word in Scots Gaelic, *ruidhle* (to reel) is used for a particular way to dance, and in Irish (Gaelic) *rince* (ring) is used interchangeably with *damhsa*.[4] It is not unusual that a society have several words for dance since they may indicate different contexts for the activity, as, for example, in Spanish, where *danza* is a ritual activity while *baile* refers to secular dance (Royce 2002: 10).

In Cape Breton Gaelic, the term *gabh danns* (give a step) is used for the act of dancing, as well as *danns* for "dance" and *a' dannsa* or *a' dannsadh* for "dancing"; "steps" are *ceumanan*. As noted by Cape Breton Gaelic teacher and singer Goiridh Domhnallach (2010), the term for dance prior to the 1970s was just *danns* because there was no need to distinguish it from anything else. When Cape Breton step dancing was advertised to be taught at a music and dance summer school at Sabhal Mòr Ostaig in the Isle of Skye in the early 1990s, the term used for it was *dannsa-ceum,* which highlights the Gaelic words for both "dance" and "step," possibly labelled thus to single out the significance of the dance style's percussive nature. Since the 1990s, the Gaelic term *dannsa ceum Ceap Bhreatainn* (Cape Breton step dancing) has also been in use. On March 9, 2015, BBC Alba, the Scottish Gaelic-language TV channel, broadcast a program exploring Cape Breton and Scottish step dancing called "Faram nam Bròg" (In Their Steps), adding yet another term for dancing.

Other Gaelic terms that occur in literature on Scottish and Cape Breton dance are in reference to the old Scotch Reels called *ruidhleadh ceathrar* (Foursome Reel) and *ruidhleadh mòr* (eight-handed Reel), respectively (Flett and Flett 1985 [1964]; Rhodes 1985, 1996).[5]

Before regional labels of styles of dance became common from the 1970s onward, it was far more important to be aware of the meaning of keywords such as "close to the floor," "neat," "light" and "old style," indicating the local stylistic and aesthetic preferences. These words would have played, and still do play, a key part in transmitting an understanding of aspects of the dance genre. For the locals growing up with the dance vernacular, these keywords act as pointers and reminders of "good" dancing from the experienced to the learner, and keep the genre coherent. Some of these words may have subtle levels of meaning that are best understood locally. Learning these shades of meanings would enhance an outsider's aesthetic understanding of the local dance genre.

The Importance of Form and Style

It is problematic to apply the English meaning of terms such as "style," "aesthetics," "art" and "dance" because they are often used in sweeping, cross-cultural statements. Their meanings differ among cultures, as indeed does the meaning in other languages of equivalent or similar terms. For example, when using the word "dance" we must remember that the term is a Western construct and that many cultures do not necessarily have the equivalent word or meaning in their own language or culture. The late ethnomusicologist Alan P. Merriam (1974) made a point of this when comparing examples of cross-cultural and Western historical definitions of the term, pointing out several pitfalls and summarizing that what we are fundamentally dealing with, from a global perspective, is human-based movement systems.

Turning to the word "style" we find that Kaeppler (2001) positions it as an emic concept,[6] part of the idea of "dance," and she draws on Schapiro's (1962) notion of style as "form, quality, or expression of whole cultures, groups, or individuals" (Kaeppler 2001: 51). Kaeppler continues:

> Style seems to refer to persistent patterns in ways of performing structure—from subtle qualities of energy to the use of body parts as recognised by the people of a specific dance tradition.... The resulting form is understood by an observer through communicative competence in a specific system of movement knowledge. (p. 62)

Linguistic concepts distinguish "competence" (a person's capacity for speech) from "performance" (the actual utterance) (Chomsky 1965), or *langue* (the system or rules of language) from *parole* (the actual utterance) (Saussure 1998 [1972]), all of which are discussed in Kaeppler's (51-54) explanation. Kaeppler posits that the notion of "dance" is understood as its "form" (or perhaps better thought of as the content entity) and that form is a combination of structure and style. The structure is the different combinations of all those little movements (elements and motifs; see below) that are conceptually understood emically by a certain group of people (insiders). When these individual movements are combined into meaningful segments that are understood in and of themselves, dance researchers call these motifs, while in Cape Breton they would be called a step or part of a step (examples are shuffles, back steps or the hop step). When these movements are strung together in a specific way it creates a dance according to the concept of a specific group of people at a specific time (51). Kaeppler continues,

> These structural elements are the building blocks—the essential elements that determine how a specific dance is constructed and how dances differ according to genre. Style is the way of performing—that is, realising or embodying the structure. (p. 52)

To draw a linguistic analogy and to better visualize this:

	System/rules	Performance	
Dance (form)	structure	style	(Kaeppler)
Language	competence	performance	(Chomsky)
Language	langue	parole	(Saussure)

Those who have "communicative competence," to use Dell Hymes's (1977) term, among both performers and observers (often the same people in Cape Breton), have learned the shared rules that apply to Cape Breton step dance in this instance. Thus, the concept of *langue* is acquired, to use Saussure's epithet—the actors in this context have been enabled to understand a grammatical sequence of movements uniquely performed. Equally, the performers must have a certain level of ability and skill to perform a similar movement sequence, or *parole*, à la Saussure (Kaeppler 2001: 53; Foley 1988, 2007). In other words, you must know the movement conventions of Cape Breton step dance to have communicative competence, which enables understanding of what is being conveyed.

The only structural form unit used for my investigation is the motif (e.g., shuffles, back steps, hop step) and, in addition to the motif unit (being the core emic structure level, what you could simply call core or basic movement material), we must define Cape Breton style (the embodied structure) in order to enable explanation of Cape Breton step dancing. To recapitulate: structural elements (motifs, etc.) are the building blocks of all form units essential for a dance genre, while style is the (unique to Cape Breton) way the dance is realized and embodied in any performance of the structure. A full inventory of form units relevant to Cape Breton step dancing would require a separate study.

Among the objectives of this study was to uncover which motifs or steps, to use the emic term, are meaningful and have taken on cognitive status (being recognized as a step) in Cape Breton. These motifs are recalled and re-embodied by each new generation of dancers. The dance may tell us something about the culture itself, based on who performs, how many perform and the interactions between performers and their audience or community. The way the dance itself is realized through the use of vertical and horizontal space, for example, and the way the dancer moves in a locally accepted fashion inform us of cultural and socially accepted norms. We begin by looking at how Cape Breton step dancing is realized with the help of certain keywords.

Keywords that Generate Aesthetic Preferences

Common keywords used by members of the dance community in Cape Breton describe—or perhaps it is more accurate to say they create and maintain—certain stylistic characteristics. Terms such as "close to the floor," "neat," "light" and "old style" are common and seem, on one level, to serve a fairly straightforward function: to describe the community's values of good dancing. But these keywords often perform a function beyond simply describing a quality of movement. The keywords serve to instil value, as can be seen in the sixty interviews contained in MacGillivray (1988), who interviewed Cape Breton dancers and musicians in the 1980s, and which reveal a number of characteristic keywords that signify attributes of a good dancer or good dancing—most of which are still in use today.

In MacGillivray's interviews, the most common word used to indicate good dancing is "neat," as in to dance "neatly." For instance, step dancer Tommy Basker, from New Victoria, and the MacArthurs, from MacKinnon's Brook, referred to the dancers in Mabou as being "close to the floor" and very "neat" (MacGillivray 1988: 26, 80). Aggie MacLennan recalled to MacGillivray the dancers of bygone days, "how neat they would be on the floor ... and they held themselves just so!" (119). Neatness is the main thing. They could dance on a 10 x 10 inch (25 x 25 cm) tile and not move from it. Today, in contrast, it is remarked to me by some dancers that while there are those who have some of the old steps, they are dancing them in a wider and higher fashion. This may also indicate that there may be a change occurring in the style (Melin 2013b).

"Nifty" is another word used, which has similar connotations to neat. Both Florence and Margaret MacPhee were labelled "nifty dancers" who were light on their toes. Florence "kept her head up and never looked down at her feet" (MacGillivray 1988: 48, 69). Willie Fraser used "nifty" to indicate the same about dancers who show qualities of lightness and dancers who hold themselves straight. Maryann (Currie) Gouthro of Frenchvale further indicates what qualifies as "neat and nifty dancing" when she remembers her mother and father dancing and learning from them:

> They stayed in the one position, the one spot. Papa told me to keep my hands down by my sides, to stand up straight and to just work my feet; that was it. And you have to listen to the tune! He did not move his arms at all; all that was moving was his feet. (MacGillivray 1988: 70)

Judique dancer Alex A. Graham said, speaking of his parents' generation, "that was just the way that they made their steps. They made them perfect and they made them neat" (72). Other words with similar meanings are "slick," "snappy" and "smooth." This variety of words in use illustrates that each individual, in their own choice of words, explains similarly appreciated qualities in a dancer. There seems to be no need for a standardized terminology, as all these words convey a similar meaning and are understood in the Cape Breton community, I surmise.

A quality inferred in the above terms of neat, nifty and the like is the lightness and precision of the dancing. Hughie "Shorty" MacDonald illustrated the importance of lightness well in his 1987 conversation with MacGillivray (1988: 85): "Big Simon Gillis was a huge man but they used to say that he could dance on an egg shell he was so light." Kenny "Neil the Islands" MacDonald was also said to be as light as a feather on the floor: "you could put a newspaper under his feet when he was dancing and he'd never tear it" reminisced Collie Beaton (154). As I understand, the Gaelic word *grinn* (neat, clean, or elegant) is also used and carries connotations of lightness and favours certain ways of moving, ultimately associating lightness and neatness with beauty. An example of the use of *grinn* and also of the word *sgiobalta* (agile, neat, tidy) would be the line from a *puirt-a-beul*, which is well suited for dancing to, "rinn donn sgiobalta mo ghiobag air an ùrlar" (Neatly-formed, brown-haired, agile, my neat one of the dance floor) (Rob Dòmhnallach 2012: 142).

Today, the phrases "being light on your feet" and "dancing as light as a feather" are commonly heard phrases in the Cape Breton step-dance community, used to signify that neatness and lightness is valued in dancing. Melody Cameron (2007) uses the word "graceful" for the same concept. Similarly, Margaret (MacLellan) Gillis singles out poise as an important quality, which she defines as when "a person holds their body in a nice position and can exercise accuracy in their feet without lifting their knees or bending their bodies with their backsides sticking out" (MacGillivray 1988: 62). Angus "Mossy" MacKinnon of Black Point is described by his niece Alice (MacKinnon) Aucoin as having good poise as well: "When he danced, Uncle Angus moved from the waist down but his upper body was straight—not stooping—straight as a die" (107). Hector Mackinnon of Cain's Mountain also danced straight and from the knees down, said Jean MacNeil in 1986, who adds, "he even did steps where he just moved from the ankles down!" (124). Hector was also protective about his steps, so he did not show all his steps too often, so people couldn't pick them

Figure 6.1 – Willie Fraser step dancing with daughters Clare and Maureen at Ceòlas Summer School, South Uist, Scotland (1996). Mairi Rankin, Joe Peter MacLean and Fr. Angus Morris on fiddle. Photo by Mats Melin.

up (124). Short-lived but famed step dancer Fr. Angus MacDonnell (1944-1977) from Deepdale was recalled as having "floating feet" and "supple ankles," and put little extra taps and beats in his nimble dancing. Jean MacNeil recalls he had very supple ankles, which enabled him to put in steps where you could hear a "triplet" sound (very quick staccato foot movements making three sounds or contact noises with the floor in rapid succession) (125). In 1987, renowned step dancer Gussie MacLellan from Inverness Town remembered St. Rose dancer and piper Alex Dan MacNeil as a

> very neat dancer; he never flung his feet like a lot of dancers do [today].... He was a very close to the floor dancer and, when he shuffled out in front, he never went out an extra foot ahead of him. (116)

Sheldon MacInnes summarizes a lot of these qualities: "*neat* sum[s] up some kind of quality that old-time dancers possessed. You can do a lot steps without much movement above the knees ... a lot of steps in a very small area" (97). Keeping in mind the above statements from MacGillivray's and my own research on "good" and "old time" dancing style (Melin 2013b), you might sum up a dancer who dances within a very small area, as the commonly heard phrases "dances on a dime" or "on your hat" indicate; who is light, neat, and nifty; carries oneself with good posture; keeps arms and head still; dances from the knees, or even the ankles, down; and uses small but precise movements as having "old style" characteristics. Furthermore, some consider it important to keep steps evenly balanced between the right and left foot, as indicated by Gussie MacLellan's observation of Alex Dan MacNeil that "what he could do with a right foot, he could also do with the left" (MacGillivray 1988, 116).

To an extent, most of these keywords relate in the first instance to the visual aspect of dancing and what is seen as good practice but, from an emic point of view, they imply aural and kinaesthetic modes of awareness that the Cape Breton music and dance community understands at a deeper and more implicit level.

When I met renowned step dancer Willie Francis Fraser, from Deepdale, in South Uist in 1996, he emphasized a number of these keywords. Willie was age eighty-one at the time,[7] and was continuously illustrating his preferred proximity of the working foot to the supporting foot in most steps: "You place your steps just so, neatly," he would say. Keeping the movements small and precise was absolutely key to achieving this neatness. Willie made a point of illustrating that only the slightest movement of the body forward, backward or sideways was required. Willie would always take great care in making the class understand exactly how he wanted the steps to be performed. His two daughters, Maureen (Fraser-Doyle) and Clare (MacQuarrie), greatly assisted his teaching at the time. In the film *God Bless Your Feet* (2004), celebrating Willie's contribution to dance, you can see how close both daughters' style of dancing is to their father's. As Maureen told me, "I have been step dancing since the early age of three with my dad at Old Home Week, Inverness.... From then on my steps were his steps" (Fraser-Doyle, 2012). Both daughters have helped keep the family style of dancing alive and in turn passed on the family dance knowledge to the next generation(s). At the top of Willie's list of important characteristics/skills were timing and musicality.

Observing him teach, and learning from him at the Ceòlas summer school in South Uist in 1996, he would not teach a class a single step until we had learned to "jig" the strathspey "Calum Crùbach" and the reel "Muilean Dubh" while Willie sang the song in Gaelic and we had reached a standard he was happy with. Thus he enabled a process where the class had to internalize the rhythm of the tunes. Even though Willie used terms such as "timing" and "interaction with the musician" on occasion, the keywords "neat," "light" and "nifty" were used regularly, and seemed implicitly to include the notion of timing and music interaction as well.

Likewise, Harvey Beaton, Mary Janet MacDonald, Melody Cameron and Jean MacNeil, just to mention four of the many Cape Breton dancers and teachers I have encountered on numerous occasions, emphasize the same qualities and the same keywords. All four use the term "close to the floor" as a stylistic marker, and neatness and lightness are always encouraged.

Some of these keywords were used on my 2008 questionnaire as suggested qualities of good representations of Cape Breton step dance. The people who filled in the questionnaire each indicated which of these terms they felt applied to each dancer. Some respondents made additional comments such as "the dancing is not showy," "light as a feather," "willingness to share the gift of dancing," "effortless" and "hold themselves well and lively dancing" (Melin 2012: 378-91). All these comments elaborate further on perceived qualities of good dancing.

In summary, the keywords highlighted above, close to the floor, light, neat, old style and so forth, do, when combined, illustrate the aesthetic preferences of the Cape Breton dance community as a whole. Today the performers of step dancing in Cape Breton hail from all the different ethnic groups that settled on the island. Even taking into account that the Scottish Gaelic settlers were the dominant group, and that many of these keywords may well have come from them, it may be better to think of these aesthetic preferences as spanning across the whole of Cape Breton culture. Having said that, I get a feeling that many of the aesthetic preferences verbalized above are simply based on family and individual taste. In her article on the concept of style, Kaeppler says that terms such as aesthetics and style are "slippery," since "these are all words that we use every day, but we do not have any common understanding of what they mean" and particularly not when applied cross-culturally (2001: 50). Aesthetics tends to infer the appreciation of beauty, but in this context I will be using it to refer to the preferences about the way certain dance movements appear, which, through embodiment and performance, create style.

As indicated in chapter 2, Gaelic terminology for dancing likely once existed to a certain extent among learned Gaels but seems to have declined greatly by the early 19th century, just as Dickson (2006: 220) suggests it did for piping in Gaelic Scotland when he refers to Fraser (ca. 1855), who compiled more than 2,000 Gaelic musical terms, particularly for fingering, and to Bunting's (1840) treatise on Irish harp music, which lists many old Irish musical terms, to name just a couple of sources. What is of further interest in this study are the historical and current "unvoiced," as Dickson (2006: 221) calls the un-spoken aesthetic values of grassroots Gaels still predominantly used in piping in South Uist and, I would add, in dance in Cape Breton. The community would organically select those movements that are deemed viable, by trial and error and by popularity, just as they did with songs and tunes that became popular over time, ensuring the survival of the aesthetic properties that were valued the most. Pleasing rhythms, economy of movement, versatility (useful at both solo and social dances) and the like would all influence the formation of aes-thetic choice over time.

It may be argued that since the dominant modes of transmission—aural, visual and kinaesthetic—are informal, there is perhaps little need for retaining any former technical vocabulary of movement, but a few keywords expressing the qualities of the movements were kept as part of the voiced transmission alongside unvoiced, both commonly understood aesthetic criteria. Indeed, Margaret Gillis (2007) of Gillisdale told me in conversation that her father, John Alex Gillis, never used technical terms for movements when teaching dances such as Dannsa nan Flurs (Flowers of Edinburgh). The relatively informal teaching methods indicated in chapter 3 of even organized dance classes in Cape Breton in the 19th and early 20th century could account for the lack of dance-related terminology in modern Cape Breton Gaelic, and for the inventiveness of English terminology for dance movements as used by today's dancers and teachers. Indeed, the proliferation of English terminology, coupled with a lack of parallel Gaelic terminology in Cape Breton today, mirror the situation of the piping tradition in 20th-century South Uist (Dickson 2006: 224-25).

So, the aesthetic preferences generated are expressed in a combination of verbal keywords and non-verbal criteria that are uniquely understood in the Cape Breton dance and music community. These aesthetic criteria are often based on personal and family notions of artistry and beauty and on social and functional values. Some islanders, for example, may prefer functional dance movements that enable a dancer to save energy and sustain dancing over long periods of time in social dances such as Reel and square sets. Also, the ultimate appearance of a dancer making his dancing look effortless is based on his ability to economize his movements, his skill of execution, his timing, rhythm and, no doubt, his ability to dance close to the floor. All these combine to create the aforementioned aesthetic preference of "lightness" in the dancing. All those keywords that indicate neat (*grinn* in Gaelic), light, tidy, upright and economized small movement from the waist or even from the ankles down, as discussed earlier, form the top signifiers of a good dancer.

Some dancers, however, do not show these aesthetic preferences, but may—due to their family connections, their ability to entertain, their charisma and energy when dancing—still be greatly appreciated as dancers in the community. If their style is the opposite of a dancer who dances close to the floor, they are sometimes referred to as a "high stepper." This term indicates someone whose movements are bigger, wider and lifted higher off the floor. The label is applied as a stylistic marker and is not necessarily negative; it does not mean that the dancer in question cannot be appreciated as a good dancer. The dancers I know who are labelled this way do meet some of the preferred island aesthetic criteria, such as excellent timing or lightness, which may make up for the stylistic difference.

Embodied "Unvoiced" Characteristics

Taking the above discussions on the voiced aesthetic criteria of good dancing (close to the floor, neat, tidy, upright), it is appropriate to now look at these, and the unvoiced criteria hinted at earlier, through my own observations. Cape Breton step dancers predominantly dance upright and erect, referred to as "dancing tall," the preferred verticality of the dance style marked by little up and down movement of the torso and head. I noted that very few people dance with their upper bodies leaning slightly forward, as would be common among some Irish *sean-nós* dancers, for example. In Cape Breton, the dancers face forward and the eyes are mostly kept level. The body's centre of gravity is generally positioned from the centre of the head through the centre of the body, down to between the balls of both feet when both feet are placed parallel and close to each other. Likewise for dancers with slightly wider stances, the centre of gravity remains in the centre between both feet. Thus, the main part of the body weight is distributed between the balls of the feet. If only one foot is in contact with the floor, the centre of gravity is shifted toward that foot to compensate for good balance to maintain the erect posture of the body. Arms are held in a relaxed manner by the sides, which allows for individual movement of one or both arms. Some dancers hold their arms quite still, while others allow them to move a bit (but not excessively or distractingly). As some obviously relax their arms to a great extent, their hands are allowed to move quite freely with the general up and down movement of the body. Some steps require a small amount of forward and backward movement, while others require some sideways movement. Any turns are generally done quite tightly on the one spot. Some steps require a dancer to make a ninety-degree turn to the right or left, and it does not seem to matter which direction is first, as it depends on the step being danced and also on which foot is leading.

Other turns can be the full way round, again depending on the leading foot and step in question. Generally, if you turn one way you do turn the other way to balance things up. There are some motifs that require the body to turn to the back with the working foot maybe one-third or one-quarter turned to enable ease of execution. Very few steps incorporate any form of diagonal travel, but steps may have a diagonal forward-and-backward rocking motion, which keeps the dancer on the spot. Hip and knee movements primarily generate the actions of the legs. Ankles are relaxed and interact with the general leg movements to provide the positions of the feet required.

Feet are for the most part held slightly turned out. Even though the voiced aesthetic criteria favour that the elevation of the body be kept to a minimum, as suggested in the phrase "dancing from the knees/ankles," the amount of elevation applied varies from dancer to dancer. The same phrase also indicates that feet and heels should be kept close to the ground. This again is very much a matter of individual preference and ability. Another individual trait is how far apart or close together a dancer's feet are positioned when dancing. Footwork is generally performed with the feet close together, with the moving foot held close to the supporting foot unless a motion or a particular shape is required. Here, though, individual styles take precedence, as some dance with feet farther apart than others; similarly, some hold heels higher off the ground than others. These are the main characteristics I have observed, and most fall in the unvoiced section of what is implicitly understood as part of the previously outlined aesthetic keywords. They apply to both male and female dancers alike. The one characteristic that tends not to vary from dancer to dancer, however, is that dancers perform from the knees down. But, even though certain characteristics are clearly valued over others, personal preference ("making the dance your own") is equally valued and should be understood when observing dancers in action because it, to some extent, allows for a range of accepted movement schema in Cape Breton step dancing. This of course is not unique to Cape Breton, as Catherine Foley similarly observed and remarked on the importance of individual style in her study of solo step dancing in County Kerry, Ireland (1988, 2012, 2013). As we are looking at a "performance" of step dance, whether in a formal or informal context, I will highlight in chapter 7 whether the dance and music community see some individual dancers as performers rather than just dancers.

The Importance of Timing

Another common word I have heard used to signify good dancing is whether the "timing" is good. Timing indicates how well a dancer is able to perform his or her movements in connection with the music (tune or song). A good sense of timing, hitting the feet on the floor exactly right to create good flow, enabling ease of dancing and creating a lift that matches the swing of the music, are seen as very important. Having good timing enables a dancer to achieve the aesthetic criteria expressed by keywords such as neat and light, for example. Indeed, many of the dancers' statements to me indicate that good timing is even more important than the number of steps you can perform. The general message is that the number of different steps counts for very little if your timing is off. Good timing is one of the highest attributes of a good dancer, and it is essential for good dancing practice.

The sense of timing is deeply connected to aural learning and the ability to know and hear the pulse or "drive," to use the local term, of the music. I touched on this notion in chapter 2 when discussing the difference in rhythm and pulse of Gaelic and English. Understanding how the local music is realized, knowing the tune repertoire, knowing individual players' ways of performing these tunes, understanding how the bowing technique, for example, of these players will assist your dancing, are all key components for a dancer to achieve good timing. A dancer's good timing also provides a point of reference for the musicians. I would see this as a counter-flow rhythm and energy to them, confirming that they are playing just right. Thus, two-way transmission is at work here, mutually benefiting each performer. What is also at play here is the ability to hear the music and the rhythm and pulse in the dance. This links in with a statement found in Dickson's (2006: 213) book on piping in South Uist, where he connects learning piping (music) by ear and the vital connection of the music with dancing and timing:

> the process of learning [pipe] tunes aurally and the performance of ear-learned tunes—*ceòl cluais*—comprise an idiom fundamentally associated with dance and by extension, timing. Therein lie both its functional value and the reason for its survival in the local tradition.

This functional value is very apparent in the dance contexts in Cape Breton. I now turn to the ways transmission through aural, visual and kinaesthetic means enables the favoured aesthetic values, such as timing, to be maintained.

Aspects of Aural Transmission

Leaving visual and kinaesthetic transmission aside for a moment, let's concentrate on what can be learned through sound. Aural learning is, in the case of this dance genre, a blend of percussive sounds relating to rhythms produced by dancers' feet in relation to music, of encouraging, guiding mnemonic verbal cues and of general contextual or ambient sounds. Taking into account how we hear sounds in all the transmission contexts, home, classroom, concert, and square dance, that we focus on in this study, these sounds help orient dancers, allowing them to stay in the middle, as they hear sounds from all around them, even from a distance, according to Ong (1967), and that they also hear with their whole bodies rather than with their ears alone (Hahn 2007: 115). This ties in with how we feel kinaesthetically through the body as it picks up sound vibrations from around us.

With this in mind, we can identify some key aspects of the Cape Breton dance soundscape. If we separate some of the main sounds in the "many layers of complexity," to use Hahn's (115) phrase, using selective attention we can begin to identify, for one, the rhythmic sounds produced by dancers' feet against the ground. Most of the examples in this study concern people's contact with the dance genre over extended periods, even a lifetime, and at regular intervals, which enables our ears to hear and our bodies to feel sound waves—as according to Ong and Hahn—and to learn to discern and make sense of sound patterns. Certain rhythmic patterns will crystallize; for example, a common reel motif known locally as the "hop step" has a rhythm pattern that could be diddled as "diddle-diddle-dum-dum"–4/4 time count ("one and, two and, three, four"; see motif reel 3). There are many variations on this motif, but all have the first four counts ("one and, two and") in common with variations on counts "three" and "four." The most common rhythm you would hear is this base or core rhythm, given above. It is also one of the first motif rhythms you would hear if you were taught the dance genre formally. Over an extended period you hear many different dancers, male and female, perform this and other common rhythms, making them recognizable as widely used rhythm patterns in the community, not confined to one particular dancer.

The next step in discerning rhythm patterns is combining the foot rhythm with the rhythm of the music (or song) to which it is danced. For simple core rhythms, 4/4 reel motifs are audibly connected to the local reel-time melody repertoire. On one level, all reel motifs can be danced to any melody in reel time. This changes, however, on a more refined level. For complex rhythm variations, a trained ear (as happens with exposure over time) discerns that certain tunes lend themselves better to certain motif rhythms. This may lead to particular melodies (or parts thereof) triggering rhythm memory in the dancer to bring out motifs with the same or similar rhythm sequences. Bringing out such motifs would, for experienced dancers, not exclude the use of other simpler (or complex) motifs to the same music, as per the individual choice of each dancer, but the possibility of connection would be there—heard, recognized, remembered.

In accordance with Hahn (2007: 115), when she says "we practice making sense of the many layers of complexity, and even learn to mask out some sounds in our selective attention," here we are concerned with remembered rhythm sequences that become associated with certain melody or song strains and reinforced every time they are realized. My own experiences of matching remembered motif rhythms with a particular tune or type of melody agree with the notion of singling out particular aural memories and matching them up. I would say that these associations are individually formed but are based on what has been heard before from other performers, and may then be seen as good practice, or simply as just making good sense. Familiarity with the local music and song repertoire enhances this rhythm knowledge. The successful ability to synchronize the movement rhythms of the feet with the pulse of the music and the song is testament that timing is the top priority in the local aesthetic preferences. The footwork should thus aim to match the rhythm and pulse of the musicians' choices and styles of playing tunes.

I observed that a higher level of awareness occurs when a musician's personal preferences of rendering a melody matches a dancer's preference, or "take" on the same tune. Each puts a personal stamp on the individual part, but they complement and enhance one another. It is here that you may find that over time certain dancers come to prefer to dance to certain musicians as they (the musicians) become familiar with their (the dancers') take on the music. As Cape Breton musicians are individually known for ornamenting tunes in a favoured or familiar way each time they play, which is in contrast to most Irish fiddlers, who change ornamentation as they go along, it becomes easier to remember how a tune will be played by a particular musician each time you dance to him or her. A certain parallel with dancers' choices of movement is found here, in that what feels right to a particular fiddler in his favoured way of playing a tune may be mirrored in the favoured way a dancer matches steps to that fiddler's style.

Another level of audible information involves the quality, or the amount of effort or strength—strong or light—with which the dancer's feet touch the ground. Though surfaces vary, and the most common surface in this context is wood, different floors give off different sound qualities. The ear may detect nuances of accent in the way the feet are placed and how lightly or heavily a dancer is hopping. Certain beats can be emphasized for effect in certain motifs. Again, these sounds become recognizable over time in this cultural context. Individual dancers may become recognized for dancing in a particular way from just hearing the sounds their feet make, as indicated in a conversation with Andrea Beaton (2009). In my own experience you can, at a square dance for example, recognize particular dancers' footwork in the hall by just hearing it. This is similar to identifying different fiddlers by hearing alone, by characteristic ornamentation and bowing technique. With some individuals, particular tunes seem to prompt them to dance more strongly or distinctly than usual, and you can isolate the sound of their dancing among the many other dancers on the floor. There is a similar familiar recognition of the style of different fiddlers without seeing them, but by simply hearing their particular soundscape (style, ornamentation, etc.).

Mnemonic keywords and encouraging or correcting phrases are another part of the soundscape. The terms outlined above—light, close to the floor, and others like them—given at gatherings, at home, at local community gatherings and/or in a class situation add to the individual and collective understanding of aesthetic preferences. These terms are often combined with visual stimuli as the prompts suggest that learners look at good practice in action. This or that dancer is neat, nifty or light, or has good timing. Other phrases, such as he or she "has the old style," often with the added statement that he or she "dances very close to the floor," recommend studying the subject visually as well as aurally. The statements always indicate a multitude of good practice. I cannot recall ever hearing a Cape Bretoner single out one dancer over many others; it is always a collective "good practice" that is indicated. Even though one dancer may be referred to specifically, a statement is commonly added that there are plenty of other dancers featuring something similar, thus indicating the collective aesthetic displayed by an individual. Again, to my understanding, this underscores the idea that personal interpretations of the genre are actively taken into account as something that enhance the dance practice in general.

The final sounds taken into account here are ambient or contextual sounds. These are all the surrounding sounds in the many contexts where dancing occurs: laughter, hollers, discussions among onlookers and approving applause when a good or difficult step is performed well or a favourite tune is played well. As Hahn (2007: 116) outlines, you become, through sound, aware of the space around you, of orientation within sound (within a melody), which helps to trace the order of events and sound relationships, and "processes of embodied social interaction" (Sparling 2004: 68) in this particular context.

Aspects of Visual Transmission

In chapter 2, I outlined recent findings in cognitive sciences research done by Cross (2010), by Cruse and Schilling (2010), by Bläsing and by Schack (2010) into the function of the human brain's "mirror neurons" in relation to the visual learning of dance. Thus, in contrast to aural learning, visual impressions are viewed from a distance rather than from the centre (Ong 1967). In the frequent absence of cue words or mnemonic instructions for the dance genre, visual transmission is a key component for embodying the movement repertoire. Visual transmission does, however, commonly occur in conjunction with aural and kinaesthetic transmission; the three complement each other.

When a dancer is being observed, the type of movement, the degree of extension or contraction of legs, the ankle movement, the part of the foot touching the ground, how high or low the dancer's elevation is, how high or low their feet are off the ground when lifted or extended, the width or the narrowness of the shape of the movements—all the dancer's movements that are performed—can be perceived. Movement sequences repeatedly performed by many dancers become recognized as essential movement motifs and become commonly known. Verbal guidelines to good practice from members of the community emphasize particular movement motifs that have preferred visual and aural characteristics. Similar to sound, certain personal interpretations of movement become accepted and predominantly used among the many ways of performing those movements; for example, shuffles in reel time are commonly performed with the heel and the toe, while shuffles in strathspey time are equally commonly done as "toe and toe" shuffles. Individual differences and preferences do occur, however.

In the case of shuffles, described above, combining visual input with the aural may inform us that when the heel touches the floor the sound is often heavier than when the toe touches the floor. The combination of sight and sound helps us identify how a dancer performs, in this case, a particular shuffle. As with the aural transmission, different dancers' characteristics can over time be detected and remembered. In many cases, individuals become known for performing certain movements in a particular way, a way that is unique to them, and perhaps not commonly used, but still accepted as part of the local aesthetic preference.

Motif combinations are, in many ways, probably first visually appreciated as a motif (or combinations of motifs) and may sound very similar but look quite different. Seeing many different dancers perform their steps you begin, after a while, to realize that certain motif combinations are common with many, if not most, dancers. However, as each individual performance is unique in motif order and interpretation, since it is generally an improvisation of

Figure 6.2 – Kelly MacLennan and Melody Cameron, Celtic Colours (2014), at Strathspey Place, Mabou, NS. Photo by Mats Melin.

movement repertoire rather than being performed in a universally set order, it takes time to learn to visually recognize motif patterns. Of course, individuals may have a basic routine in mind that they work around, but these choices still remain individual. Visually appreciating which motif can follow which, and how visually different but recognizable motifs are linked together, is learnt by watching many different dancers perform. The appreciation of step- or motif-linking is a learning process that takes time. Combining visual input with the sounds of the feet and the kinaesthetic appropriation of the movement completes the process of understanding these motif combinations.

When observing a person who dances with ease, flow and lightness, and whose timing of each movement done in relation to the music is absolutely "right," it is then that you feel you want to be able to dance along the same lines yourself. I yearn to understand how these patterns work, how they are constructed and, by extension, I would also like to be able to perform the particular movements with similar ease and insight. Answers to questions such as which motifs fit well together, which can be "doubled up" (repeated twice on the same foot), which are more frequently used to certain melody types, and similar questions are answered initially via visual impressions. Repetition of visual impressions by observing many performers (and over long periods), in conjunction with aural and kinaesthetic transmission, constantly informs and reaffirms good practice. It is then that personal, and also family, versions of popular motif combinations become apparent.

Taking motif reel 1 and reel 2 as examples, and depending on a number of factors, such as personal preference or music connectivity, these two motifs can be danced in the order reel 1+reel 2 or reel 2+reel 1. It is a small difference, but it can be significant in relation to melody rhythm. I have observed that some dancers prefer one way over the other, while other dancers use both interchangeably. Certain individual movement combinations are associated with a person as a signature or characteristic step they perform(ed). Some of the Cape Breton step-dance style's most common motifs are described in Melin (2012: 171-95).

Observing whether dancers start a movement (motif) with their right or left foot is also part of visual aesthetic. When formal teaching started in the 1970s, it became common for dancers to be taught to start dancing off the right foot. This occurred, while at the same time their teachers would revert back to what they were used to doing when performing or sharing their steps, by starting using either. Some dancers, I have observed, always start with the left or always with the right foot when they dance. Using a different starting foot interchangeably through the routine for different motifs is also common with some dancers. Here the change of starting foot for a motif can be seen as a seamless transition between motifs: one foot starts certain motifs; the other foot starts other motifs. Hearing comments by members of the Cape Breton community, it becomes clear that it is acceptable to use either foot as the starting foot.

I have observed that the island dance community more or less observes the general aesthetics of how the upper body, head and arms are held when dancers are in action. Even though certain individuals differ from the norm, by leaning forward while dancing, for example, or swinging one or both arms, the generally accepted stance is that the body and head are held upright. The interaction between dancers and musicians, and between dancers dancing together is also perceived visually. How are they interacting? What can body language tell us about their relationship to each other? When does a dancer respond in a particular way to the way a musician is playing at a certain moment? Again, sight and sound combined provide us with certain data that informs us about good practice. What was it that visually indicated that the music was "just right" for a dancer at a particular moment? Did the dancer look relaxed, at ease, or even happy? Did the movement flow with apparent ease? Did it seem to match the melody or part of a tune? How did the onlookers respond to the performance? Were they nodding, smiling or applauding, or perhaps shouting encouragements approvingly? Or did we see a small shake of the head accompanied by leaning over to the neighbour to pass on a comment? All these, and many other, questions can be answered in part, or in full, through visual input. They all provide different aspects of the whole that have to be perceived, the better to understand the dance genre.

Aspects of Kinaesthetic Transmission

In all the contexts studied in this book there are instances where some sources state that they have held hands with another dancer while teaching them, allowing them to "feel" how it should be done. Others refer to feeling the steps transmitted through the floor or stage into their own bodies, or being "jigged" on their mothers' laps as small children, thus getting a feel for the rhythms in connection with songs or music.

In Tomie Hahn's (2007: 1) first dance class, her headmaster (dance teacher) Tachibana Hiroyo told her—"know with your body"—which aptly sums up the complicated processes involved in what Deidre Sklar (2008: 103) suggests: "gesture [movement] requires not only association with movement's kinetic qualities of vitality but also an accounting of the way the sensations of kinetic vitality are socially structured, transformed, and mediated." In other words, to understand the sensations of movement on this level we must understand the context and amplify it through analysis. What we refer to here is that we must study and understand the transmission of cultural knowledge: kinaesthetic transfer and proprioceptive awareness alongside visual and aural processes that should be seen as key components in shaping the aesthetic, stylistic, and movement preferences of this dance genre. In chapter 2, I outlined the complex ideas and problems of describing kinaesthetic transfer, both within the body and from body to body. In the following examples I will try to illustrate, using my own experience and movement sensations, how Cape Bretoners show that they know with their bodies when they dance.

In Cape Breton and elsewhere, when I have met Cape Breton dancers, I have first subconsciously but later consciously become aware of the bringing out of somatic, or felt, dimensions of movement; in other words, the proprioceptive or kinaesthetic awareness of movement's kinetic vitality. This flow within my own body, as well as from other dancing bodies, has informed me, probably at the deepest personal level, of what movement in this dance genre is. It is perhaps the closest I can get to dancing as a "Cape Breton dancer," but I dance on my own terms and as my own person, both outside and within their context(s), to follow Rice's (2008) outline of experiencing the culture through phenomenological hermeneutics (see chapter 1). A few instances will serve here as good examples of when I could consciously recall "feeling with my body" what another dancer was doing. This one concept of transmission, I feel, might well warrant a specific and deeper study in itself.

When a dancer holds both my hands, as sometimes happens when "stepping it out" in the reel part of a square set or maybe in a class or learning situation, the feel of her movements is transmitted to you. It is not only a question of how much she moves up or down, or any other direction, but also of how much energy or vitality she put into the movements. Combine this feeling with the sound and the sight of it, and you have a multitude of data to process and consciously analyze in order to make these movements in a similar way but on your own terms.

This direct contact goes further, all the way around a circle of people holding hands; as in the jig figures of the square sets, this type of information flows not only from the people nearest to you but from almost all in the circle. You may initially see something, or even hear a rhythm or steps done in the circle, and then everybody's senses collaborate and it becomes possible, on one level, to concentrate on "feeling" what the other bodies are doing. I have learned the particular "swing" and amount of contact between feet against the floor for jig shuffles in this way.

Dancing next to dancers in a line, or cutting through the figures of a Scotch Four has similarly informed me of the vitality in the other dancers' movements: how light or strong they are on their feet, how much effort they put into their dancing, how they hold themselves when moving from one place to another, how they shift their body weight to move around in the most economical way, or how the energy/vitality changes when transitioning from one cell or motif to another. It is about letting one's own body "know" and feel the flow and pulse of the dancing. Two of my most intense memories of this type of feeling are of dancing a Scotch Four flanked by Mac Morin and Wendy MacIsaac, and once with Kelly MacLennan and Melody Cameron on either side of me. Their full awareness of the movement repertoire and their ease of moving within the genre's aesthetic parameters greatly influenced how I danced at those particular moments. Upon reflection, I can recall certain bursts of energy emanating from them, which made me aware of how certain movements could be performed.

Kinaesthetic transmission also occurs from a distance. At a square dance, all the dancing bodies emit a level of kinetic vitality when moving. Along with seeing and hearing them, you feel rhythms through the floor as vibrations, especially if it is a good sprung wooden floor. Feeling floor vibrations occurs when actively taking part in the dancing or when simply observing on the sidelines. A group of bodies moving together in approximate unison, but with individual takes on the same motifs, will provide a flow that one's own body picks up. As one local dancer once said to me after an evening of square dancing, you would definitely have a feeling for the "diddle-diddle-dum-dum" rhythm of the reel-time hop step, even if you just observed. "You just can't miss it!" Reflecting on this statement some sixteen years later, I realize that he was talking about kinaesthetic transfer as much as he was talking about the more obvious visual and aural ones.

When I first encountered Cape Breton step dancing, in 1992 in Scotland as detailed in chapter 1, I would observe the movements shown in class, listen to the sound and the mnemonic keywords provided and try it out slowly for myself. However, when watching these same dancers perform the steps up to speed in a performance, improvising round the movements I had just learned, a different level of transmission occurred. Seeing a multitude of variations of common motifs danced, hearing the sound and the connection with the music, I began imagining at a subconscious level what their movements would feel like if I tried something similar. Questions in my mind would form, alongside renditions of a movement sequence in my mind's eye. How strong, light, fast and so forth would I have to perform the same to achieve something similar? When trying out the movement for myself, these questions and these "felt" experiences would help me inform my own body of how to execute a particular movement. Did it feel right, look right and sound right in comparison with what I had observed before? Only constant repetition and contact with the movement repertoire over time has helped me to shape my own performative ability of the genre. This ability is in a constant state of change as every new perception of the dance form adds yet another layer of understanding.

One final level of kinaesthetic transfer between performers and audience can also be found. When dancers and musicians, at concerts, dances, gatherings at home, wherever it may be, perform particularly well, their efforts are appreciated. This appreciation often takes the form of spontaneous applause in the middle of a dance or tune. The performer can feel the flow of energy transmitted from the clapping of hands (not only heard and seen). A couple of times, when I have solo danced at a square dance, and been given an encouraging applause by those watching, I certainly felt it inside me as encouragement but also as a surge of energy that made me relax deeper into the music and dance even better. It confirms at some level that what you are doing movement-wise is, at that particular moment, appropriate; the timing, lightness, neatness and movement combination have stood the test of local appreciation and have complied with their aesthetic preferences.

The Drive

As an example of how visual, aural and kinaesthetic senses work together, I shall use my own experience of learning motif Reel 1, or the "backstep." Note that motif Reel 1 also forms the predominant section of all hop-step variations (Reel 3), which may be the reason it is possibly the most common motif performed in reel time. The following understanding has never been explained to me in a class or in private. It is my own consolidated understanding of visual, aural and kinaesthetic transfer that has developed from watching Cape Breton dancers in action over the years.

In its simplest realization, backstep motif, Reel 1 (performed on the right foot), is a step with the left foot (count "one"), a shuffle with the heel and toe with the right foot (count "and two") and a hop on the left foot (count "and"). If performed mechanically, this movement would most likely be devoid of life. Using the three sensoria in combination, other levels of realization occur. To bring life or, perhaps better put, drive—to use the Cape Breton term—into the step(s), a number of matters have to be understood. How strong or light are the feet when striking the ground, for example? By hearing the step performed numerous times you get a sense of the "right touch" to the ground. The contact with the ground should be neither too strong nor too light, but as the heel is being used in the shuffle, that particular beat has a deeper, slightly heavier sound, as a rule. This adds nuance to the soundscape. Maybe the drive could also be equated to an energized form of "pulse," being that added element that vitalizes the proprioceptive understanding and execution of a particular movement.

In appendix 2, I give one example of a strathspey motif, sometimes known as "1, 2, 3, kick" or "shuffle-slide-step," where a series of tapsprings on alternate feet is followed by a brush kick. The individual movements need to be energized in a similar way to strathspey music as to that of a reel; as a dancer, you use the pulse to vitalize or realize the drive needed to bring life into your strathspey steps.

By observing the movements, you realize that few dancers use their ankles to any great extent to generate the shuffle; rather, their hips and knee joints flex and straighten the legs, while the foot is held almost parallel to the ground. Following observation, sensing what I do myself kinaesthetically confirms what body parts are active for these movements. Finally, visual observation can detect that different types of effort or energy are used for each element of the motif, particularly at the moment of the motif's transition into the next motif, or when it is repeated on the other foot.

It is here that an understanding of the movement's kinetic qualities of vitality comes into play (Sklar 2008). It took me a long time to internalize what I was doing in this motif. The movement actions I "felt" immediately, but I could not initially make them look the same as what I perceived the Cape Breton dancers to be doing. Nor did I feel completely relaxed or comfortable dancing the motif. I now analyze what I do, as exposure over time has enabled me to feel the step—to feel that my bodyweight is light enough to mirror what has been kinaesthetically and visually transferred to me. Likewise, I have learned to feel the tension and release in my hip and knee joints when performing a shuffle and listening to the sound as my heel and toe brush the ground to hear if it matches the soundscape memory in my head. From a visual point of view, this memory has to conform with my visual "gesturescape" memory as well—not lifting the foot too high off the ground, not pushing it too far out, and so on, thus also making the movement fit in with the rhythm and the music (aural and visual information combined). Finally, the concluding hop of the supporting foot of the motif, I now realize, is not a final movement element but a transition of energy, or effort, to the next movement element. By building up energy over the first three counts of the motif, the energy is released or, rather, transferred to the next movement during, and just after, the concluding hop. This, to me, is applying the kinetic vitality or energized pulse, or drive, to use the vernacular.

This energy transfer can be visually appreciated when watching a series of backsteps being performed, and with the hop not landing in place but a bit ahead so the transfer of energy to the other leg/foot appears as you spring onto the other foot "in place." This transferred energy can then be channelled to the subsequent movements, built up further again, thus creating a stream or pulse of energy right through the dance. This movement energy, combined with the drive in the Cape Breton–style music, is what energizes me when I dance. From a strictly personal perspective, this energy flow seems different when dancing to music played by musicians outside Cape Breton. It is not the same if an Irish or Scottish musician plays a reel, for example. Their renditions may be excellent, but the music style and pulse does not have the same connection with this style of dance as the Cape Breton music has. Simply put, it feels different and each rendition gives you a different type of energy flow. This exploration would be a matter for a follow-up study on energy transfer, pulse and rhythm, but here it will at least serve to illustrate how visual, aural and kinaesthetic movement transfer has informed my own dancing. I feel I have found the kinetic qualities of vitality, or drive, for this movement combination.

Chapter 7

Dancing the Music and "Musicking the Dance"

The Distinction Between a Dancer and a Performer

There is, according to Harvey Beaton, a vernacular distinction between people who are considered dancers and people who are considered performers. When Cape Bretoners use phrases such as "got the old style," "has a close-to-floor style" or "is a neat or tidy dancer" they often refer to people who are performing or sharing their steps. Harvey Beaton, for example, says that the number of motifs (steps) you have is relatively unimportant, compared to what you do with them: "One should not take the dancing too seriously"—the dancing is about developing a unique style and becoming comfortable with the steps one knows (H. Beaton 2005). Jenny Tingley (2007), who resides in Boularderie, says that to her, "dancing is your 'language,' your choices of combining 'steps,' [and] knowing how to use it. Subtle things can speak louder than big fancy steps."

Many dancers participate in public squares, but will only get up and dance solo in a private environment, such as a house party. Their repertoire of steps may vary but they are comfortable with their dancing and, as indicated above, it is not the number of steps that is important but the quality (timing and musicality) of the dancing. Rodney MacDonald speaks of his own relations, Donald Roddy MacDonald, Angus D. (Daniel) MacDonald, Harold MacDonald, Angus Donald MacDonald and others from the same area of Mabou Coal Mines/ Mabou Harbour, who are all good square dancers but will not dance solo in public. All are known locally for their good timing and rhythm (Anita MacDonald 2009).

Keeping the unique style of the individual in mind, Harvey Beaton continues to talk about the concept of "owning a step," a kind of hallmark motif for which certain dancers are known, or by which they are recognized (see also Foley 1988, 2012, 2013):

That [hallmark motif] occurs when you have practised a step so much that it becomes a part of your repertoire. It occurs when you no longer think about how the step goes, who taught it to you, or under what circumstances you learned it. After a while that step becomes yours so to speak. Again the number of steps a dancer has does not determine how good he or she is ... it is all to do with the execution of the steps, with the timing to the music, which is so important. The dancing has to look natural, not mechanical. (H. Beaton 2005).

Many dancers have steps that I understand are regarded as their characteristic or signature steps, including, for example, Willie Fraser, Rodney MacDonald, Mary Janet MacDonald and Harvey Beaton. As I have observed Cape Bretoners taking to the floor in both formal and informal contexts since 1992, I have come to understand that some individuals are appreciated for that very quality of sharing their love for dancing with all around them. To my mind, it is not about "showing off," but instead is about sharing their "take" on the dancing and, for some, reiterating to the community their ability to dance certain steps associated with them personally, or with their family. You recognize this as you see them frequently get up to do just that—share their dancing. Others you may see less often in public, or not at all, but you know from conversations that, outside the public spaces, they will get up and share their steps at a house party, for example, and that many in the community are well aware of their ability to dance solo. Regardless, their ability to dance can be spotted when they dance a square set, as often their dancing stands out as having an excellent quality about it. Then there are other individuals who will dance in public without necessarily having these hallmark qualities. This provides the observer with quite a mosaic and range in the dancing on display in Cape Breton. I do feel that having some insider knowledge enables you to see the often subtle differences between these individuals when dancing.

Routine or Improvised Dancing

Whether dancers improvise or dance a routine depends on context and personal preferences. Context is important. A dancer who is quite happy to dance "off the cuff" in the private setting of a house party may have a routine or at least an idea of what to share in a formal context, such as a concert setting. According to MacGillivray (1988), Aggie MacLennan would, for example, always improvise her dancing, letting the tune guide her with regard to what steps would follow. In contrast, Gussie MacLellan stated that he would improvise at parties but have a routine or idea in his head for a performance. Observing dancers performing over the years, I have noticed that indeed some seem to dance in routines. This is particularly common when siblings, such as the Warner Sisters or the Pellerins, who perform a predetermined routine, dance in synchronization. These two sibling pairs are indeed known and appreciated for their skill in performing synchronized routines. As individuals, Melody and Kelly (the Warner Sisters) and Bill and John (the Pellerins) will, however, dance differently.

Another observation I have made is of young dancers dancing a sequence of steps, and, when they come to the end of the sequence, they start again from the beginning and go on until they decide to stop. Other dancers mirror the music better and will be intuitively guided movement-wise by their musical insight. Still, dancers with a small repertoire of motifs may be appreciated for their ability to vary them to suit the music to perfection. In one respect, dancing a routine has always been part of the dance tradition, as the old set solo dances had set steps, even if the order in which they were danced could be altered. Irrespective of what type of routine is danced, it is timing and musicality that are always at the top of people's stylistic preferences. Following these favoured qualities comes the performer and where he or she fits into the local community fabric. These are the paramount factors determining the level of local and individual appreciation.

Gendered Steps?

Through my research I have not encountered any movement that is exclusively used by one gender only. All movements and steps are equally used, something Frank Rhodes (1985) also noted in 1957, when he stated that the steps in Reels were the same for men and women. What is more apparent is that particular movements are favoured by certain age groups due to their level of difficulty or the ability of the individual dancer to perform them. It is also conceivable that the movements popular at the time of learning play a role.

Most important, however, are overall personal preferences guiding what aspects of the movement repertoire to express and how these are combined. Mary Janet MacDonald (2010) gives her personal opinion on gender:

> To me—there are definitely steps that are more male based—like the "train step" (heel, heel, toe, toe, and then creeping forward to a 6 count)—that step is better done by a man; also some of the steps that Willie Fraser does—I think of how he begins his strathspey sometime—heels together and toes together going around in a circle—much more male dominated.

However, women frequently dance both of these steps. The issue here is probably related to the idea of the "power" men can put into their steps, but that calls for a separate study.

What is clear is that there are currently more women dancing than men. Good male step dancers are becoming a rarity as few young males step dance, while many excellent young girls are coming forth. This is probably part of the general Western trend of dancing not being "cool," and also that dance teaching is less commonly done naturally in the home and at unofficial classes but conducted in public classes, where women teachers predominate.

When it comes to role models for step dancers, the male dancers seem to dominate. Jackie Dunn-MacIsaac (2010b) says:

> When I think about my favourite step dancers of my peers, my top choices *are* male, I love many female dancers but there is something so captivating and so much drive in an excellent male step dancer. [...] I don't think it means on the whole the male dancers are better than female, there is a difference in the "attack" of the males' style which makes it flashier in a sense. My mom [Margaret Dunn] always said that when she was a little girl that it was OK for girls to step dance so they couldn't have been stopped from dancing. Girls were also encouraged to play piano (accompany) but girls were not encouraged to play the fiddle.

In past generations in Cape Breton, girls were encouraged to play the piano (taking the back seat of accompaniment) while men took the lead on the fiddle. Today we see almost a reversal, with many male pianists at the fore and up-and-coming fiddlers being predominantly female.

Returning to the discussion on role models, Mary Janet MacDonald (2010) adds:

> I would definitely agree that the men had the upper hand years ago and were held in very high regard. In my own personal opinion—I have rarely, if ever, admired female dancers—other than to comment on how lovely they were to dance—but all of my own personal idols were men (Willie Fraser, Thomas MacDonnell, Fr. Angus Alex MacDonnell—plus today—Rodney MacDonald; Harvey Beaton; Gerard Beaton). Having said that, I would also say that today—two of my favourite dancers are Melody Cameron and Dawn MacDonald—leaning more to Dawn's style and footwork as closer to what I like myself—and yet respecting Melody for her lightness, deliverance, yet amazed at how her steps which might not finish with the phrase—end up working—just lovely.

It should nonetheless be remembered, as piper John MacLean (2010) points out, that women in Gaelic society were equal in passing on the oral traditions. Even though written sources list more men as dance teachers, for example, it is commonly known within Cape Breton Gaelic culture that women at home passed on dances and other traditions before the 1960s and 1970s, when it became more common for women to teach and perform in public. This is partially substantiated in MacDougall's (1922) *History of Inverness County* and in Rhodes's 1957 observations (1985, 1996), which mention, among the many men, some women as dancers and teachers. For example, Mary MacIsaac MacIntyre (Nighean Illeasbuig Oig, daughter of young Archibald MacIsaac) lived in Broad Cove Banks and taught step dancing in the late 1800s. Mary "Tulloch" MacDonald Beaton (Mairi Aonghuis Thullaich, 1795-1880) had been a distinguished dancer in Lochaber, Scotland, and, after immigrating to Cape Breton, set up a school near MacKinnon's Brook for the purpose of teaching that skill (MacGillivray 1988: 24; Gibson 1992: 9).

Regarding women fiddlers and dancers, John MacLean (2010) further says that they may have been less common owing to the structure of the society before the 1970s.

> Women were less mobile and independent—less likely to drive cars or travel alone for example. As in all of Western society, women were the keepers of the household. When my father died,

a part of my mother's identity died too. Although, as a couple my parents shared the same friends and acquaintances, my mother was more likely to be known as "Johnny's wife" as opposed to Sarah Jean MacLean, a good dancer and tradition bearer in her own right. [...] I grew up immersed in the community of fiddlers and dancers like Winston Fitzgerald, Bill Lamey, Margaret, and Maybelle Chisholm, etc.—and I never once heard any sort of sexist comment. In fact, my father always praised Margaret Chisholm as the most wonderful musician of that legendary family. Consider names like Tina Campbell, The MacDonald Sisters, Theresa and Marie MacLellan, etc. ... in terms of cultural outlook, there is a great recognition among all of the tradition bearers about the importance of their mothers in passing on songs and tunes.

MacLean himself learned many pipe tunes from his mother singing in Gaelic or jigging tunes while doing her work in the kitchen. More specifically, MacLean feels there was never any devaluation of female dancers. All MacLean ever heard was praise for neat and tidy dancers—"close to the floor" or "from the ankles down"—male or female. On the contrary, he would hear criticism of "rough" dancers, of both genders, who were heavy on their feet. Praise for women like Aggie Red Rory MacLennan, Margaret MacPhee and Maryann (Currie) Gouthro was common (MacLean 2010).[1]

The Changes in Gender Roles in Social Dancing

I have described how step dancing featured in the Scotch Four of the past, which was the favoured dance until square dances (quadrilles) became popular. John MacLean earlier shared the insight that his grandparents' generation preferred the Scotch Four above all else and they observed strict decorum—even at home (chapter 2). By the 1930s and 1940s, square dances had taken over as the social dance of choice. In the 1960s and 1970s, the strict four-couples-to-a-set and the prompting of figures began to disappear, and each community started to favour a single 3-4 figure dance, which is repeated several times throughout an evening's dancing in a local hall (chapter 5). In this later era of square dancing, many of the older generation would sit down if extra couples attempted to join a set. They would be quite mortified to see the rough-and-tumble dancing that goes on now—which includes women dancing together. MacLean says that step dancing through the set, except in the Scotch Four, was unknown until the 1970s. "My parents' generation did not really agree with it." He continues:

> Where there was dancing, it was a social occasion for the sexes to mingle and the decorum was quite formal—including the notion of getting cleaned up and wearing good clothes. In fact, my father often spoke of carrying his shoes over his shoulder and walking to a dance in bare feet so his shoes [wouldn't] get dusty on the dirt roads on the way to the dance. Of course, dances were an important part of the courting rituals for these people. (MacLean 2010)

The Cape Breton music and dance community could be said to form a constructed "communitas," to use Turner's 1974 definition, referring to the sense of togetherness that is created through ritual behaviour and in which the hierarchical structures that form part of everyday life, differences and distances are abolished within the larger Cape Breton community. It is no longer just the immediate local or parish community that will attend locally organized music and dance events, but participants and audiences, in the case of festivals and concerts, come from all over Cape Breton and Nova Scotia and further afield. In our postmodern times we see the decline of "traditional" communities deeply rooted in the interconnection of people living within locally understood boundaries. In my research, many lament this loss. With once-strong parish and village communities in decline, our sense of time and space has been altered by ongoing capitalist and technological developments (Giddens 2004; Urry 1995).

Dawn Beaton (2010b) points out in correspondence that the strict decorum and certain local men—e.g., the golden boys, Second World War veterans who once were the dominant figures on the floor and kept things going—are long a thing of the past. With fewer boys participating, young and teenage girls are often seen dancing together, and some women are occasionally seen to ask men to dance, something which was once greatly frowned upon.

> There may be several reasons why women now dance together. It may be an age thing and small children are often more comfortable dancing with their sister or their friend, who they have attended the dance with. Teenagers can be hard to come by at

a dance—social awkwardness and a lack of boys and shyness of those boys in attendance to ask a girl usually mean two girls dance in a set. Finally we have visitors … having not been brought up in this community, don't feel any social stigma of dancing girl to girl and may choose to dance with their travel companion rather than seek out a local in the situation where a local doesn't first ask them to dance. (Dawn Beaton 2010b)

That said, local men are still on the whole the ones who take the lead in the sets; they are the first on the floor, having asked women to dance.

Dancing the Music and "Musicking the Dance"

Of the many qualities regarded as paramount in the Cape Breton step-dance genre, a dancer's good timing and musicality are perhaps the most important. "Timing is number one. You have to be right on with the music. The dancer must be one with the music," Fr. Eugene Morris told me as we were watching the dancers at the Chestico Annual Dance Festival, in Port Hood, in July 2007. Fr. Eugene's words are only meaningful if they are taken in connection with the stylistic and aesthetic preferences of the dance genre. Indeed, Hungarian ethnochoreologist László Felföldi (2001: 160) points to these overarching connections between dance and dance music:

> In order to uncover dance and music connections, we must pay attention to all the factors serving music and dance expression and how these factors participate in their connections. We must take into consideration that dance and music are

Figure 7.1 – Mac Morin with fiddle during Celtic Colours (2014) at Strathspey Place, Mabou, NS. Photo by Mats Melin.

special phenomena that take place in time and space, thereby creating communication between the dancer and the musician and between the performers and the audience, while operating within a socio-cultural context, using kinetic, visual, acoustic and proxemic channels. [...] In research on dance and music connections we must determine different levels of methods and analysis. The analysis of dancing and playing music as a process needs different viewpoints than the analysis of dance and music as the products of this process.

The role of the musician in the context of Cape Breton square dancing is highly important and not extractable from the dance. As stated earlier, most of these musicians are also step dancers—the two cultural expressions embodied in the same person. The musicians have intimate knowledge of what must be played. They know the ideal speed, timing and choice of tunes for step dancing. It is often the case that musicians know what particular tunes, style of tunes and what speed is preferred by particular dancers, and will often include those dancers' favourite tunes. If the fiddlers do not know, they will ask the dancer what they prefer to enable them to provide the best music for the dancer. The relationship between individual musicians—fiddlers in particular—their individual styles of playing, their family affinity and their status within the community plays a significant part in their relationship with the dance.

While some musicians on the island are regarded as players that you mainly listen to, others are known as particularly good players for dancing. Some players, of course, fit both categories. The musicians' ability to provide "drive" or lift in the music and their ability to get the tempo right for individual dancers is essential. As fiddler Mike Hall (2009) said in conversation, "know the dancer [and] you know the speed to play." Certain fiddle techniques, such as cuts and upstrokes or up-driven bows, are employed to create this trademark drive in the music. Fiddler Glenn Graham (2006: 126) further writes that

> to complement dancing, bowing is very rhythmic, often one bow stroke being applied in one direction for one note. Upstrokes are often as powerful as down strokes with a variety of pressures being exerted on the bow for dynamics and accents. A type of reel called the strathspey features a characteristic stuttering rhythm

called the Scotch snap ... [which] provides an accent similar to that found in Gaelic song and pipe music.

The Cape Breton music repertoire is predominantly geared toward dancing, and the symbiotic nature of the music and dance has developed together over time. For instance, if the speed of the music is not right, then the dancer struggles to dance well. When he dances well, then the fiddler is producing the right "drive" or energy and thus the dancer provides energy through his performance back to the fiddler in turn. Sheldon MacInnes expressed his view in 1986 in an interview with Alastair MacGillivray (1988: 97-98):

> If the dancers are in tune with the Fiddler, then they engage in some kind of non-verbal communication with him. That mutual support, going two ways, he's always there whether you are looking at the solo step dancer, or you are looking at the dancer in the square set.... That rapport is a give and take all evening. Buddy [MacMaster] cannot get away with playing a new tune without a good sector of the dance floor picking that up and in some way letting him know, "hey, I like that!" It might be just a smile, it might be just a little twitch of the head, but Buddy gets that message—and I am sure that Donald Angus Beaton in his day and Kinnon Beaton today have sensed that same thing. That folk

Figure 7.2 – Mary Elizabeth MacInnes and Joey Beaton, Celtic Colours (2014) at Judique Community Hall. Photo by Mats Melin.

exchange as we know it here in Cape Breton is *very* important—a mutual recognition between the dancer and the fiddler. I can't emphasize enough how important that is and how *that*, to a large degree, is going to determine the quality of music and the quality of dance! Without the mutual recognition, something great would be lost.

Fr. Angus Morris simply describes this relationship in an interview thus: "a good fiddler brings out the best in a step dancer and a good step dancer will bring out the best of the fiddler" (Morris 2007).

Almost all those who step dance solo either play music (fiddle, piano, etc.) or sing. I have come across very few who do not. A majority of these individuals thus embody the roles of musician and dancer in one. There is a certain crossover point of individuals who are experts at both, while others prefer to do one or the other, even if they have the ability to do both. This gives them a particularly deep knowledge of both music and dance structure and tune repertoire, and it strengthens the connection between these individuals when they perform.

Dancer and pianist Harvey Beaton comments on the importance of this teamwork between dancer and the fiddler: "I always say that the dancing is only as good as the music because the music determines how well you dance" (MacGillivray 1988: 33). He also points out that you have to listen to the music all the time, "you have to be really familiar with the music before you can do the dancing well because the timing is crucial" (34).

This teamwork happens not only between dancers and tune players but also between dancers and accompanists. A piano player (who is also a dancer) once said that dance rhythms influence her playing and that she is often inspired by the rhythmical sequences and sound produced by a performing dancer (Melin 2006). Dancer and pianist Joël Chiasson (2009) said that when he plays he does not think about what he is doing; he is just responding to the music. However, when he listens to recordings of himself, he feels he is mimicking step-dance rhythms naturally in his accompaniment style. "That sounds like that step," he says—it is like the dancer in him comes out subconsciously. "[It is] not a conscious action; it just comes out."

I would argue that the musicians in Cape Breton in one sense subconsciously dance with their bodies while playing. Just as *binou* (folk oboe) players for traditional dance in Brittany, France, move their bodies vigorously and often mimic dance steps while seated and play-ing, to a certain degree so do musicians in Cape Breton. Some dance fiddlers move their bodies quite a lot when playing, I have observed. While sitting down, most of them beat their foot or feet in time with the music. Of course many musicians from various music traditions indicate rhythm with the feet, so there is nothing unusual about this per se, but those playing for Canadian forms of percussive dance (Québécois, Ottawa Valley and so forth) do so in a vigorous way, en-hancing the dance rhythms (Melin 2013b). As this is such an integral part of the music soundscape, the tapping of the fiddlers' feet can be heard on most live and many studio recordings of Cape Breton fiddle music rather than being edited out. In addition, most fiddlers can be observed swaying gently forward and back as they play; a few can be seen on occasion leaning forward so as to come closer to the dancers. There is movement communication constantly at play here among all the actors in this context. With such a deep embodied knowledge, this community could be said to "dance the music" and "music the dance," which are both related to the central notion in Christopher Small's (1998) term "musicking," regarding the action or culture of making music. Musicking, according to Small, is to always see music as an activity rather than a thing, where its function provides insights into relationships: between and among notes, rhythms and metres, to mention some aspects, but also between musicians, listeners, dancers and dancing. Musicking is about embodying relatedness, which is an essence of social and perhaps also of human life (1998: 9). I find New Waterford–based Anna MacEachern Grechuk's description of some of these active embodied relationships quite good:

> I just get up and dance; the more the music comes, the more I drive 'er. The tune brings you on. You dance with the tune, and you have to have the feeling; the steps look like nothing with no feeling for the tune! And when I dance and feel it, then the audience feels it too. Also, I feel that your steps have to fit with the turns of the tune. Sometimes I have a step in mind but it just won't fit the tune. And, if you don't know the piece of music, I do not get as many steps out. (MacGillivray 1988: 76)

Here the music (tune) knowledge is put into practice as an ex-pression of movement that has feeling and meaning, and hints at the intangible relationship among dancer, musician and audience, and between movement and rhythm.

The relationship between the Cape Breton musician and dancer in performance is not unique, but the intensity is. I have observed, for instance, a Norwegian halling dancer and fiddler perform together with a great understanding and respect of each other's need in a similar, yet different fashion to that occurring in Cape Breton.[2] It comes down to the embodied knowledge of tempo, suitable tunes, bowing and fingering that, when applied, will provide the best conditions for a dancer to thrive and to perform. It is a symbiotic relationship that allows dancer and musician to feed off each other's energy in the performance. This is reflected in the terms "lift" and "drive" in reference to playing music. Both terms are meaningful, but very difficult to conceptualize. In short, when applied to the music they are said to inject a surge of energy toward movement in general and dancing in particular. A fiddler applying lift and drive to the music makes you tap your feet as a listener, or makes you dance lighter and with increased energy. These two terms are part of the core components that bind the music relationship to the dance in what is often referred to as "old style" sound. Doherty (1996), Graham (2006) and Herdman (2008) analyze the relationship between the music and the dance in Cape Breton fiddling. Herdman (2008: 93) looks at the notion of the old-style sound and its link to the dance and the fiddle techniques employed to provide the "correct" music stylistically and rhythmically for the step dancer.

> Playing for dancing requires particular techniques that become concretized as stylistic attributes. While some of these features may have a rootedness elsewhere—in imitation of bagpipes, or from the nature of the Gaelic flavor—their perpetuation has been demanded by the practical needs of dancing. Some of the techniques that are associated with the "old style" are almost exclusively employed in dance tunes. For example, the "up-driven" bow, "high bass" tuning, "cuts," and "cutting." In particular some of these techniques—"up-driven" bows and "cuttings"—are generally only used in the performance of strathspeys. Thus, this "old style"-dancing relationship seems particularly close with solo step-dancing, which necessitates the use of strathspeys.

As the scholars mentioned above point out, the term "old style" is often equated with Inverness County and with Mabou Coal Mines style in particular, both linked to the music-dance connection. The reason for this, according to Herdmanm (2008: 94) again, is that Inverness County (Mabou Coal Mines area included) is linked to the "dominance of the Scottish diasporic communities" and "may be rooted in an integrity of dance within these community practices." As Addison (2001: 24) stated, in the late 1990s and early 2000s were at that point "the highest concentration of music and dance culture is in central Inverness County." These observations about this deeply intertwined relationship would no doubt sound redundant to most Cape Bretoners, for whom the intricate relationship between music and dance goes without saying. To conclude this section on the music-dance connection, I will leave you with something Glenn Graham told me during a conversation at the Gaelic College (now Colaisde na Gàidhlig) at St. Ann's in 2007: "it [the music and the dance] is an expression for people, who you are and where you come from. It just comes out at these occasions.... There is a strong connection between musician and dancer ... [they] feed off each other" (Graham 2007).

Religion and its Relationship to Dancing

In close-knit communities such as those of rural Cape Breton, the influence of the church and religious beliefs on all aspects of life is strong. In Cape Breton, the number of local priests that excel in music and step dance is a prominent feature in the local context. Fr. Eugene performs, promotes and taught step dancing. His brother, Fr. Angus, is a prominent local fiddler, and it is maybe fitting that I conclude this chapter with a few observations on the influence of the church on the Cape Breton dance tradition, considering that it was Fr. Angus whom I initially met during the first day of my first visit to Cape Breton in 1995, and who advised my wife and I where to seek out the real music and dancing in the Cape Breton community.

In MacGillivray's *Cape Breton Ceilidh*, a number of priests are mentioned as examples of good dancers, including Fr. Donald Michael Rankin and the late Reverend Angus MacDonnell, who was a highly acclaimed step dancer whose flowing steps sometimes got him referred to as a "showstopper" (1988: 93). As the noted Cape Breton folksinger John Allan Cameron once said, "when I was growing up, the most important people in the community were the fiddler and the priest" (Thompson 2003: 23).

As educated men, the local priests are seen most commonly in a positive light in both local lore and written records. However, in local lore there is also an aspect of negativity directed towards priests who did not conform to community expectations. In the essay "The Fiddle Burning Priest of Mabou," Jodi McDavid (2008) analyzes the local legend that claims that Fr. Kenneth MacDonald, first pastor at Mabou, Cape Breton, from 1865 to 1894, collected and burned fiddles. The common strands to the story are that the pastor collected or confiscated fiddles, later to destroy or burn them. He was against the drinking associated with events where music and dance were featured.[3] Whether he actually burned fiddles or just confiscated them remains unclear. The moral of the story is that no matter who abuses their authority, in this case a priest, the music tradition and fiddle tradition survive against all odds.

The fiddle is today iconographic in Cape Breton. It is very much the symbol of the local culture,[4] appearing on signs, as sculpture, on book and CD covers, and so on, and McDavid suggests that the story represents a deeper level of meaning than the surface would suggest, illustrating the challenges, perseverance and belief in the local musical tradition (and, by extension, the dance tradition). Memories of general suppression may be an aspect of this iconography—and thus the legend an "expression of tension not only between clergy and parishioners—but between official and vernacular culture" (2008: 133).

The legend of the fiddle-burning priest does feature in the literature with regard to dancing, as music and dance occur at the same time. Frank Rhodes most certainly heard the story and added that a Cape Breton bishop at the time put a temporary ban on dancing, which led to the discontinuation of the dancing of the Wild Eight (1985: 271). What Rhodes is referring to is likely the only official statement against dancing featured in a letter to Inverness County parishes (Acadian, Irish and Scottish parishioners all included) in the diocese, sent by Bishop John Cameron on February 27, 1894. The letter negatively concerned the occurrence of "round dances," but does not mention the dancing of Reels, Quadrilles or step dancing.[5] Even if this letter did have a negative effect on the dancing of certain dances, as Rhodes claims, it did not stop people from dancing. Indeed today, as mentioned earlier, the Roman Catholic Church is one of the main promoters of music and dance in Cape Breton, with square dances and other events such as concerts and festivals organized in parish halls and on parish grounds.

Chapter 8

The Importance of Transmission and Observed Changes to the Tradition

This book's contribution to dance research has so far concentrated on various modes of movement and musical knowledge, transmitted via aural, visual and kinaesthetic processes, and on some aspects of practices being transmitted in the Cape Breton community. The emerging picture is one of a holistic transmission environment, where the processes of sights, sounds and movement come together harmoniously, subconsciously, to inform each actor in this cultural context. These transmission processes take place over an extended period, and in one sense they never stop; they develop into an ongoing process that forms an integral part of daily life. The transmission of movement and awareness of rhythm and pulse (in the local music tradition) from a parent or family member, most commonly the mother, becomes or more likely initiates a natural part of this process. Learning at home is further reinforced by social dancing and performance in the community as a whole. Initially, Scotch Fours (or Reels) would mainly have been danced at home, but when square dances became more popular, dancing in local schoolhouses, and later in halls, became the more prominent gathering contexts. Solo dance performances at both social dance events and community concerts added further to the opportunities of knowledge transmission. This study also shows that the Cape Breton dance (and music) traditions keeps evolving and that new ways of its rendering emerge and are slowly incorporated, which keeps the tradition alive and invigorated.

Even though there is plenty of evidence of the cultural importance of the house ceilidh in Gaelic society as a learning environment, as discussed in chapter 2, dance is seldom, if ever, recorded in detail by scholars and is generally mentioned only in passing. One can, however, assume it to be present, as those discussing music and song-making in the house ceilidh context in articles and books imply that they think of music and dance as one entity (Dickson 2006; Graham

2006; Kennedy 2002; Shaw 1992-1993). According to my sources' accounts, the informal nature of transmission in the home, at ceilidhs and in other community contexts continued even after formal classes became prevalent from the 1970s onward. Dance classes are nothing new to Cape Breton, as chapter 3 on the classroom contexts outlines. We have a record, through Rhodes's 1957 two-week research visit, of what dances were taught in some of these early classes. Rhodes (1985, 1996) outlines both the use of named solo dances and improvised step dancing. He also gives accounts of various Reels in use, as well as some Gaelic dance games, as he was searching for parallels to his findings in the West Highlands and Island of Scotland, where most of his Cape Breton subjects' ancestors had come from. So, we get an idea of what dances were in use, but little detailed knowledge of what transmission processes were at work in passing them on. We can only speculate that the ways of transmitting movement in dance classes prior to the 1970s shared similarities with those described by the sources for this study. A clue about the continuity of dancing style is provided in some of the recollections noted in my research (2013b), which mentions members of the older generation having attended dance classes in the late 1800s and early 1900s, all of whom displayed clearly recognizable stylistic features in their dancing. This supports the idea that the way dance has been transmitted since the 1970s, in both home and class environments, carries on essential elements of previous generations.

The first generation of new dance teachers of the 1970s brought the subconscious transmission processes of the home into the formal class environment. They found individual ways of passing on movement repertoire to large groups of people, often of different ages. The individual naming of steps became a necessary tool in assisting efficient teaching and in providing a focus toward learning movement sequences. For many, dancing became a classroom-based learning experience, enhanced by square dances and concerts, both as observers and as active dancers. The transmission processes of the Cape Breton dance style thus shifted from predominantly home contexts to predominantly public-space contexts. Of course, for some families, learning in the home continued but, from a general standpoint, a change of the primary transmission environment took place. The home became, for many, a place of first learning and of reinforcement of what had been taught (by other community members) in class. Note that the common denominator for almost all of the primary sources of this investigation (except for two) is that they learned their initial dancing skills in the home environment, which would have had a significant impact on how and what these individuals were teaching in their classes during the 1970s and 1980s.

Another related factor in the processes is the full integration of musical knowledge, from an often full and general awareness of the local tune repertoire down to Gaelic song pulses (*puirt-a-beul* in particular), which reinforce understanding of dance rhythms in the music, to the knowledge of an individual player's particular take on, or style of, rendering those melodies. All the sources in this study are dancers and accomplished musicians or singers. Each one of them embodies both movement and music (song) knowledge, which fully informs their own internal beings of the relationship between these particular proficiencies. Their own individual understandings of these relationships also informs, through their performances of both dance and music, those around them through the same transmission process, as outlined above. The different proficiencies, picked up by different senses, migrate within these individuals' own bodies, and from body to body, as described by, for example, Sklar (2008) and Hahn (2007), and develop into a shared experience both close to and away from each other.

My study provided snapshots of different transmission processes at work, asking questions about their particular function. From a general point of view, the interaction of the senses among eye, ear, and "knowing with one's body" is illustrated. On an individual level, however, we find that we occasionally emphasize one of our senses as more prominent in the transmission experience. This is natural as different situations will call on different sensoria, but also as different cultures prioritize different sensoria, according to Hahn, in how we learn to know with our bodies. Even though Hahn looked specifically at how movement is transmitted in Japanese dance culture, many of the manners she describes I found also applicable to dance transmission in Cape Breton—such as picking up on sounds around us (soundscape) and movement knowledge passed from one body to another, by holding hands, for example. Most of my sources seem to indicate that all the senses contribute to their ability to perform the movements of the local style in an aesthetically correct way, as deemed by the community. Few of them indicated that they were aware of one sense being more prominent when learning, but their stories indicated what information each sense prioritized when recalled.

The importance of well-placed verbal comments (or keywords) that seem to suffice to keep each individual on track and within the boundaries of the style aesthetic, as set by the collective appreciation of the community, was another topic outlined in some detail. Keywords keep the general aesthetic framework clear in the local mindscape. As Sklar (2008), Hahn (2007) and Bull (1997), for example, all argue, there is an ongoing refinement process of the senses (visual, oral/aural and tactile) as vehicles of transmission. Learning to "know with your body" over long periods and complete immersion in the embodiment of the cultural expression are some of the key concepts expressed through this study's source accounts.

Examining all the information gathered from a broad perspective, I see a presence of *shared commonalities* in the various aspects of transmission processes and key components of what is transmitted. In the featured cases of this study, these shared commonalities are present whether transmitted predominantly through a primary source, such as a teacher, or by a dancer's general impressions of many individual dancers in the community. The most common scenario is a combination of particular transmission sources, and general impressions of the dance community's actions as a whole. My experience of asking Cape Bretoners to name some good local dance exponents yielded numerous names, rather than one or two, which helps to illustrate this.

One then sees that what is being shared among this group of people evolves and changes over time, but certain aspects remain recognizable as core elements. These may be certain visual patterns, movement combinations, interaction between people and so forth, all with an individual interpretation, which over time may evolve but remain recognizable by what I would call a common sameness. The sameness applies to the aural and kinaesthetic aspects of the movement combinations: rhythm patterns of the feet either on their own or in relation to music and song, for example. As active participant, observer, or both, embodied knowledge is passed from person to person and strengthened within one's own body during each moment of realization. The movement building blocks of common motifs, with their accompanying keywords or phrases and with individual takes on their realization, provide shared commonalities in this community.

I believe it is the great volume of shared common values and expression of movement and sound that allows individuals to improvise their realization of the dance and music style around a strong body of core dance-rhythm understanding, suitable tempos and melodies. By "volume" in dance, I do not mean the number but the frequency of, for example, the step-shuffle used in a reel motif that one sees (and hears and feels), or the frequency of the few keys being repeated. The transmitted core movements and aesthetic keywords keep the general realization of the dance style coherent for the community, and at the same time this general realization allows, at an individual level, for personal interpretations within the defined verbal and non-verbal boundaries. The boundaries of the style are thus continually made clear and are even further reinforced through each realization of the dance. The silent transmission processes work hand-in-hand with the few choice keywords that emphasize the essence of the dance style. To me, the ability to improvise around these core movements and aesthetic values brings life and meaning to both the dance and the music. As Melody Cameron (2007) aptly puts it, "the music and dance nourishes us." The processes described above keep the dance style not only alive, but also recognizably distinct.

Another strand of the discussion in this book includes arguments for and against the relevance of the rhythm of Gaelic language and song to the local musical style. With the Gaelic language having declined in favour of English in Cape Breton, the question was posed whether the music itself has absorbed elements of the Gaelic-language rhythm, thus keeping alive some of the core rhythms that distinguish the local music and dance style. I would like to pose a new approach to this topic: rather than singling out language, might it not be more relevant to look at the many aspects of commonalities (which would include language as a primary element) as a key to the realization of the music, song and step dance in Cape Breton? According to the Nova Scotia Gaelic-language teacher Joe Murphy, the "idea of shared commonality among the people is a very important aspect of the whole psyche of the Gaelic people" (CBC News, January 31, 2012). My observations suggest that these common notions of rhythm and pulse (in language, song and music), and the timing of dance movements in relation to these, lie at the heart of meaning-making in the local dance community.

To summarize, I see the following aspects as defining Cape Breton step dancing as a style at present, which are essential to enabling particular transmission processes, as outlined:

Settlement patterns—the current communities in Cape Breton are largely based on the early settlement pattern of the 19th-century immigrants. Often, the strong community bond that existed in their home country continued in Cape Breton. Even though outmigration to other parts of Canada and the United States, as well as resettlement within Cape Breton to the urban and industrial areas around Sydney, has affected the coherence of the early community settlements, the pull of home brings people back to visit as often as they can. This pattern of summertime visiting and the clear idea among "displaced" Cape Bretoners of where "home" is helps to strengthen the community traditions. It is also significant that in many areas, geographical references, such as responses to requests for directions, often relate to dance contexts such as the whereabouts of dance halls (see Addison 2001).

Contexts—the main contexts or locales where transmission of the style occurs: primarily the home, though since the 1970s increasingly in the formal class situation. Both of these contexts are reinforced in so-called third places, such as square dances and community concerts.

Time—long-term and frequent exposure to the style and related cultural aspects in evolving community-defined contexts.

Transmission processes—the particular ways, outlined in this study, in which transmission occurs through one's senses by visual, aural and kinaesthetic means. Where context, time factors and often close proximity between those performing the style play a role in what and how movement schema migrate from body to body and develop within bodies.

Music and song knowledge—the close relationship between movement and the local expression of music and song, often embodied within the same person, as the dancer tends also to be a musician, singer or both. This is deeply tied with the Cape Breton understanding of rhythm and pulse.

Motifs/steps—the movement repertoire. Certain core movement combinations amalgamated according to the community's aesthetic preferences, establishing the form of the style.

Lack of quantity of mnemonic keywords—only a few keywords or phrases convey a deep non-verbal understanding of what the preferred aesthetic style criteria are.

Flexible boundaries—the combination of core motifs and aesthetic preferences creates a framework that the individual dancer can improvise around and within what are, to a certain extent, flexible boundaries as understood by the community. These flexible boundaries carry meaning as to what the style is and what it is not. They have a degree of fluidity as the dance style slowly evolves.

The transmission processes at work, as outlined above, are essential for how both the aesthetics and the structural elements of the dance style have been and are maintained. Not only is a deep embodiment of movement and musical rhythm enabled, but the community consensus of the style boundaries is maintained. Recall how, in chapter 2, I illustrated that Cape Breton communities continually view many good dancers who provide fluid and continually refreshed guidelines for the "best practice" as conforming to the unspoken boundaries through their individual performances over time. At the same time, this view allows for personal interpretation of common motifs and, by extension, for gradual innovation and gradual change. Still, despite changes, certain constant identifiers, which define both the aesthetic and structural (form) parts of the dance style, are maintained.

Whether and how these given criteria will change when transmission processes change—whether the number of core motifs might expand or the aesthetic criteria might alter—is for further studies to determine in detail. This study is only a snapshot of a certain group of people identified by their community as good representatives of the Cape Breton step-dance style, within a particular timeframe, and of how they experience transmission processes, perform the motif repertoire and uphold a certain set of aesthetic preferences.

It should be noted that the dancers featured as primary sources in this exploration, with few exceptions, should be seen as representations of particular transmission processes at work, and these sources' frequent interaction with certain contexts (particularly the home context) is not necessarily the norm any longer. Many of the sources have expressed concern that the level of understanding of fundamental values of the music and dance tradition by young musicians and dancers in Cape Breton is no longer as grounded (or interconnected) as it once was. Maybe the snapshots in this exploration will serve as a reminder of a certain level of natural harmony in transmission processes and shared commonalities at work in the Cape Breton music and dance community. This study should be regarded as an overview of a period of transition into another phase of the development of these local traditions. It is often said locally that the ability to play music or dance "is in the blood." This phrase, in my opinion, refers to the non-verbal understanding of shared commonalities through dance (movement) and music.

In my personal journey of discovery as an outsider to the tradition, I moved away from simply learning and recording different motifs, and how they are combined into a meaningful flow in relation to the music or Gaelic songs, to a better understanding of the nuances positioned around the actual rendition of the physical movement. For me, the realization that family, community and the contexts that movement processes are transmitted in, are equally important. Getting the movement right is only one aspect—almost a product. The processes involved in feeling, seeing and hearing how movement fit in with the music, the songs, family and community life added to my own ability to realize the dance style when performing. I am no longer simply dancing a set of movements as learned in class; I am dancing memories, I am dancing movements from specific people, I am responding to certain tunes in a particular way because someone told me to listen in a specific way. I am dancing, not only for my own pleasure, but for everybody around me to share my experience, while always keeping in mind some of the aesthetic keywords I have been told many times—"dance close to the floor," "dance lightly," "make the dance my own," "keep time with the music" and keep those core movements "right in there."

My own understanding of Cape Breton step dancing today is fundamentally different to what I experienced in 1992 in Scotland, when I first encountered the style. Today I see it differently: I look for nuances in the footwork or maybe how a dancer carries himself or herself to produce a great performance. Presently, I frequently hear a step rhythm before I see what the feet are doing, while in 1992 it was the other way around. Now I listen to the strength and lightness of a dancer's feet touching the floor; I listen to the sound of the feet in relation to the music. Foremost, I have learned to feel the dance in the core of my body, in my heart. I have felt steps transmitted to me by holding a fellow dancer's or mentor's hands while dancing and have learned to allow my body to feel and interpret that movement so I can produce my own take on it, for example. This is what Cape Breton dance is to me now, to spend time in that place, travel around the island, socialize, have discussions, go to the square dances, laugh, enjoy the summertime concerts, dance at house parties and be allowed to share the dancing memories of friends and the dancing community.

Cape Breton step dancing keeps evolving and changing. It is not static, it is a healthy, living tradition. One should compare the changes in the dance tradition to the changes in the fiddle and piano music as described in Doherty (1996) and Graham (2006), to name only two sources. If the music and dance are so closely related, as is indicated in this research, then the dance tradition has changed considerably over the years, alongside the changes in the music. Having said that, Cape Bretoners are no different than any other group of people; they are often hesitant to embrace change, especially if it is perceived as happening too quickly, or if they feel concerned that something about their cherished tradition will be lost if change occurs. To my way of thinking, these are very natural responses to change of any kind. Even though observing change was not the main topic of this study, inevitably the notion of change was discussed in conversations and interviews. I observed it occurring over time through my own experience and by watching video clips, and by looking historically at the information available to us about patterns of change that have emerged in characteristics of the step-dance tradition.

Some Changes of Characteristics in Cape Breton Step Dancing from the 1970s to the Present

Although this investigation was not primarily concerned with observing change in the tradition, I inevitably noticed it in the process of doing research. Change is inevitable in a living tradition, as Andrea Beaton (2010) told me:

> I believe that the dance scene is changing, as is every aspect of the tradition. But I am now convinced that is what a living tradition does.... It's how it can continue to be a living tradition. I believe there are a lot of aspects that have changed through the years.

Observers of change in traditional ways and practices often lament it, especially if the changes are seen as not occurring slowly and naturally within that tradition (see, in particular, Gibson 1998, 2005, 2008; Shaw 1992-1993; Kennedy 2002). Indeed, loss of whole aspects of a culture, like daily use of the Gaelic language in Cape Breton, is part of this process of change. Because of the general process of globalization, contact with other traditional expressions in music and dance has increased, and with it change occurs, probably faster than it did in previous generations. Workshops, formal classes and technology are factors that increase the pace of learning and the scope of what can be learned, thus increasing the range of possibilities of change. Sklar (2008) and Hahn (2007) comment on the implications of an increase in the transmission pace and suggest, as I understand them, that this might change subtleties of what can or cannot be perceived during transmission processes of different lengths.

What became clear to me by conducting this study is that generational preferences in the dance content do exist. Different generations of dancers have slightly modified and developed a framework of dance knowledge, particularly in relation to the motif repertoire they use. For example, the range of motifs in play has expanded over the years, while it seems that in the past only some dancers had extensive motif repertoires; the majority perhaps had core repertoires, but they were likely less extensive. This points to individual creativity, but also suggests that there was no need for an extensive motif repertoire in the first half of the 20th century. The transmission processes and the different locales in which they occurred surely had an impact on a dancer's repertoire and how it was used. A comparison of different generations of dancers' preferences and motif repertoire will, in one sense, always be a generalization; changes do not occur in a straightforward manner, nor in isolation. The following categories of dance characteristics I have made are based on my recent research, and are by no means exhaustive (Melin 2013b). The division below is only helpful for observing the patterns of change in certain characteristics, such as in the dance–music relationship, the use of different lengths of motifs and some aesthetic preferences. Many dancers do not fit into such divisions in reality, and the majority straddle the second and third or the third and fourth categories, which should be kept top of mind.

Categories Based on Dance Characteristics

Set Solo Dances Associated with Particular Tunes

The first category includes dances associated with particular tunes and is an aspect of the dance tradition that has almost completely disappeared in Cape Breton. It is represented by dancers such as Margaret Gillis, one of the last people in Cape Breton who can still remember the set dance *Dannsa nan Flurs* (Flowers of Edinburgh), and she is the daughter of the late John Alex "the dancer" Gillis, of Gillisdale. Flowers of Edinburgh requires an analysis of its own, but the two most striking aspects are the close correspondence rhythmically to a particular tune and the very "close to the floor" style of floor movements. This particular dance has a pattern where a circle using percussive chassé steps is danced to the A part of the tune, and a percussive step is danced to the B part. The steps to the A part stay the same right through the dance, while the steps to the B part change each time. The order of the steps seems not to have been strictly set. In Margaret's case, this dance was learned at home from her father (see Rhodes 1996: 189).

Solo Extemporaneous Dancing with a Limited Motif Repertoire

The second category is limited motif repertoire. It is representative of dancers such as the late Alex Hughie MacDonald, from Judique Intervale, whom I observed dancing in both 1995 and 1996. Alex Hughie features in the 2006 film *Highland Legacy: The Music of Cape Breton*. He effectively used a fairly limited number of one-bar and two-bar motifs when he danced, and there was only a small difference between his strathspey and reel steps. His right foot dominated his dancing. He did not repeat all motifs evenly between the right and left side. His timing was perfect, and he leaned very slightly forward and gently moved his left hand all along the sequences. His trademark steps involved a lot of heel taps to the ground, and he used his legs quite vigorously (putting a lot of energy into the leg work) when dancing them. He would be termed a "high stepper," to use a local phrase. Alex Hughie always got the crowd cheering when he danced. He radiated pure enthusiasm, and the more the crowd cheered and applauded, the bigger his smile grew.

Solo Extemporaneous Dancing with an Extensive Motif Repertoire

The dancers in the third category all have a fairly substantial repertoire of motifs/steps that they combine. All the dancers featured in this study are part of this category (and some also fit into category four). If generalizing, this group predominantly features dancers who learned at home from family and friends. In addition, some of them might have attended community dance classes from the 1970s onward.

Characteristic of them all is the use of combinations of one-bar, two-bar and four-bar motifs and phrases (steps). These motifs are generally evenly repeated two or four times, depending on the motif in use. This is not a strict rule, however, as most will deviate from it at some point and break up the evenness with singular motifs, placed at points when either the mood or the music so dictates. All these dancers may also change their minds mid-flow and, a step that does not feel right for whatever reason may be changed. In fact, many musicians deal with tunes in a similar fashion. If a tune is not right at any particular moment, it is either played short or a new tune is started at a convenient place; in either case, the flow of music and dance is never interrupted.

The extent of the repertoire of motif and phrases (steps and step combinations) that these dancers use varies from individual to individual. What is of higher importance, and what they are generally recognized for, is their good use of these motifs (steps), their timing and musicality. Many of these dancers are the ones called upon to share their steps, as I would call it, with the community at public events.

Young and Predominantly Formally Taught Dancers Who Use "New" Motifs and Aesthetics

The fourth category of dancers consists mainly of younger dancers who have learned their dance skills predominantly in a class environment. That being said, they also learn steps by observing others at dances and concerts. Note that many young dancers fit better into the third category. The observations below only serve as illustrations of differences from the other categories.

One of the characteristics I have observed is that these dancers use longer steps. Four- and eight-bar combinations of motifs and phrases are common, and many seem to dance with a plan in mind rather than "off the cuff," as those in the other categories predominantly do. Some of these dancers also draw upon motifs and phrases from other dance forms, such as other percussive forms (Irish and other Canadian styles, such as Ottawa Valley and Prince Edward Island, among others) and movement repertoire derived from modern Highland dancing, for example.

Some do not dance close to the floor, but lift their feet quite high and use more lateral movements. In the mid-1990s, I observed how many of these dancers used steps that mostly consist of "broken ankle" movements (that is, rapidly twisting the heel forward and downward, or twisting the working foot onto its outside). Some dancers use this particular movement in every other step they dance. When Willie Fraser refers to a step as a "quiver," implying that there is something new and modern to the style, he probably means this kind of movement. Some feel that these "flashy" steps only started emerging when solo dancing predominantly migrated from the house party to the concert stage.

Another aspect of this category is the creeping in of different rhythm patterns, some more complex and others of a cross rhythm or "broken" nature—for example, dancing five-count rhythms in 4/4 time or dancing certain steps on the "off" beat (emphasis not placed on the main beat). Of course the dancers in the third and fourth categories use complex and cross-rhythm steps, too, but the frequency of the use of these types of movements increases in five-count beats. Fr. Eugene Morris remarked that the use of "broken timing" steps would have started around 1980, and he compared these rhythms to "something like the kind of thing you'd hear Sheumas MacNeil playing on the piano.... It seems to be going hand in hand.... Harvey Beaton is someone that is good at that.... It's an innovation" (MacGillivray 1988: 144).

Some Comments on What Has Been Lost, Modified and Gained

I met Maggie Ann (Cameron) Beaton in Mabou in 1995, and she commented on some of the changes she had observed over the years. She said that some steps had gone out of use altogether. She recalled, for example, some strathspey steps that involved movements performed higher up on the toes than what she had seen in recent years. She indicated that these steps were close to the floor but that the positioning of the feet was different. Sadie MacNeil echoes this observation of dancing on the toes in the strathspey (MacGillivray 1988: 128).

The use of touching or placing the heel on the floor, particularly in reel time, seems to have changed as well. It might be a matter of personal preference that influences the use of heel taps, particularly in shuffle motifs, and in movements where you dig your heels into the ground to give extra emphasis. Rhodes (1985) describes some of these characteristic heel movements. Certainly some dancers use more heel-based movements than others. Mary Janet MacDonald (2009) also indicates in conversation that the current use of shoes with no heels (trainers or sandals) or even dancing in bare feet—and the lack of hard-soled shoes and hard heels in general—may affect the use of steps that use the heels. As a result of the absence of heavier sounds of heels hitting the floor, the soundscape of the dance style changed.

Glenn Graham (2006) raises the subject of speed and suggests that by adding percussive footwork to the square sets they became Gaelicised, which led to them being danced at increased speed. On the subject, he remarks that

> change in tempo could correlate to society itself—efficiency and speed of application in any task seems to be more valued now. Or perhaps it is the younger dancers, both as individual performers, and at dances, prefer a livelier tempo; this may have been a trend since as early as the 1930s. (p. 129)

Graham (129-32) goes on to quote Dunlay (1992), among others, who concur on the subject of increased speed, and engages in a discussion about the various reasons for and perceptions of the changes in tempo. Maggie Ann Beaton also commented on the increase in speed, saying that the strathspeys were certainly danced at a much slower tempo when she was young.

In the mid-1990s, I observed that many, in particular younger, dancers kicked and lifted their feet higher off the ground, and I speculate that perhaps this was for bigger visual effect and possibly also reflecting the popularity of the touring Irish dance show *Riverdance*. The increase in speed and the way some young people dance are also commented on in MacGillivray's interviews a decade earlier. Johnny Stamper, of Scotch Lake, for one, lamented in 1987 that the close-to-the-floor style was disappearing and, along with it, the musicality of the dancers: "they don't give a darn *what* tunes are being played or anything else!" (MacGillivray 1988: 157). This sort of comment indicates that change is not always accepted readily when it comes to tunes in use, speed of playing and the manner of dancing.

Finally, I got a couple of comments from dancers from the Boston area with connections to Cape Breton but who predominantly learned to dance in the United States. One felt that, when dancing in Cape Breton, he or she would not include all the different steps in his or her repertoire, particularly not those with an Ottawa Valley, Québécois or American influence, that she would incorporate at home. Another said that more individual dance styles were apparent many years ago, but that the step-dance style has become homogenized through class teaching by a relatively small number of teachers.

Summary of Changes Observed since the 1970s

Taking into account all that has been pointed out above, I will try to summarize the main changes to Cape Breton step dancing:

- an expansion of, and an increase in, the number of motifs in use in addition to the core repertoire;
- taking one- or two-bar motifs and lengthening them to four- or eight-bar motifs (phrases), thus adding to the amount of recognizable motifs in use;
- the introduction of new movements into fairly common usage—for example, so-called broken-ankle steps;
- a degree of increase in tempo;
- a certain degree of disconnect between the dancers' steps and the music to which they are danced, often in relation to the dancing of routines (note that this is not always the case as it depends on the individual dancers);
- a lack of adherence to key aesthetic concepts, such as close-to-the-floor style;
- a reduced use of movements involving the heel striking the floor;
- the almost complete disappearance of set step dances performed to a particular tune; while the tunes remain in use, the dance

arrangements are not in active use anymore. In contrast, core aesthetics, such as good timing, neatness and lightness, as explained in chapter 6, seem to remain constant.

Recommendations for Further Research

During the research period of this book a number of future research questions about dance emerged. Some are related to the fear of quicker change to the tradition and the loss of cultural expression, as those concerned know it. Further questions may be asked about the stability of current transmission processes. I would suggest that morphological and structural analysis is needed to map and record the Cape Breton dance style, while other questions have to do with historical aspects of dancing or other related expressions of step dancing.

This investigation is only a snapshot of a particular group of people within a particular time frame. As most of the sources experience similar transmission processes and have similar aesthetic and movement preferences, their insights were necessarily also quite similar. However, from when I started step dancing in 1992 and throughout my research period (2006-2012), I have always come across comments reflecting a fear of losing the transmission processes and the particular cultural understanding they reflect. Without quoting anyone in particular, but amalgamating sentiments of numerous comments and discussions with Cape Bretoners, the following questions and concerns arise:

- Will the level of understanding of this cultural expression change? If so, to what extent?
- What might be the conditions for, and also the speed of, transmission change?
- If less learning occurs in the home, and more takes place in organized weekly dance classes, will change occur?
- When the community members who belonged to the generation when transmission at home was part of daily life are gone, how will this affect all aspects of the dance style?
- When those who primarily learned in class environments take over the roles as teachers, what level of disconnect may then occur between the transmission processes and the core matter passed on, as outlined in this study?

- Will the emphasis perhaps be on increased and advanced technical ability, incorporating, to a greater degree than before, movement ideas from other related or non-related dance forms?
- Is it possible that solo dancing is moving toward a more perfor-
mance-oriented activity rather than something that is done as
part of a social gathering, whether that be a house party and/or
a community concert?

Deidre Sklar (2008) mentions, for example, the speeding up
of transmission processes having possible effects on what is being
learned, and also the level to which full embodiment of movement
takes place. If the learning process is contracted to a short timespan,
our bodies have less time to adjust and pick up the nuances of particular movements. If class learning occurs over short periods, with
only certain aspects of the tradition being emphasized, resulting in
short bursts of concentrated movement learning being passed on—in
opposition to comprehensive and sustained gradual learning—then
what will be the result with respect to aesthetics as well as movement?
What will be missed and what will change as a result? One may ask, for
instance, if the class scenario emphasizes learning routines, will the
skill of improvising decline, as the transmission norm of experiencing
many different versions of the same dance would not be present? The
multitude of surrounding sensory stimuli would possibly be largely
absent. A scenario to illustrate this, to provide one example, would be
to learn a step-dance routine in class but never experience dancing it
in the home, concert or square-dance context, and thus miss out on all
the sensory stimuli these contexts naturally provide through sounds,
sights and feelings, which all add layers of meaning to a dancer.

If the connection between music and dance were to decline,
perhaps because of the attraction for young players to perform on
stage rather than make music for dancing, what will be the resulting
changes for both the music and dance style? Will we see a divorce
between aspects of the music and dance traditions, as is evident
in both Scottish and Irish music today? A number of voices in the
community have expressed great concern regarding this particular
disconnect between music and dance and any resulting changes to
the tradition. One concern is that by not honing the finer nuances of
driving dance-music playing, a result of watching dancers in action

over many years, the music, speed, and suitability of tunes played will change, and slowly divorce itself from the dance.

There are currently no public competitions in the Cape Breton step dance, although they appear to have been fairly common at one point in time as we find scattered references to these occurring in the early 20th century in MacGillivray (1988). The context and role of those competitions would be an interesting historical investigation. There is perhaps an element of step-dance competition occurring within Highland-dancing schools at present. However, comments I have heard on the matter suggest that the Cape Breton dance community is proud of its non-competitive dance form and generally would like to keep it that way. Only further studies can unearth answers to the above and other similar questions.

From an analytical point of view, this study does not deeply engage in the ways dancers improvise around the core motifs described. I have merely stated that improvisation occurs around these core sets of motifs. There is scope for looking at particular patterns of motif combinations, carrying out a study of a particular repertoire as a representation of the Cape Breton dance style, and looking at particular motifs associated with either individual dancers or certain families in a geographical area.

As mentioned above, I did look at some aspects of change with regard to the span of, and changes to, motifs in use during the research period. This is an area of research that could well be analyzed in further detail. Questions to be looked at, for example, could be: Exactly why do these changes occur? What are the primary influences to these changes? Following a comprehensive morphological (form) and structural analysis of Cape Breton step dance, a comparative study could look at similarities or differences between Cape Breton step dance and, for example, existing notation of Québécois step dancing (Chartrand 1991) and notation of step dancing in County Kerry, Ireland (Foley 1988, 2012, 2013). Another study could look specifically at stylistic identifiers in the step dancing done by dancers with an Acadian background, as their style has influences from New Brunswick and Québec, for instance, and has certain rhythmic characteristics that may set it apart from general Cape Breton step dancing on a structural level.

From a historical point of view, a study could be built around Rhodes's 1957 findings, as published in 1985 and 1996, looking at how the Scotch Reels have since evolved and further explore the changes in society that led to the old set solo dances falling out of favour. The presence of the genre of Highland Games dancing was not explored in depth in this study, but during the research period I uncovered some evidence that suggests that forms of flings and sword dances may have been more common on the island than previous research has revealed. Perhaps a closer look at the influence of mainland Canadian traditions, the many Highland societies in Nova Scotia and the Nova Scotia Highland Games may have had on Cape Breton dancing as whole is warranted.

Gender balance could be another line of inquiry. This investigation touched on some gender issues, such as the change in the role of women in transmitting dance knowledge, women dancing more in public and women teaching dance in increasing numbers. Since the 1970s, women have come to the fore in all these aspects while the number of men involved is declining. The shift in gender balance in the dance community is as apparent in Cape Breton as in many other cultures, including Ireland and Scotland. A detailed study could reveal further aspects of the influence women have had on the dance tradition, as well as the reason the number of male dancers is declining, even as their popularity as primary exponents of the dance style remains strong.

Figure 8.1 – Step dancers at Celtic Colours (2014) at Strathspey Place, Mabou, NS. Photo by Mats Melin.

Finally, contextual changes in social dancing could be further explored, from the dancing of the Scotch Four in the home to the current square dancing in local parish halls.

- What remains of the Reel dancing of old?
- What place does it have in today's dance contexts?
- Has the Reel, or Scotch Four, become a performance dance only, or does it still have a social function?
- What changes has square dancing undergone?
- We have touched upon the watering down of figures and the decline in local versions of square sets in this study. What other changes can be observed?
- What about gender balance in the dancing at present, with more women than men attending square dances?
- Is the use of stepping in square sets on the increase or in decline?
- What impact have tourists attending summertime festivals had on this style?
- With many of the older generation of dancers attending fewer dances, is the nature of what is being done changing?
- Further studies would no doubt raise further questions.

The social scene is changing in Cape Breton. Gathering places such as The Red Shoe in Mabou and Governor's Pub in Sydney regularly feature fiddle music with the occasional step dancing taking place. One may ask what impact this may have, if any, on the tradition. Is there a danger of step dancing losing its connection with the music? Do big festivals, like Celtic Colours, have a positive or negative affect on the dance tradition? A positive sign was that both of the artists in residence in the 2014 Celtic Colours were dancers. Other positive signs are the formation of the Gaelic piping group Nuallan and the Gaelic traditional dance and music group Fileanta which both invigorate the current music and dance scene in Cape Breton, appearing at concerts and square dances. One may ask whether the core function of future generations' playing and dancing will be one of performance rather than a social activity, as it is today.

Indeed, there is plenty of scope for further dance research in Cape Breton. In the meantime, we should perhaps follow the slogan I once saw on a T-shirt at a Glencoe Mills square dance: "Step dancing is life, the rest is only details!"

Chapter 9

Biographical Sketches

The following biographies are of dancers I interviewed for this book regarding their views on transmission processes in particular and Cape Breton music and dance culture in general. I previously analyzed their motif/step vocabulary for my PhD dissertation, the notations of which are available online (http://insteprt.co.uk/cape-breton-step-dance/.

Their stories are, in many ways, central to an understanding of Cape Breton dance culture and its community's aesthetic preferences. To me, these biographies represent snapshots of the complex mosaic that constitutes the totality of Cape Breton dance culture. In many ways this book highlights aspects of their combined stories. A future study could perhaps focus its biographical sketches on the many current younger step dancers, such as Dawn and Margie Beaton, Gerard Beaton, David Rankin and Stephen MacLennan to mention just a few to add to this mosaic of dance culture in the making.

Willie Fraser (1915-2015), Deepdale
Step dancer and Gaelic singer

Willie Francis Fraser (Willie mac Shiomein), a singer, storyteller and internationally noted step dancer, was born in St. Rose, Inverness County, an area in Cape Breton known for its vibrant Gaelic heritage. His father, Simon, who played the fiddle and step danced, came from the now-abandoned community of Lowland Cove on the northern tip of the island, and his mother, Mary Belle MacKinnon, whose family had musicians and step dancers among them as well, was from St. Rose. He grew up in a family of ten children, inheriting a rich cultural tradition from Gaelic Scotland. His maternal grandmother, Kate MacLellan, was a singer and step dancer from Dunvegan, Scotland. As a young boy Willie used to watch her showing him steps while she sat in a chair, as she was too old to dance by then. His love for the music, the Gaelic language and song tradition, and his ability to step dance would have come down from these people and their relations who provided music, song and dance in the community when Willie grew up.

> Over the years, Willie has fished, worked in the woods and been employed as a stevedore—but his passion has always been the music of Gaelic Cape Breton. For decades, Fraser step danced at church picnics and community fund-raisers around the province—all the while helping his wife Kay raise their family of twelve. (Comhairle na Gaidhlig 2015)

Another and perhaps unique aspect of transmission in Willie Fraser's case that has been well documented (MacGillivray 1988: 56; W. Fraser 2004; Comhairle na Gaidhlig 2015) and often recalled by Willie himself (Melin 2006) is a series of dreams he had when he was about six years old in which a young, well-dressed boy shows him steps, which Willie is able to dance straight away. Willie "got" some twelve steps in this fashion. The notion of receiving aspects of one's culture passively, or that such comes from an outside force, is not unknown in Cape Breton. The fiddler John MacDougall claimed that most of the 42,000 tunes he wrote down "just came to him [from the dead]" (R. MacDonald 2009) and that the music in the MacLellan family (Theresa, Donald, John, Marie and their father, Big Ronald) had partly been acquired through "fairy magic" (Caplan 2006: 116-7).

Willie was also influenced by a number of contemporary dancers and by dancers of the older generation, notably Angus "Mossy" Mackinnon. He would see the Deepdale MacDonnells (Peter and Hughie Dan among

Figure 9.1 – Willie Fraser dancing at a Ceòlas Ceilidh on the island of Eriskay, Scotland, July 1997. Photo by Mats Melin.

others) dance at their "open house" every Sunday, and many more influences are mentioned in MacGillivray (1988: 56-57). Over the years, Willie danced at numerous picnics, weddings, concerts and dances and, in doing so, he danced to most of the well-known fiddlers of his day: Winston Fitzgerald, Donald Angus Beaton, Angus Chisholm, Sandy MacLean and, more recently, Buddy MacMaster, Fr. Angus Morris and Kinnon Beaton, to name but a few.

Willie noted that, in his day, there were more men dancing in public compared with today, even though there were always many good female dancers. Another recent change that he conveyed directly to me (Melin 2006) was the inclusion of many new, flashy movements by contemporary dancers, which he felt had changed the visual and rhythmic aspects of the island's step-dance genre.

Willie has passed his love for dancing on to his children, grandchildren and great-grandchildren. His movement repertoire and subtleness of dancing has been transferred in particular to his two daughters, Maureen and Clare, and to his granddaughters Heather and Melanie (Clare's daughters).[1] The granddaughters learned both in classes from Clare and Maureen and informally from Willie, often in his kitchen. Willie would be quite precise in how he wanted them to move in order to project the family style. Even though over the years a number of dancers in stage performances have introduced more flashy steps, with "quivers," a term Willie is known to use to signify

Figure 9.2 – Willie Fraser and his daughters and granddaughters, Broad Cove Scottish Concert, July 30, 2006. Photo by Victor Maurice Faubert.

movements such as "ankle bends" and "ankle twists,"[2] the Fraser girls of both generations have kept to the family style, in a way keeping the house-ceilidh-style alive, a style that prioritizes subtle rhythmic nuances over flashy visuals (C. MacQuarrie et al 2007). Willie Fraser's name will live on to be associated with "good dancing" in Cape Breton. MacGillivray's (1988) book contains many quotations referring to him as a role model for many dancers, and frequent references to him in the community bear testimony to his ability as a dancer and his character as a humble gentleman. In 2006, Willie received an award from Nova Scotia Lieutenant-Governor Myra Freeman at the East Coast Music Awards in Sydney for his volunteerism and commitment to Gaelic language and culture.

Willie Fraser, who beyond his artistic accomplishments was a farmer, fisherman and coal miner, passed away peacefully on March 22, 2015 at Inverary Manor in Inverness, NS. He was 100 years old.

Harvey MacKinnon, Whycocomagh (Hays River)
Step dancer

Harvey MacKinnon was born in 1935 in Hays River, southwest of Lake Ainslie, Inverness County. His parents and older brothers were Gaelic speakers, but as his parents' generation were discouraged to speak the language in school, it was not actively passed on to his own generation. While his older brothers could not step dance, his three younger sisters could. Harvey was not involved directly in music when he grew up, other than hearing it at the local dances. His father, Neil Sandy MacKinnon, played the violin, though as a party fiddler, not as a performer. His mother's side of the family (MacInnes and MacKinnon) were also very musical. Harvey said in an interview that he never heard his father play growing up:

> I think the first time I ever heard him really playing was one night, I was probably 16 or so, there was an old fiddle hanging on the wall at home and I got my mother to send to Eaton's [mail-order and department store] for strings and for a bridge and for hair for the bow, and I took it to one of my neighbours, who was a violin player, and he strung it up and put it all back together. And, of course, the fiddle was after drying out and spreading and he glued it back together a little bit and I took it home and my

Figures 9.3 (left) and 9.4 (right) – Harvey MacKinnon dancing on stage at Karen and Joey Beaton's Ceilidh, Mabou Community Hall, June 28, 2011, and at a Brook Village square dance, June 30, 2009. Photos by Victor Maurice Faubert.

father played it that winter for me. Quite often, pretty well every night he'd take a spurt at it, and he was starting to remember some of the tunes he'd played. He was an ear fiddler—he didn't play any notes or anything. I never did try to dance to him or anything, because I wasn't dancing at that time (MacKinnon 2007).

In an interview in 1987, Harvey recalled that his mother's uncles, Farquhar Beag and Farquhar Mòr MacKinnon from East Lake, were good pipers and could step dance a bit. Other relations were also dancers and fiddlers (MacGillivray 1988: 112).

Harvey remembers being impressed by fiddlers Lauchie Meagher (1881-1942, Brook Village) Alec MacDougall, and step dancer Donald Walker playing and dancing at a pie social at the school in Hays River, attending with his mother and father sometime around 1941. Around 1952, when he was about seventeen, he started going to the local square dances—so in addition to the aforementioned Hays River Schoolhouse he would then often attend Kenloch and Centerville, as the Brook Village hall was being rebuilt after burning down in 1939; the current hall opened in 1945 (Addison 2001: 38).

> Besides the dances in Kenloch there would be dances in Whycocomagh at the old Legion Hall where Fitzgerald often played, dances in Inverness Legion Hall and the Labour Temple Hall and in Glenville as well during the 1950s. A fiddler who often played for me besides Buddy MacMaster was Theresa MacLellan. ... Once I got started myself and people started seeing me, I'd dance at the Highland Games in Antigonish—that was in 1956 or '57. I danced there for 25 years straight. (*Inverness Oran* 2015)

He learned the hop for the reels and the jig shuffle for the square sets. By age nineteen, Harvey slowly started picking up steps from here and there. He saw dancers locally like Francis MacLellan (Centreville), John Hector MacLean and Ronnie Sutherland (Orangedale) and Peter Parker (Brook Village), and occasionally Thomas MacDonnell and Willie Fraser performing at Broad Cove and at other concerts. It was not as common then for good dancers to take to the floor during a square dance to perform a solo. At the Kenloch dances on Thursday evenings during the summer, where Buddy MacMaster and one of his sisters generally provided the music, the Gillis brothers used to step dance.

> John Archie and John Charlie and John Robert, they were all "Johns," and they used to get up, the three of them, and dance every Thursday night in the summer time. For two or three months in the summer ... they would have the dances. I would never miss that. I was outside and I heard the strathspeys starting and I just ran for the hall because I wanted to see the step dancing. I just thought I would give anything in the world if I could do that. Of course there were no teachers around. There wasn't [sic] people that you could go to and they would teach you. (MacKinnon 2007)

Harvey admired the Gillis brothers and they became quite an influence on him. Then, in the autumn of 1954, he started dancing himself:

> A violin player [John MacLeod of Mull River] started playing strathspey and reel, well a strathspey, so I just was carrying on

with the group that was with me ready to start a square set and I started step dancing and the first thing—at that time you didn't see too many people getting up as you do today, just the odd time there'd be a dancer in the hall that would dance or play for step dancing so I just started fooling around and doing a few steps—and the first thing I knew everybody that was sitting down, because they hadn't been seeing a lot of dancing, they all jumped up and came over to see who was dancing and I thought to myself that I got myself into this I may as well get out the best way I can. Oh I danced for them, and before the night was over they got me out on the floor again to dance.... And then as I went to each dance after that I had to step dance, you know. Of course, then I decided I had better take this serious and I worked at getting new steps and ... putting combinations together. Of course you come up with the odd different step too because as you go through life you come up with something ... I worked it out myself.... For that reason I probably wasn't involved very much in the music, you know, other than just hearing it at the dances. (MacKinnon 2007)

Harvey also learned his dancing at his neighbours' house, the Walkers. The father, Dan Malcolm Walker, played the fiddle and his son Vincent was a good step dancer and played the guitar. The other boys and girls in the family played instruments and danced a bit too. Dan Malcolm would have been an uncle of the man in uniform Harvey had seen dancing at the picnic mentioned above, and he recalls the weekly ceilidhs at the Walkers' house:

When I did start to dance and I was taking it really serious and I was wanting to teach myself steps and get into different things, I used to go down there about twice a week in the winter time. Walk down through snow to my middle, and when I got there Dan Malcolm had a pair of shoes that would fit me, and I'd put them on and two or three times through the night, I'd dance for them. 'Course I was getting a lot of practice in.... There was nobody else. I'd be the only person that didn't belong to the household. But they were a really fabulous family and just loved the music themselves and loved the dancing and I think even the gentleman, the father, I think he was very good on his feet too. So the Walkers were all pretty good dancers. (MacKinnon 2007)

Finlay Walker, an older son of the Walker household, used to take Harvey to summertime square dances. This would then characterize Harvey's dance experience, and how he danced at the house ceilidhs and local dances. Once Finlay pushed Harvey onto the floor as the three "Johns"—the Gillis brothers—were step dancing, and so he became the fourth dancer after that. Harvey recalls with amusement that the Gillises always called him "John Harvey." After the summertime dances it was quite common for five or six cars to follow the Walker car home for a house party. Sometimes the parents were not with them but would be woken up by the arrivals. The fiddles would come out and the party would start. Their mother would get the tea and sandwiches out. This, Harvey recollected, also took place when their boys were home to help their family and neighbours make hay in the summer, as they all worked away from home. When the work was done, the entertainment was music and dancing. Harvey felt that a balance of life was established, of hard work and good parties:

> It was a nice place to grow up. There wasn't a lot of activity, but we made a lot of our own fun and so that's I guess really learning to dance, it was probably in that household and ... my parents probably weren't even getting a chance to see me dance because they didn't go out much. I think the first time my father ever saw me dance we had a party at the house for their 25th or 26th wedding anniversary and I danced there.... He was quite taken up with that. I know he was very pleased, you know. I guess it's been a great ["asset"?...inaudible] to me. I have many friends and an awful lot of them were because of the music and the dance. (MacKinnon 2007)

According to Harvey, when he began dancing he danced rather flatfooted, using both his heels and his toes, but over time he picked up more steps using just the toes. After seeing Willie Fraser dance at Creignish once, he saw shuffles done with the toe, but he spent quite a while working out what it was until he got it:

> I couldn't get in; the place was packed.... But you have to go down three or four steps off the side of the highway and of course I couldn't get in. I was standing back on the road and I was bent down looking in under the door and they had a stage, and all I could see was Willie's feet halfway from the knees to the ankle, and he did one step that I thought was just something else and

I couldn't do it, but I was thinking some day I will meet Willie Fraser and I'll get him to show me that step. But after I started dancing for years, so I don't know how long, I was just fooling around trying to do different things and all of a sudden I did the step and I knew right away that it was the step that I liked so well. I did it, and it was with my left foot and of course I always learned a step with my left and taught it to the right, you know. (MacKinnon 2007)

Even though Harvey is right-handed, he always danced his steps starting with the left foot, his stronger foot, but he is not sure why it ended up that way. He says he did not learn to do the steps to the music; he always more or less danced to the rhythm of the music—that is to say internal rhythms rather than particular tunes. He states that other dancers may start a step with the music and repeat evenly on either foot:

I could change in the middle [of a tune] because of being self-taught and not really knowing the music when I was learning to dance.... But I always thought that one of the real important parts of dancing is the timing. I always loved the timings. If you have impeccable timing and you can hear the feet.... If someone's dancing and I can hear their feet and you hear that it's right with the music, it makes it that much better (MacKinnon, 2007).

In the early days of learning, Harvey constantly had the music in his head and thought of steps. In a 1987 interview he added:

We had an outhouse at home and I used to go out there. I'd catch onto the beams, get my balance, steady myself, and learn the steps that way.... I danced in the cow stable and on the thrashing floor—everywhere you could think. I always had music in my head! I danced on wooden bridges, mostly at night when I'd be coming from a dance or something. (MacGillivray 1988: 112)

Harvey's memories above allude to the hallmark Cape Breton symbiotic relationship between the music and the dance, and between musicians and dancers. He continues by stating that in his experience:

...a good dancer makes a better fiddler and a good fiddler will make a better dancer—they'll just ... they complement one another. So, lots of times I remember going to dances years ago and you'd start the dance and it was maybe a little kind of draggy or wasn't quite up to par and you'd get three or four good couples on the floor, right up close to the stage, and before that set was through, boy, the fiddle was just coming back ... give him a lift to get him over that hump starting out. The music would be just great after that. (MacKinnon 2007)

Harvey worked shift work for thirty-four years at Stora Forest Industries in Port Hawkesbury, retiring in 1996, Work often interfered with dancing, as did having and bringing up a family of three. So, for a good number of years dancing took a backseat, but in the mid-1980s family square dances started up again in West Mabou, and Harvey and his wife started attending and have been regulars ever since. He still performs at concerts and square dances. He has appeared on television and in concerts outside Cape Breton, and there are currently several clips of Harvey dancing on YouTube for all to enjoy. Despite his becoming relatively well known, Harvey MacKinnon remains humble: "You're only as good as the people that are watching you think you are."

John Robert Gillis, Halifax (Kenloch)
Step dancer and fiddler, member Cape Breton Fiddlers' Association

John Robert Gillis was born and brought up in Kenloch, on the north side of Lake Ainslie, Inverness County. There was always music in his house as he was growing up. His two older brothers played the fiddle and all four brothers step danced, especially after they had started going to the local square dances. They picked up steps at the dances as there were some good step dancers around at the time. John Robert learned his first steps from his older brothers, and later from going to public dances in Kenloch. Buddy MacMaster played there on Thursday nights in the 1950s and early 1960s. There was always some step dancing at these dances, and both John Robert and his brother would get on the floor. Growing up, he remembers watching good dancers, such as Willie Fraser (Deepdale), Thomas MacDonnell (Judique North) and Gussie MacLellan (Inverness Town). Gillis "picked up" or learned steps that he still uses from dancer Dan Joe Cameron. Dan Joe would be step dancing on the stage and calling (prompting) the sets at the same time. Dancers were always told to dance "close to the floor" (Melin 2013b). Another older gentleman, Murdock "Murdie" MacQuarrie from Kenloch showed John Robert quite a few steps: "Murdie once told me to take my hands out of my pockets. You didn't dance with your hands in the pockets, shy or not, I was told. That's how I learnt to hold my arms down by my sides" (J. R. Gillis 2009). John Robert also recalls that Murdie MacQuarrie danced the really slow strathspeys, like "The Ewe with the Crookit Horn." Today, John Robert says you see many different styles, and observes that some dancers move their arms quite a bit; "we didn't" (J. R. Gillis 2009). Another influence was Mary MacDonald Letho from Mabou, who taught both John Robert and his daughter Cheryl a good number of steps (J. R. Gillis 2012). In addition to all these steps learned over the years, he uses some that he has made up himself.

John Robert feels that certain tunes are better suited for step dancing than others, "lively tunes but not too fast" (J. R. Gillis 2012). When John Robert teaches dancing there is a pattern to it. Some steps are put to a certain round of strathspey and reels. (A round of music is commonly 32 bars with the tune played ABAB, for example, but this depends on the melody length.) When John Robert was teaching with his daughter Cheryl, they used to make up routines to each "round" of music. But when performing, John Robert mixes his steps quite a bit, depending on the music and the players. "When you hear a good tune, you don't follow a pre-set pattern but just do what

Figure 9.5 – John Robert Gillis, Chestico Days Annual Dancing Festival, Port Hood, 2011. Photo by Victor Maurice Faubert.

comes to you" (J. R. Gillis 2009). He feels one has to vary the steps when performing to make it look interesting. "I like to complete the step on [the] right foot [and] then [the] left; when moving from the strathspey to the reel I like to start on my right foot" (J. R. Gillis 2012). He adds that playing the fiddle helps him anticipate what steps to do, as he knows what is coming next in the music (J. R. Gillis 2009).

During the 1950s and into the 1970s, when John Robert was taking a turn on the floor dancing solo, three rounds of strathspeys used to be danced. Today, commonly, only two rounds are. Once, John Robert had to dance four rounds of strathspey and he "had to dig down" to get through it (J. R. Gillis 2009).

John Robert cannot recall many female dancers from his younger days. The role models were all men. They all had a pattern to their dancing. The dancing had to be balanced, the "steps" repeated evenly on each foot and the steps finished with the music. The steps John Robert remembers were all with the beat in the music. The offbeat steps commonly danced presently are a later introduction and are not typically used by John Robert himself (J. R. Gillis 2009).

John Robert and his wife are frequently seen at the summertime dances around Cape Breton and sometimes in West Mabou at other times of the year. He takes a great interest in the Cape Breton Fiddlers' Association and, in 2008, went on tour with them to Scotland.

Mary Janet MacDonald, Port Hood

(Including biographical notes on her great-aunt Maggie Ann [Cameron] Beaton and her cousin, Minnie [Beaton] MacMaster).
Step dancers

Mary Janet lives on East Street in Port Hood, Inverness County, with her husband, Cecil Jude MacDonald, a retired schoolteacher. She has raised seven children, five of whom (in 2011) still live in Nova Scotia. She now also enjoys the visits of five grandsons and two granddaughters. She is a noted step dancer and teacher, and has taught thousands to step dance since the late 1970s. She is also a good singer; in fact, the whole family enjoys singing together in the house and sometimes in public. Her youngest son, Mitch, is a singer-songwriter who was runner-up in the 2008 *Canadian Idol* reality TV competition. All her children step dance at some level, and one of her proudest moments was when she appeared on stage with all seven at the Dancer's Dream concert at the Celtic Colours Festival in 1998 (M. J. MacDonald 2007). She has released two instructional videos on step dancing (*One Step at a Time*, 1992, and *Cape Breton Stepdancing: A Family Tradition*, 1999).

Mary Janet was born in 1952 and grew up in Southwest Mabou, the second youngest of five children of Margie MacDonnell of Glengarry and Donald MacDonald of Mabou. During the time, from 1952 to 1955, that her mother battled with cancer, she was looked after by her great-aunt Margaret Ann (Cameron) Beaton, who lived just two miles away. When Mary Janet's mother passed away in 1955, she continued to live with Maggie Ann, who became her adopted mother, or "Mama," and "Red" John Beaton (Iain Ruadh Aonghais Dhòmhnaill Ôig) of Mabou Harbour, who became "Papa." She still maintained close contact with her father and siblings, but the Beaton household was now home. John Beaton was a quiet man by nature but there was a lot of music in his family. Maggie Ann came to pass on music and dance to all her children, especially daughter Minnie and, of course, Mary Janet.

Maggie Ann was witty, sincere and sensible, according to Mary Janet (M. J. MacDonald 2007). She told stories—she told it "like it is," and often stole the show. Her English was colourful and expressive and full of Gaelic words and sounds, as Gaelic was her second language. Maggie Ann spent some years in Boston in her younger days but returned home to Southwest Mabou to marry John, a fisherman. She looked after the farm while he was away fishing, handling teams of horses and the raking machine. She raised their six children, along with Mary Janet.

Maggie Ann had grown up surrounded by music in the household of "Big" Dan or Dhòmhnull Mòr (Iain 'Ic Aonghais) Cameron, born in 1850 in Mabou, and whose ancestor Angus Cameron had come from Lochaber in Scotland in the early 1800s to settle on 500 acres (200 ha) of leased land in Mabou. Dhòmhnull Mòr was a big (240 lb, 108 kg) jolly man known for his ability to step dance "as light as a feather," (M. J. MacDonald 2007), and for his fine Gaelic singing, according to family tradition. He went to a dance school in Mabou but little is known about the nature of his schooling there. Because of his skill, Dhòmhnull Mòr was always sought after to dance at local weddings, picnics and public dances. He would often be seen having good-hearted step-dance duels with his friend Dr. Kennedy of Mabou.[3]

Maggie Ann and her brothers and sisters had no access to fiddles, but she carried on the tradition of Gaelic song and dance, which she in turn passed on to her own children. As a young woman, Maggie Ann accessed a knitting machine and started producing socks and *drathaisean* (underwear) for family and for the local community. Maggie Ann's daughter Minnie recalls her mother's great rhythm. Minnie would be sitting upstairs listening to her mother jigging or singing in Gaelic as she was turning the wheel of the knitting machine. Her feet and hands would match the rhythm of the songs (M. MacMaster 2009). Indeed, when Dhòmhnull Mòr was still alive, when taking a break from working outside he would sometimes ask his daughter to sing or jig a "string" while she was working. This was the singing or jigging of tunes, "stringing" together particular tunes that flowed well after each other. These strings could consist of fifteen to twenty tunes and were often rounded off with a Gaelic song.

Maggie Ann recalled that her father would get up to step dance while she sang "the strings." Maggie Ann always emphasized the importance of the flow of tunes and the relationship between musician and dancer, as well as the importance of a dancer's ability to fit the right steps to a tune (M. J. MacDonald 2007). In an *Am Bràighe* newspaper article from 1994, Maggie Ann, then aged ninety-two, recalled an even bigger treat than being able to sing the songs herself: house sessions featuring, for example, Mabou Coal Mines fiddler Danny Johnny Ronald (Domhagan Iagan Raonul) and his brother, Angus (Aonghas Iagan Raonul) the piper (both cousins of the late Mabou fiddler Donald Angus Beaton), and many more who would gather in the house on a Sunday for tunes, songs and step dancing.

Figure 9.6 – Maggie Ann Beaton at her knitting machine (n.d.). Photo by Mary Janet MacDonald, used with kind permission.

Dhòmhnull Mòr tells a story about his uncle, also a good step dancer, from this period:

> Angus the piper went to play for this [uncle] ... and the [uncle] was making all the tunes [steps] match every turn in the tune and the piper went and he made two mistakes in two turns of the tune and the dancer [the uncle]—his foot went up and it wouldn't go down. He made the wrong turn. He knew the tune that well. (MacEachen 1994-95: 8)

The story illustrates well the intimate knowledge aspired to in music and dance. Maggie Ann was of the strong belief that the "music must be in you," that it is "in the blood" and that it comes down the family lines. Dhòmhnull Mòr's wife, Mary Campbell (Mairi Shomhairle), sang Gaelic songs and knew the music too, even though Maggie Ann felt it was from her father's side that she and her siblings had got the music.

Both Mary Janet and her older "sister" Minnie (who would have been about ten years old when Mary Janet arrived, at age two or three) recall their mother, Maggie Ann, lining the children up at home, oldest to youngest, and first showing them steps, then turning around making them copy her dancing. She would give them basic jig, strathspey and reel steps and would sometimes point out if she was showing them one of her father's steps. She would constantly jig the tunes or sing Gaelic songs while doing this. In addition to their mother's singing, there was constantly music on the wind-up gramophone, as the family acquired the latest 78 rpm records of local fiddlers when they became available. In the early 1960s her brother Donald Alex got one of the first reel-to-reel audio tape recorders in the area. Minnie recalls her mother's singing/jigging and that she "had what you call the flavour in it. She could do all the cuts 'drrrm'—you know.[4] To have her jigging was sometimes better than

Figure 9.7 – Minnie MacMaster and Mary Janet MacDonald (n.d.). Photo by M. J. MacDonald, used with kind permission.

what you heard on a recording" (M. MacMaster 2009). Of Maggie Ann's own children, Minnie was the one who excelled at step dancing:

> She [Maggie Ann] would have us up dancing lots of nights. In the wintertime, cold and windy nights out, Mama would jig for us. That's what I grew up with. As I grew older, fiddlers from the local area kept coming in on Sunday nights. They would open up the fiddle cases and get their fiddles out. Sometimes there would be a piano player too. You had music for all hours.... John Campbell and Dan Hughie MacEachern came to the house. John Allan Cameron and his brother John Donald both played the fiddle, but often John Allan was on the guitar. There were times that my mother's brother, my uncle Findley Cameron and his wife Sadie would come over to visit from Boisdale. They would always want me to dance and that was such a joy for me because his jigging was so full of life, I would want to dance many times during the evening. (M. MacMaster 2015)

These frequent parties featured Gaelic singing, stories, fiddle music and step dancing—they were said to be amazing. Minnie was keen to learn new steps because she was asked to dance at various concerts in the surrounding communities. She used to watch other dancers perform:

> You'd see another step dancer there, and you would get home and think, "Oh my gosh, see if I can remember that step." You'd come up with a step but maybe it wouldn't be quite the same as the dancer you saw. But that would be what I called my step. Then at the next concert you'd do the same thing.... That's how I learnt it. (M. MacMaster 2015)

It's important to note that what Minnie describes is not a rushed process but one that requires constant reinforcement. In this process, movements, sounds and sights are embodied, allowing Minnie to become proprioceptively aware over time. Minnie enjoyed watching dancers like Willie Fraser, Harvey MacKinnon, Fr. Angus Alex MacDonnell and Margie Dunn, who had some beautiful and unique steps of her own, which of course Minnie tried to mimic.

Minnie always remembers Thomas MacDonnell for his poise—he had the most beautiful posture when he danced. Minnie's father, John, supported her dancing too, but in a quiet way. She recalls his beautiful proud smirk on his face, which is all she ever needed to see to know how proud he was of her dancing at the concerts and parties. Going out was a novelty, as most of her childhood was spent at home playing and fighting with her siblings. Going to the concerts was therefore a big event. The local parish would send a car up to take them to the concert:

> We did our thing and sometimes we would get fifty cents. One time I got a dollar. I remember going to school the next day feeling I was really wealthy and I would spend it all on candy. That was one of the nice perks of being able to dance. (M. MacMaster 2009)

As Minnie grew older and her reputation spread, she was asked to go farther afield. Getting the ferry to cross the Strait of Canso to the mainland to travel to the Highland Games in Antigonish is one of many memories. Payment was never an issue; just being asked by another community to dance, and being allowed to go, was very exciting. Compared to today, when many dancers are readily available to get up on stage to perform, in the 1950s and 1960s there were only about seven or eight dancers who danced regularly at public events. Many more, of course, danced socially and step danced at house ceilidhs.

> I remember going to a wedding with my parents and it was held on an outside stage connected to the bride's home ... it was built especially for the wedding. I was only thirteen at the time and that night I had the chance to dance my first square set and I remember having so much fun. As I grew older (15 or 16) a number of times I was allowed to go to a few of the local square dances with my older sisters at the dance hall in Mabou and the "Seaside" dances in the Port Hood area.... (M. MacMaster 2015)

The sets were prompted, with only four couples to a set, and so some twelve sets could be danced in an evening. Two jigs and a reel figure were the norm, and Minnie was disappointed if she did not get to dance every set.

When Mary Janet arrived in the household, to Minnie it was like getting a real live doll. With Minnie constantly dancing around the house and there being both music and dance in Mary Janet's family, it was inevitable that she should dance. Minnie recalls:

I remember teaching her not only the footwork but also taking her by the hands ... to get the beat from what you are doing. She was really quick to catch on. And then came the point when Minnie felt she was ready to dance on stage together with her. It was in Mabou and I'll never forget that night. She got along just beautiful. So we danced together at a number of places after that. Holding hands at times. But mostly just dancing. She grew up and kept the dancing going. (M. MacMaster 2009)

Mary Janet has the same memory:

She [Minnie] said that I'd feel the rhythm through our joined hands and would copy the rhythm while watching her—all this while Mama jigged the tunes. I guess I danced in my first concert in Mabou when I was about four. I was with Minnie on stage. I recall being up there with my finger in my mouth and Minnie's many attempts to remove it. I also recall the applause afterwards and how I cried—I guess I got scared. (M. J. MacDonald 2007)

Both Minnie and Mary Janet went on to teach step dancing. The community (in Creignish, just next to where Minnie lived in Troy) started asking Minnie to teach at the local school in the early 1970s. Even though she did not feel confident, she decided to give it a try. At first, she found it hard to teach and keep the youngsters under control at the same time. By the mid-1970s fellow dancer Geraldine MacIsaac (mother of fiddler and step dancer Wendy MacIsaac) suggested that they teach together. They taught in Creignish and Glendale for a couple of years. By the late 70s family priorities took over and Minnie stopped teaching, but she continued to dance at concerts. Her daughter, Natalie MacMaster (b. 1972), has very successfully continued the family tradition since the 1980s, now internationally acclaimed as a performer and ambassador of fiddle music, and deeply rooted in the local Cape Breton culture.

Mary Janet would, in a similar fashion, watch the same dancers perform, "imprinting each step into memory" until she could do them herself (M. J. MacDonald 2009). For a time, Minnie went to work on the Nova Scotia mainland, while Mary Janet continued to dance at summer concerts.

Mary Janet got married in the early 1970s and started a family soon after, which meant less time for step dancing. However, with the increased interest in the fiddle and dance tradition following the 1971

CBC-TV documentary *The Vanishing Cape Breton Fiddler,* her dance career got a new lease on life. Pianist Joey Beaton from Mabou encouraged her to start teaching classes locally. She had to teach herself a comfortable way of passing on her skills and eventually found one that worked. At one point, she was teaching weekly classes in both Port Hawkesbury and Chéticamp:

> [Step dancing] was absolutely huge in the late seventies and early eighties.... You know you just couldn't keep up with the demand. Everybody wanted to learn to dance. I taught classes in Port Hawkesbury, Judique, Port Hood, Mabou, Whycocomagh, Orangedale, not in Inverness, because one of the Fraser girls was teaching there ... [and in] Margaree and Chéticamp ... year after year after year. I mean, in Port Hood I had my regular classes and I'd do ten-week sessions—spring and fall in ten week sessions—that's all I could do, you know.... I was meeting a demand that was there and there were not very many dance teachers.... There were very few that could do Inverness County, right? Betty Matheson, Father Eugene were doing it over on the other side [in the Sydney area].... Minnie was just sticking to Creignish, Margaret Dunn was in Antigonish.... I was out every night of the week teaching dancing. Every night. Working by day, teaching by night. Just to make ends meet, basically.... It was great seeing all these people dancing.... [On] Saturday afternoons I'd go to Chéticamp and teach. Huge classes. Those poor people that accepted the way that I was teaching at that time. I'd be standing in the middle of the gymnasium and there'd be people all around in a circle. Fifty, sixty, seventy people.... The demand was huge.... I don't know if you'll ever see that again. (M. J. MacDonald 2007)

Mary Janet was made aware of the impact that her teaching these classes had when she was asked by Fr. Eugene Morris to go to Scotland in 1983. The destination was a *feis* (Gaelic festival) on the Isle of Barra. She relates:

> I would have been thirty-one when I went to Scotland and at that time I had been teaching a few years.... Prior to that I had worn taps on my shoes because it was the thing to do, you know. You didn't have that responsibility to your traditions at that time, because it just wasn't important or you didn't think of it in that way, or I didn't think of it in that way and then all of a

sudden when you're teaching and you're passing it on then you're going to Scotland, all of a sudden, Father John Angus Rankin, who was the biggest fellow on traditional music and dance—he took that stuff very, very seriously ... said, "Well, if you're going to be teaching this and influencing so many people"—because he could see this wave beginning—"you'd better be doing it the right way." Honest to God! I can't say that I was hurt by that but the absolutely physical blow that I felt inside me was all of a sudden, Oh my God! I have such a responsibility. It was within hours that I ripped the taps off my shoes.... I started thinking, teaching classes.... I absolutely went the opposite way then.[5] (M. MacDonald 2007)

During the 1960s and 1970s it was quite common for people to wear taps, as one could hear the dancing better at outdoor concerts. For instance, everyone on CBC-TV's *Don Messer's Jubilee* was wearing taps because the core members were largely from Prince Edward Island.[6] A lot of people liked the PEI-based dancers, who all wore taps, and so they mimicked them. It is an early example of visual media's influence on a tradition. However, the fashion changed. That Mary Janet stopped wearing them for classes and performance may have influenced many dancers to also stop wearing them.

Mary Janet reflects on the impact of teaching the tradition, not just locally but also internationally, and how her teaching may have changed aspects of the genre:

As you brought the dancing to ... the wider world then ... you moved out of your comfort zone—you went to Scotland and then went to California and then ... Seattle and Utah and Chicago those places. All of a sudden people start[ed] questioning what you're doing. They want to find out; they want to get inside it; and they're coming from all these other kinds of backgrounds and examining and everything else. Because of that I changed how I do things in my dancing. Where once I was totally spontaneous, all of a sudden I know that I changed the way I do things, so that it would be more correct. Now, what I mean by that is: when I would get up to step dance, I don't know if I would start with my left foot or my right foot. It didn't matter. Would I start at the beginning of a phrase or in the middle of a phrase, or would I do three steps instead of four? Would I do them all evenly? I don't know ... that was not something that was taught, it wasn't structured like that.... Now I will teach: start every sequence of steps with your left foot and that will keep everybody on the right/correct foot, whatever. Did I do that? Absolutely not! I ... [reflecting pause] ... examining what you're doing, so I taught a lot of, a lot, a lot, a lot of people in those early days. Goodness knows what I taught them. (M. J. MacDonald 2007)

Mary Janet accepts that the tradition is changing, but she feels that aspects of what she is doing are the same as what her mother would have danced in the 1920s and her maternal grandfather would have done in the late 19th century. Every step that she ever learned from Mama Maggie Ann and her sister Minnie are on her two instructional videos, as well as some of her own input.

In October 2008 the Celtic Colours Festival put on a tribute concert—Close to the Floor: Mary Janet's Bunch—at the Strathspey Place in Mabou, celebrating Mary Janet's life and achievements as a dancer.

Harvey Beaton, Halifax (Port Hastings)
Dancer and pianist

Harvey Beaton was born in 1962 in Port Hastings, Inverness County. His mother's family, the MacDonalds from Troy, Inverness County, danced, but were not considered performance dancers except for his late mother, Marie Beaton, who did dance in a few concerts either solo or in an eight-handed Reel when she was a young woman. Harvey never saw her perform in a concert. His mother had brothers, uncles and one sister who could dance as well. They would have gone to schoolhouse dances in Troy. His maternal

Figure 9.8 – Harvey Beaton dancing to fiddler Andrea Beaton, Broad Cove, July 29, 2007. Photo by Victor Maurice Faubert.

grandfather, Duncan Francis MacDonald, used to play the fiddle for dances, prior to the 1930s.

Harvey cannot recall the first time he heard a fiddle tune or saw a step dancer; Scottish music and dancing was simply part of his up-bringing. Although no one in his family played the fiddle when he was young, he used to hear tunes on the local radio station. As a child, he witnessed the music and sets being performed in his parents' house. Even though the parlour was small, they would make room for a square set during some of their house parties. The first fiddler Harvey ever heard was probably Donnie "Dougald" MacDonald of Queensville. He was a friend of the family and a regular at these parties. His cousin Howie MacDonald and his family, who were a big musical influence on Harvey's life, would also be at these parties. Naturally exposed to all the fiddle music and step dancing awakened Harvey's interest in music and dance. In addition, the family had a piano, which has resulted in Harvey being known not only as a dancer, but also as a piano accompanist for fiddlers.

His mother, Marie, was most likely the first step dancer he saw, and she taught him his first few steps when he was about thirteen years old. Harvey vividly remembers trying to learn a step in the living room in their home in Port Hastings:

> Well, maybe "vivid" isn't 100-per-cent correct, as I can't recall if it was the back step or another one (step, heel-toe, hop shuffle, back) ... [reflecting pause]. Anyway, I remember dancing in earnest and then calling out to my mother who was in the kitchen, "Is this it?" "No!" came the reply. "How do you know?" [I asked]... "Because I can hear it. You're missing something," she answered matter-of-factly. (H. Beaton 2007)

The recollection serves as a good example of aural transmission and how fine-tuned Harvey's mother was to the tradition and its aesthetic requirements of impeccable timing and execution.

Harvey also remembers going to outdoor "Scottish concerts" in the summers in nearby Creignish and Glendale when he was growing up—his first recollection of a concert is from when he was about nine years old. The Catholic parishes sponsored these events, and they essentially consisted of fiddling, step dancing and Gaelic singing. Harvey recalls being at a closing party of a step-dancing class in Sydney when he was about thirteen years old.

I watched the students dance that evening and wished that I had the opportunity to take classes. My cousin and good friend, Evelyn MacDonald, was in the class, and she was learning to dance from Father Eugene Morris. Since Evelyn and I often went to summer square dances in Glendale with our parents, we were both anxious to learn some steps. While there were lessons being held in Sydney, there were none to be taken close to Port Hastings, nearly two hours away. This was a great irony considering the number of step dancers who lived in Inverness County! (H. Beaton 1994)

At the time, most people just picked up steps from other people in the home, perhaps at dances or at parties. In 1976, however, classes were set up closer to Port Hastings, in Glendale and Creignish. The lessons were very popular and space was limited, but Harvey managed to enrol in the class at Creignish, which Minnie (Beaton) MacMaster and Geraldine MacIsaac were teaching. For eight weeks at $1 per lesson, Harvey took the one-hour class at the community recreation centre. He had just turned fourteen and was thrilled to have those two for teachers because they were both considered excellent dancers. Another early influence was Margaret Dunn, who taught him informally on occasion but never in a class.

In the autumn of 1976 Harvey first danced in public at a Halloween party in Glendale:

I believe Carl MacKenzie was playing that evening and when the dance was almost over he started playing some really great Strathspeys. I was in the car ready to leave when I heard the lively music and decided to run back inside to see who was showing their steps. After I was inside, someone pushed me out onto the floor and I step danced in front of the crowd for the first time. (H. Beaton 1994)

His first concert performance was in Glendale hall in 1977 or 1978. After that, he was asked to dance at local concerts in community and church halls, and eventually at big outdoor concerts like Glendale, Broad Cove and Iona. During his teenage years, Harvey danced at a concert every weekend in the summer. He enjoys performing at such events to this day.

Although Beaton went to his first square dance at Glendale in 1974, at age twelve, he did not start going to dances regularly during summers until he was fifteen. Before then it was difficult to access local dances, as there were none organized either at Port Hastings or Troy in the mid-1970s. The nearest dance was the Thursday night square dance at Glencoe Mills, with music by Buddy MacMaster, who was accompanied by his sister Betty Lou. Dances were also held on Monday nights at Brook Village, where fiddler Cameron Chisholm and pianist Maybelle Chisholm played. At these dances it was common for a solo dancer to be asked to dance if the fiddler began playing strathspeys between the square sets. Harvey often danced solo at these functions, especially in Brook Village, where the pianist Maybelle Chisholm insisted he get on the floor. Even though Harvey enjoyed attending the Scottish concerts and seeing other dancers perform, he learned the most at the square dances:

> It was really at the square dances where I took [the] most interest in it [the step dancing in the Square steps] and [it] kinda honed my steps and you watch other people and that's really the environment where I first saw it as being a social dance, you know, and not something that was structured, or you had to have certain routines or anything else—you just did what came from the heart. (H. Beaton 2007)

In 1994, Harvey commented on the state of and growing interest in step dancing since he had started in the mid-1970s:

> When I was a teenager in the 1970s there weren't many others my age dancing. This has changed a great deal over the past ten to fifteen years as more and more young people began playing Cape Breton Scottish music and appreciating it. These days, there are step-dancing lessons in virtually every community in Inverness County and in many other parts of the island and on the mainland. At my home in Dartmouth, Nova Scotia, I get calls very regularly from people wanting dancing lessons. (H. Beaton 1994)

Harvey began teaching step dancing and square dancing when he was fifteen and has been doing so on and off ever since. In 1977, one year after he started dancing, he set up a class in Port Hastings and at one point had seventy students (MacGillivray 1988). He has taught dancing in several provinces in Canada and in many places in the United States, including Washington, DC, Boston, Washington state, California, and New York. Harvey has also performed and taught in Cork, Ireland, and in several places in Scotland. He first went to Scotland in 1991 with fiddler Sandy MacIntyre. They did workshops (fiddle and dance) in places like Inverness, Dingwall, Thurso and Portree. In July 1992, Harvey went back to teach with Buddy MacMaster during Alasdair Fraser's week-long summer school at Sabhal Mòr Ostaig in the Isle of Skye. In a letter from 1994 Harvey wrote, "[It] is a real treat—to teach my style of step dancing in the very place from which it originated" (H. Beaton 1994).[7]

Harvey no longer lives in Cape Breton; he lives about 300 km away in Halifax, where he is the principal of Millwood High School, Lower Sackville. He visits Cape Breton regularly and does not see any striking changes in Cape Breton step-dancing styles in the past fifteen years. People do, however, continue to develop their own steps. Harvey, among many others, did the same some thirty-five years ago, so nothing has changed in that respect. It is an ongoing process. He asserts that "as much as dancers develop and learn new steps, you can never replace the standard steps from generations ago. They are the foundation of the step dancing in Cape Breton. Those steps

Figure 9.9 – Scotch Four at Broad Cove. L to R: Melanie (MacQuarrie) MacDonald, Bill Pellerin, Harvey Beaton, Maureen Fraser-Doyle. Andrea Beaton (fiddle) and Robbie Fraser (piano), July 7, 2007. Photo by Victor Maurice Faubert.

will never be replaced—simply complemented with other steps" (H. Beaton 2005). In 1994, Harvey wrote in a letter that

> there are still enough original steps to make everyone a unique performer. Some people, however, fear that Cape Breton may lose its unique style of dancing as young people in particular begin to experiment with other style[s] of step dancing, Irish for example, and integrate it into the Cape Breton style. I am not yet too concerned about this as I feel experimentation is a natural curiosity and that there are plenty of dancers carrying on the "pure" Cape Breton dance form. (H. Beaton 1994)

Only after he started dancing himself did he begin to pay attention to what other dancers were doing. He observed their differences and individual styles, even though they often danced the same steps. He does not recall asking too many dancers for steps, but observed more than anything else (MacGillivray 1988: 34). The dancers who had the most influence on him in the early days were Minnie MacMaster, Geraldine MacIsaac and Margaret Dunn. Others, like Willie Fraser from Deepdale, taught Harvey to dance the Scotch Four (34).

Step dancer and teacher Margaret (MacLellan) Gillis, from North Sydney, summed up Harvey Beaton's dancing rather aptly in a 1986 interview:

> My favourite dancer in Cape Breton is Harvey Beaton. He can execute the steps with very little effort. He can get around the steps very neatly and get a lot of taps in … that's what I admire: his poise and his deliverance of steps. But there are a lot of good dancers. (MacGillivray 1988: 63)

Rodney MacDonald, Mabou
Step Dancer, Fiddler, Politician

Rodney Joseph MacDonald was born in 1972 to Elizabeth Ann Beaton from Mabou and Alec Angus MacDonald from Mabou Harbour. He was raised in Mabou and has a strong musical heritage: his maternal grandfather was the renowned fiddler Donald Angus Beaton; his maternal uncles include Kinnon Beaton (fiddler), Joey Beaton (piano player) and Mary (Beaton) Graham (piano player, step dancer and mother of fiddler Glenn Graham). Rodney adds:

and my grandfather's [Donald Angus Beaton's] sister, Janet Beaton, was a piano and fiddle player and her father, Angus Ronald, was a fiddler and a piper.... I have other uncles that play too. There's a lot of music on the Beaton side and they're also connected to the Campbells in Mabou, which are a well-known musical family, and the Rankins. The Rankin Family [musical family group], ... we all tie in together. On my father's side, there were a lot of dancers and a few fiddlers and such as well: Kenneth Johnson MacDonald, who recently passed away.... So, in my house there was always music. We'd be listening to an old recording of someone playing, or a new record that came out and my mother and my father loved to dance, and would be dancing in the garage, in the house, would be dancing when my uncles came. We'd be dancing out in the yard and my mother would always be jigging tunes. So, I was dancing in the kitchen when I could walk. We were dancing before we were walking.... It wasn't something you went out and learned how to do. It just was. (R. MacDonald 2009)

When referring to Rodney, members of the Mabou community often say that he carries on the Mabou Coal Mines fiddle and dance style. There are certain steps that all the MacDonalds—Alec Hughie, Benedict MacDonald, Benedict's son Blair MacDonald, Rodney's uncles Angus Daniel, Harold Donald and Angus Donald—often do, according to Rodney. Joe Rankin from Mabou Harbour also does them. Kinnon Beaton calls these regional differences in step-dancing style "a language":

An accent is a good word for it. You know, if you talk to somebody from Glencoe Mills, they're going to talk

Figure 9.10 – Fiddler Rodney Mac-Donald step dancing. Broad Cove Annual Concert, July 25, 2010. Photo by Victor Maurice Faubert.

different from somebody from Mabou. Somebody in Margaree is going to talk different from somebody in Mabou. And their music is the same.... Each community has ... "regional" sounds. (K. Beaton quoted in Herdman 2008: 36)

According to Herdman (2010: 167), pinning down the Mabou Coal Mines style is difficult for outsiders, but Rodney provides a helpful glimpse into the context of this particular stylistic sound:

It was just natural and it wasn't just the dancing. You were hearing the Gaelic and you were hearing—my grandmother's first language was Gaelic, so it's pretty common around Mabou—so if you were at my grandmother's, at Elizabeth Beaton's, she'd be playing the piano, my grandfather would be playing the fiddle and then you'd dance or you'd do something else at parties, and so it was just part of life. (R. MacDonald 2009)

It was not, however, just the general surroundings that influenced Rodney—many specific people had an impact on him as well.

My parents were an obvious influence on some of the basic steps [his mother in particular], and my uncles—one in particular: my father's brother, Donald Roddy MacDonald, who's a very good dancer and has some great steps and he watched a lot of dancers, and I really enjoyed his dancing, so I learned a few steps from him.... My other uncles, people like Francis Beaton and others ... loved to dance as well and I'd be watching them, but Donald Roddy in particular of my direct uncles had the biggest influence on my dancing. Then, of course, I went to a few lessons with people like Mary Janet MacDonald, but most of my dancing wasn't from formal lessons; it was mainly from watching different dancers. Especially on video. When video became popular, I watched a lot of videos [of] people like Harvey Beaton. Harvey was one of my favourites. The Pellerin brothers, John and Bill Pellerin from Antigonish. Willie Fraser. [...] I was a big fan of Willie Fraser, and I would watch him and Harvey Beaton over and over and over again on video and try to figure out how they did a step. Harvey MacKinnon, Mary Janet MacDonald and a whole host of others ... I was just impressed with their dancing. ... I would stand in front of the mirror and practise steps or stand in front of the fridge, because I could get the reflection in the fridge, and I would do it for hours and hours and just practise steps. (R. MacDonald 2009)

Rodney started dancing in the young square set,which was taught in the Mabou school when he was about eight years old. Maureen MacKenzie from Mabou and her partner Heather Rankin from the Rankin Family were running it. They went to places like the Mayflower Mall in Sydney, where Rodney would perform a lot. He started dancing solo when he was about eleven or twelve years old. He started playing the fiddle at age twelve:

> I loved the fiddle.... When I turned eight or nine, I started just sitting there for hours just doing the bow. Just doing the bow over the strings, and then when I was about twelve, my uncle [Kinnon Beaton] came in and gave us some lessons. And I learned from there. (R. MacDonald 2009)

Although Rodney acknowledges the influence of many great female dancers, like Mary Janet MacDonald and the Warner Sisters, he concentrated on older male dancers, picking up steps here and there. Eventually Rodney started to teach dancing. While he kept honing his skills and pursuing a career in music, he studied and received a Bachelor of Science in Physical Education at St. Francis Xavier University, Antigonish, where he had well over one hundred dance students. When at home during the spring he taught in Mabou, Port Hood, Judique, Inverness and Whycocomagh. In the summers he was a tutor at the Gaelic College in St. Ann's (where he is the CEO). Some of the students who Rodney once taught are carrying on the dance tradition—Dawn and Margie Beaton, Gerard Beaton and his cousin Blair MacDonald, to name a few. He also taught in Scotland in the mid-1990s.

For a time Rodney pursued a career as a teacher before venturing into politics. He served as member of the Legislative Assembly for the riding of Inverness from 1999 to 2009 and as premier of Nova Scotia from 2006 to 2009. He has one CD in his own name, *Dancer's Delight* (1996), and appears on two others: *Traditionally Rockin'* (1997), with his cousin Glenn Graham, and the 2004 Smithsonian recording *The Beaton Family of Mabou, Cape Breton Fiddle and Piano Music*. He received two nominations for the East Coast Music Awards in 1998. He has toured in Atlantic Canada, central Canada and the northeastern United States.

Rodney recalls growing up spending much time playing music with Natalie MacMaster and playing music and dancing with Ashley MacIsaac. Rodney would watch Ashley, Natalie, Wendy MacIsaac, Jackie Dunn and Jackie's mother, Margaret Dunn, as they were all good dancers. Gradually he formed his own take on the dancing:

> Growing up, I practised certain steps, so I'd have them together, but I never really had [a] routine ... that I stuck to. I'm one that ... like[s] to do certain steps one after another. And I have an idea where they'll go but I really like to follow the tune. So, if the tune has a cut in it, I like to do a step that fits with the tune. Or if the tune I know is going to change, I try and fit a step that will change with the tune, that people can see the change and hear the change at the same time.... To me, it's not the number of steps anybody has, and even when I teach kids or adults or anybody, it's the timing. I'd rather see a person with one step that can do it on time than do a hundred steps and not have the time.... I think people, when they're watching ... notice if the step goes with the tune and especially in Mabou here ... a lot of people understand the music.... They appreciate it and really listen a lot to it.... They have a pretty good feel for it if something is on or if it's not.... And then, it's not how complicated the step is ... but ... [it's about] watching someone, how they hold themselves, feet close to the floor, the types of steps—it's very important in my opinion. (R. MacDonald 2009)

Rodney feels quite strongly that the relationship between the dancing and the fiddle music is symbiotic and keeps the music at a certain speed, preventing it from being too fast or too slow. The fiddler is forced to play for the dancer and, according to Rodney, "that's a good thing, so we each keep each other honest" (R. MacDonald 2009).

Melody (Warner) Cameron, West Mabou
Step dancer and fiddler

Melody (Warner) Cameron grew up in River Bourgeois, southwest of St. Peter's, in Richmond County. Alongside her sister Kelly (MacLennan), she absorbed music and dance at home, encouraged in particular by their father, Norman Warner Jr. There is music and dance on both sides of the family. Their grandfather was piper, fiddler and step dancer

Norman Warner Sr., from Port Hawkesbury. Their great-grandmother Annie (Steel) Warner, hailing from the Cleveland area in Richmond County, was a Gaelic speaker and used to jig tunes and sing *puirt-a-beul*. Melody's great-great-grandfather was Levi Campbell, who was adopted by the Warners at the age of eleven. Melody's grandmother Georgina (Kelly) Warner was a step dancer who performed regularly at local concerts in Richmond County. Georgina had an Irish father (George Kelly) and a Scottish mother (Rosella MacDonald). They lived in St. Peter's, Richmond County. Melody's maternal grandparents, Roderick and Viola Touesnard, are of Acadian descent. They had kitchen parties over the years with local fiddlers dropping in. Melody often stayed with her grandparents while growing up, and was present at many of these gatherings.

In an interview, Melody says that her father, Norman, who danced in the square sets, taught the sisters their basic steps at home. Shuffle steps would be danced sitting down at the kitchen table, even during dinnertime, or just walking in time with music while carrying a grand-child. These, more current, natural and continuous encouragements of music, timing and rhythm bring back memories to Melody of her father and grandfather doing the same to her and her sister. Indeed, her sister Kelly's children are now step dancing alongside their mother at local concerts and dances, as this dancing is naturally encouraged at home. Melody also recalls a story of herself and Kelly as very young girls lying in bed at night practising steps. They would push their beds up against the wall and put their feet on the wall and work out step patterns together. This would regularly end when their father would ask them to stop the racket and go to sleep! Still, their father wholeheartedly encouraged

Figure 9.11 – Melody Cameron danc-ing to the playing of Ashley MacIsaac (n.d). Photo by Fran O'Brien.

them to step dance, an encouragement that meant they did not really engage with other types of dancing as they grew up; step dancing was the main thing. Because of this, as Melody grew older she would step dance at rock concerts, as step dancing felt natural. The music would conjure up dance steps in her head, she reminisces (Cameron 2007).

After their father had taught them his repertoire of basic steps, they went on to learn more dancing locally from Gladys Cote and later from Linda MacMillan, from Glendale, in the late 1970s. Linda MacMillan would have had a similar style and choice of movements to Harvey Beaton but with her own personal twist, such as particular ankle rolls. Linda's teaching was a mixture of showing steps to music and breaking them down slowly at first before trying them out to music, depending on the complexity of the step in question. As mentioned above, the Warner Sisters, the name under which Melody and Kelly danced together, also made up their own step (motif) combinations as they grew older and became more confident in their dancing. The Warner Sisters have over the years become synonymous with "good step dancing" in Cape Breton. They appear in a number of clips from the 1980s onward on YouTube, and some of the clips have been viewed thousands of times. The Warner sisters appeared on the British Channel Four documentary *Down-Home: Cape Breton and Québec*, presented by Shetland fiddler Aly Bain and recorded in 1984-1985 (Alexander 1985).

Furthermore, the sisters performed synchronized step-dance routines at numerous venues throughout Nova Scotia, Prince Edward Island and western Newfoundland in the 1980s (Cameron and Cameron 2011). In December 2005, for example, the Warner Sisters appeared in the Rankin Sisters' televised Christmas special, *Home for Christmas*, broadcast on Canada's Bravo channel.

With their choreographed synchronized routines, they often appear in matching outfits, sometimes sporting tartan waistcoats or tartan skirts with a tartan sash draped over the left shoulder and diagonally across front and back. In later clips, the tartan element of their costume is less visible. A hallmark of the Warner Sisters' synchronized routines is their combination of older motifs, recognized by the community, with their own motifs. Melody told me in a conversation that the trick is to "keep the performance interesting to look at without doing too much"; the routine should catch the eye and then keep moving on without being overloaded or boring (Cameron

2007). This concept of balancing old and new motifs has kept audiences happy and kept the dancing within the local boundaries of the dance tradition. Melody's father, Norman, was taught to dance on a small board—introducing boundaries of neatness and spatial awareness. The aim was to keep the dancing neat and not to move about too much. Norman's ideas of boundaries in turn passed on to Melody. The key element, Melody was told by her father, was to "keep the feet close to the floor but look lively, stay relaxed with your hands down by your side. Just do the movements and keep the bounce" (Cameron 2007). Her father danced his shuffles using both heels and toes, as does Melody, to keep the correct beat. It is interesting to note that Melody does not think of the movements (steps or motifs) as corresponding to particular bar lengths, or to parts or segments of tunes. The music is so engrained in her that suitable movements and music just naturally fit together. She just responds to the music. The Warner Sisters used to wear taps when they performed, but this was often frowned upon in Inverness County and today both Melody and Kelly wear shoes without taps when they dance. Melody believes the wearing of taps was never part of the tradition on the west side of the island.

Since marrying Derrick Cameron, Melody has made her home in West Mabou, on the property of the farm where Derrick grew up. They are strongly involved with the local music and dance scene. It

Figure 9.12 (below) – Melody and her sister Kelly and her daughters at Broad Cove. Fiddler is Andrea Beaton (n.d.). Photo by D. Cameron.

is worth noting that Melody is also a very accomplished fiddler in the local style. They focus their efforts on keeping the local traditions alive, as the current out-migration from Cape Breton and the changing priorities in people's lives mean that less music and dance is transmitted in the home environment. Melody is in great demand as a step-dance teacher in her own right, and as a duo Derrick and Melody perform together, particularly during the summer months, all over Cape Breton and beyond. Since 2004 they have been involved with the local Comunn Fèis Mhàbu,[8] a project that aims to support local adults and children in helping them access their Cape Breton Gaelic culture, and participants come from all over Cape Breton and beyond. One successful initiative has been the Mabou Musical Mentorship Program. Since 2005,

> this mentoring program's focus [has been] on using house sessions to bring together talented young performers of Cape Breton music and dance and well established tradition bearers. The relaxed, informal atmosphere of the house sessions is well suited for the passing on of music, dance, and stories.[9] (Cameron and Cameron 2011)

Derrick and Melody host these sessions in their West Mabou home, and it is not just the informal aspect of the occasion that is of importance, but the integrated nature of the music, dance and associated stories as passed on from local tradition bearers to the younger generation. Many of these youngsters would otherwise not be exposed, in the current more formal learning environments, to the totality of this particular form of cultural transmission (Cameron 2007).

Joël Chiasson, Sydney and Chéticamp
Piano player and step dancer

Joël was born in 1973 and grew up in Chéticamp, Inverness County. His family was musical but neither of his parents played an instrument, and so he did not experience fiddle music or dancing in the home. Joël and his younger sister learned to dance and Joël took an interest in music, too. Today, Joël is not only a highly respected step dancer but also a piano player in great demand. His playing has been strongly influenced by the masterful playing of Hilda Chiasson, Maybelle Chisholm-MacQueen and John Morris Rankin. Joël toured with

Ashley MacIsaac and the Kitchen Devils for five years, and later with Natalie MacMaster's band, in which he both played the piano and step danced. He has taught workshops in step dancing through the United States and Canada. He continues to perform, playing at concerts and square dances around Cape Breton. Joël is currently working as an educator at Étoile de l'Acadie, the French-language school in Sydney.

The first impression that caused the spark that made him dance occurred when he, aged twelve, went to a social event in the local parish hall. It was a variety show and it included fiddling and step dancing. The dancer that night was Lucienne Lefort from Chéticamp. At the time, Mary Janet MacDonald was teaching local classes in step dancing, but she did not teach young children at the time, and so Joël did a beginners class with one of Mary Janet's former dance students, the late James Cormier, where he learned the basic steps.

Because he was sixteen years old and had his driver's licence, he was able to go further afield to seek out dance and music venues, as Chéticamp had none of that to offer at the time. The Normaway Inn in the Margaree Valley was popular, as was Alice Freeman's Thursday night youth sessions in Inverness Town. In that environment Joël came to meet and learn his music and dance skills from Wendy MacIsaac, Rodney MacDonald, Natalie MacMaster and Ashley MacIsaac, to

Figure 9.13 – Joël Chaisson step dancing to Nuallan during Kitchenfest (2014) at Colaisde na Gàidhlig. Photo by Darcy Campbell, Nova Stream.

name but a few. In such an informal context one watched, listened and learned. Having gotten to know the others better, Joël started informally "trading" steps with them. For example, he recalls jovial step exchanges with Natasha Roland from Alder Point. Thus, the style of his peers became highly influential on his own style. He went to the square dances at West Mabou or Glencoe, but, being an outsider to the area, he did not share the common cultural heritage and family ties expressed by this dancing and music community. At the time, he simply "got a kick out of the dancing" (Chiasson 2009). In a way, Joël's place in contemporary Cape Breton culture reflects one of a dual identity. He is very proud of being Acadian, but his dancing does not express his Acadian identity or heritage. His dancing is purely an expression of his enjoyment of the movement style and his passion for dancing and everything that goes with it—the social and the musical. Joël sees himself as an Acadian who dances in a traditional Cape Breton step-dancing style. He feels it is the dancing that transcends everything he does, especially musically. He has noticed "some rhythms creeping up through his hands from the rhythm of a step" while playing piano (Chiasson 2009). Today he has come to appreciate and respect the deep connection his peers have with the music and dance, but he is also grateful that the Gaels communities accepted him, allowing him to take part and interact with them.

Joël started playing the piano before he started step dancing. He did some ten years of formal classical piano training in Chéticamp, but when he "discovered" traditional music this changed. He wanted to accompany fiddle music, but he could not find anyone playing or teaching this particular style in Chéticamp, and so there was no way for him to learn locally as a teenager. Joël explains how he used a few tools to enable him to learn by himself. He watched the weekly TV show *Up Home Tonight*, watching for the episodes that featured Cape Breton musicians in the mix of Nova Scotian, New Brunswick and Prince Edward Island performers.[10] As he would record the show, he could study the few seconds of Hilda (Cormier) Chiasson playing a chord transition, and then work with that until he got another snippet of information a week or two later. He says that he learned to accompany dancers by getting the pieces of the jigsaw one at a time. He had never been able to sit down next to a piano player, watch and just pick up.

Initially, when listening to the music he found it hard to break down what was going on—it made no sense to him. After ten years of classical training he was dependent on sheet music. He felt he was learning a completely new instrument and he had to deconstruct his former learning. It was very challenging, but he didn't think of it along those lines. He had a few cassette tapes, to which he played along at maximum volume. An uncle played the fiddle a little, and so, with his limited repertoire, Joël's accompaniment improved. The biggest challenge was learning the huge repertoire of local tunes, Joël states. Fiddlers like Rodney MacDonald kept asking him to accompany them, which helped greatly when he was first learning. The significance of Joël's and his peers' learning experience is that they learned by using their senses subconsciously, using visual, aural and kinaesthetic transmission modes. In addition, this transmission took place over a fairly long time and through a process of interaction with peers, where high standards of competence were aspired to and deeply understood.

Mac Morin, Troy
Step dancer and piano player

Music was a permanent fixture in Mac's household as he grew up. He remembers the fiddle and guitar playing of his father and brothers, and the piano playing of his mother, Mary Catherine (MacDonald) Morin. She was a noted step dancer, and her father, John R. ("Roddie Eddie") MacDonald, was a well-known step dancer/fiddler in his day. Mary was the first one to expose Mac to Cape Breton step dancing and later encouraged him to take a few sessions from Melody Cameron and Kelly MacLennan (the Warner Sisters).

Mac began playing piano with a year of classical lessons from Imelda Fougere (Port Hawkesbury) when he was six, but, because Imelda's husband fell ill, she was unable to continue with her students. It was not until years later, before his seventeenth birthday, that Mac took up the piano again, prompted by Tracey Dares, whom he had met while attending the Gaelic College for Gaelic language. There, fortunate to be surrounded by so many talented musicians, Mac was able to watch and learn, accompanying them for occasional sets at house parties. According to Mac's own website, "his first, real, 'public' gig was at a wedding where Buddy MacMaster was playing. Buddy's piano player couldn't make it, and Buddy convinced a very shy Mac to jump on the piano" (Morin 2011).

Mac has toured with many musicians over the years, including Natalie MacMaster (1999-2001, 2006-present), the Rankin Family, and with various local fiddlers, including Howie MacDonald and Ian MacDougall. He is still a member of the Cape Breton band Beòlach, formed in 1998. A self-titled album was released in 2003, and he can be heard on a number of recordings released by other local musicians. He is also a sought-after step-dancing teacher, both locally and internationally. He has travelled across North America, the United Kingdom and Ireland teaching the Cape Breton genre.

Mac's mother seems to have had the biggest impact on his opinions and attitudes toward the Cape Breton style of dancing. He would be the first to say that the way he thinks about the style and the way he approaches the motifs (steps) have been shaped by his mother—never overtly, but subtly. Mary's own father, Roddie Eddie, a great dancer himself, helped Mary along with pointers and encouragement in her youth. Mary would watch people at dances, and then later recall the steps from memory at home, using the TV screen as a mirror (a story Mac remembers her telling him). Her father was no longer able to dance or play the fiddle due to a Second World War injury that left him partially paralyzed. Mac remembers his mother telling him that his grandfather used to walk home from the dances barefoot, preserving his only pair of shoes. Roddie Eddie is still remembered as a great dancer from his younger years. Mac tells this story about being compared to his grandfather:

> I remember dancing in a concert in Glendale one summer and someone came up to me after I was finished to let me know "you've got your grandfather's forehead when you dance." Now, I know it was a compliment ... even though it's a little strange when someone is comparing your forehead to your grandfather's when you are dancing ... it's a little odd. They aren't exactly in close proximity on the body ... but I know what they meant and understood the sentiment. So I took it as a compliment. (Morin 2008)

Mac remembers his mother dancing around the house and kitchen whenever fiddle music would come on the radio or if his father was playing a tune. She would show Mac and his brothers the basic movements; they were all quite shy, but she wasn't deterred and continued to coach and encourage. Eventually Mac became interested, and after

Figure 9.14 – Mac Morin, flanked by fellow step dancers Mairi Rankin and Wendy MacIsaac, performing with Beòlach (Ryan J. MacNeil and Patrick Gillis) in Pennsylvania, September 24, 2006. Photo by Victor Maurice Faubert.

getting a few basic steps from Mary (once she convinced him), went to the Warner Sisters. Melody and Kelly alternated teaching in six-week sessions, and so Mac was able to get instruction from both sisters during the two sessions he attended. Mac recalls that his mother never used the same terms that the Warners used, but had a different way of explaining the steps:

> She would describe the shuffles as "a long" and the hops as "a short," so that we were doing the movements before they were described as shuffles and hops. I can still hear her saying, "Long, short, short," over and over. It worked and I know my brother David is teaching his kids the same way! But there was always encouragement.... Mom just had a way about her.... I never felt like I wasn't gonna be able to do it.... I just knew because she knew. (Morin 2008)

After the two sessions with the Warner Sisters, Mac started to learn by watching others:

> Then I was able to recognize things on my own. I now had more

confidence.... I knew how to do what I wanted to do with my feet to make the sounds I was hearing. Whenever I'd come home after seeing a step or after making a step, Mom was the first person I'd show. And then she'd either okay it, or "no, I don't think" ... and then I'd ask her why and she'd ... well, sometimes she'd have an answer and sometimes she wouldn't [be] ... specific. She would never say, "Your foot is doing this and I don't like that." It was more of a generalism [sic]. (Morin 2008)

Mac would frequently dance a sequence of steps to music and include any new steps he had learned, and wait for his mother to comment. He feels his mother's opinion of what makes a good dancer or how good steps should be danced greatly influenced his own opinions and style. Mac feels the steps and the music are intertwined and they influence both musicians and dancers and the music and dance genre of Cape Breton. He says the music almost always inspires him in his choice of steps while dancing, making a new step, or creating a performance routine. The steps can't be based on their internal rhythm alone, as they have to fit somewhere.

Mac has a great respect for many dancers on the island and appreciates all the individual styles there are under the umbrella of the Cape Breton dance style. He respects and admires the Warner Sisters (as they taught him directly), Mary Janet MacDonald, Harvey Beaton, Joël Chiasson, Harvey MacKinnon and two of his fellow Beòlach band members Wendy MacIsaac and Mairi Rankin. He confesses that he wishes he could spend more time with the dancers he does not get a chance to interact with on a regular basis.

Mac will admit concerns regarding the changing nature of the Cape Breton step-dance genre. In his view, there seems to be a watering down of the fundamental movements and characteristics of the style, a kind of blurring of unspoken boundaries by some. They do not take on board, as it is sometimes perceived, all the characteristics of the Cape Breton step-dancing tradition. He reflects:

The thing with Cape Breton step dancing is there is no accreditation process, no standards that are set and required for the style. Not that that is the answer.... I think the fact [that] there aren't any of those requirements really sets this style apart from other styles. It has always been more relaxed, more social. That in itself is part of the style—what makes it unique. But standards help in other ways.... For instance, Irish dancing... For Irish dancing, it has to be a certain way, a certain movement only and if it isn't, then it's not really Irish dancing, but some other form or hybrid. Or at least with standards, people are required to perform at a certain level to be thought of as an Irish dancer.... We don't have more rigid standards in Cape Breton music or dancing, other than people's opinions.... Now ... people from here will have a spot-on opinion of what's right and real.... They may not always say it out loud, but they know.... Maybe that's because they've lived it, or lived here for so long, surrounded by it. I'm just more concerned about those that may not have the same resources and background to draw from; that there are those who don't truly understand—and that don't care to *try* to understand.... That's where I get concerned about the style. That it will be changed by some who don't understand they may be changing it ... and be taught to others who take it as authentic and then change it again... without knowing where it has really come from.... "I just learned this form of dance and these steps," but this individual doesn't have any frame of reference as to what they should truly look like or sound like.... It's like a dance without an origin. That's my concern. (Morin 2008)

Mac's comments illustrate thoughts on, and often complex feelings about, the natural processes involved in a constantly evolving dance style.

Brandi McCarthy, Port Hawkesbury
Step dancer and fiddler

Brandi McCarthy was born in 1987 in Ontario but raised in Port Hawkesbury, Inverness County, from the age of four. Her father came from Cape Breton while her mother was from Ontario. Brandi was not brought up in a household full of live music, though she did hear tapes of the Rankin Family, Natalie MacMaster and Ashley MacIsaac. She says that these recordings made her want to start learning how to dance and play the fiddle. Brandi started in a creative (modern) and ballet dance class at the age of five. Sally Clark came up from Antigonish to run this weekly class in Port Hawkesbury. Observing step dancers perform in a dance recital when she was about six, Brandi got enthused and quickly switched to step-dance classes. She went on to take a series of lessons from Mary Janet MacDonald. From then on she joined various workshops, taught by various teachers, including Sabra MacGillivray and those teaching at the Gaelic College in St. Ann's—Betty Matheson, Jean MacNeil and Cheryl MacQuarrie. She would go down to the annual Chestico Days dance festival at Port Hood. When she was old enough to attend, she would regularly go to square dances.

At age nine she started to play the fiddle and took lessons in that as well. John Donald Cameron (Port Hawkesbury) was her first tutor for about a year, and then she had Dawn Beaton from Mabou, who came down weekly (together with Mary Janet MacDonald) to teach. Then followed many other teachers at workshops around Cape Breton and at the Gaelic College, including Andrea Beaton, Eddie Rogers, Sandy MacIntyre, Glenn Graham, Troy MacGillivray, Stan Chapman and Buddy MacMaster. According to Brandi, the Gaelic College is an excellent place to interact with peers and the sense of community it creates is what motivates one to practise and learn further steps and tunes.

Acquiring the particular "Cape Breton sound," with its characteristic swing and drive, is fundamentally important to Brandi. Once one has the core material and that embedded sound right, it is all right to add newer material. Tunes from other traditions and locally composed tunes all add to the repertoire. Brandi feels that the Gaelic sound, often discussed in reference to its relevance to the Cape Breton sound, is now embedded and mimicked in the music itself. One does not need to have the language to play in the style; one can pick it up by listening to local players and old

Figure 9.15 – Brandi McCarthy, Glencoe Mills, August 1, 2008. Photo by Victor Maurice Faubert.

recordings. In Brandi's mind, music, song and dance are all linked. She likes to step dance to *puirt-a-beul*, as sung by Mary Jane Lamond, Colin Watson and Jeff MacDonald, as this type of song provides particularly good rhythm to step dance to.

As mentioned above, female dancers have primarily taught Brandi, but she did a few workshops with Harvey Beaton, and has watched YouTube clips of various male dancers. She likes Ashley MacIsaac's style, step repertoire and stamina in the clips from when he was young. Brandi says that her favourite dancer stylistically is probably Rodney MacDonald. She likes dancing in strathspey time and favours putting in as many beats as is comfortable in her steps. Brandi also engages in Irish solo dancing, and has spent time learning this style both in Cape Breton and Ireland.

Anita MacDonald, Little Narrows
Step dancer, fiddler and piano player

Anita was born in 1991 in Little Narrows, Victoria County. Her family is musical, and she was brought up surrounded by Cape Breton music, both played live and on many records and tapes at home. She says it is "her blood." Her background is a mix of English and Scottish. Her grandmother's people, for example, came from the Isle of Barra and settled at Christmas Island. She says the music came from her grandfather's side; his father was from England and his mother had Scottish and Italian roots. Her grandfather plays a bit of fiddle, plays a bit of guitar and sings, while her mother is similarly gifted and dances as well. She started step dancing at age four and initially learned from her mother at home.

Her grandfather was also an influence on her dancing. She never saw him dance, but he gave her constructive advice, like how to hold herself, and verbally taught her steps. He used terms such as "close to the floor" and "hop step." He diddled, or jigged, and showed her steps by making reference to what she should do. He moved his body to indicate what he wanted and then when she successfully performed the step he would say so. She would watch herself in front of the dishwasher to see her own reflection. For a while, she had a specific routine that she kept repeating in order to get used to moving from one step to the next. One strathspey, followed by a number of reels, was her usual routine, even though she now improvises the order of movements according to what the music dictates. As a teenager she took dance classes from both Jean MacNeil and Bonnie Jean MacDonald-Cutliffe. She is still involved in the many events, activities and workshops that take place in Cape Breton.

Anita did not grow up in a Gaelic-speaking environment, but was aware of the language through, for example, her paternal grandfather, who sang in Gaelic, and her great-grandmother, who spoke it. Anita took up the fiddle at age eight and was initially influenced by her grandfather, Charlie Ellis, and her great-uncle, Raymond Ellis. She then learned from Kyle Gillis, Jerry Holland and Kimberley Fraser. Other fiddle influences include Sandy MacInnes and Andrea Beaton, and on the piano she admires Allan Dewar and Susan MacLean.

Anita feels step dancing is the basis for her musicality, as it is the first thing she learned. She personally likes that it is close to the floor. The style is very relaxed and allows her to express herself. When she was learning, she was told to pick a spot on the wall and focus on it. It is precisely the relaxed way in which Jean MacNeil and Bonnie-Jean MacDonald-Cutliffe dance that she admires. She feels the steps they both do are very traditional, which is what she wants her own style to be. She dislikes lateral movement or the motion of flicking, or kicking, her legs up and forward and back. She prefers medium-length steps rather than stringing long sequences of movement together on the one leg before repeating on the other leg. Her grandfather's style was very traditional, but it involved a lot of complicated movements. However, the movements were strung together done in a relaxed flowing manner and were not "too flashy" according to Anita (2009). One current dancer she admires is Harvey Beaton. Harvey's steps are well balanced, just like her grandfather's.

Playing the fiddle and knowing the tune repertoire works greatly to her advantage, Anita says. It creates a larger repertoire in her head, and she knows what is coming next, making it easier to find steps that fit the tune well. Anita feels the music suggests steps to her, but it works on a subconscious level: "It just happens; it's automatic." She refers to the music as "dirty" or "gritty," and says that it has a particular swing and requires drive in the bow action, citing "King George" as a tune that has inherent drive. Music and dance go together, and if you lose the dancing tradition you also lose part of your music, she says. A deep local cultural knowledge is vital for creating the right feel for the music and dance to thrive symbiotically.

When a dancer gets up it gives the fiddle player and the dancer a chance to feed off each other. The fiddler may start out very strong, but with the added dancing, it will end up with much more drive, as you are going to feed off that energy. It is more powerful. It is a feeling, not a visual thing.... You can almost touch that connection at times. (A. MacDonald 2009)

Anita does not feel that there is such a thing as gendered steps but that there is a personal preference in how the dancing is presented. Men and women hold themselves differently, in Anita's opinion. She refers in particular to the older men who grew up dancing. According to her, they are extremely relaxed and their movements very loose from the knees down. Anita's goal is to imitate the style of these older men, like her grandfather and Harvey Beaton. The main difference between women and men, she believes, is that the men are more relaxed when they dance. She is always observing dancers, at concerts and square dances, to see what she can "pick up," and she watches all dancers, not just those who dance solo.

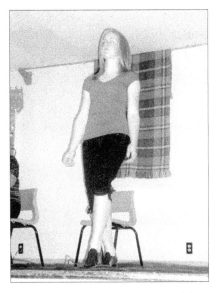

Figure 9.16 – Anita MacDonald at Mabou Parish Hall. Photo by Victor Maurice Faubert.

Anita wore shoes with taps for dancing when I interviewed her in 2009, but she said the only reason she used them was because she could not find a pair of good hard-soled leather shoes. She is currently passing on both her fiddle and dance skills to her two younger sisters. In the end, Anita concludes, it is all about having fun while continuing to preserve what the community knows as being their heritage.[11]

Jean MacNeil, Washabuck and Sydney Mines
Step dancer, teacher and pianist
Jean (MacKenzie) MacNeil is originally from Washabuck, Victoria

County, and comes from a very musical home. Growing up in a family of twelve children, seven sisters and five brothers, all were "able to produce fine Scottish music on a variety of instruments"

Figure 9.17 – Jean MacNeil step dancing at a house session. Kyle V. MacNeil.

according to brother Carl MacKenzie (MacGillivray 1997: 132). The most notable fiddlers in the family were Jean's brothers Carl and Hector, both with commercial recordings to their name. According to Jean's daughter Lucy, the eldest brother, Charlie, had a "tremendous singing voice and also played the fiddle" and brother Simon played the fiddle too (L. MacNeil 2014). The MacKenzie siblings learned music and dance in the many household and community gatherings of the area. There were about a dozen one-room schoolhouses in the Washabuck area and each one would have a dance, and then there were house parties and weddings, according to brother Hector MacKenzie (born 1933) (MacGillivray 1997: 134).

After marrying Columba MacNeil, Jean moved to Sydney Mines, where they raised six children. In 2011, the couple and their children, who make up the internationally acclaimed Barra MacNeils, celebrated more than twenty years in an outstanding recording and performing career. Jean learned her step dancing and music at home by watching her older siblings and visitors to the house. She cannot consciously remember learning the hop step, but feels she picked it up at home. There were many good dancers and musicians in the Washabuck and Iona area when she grew up. One visitor, Hector MacKinnon from Cain's Mountain, she recalls as a "great dancer with nifty feet." He did a lot of steps on his toes and with great ankle movement (J. MacNeil 2007). Travelling to picnics and concerts influenced her too. She recalls Willie Fraser and Angus MacIsaac dancing at Broad Cove when she was about seventeen or eighteen. Dancers like Bernie Campbell and his brother used to show her steps at the Highland Village, in Iona. When she moved to Sydney Mines, she interacted with fiddlers Robert and Lauchie Stubbert and Winston Fitzgerald, and she used to step dance to them at the house parties (J. MacNeil 2007).

When Fr. Eugene Morris set up dance classes in the Sydney area he encouraged Jean to start teaching. She was at first reluctant but eventually taught in Big Pond, North Sydney, Bras d'Or, Whycocomagh, Washabuck and, of course, at home in Sydney Mines. She has also taught annually at the Gaelic College in St. Ann's for many years. Some of her students are admired as good dancers, such as Natasha Roland, Jennifer Roland, Bonnie Jean MacDonald, Kimberley Fraser and Leanne Aucoin. She taught all her multi-instrumentalist children to dance, even though the two older boys do not dance much. Step dancing is, however, fully integrated in the Barra MacNeils' performances. Jean has made an instructional step-dancing video, *Spring in your Step* (2005).

Margaret (MacEachern) Dunn, Queensville

Step dancer

Margaret grew up in a musical household: her father, John Willie MacEachern, was a fiddler, her aunts danced, and her uncles played the fiddle. Uncles Dan Hughie MacEachern (a well-known composer of fiddle tunes), and Alex MacEachern, who lived in New York and who played the fiddle for dances in the United States, are noteworthy. There were always square sets and solo dancing around when Margaret grew up—"It [the dancing and the music] was with me as I was growing up" (Dunn 2007). Margaret learned her first step from her grandfather John MacMaster. Her father and her father's sisters also helped her. They had a fairly limited repertoire of steps, but it was enough to get her started. She learned more steps from watching others. She first danced in public at the age of four at a dance in Creignish, where her father, John Willie, and uncle Dan were playing: "Someone put me up on stage to dance and people started throwing change at my feet. An elderly lady, Charlotte Cameron from Creignish, gave me a dollar all folded in a small square. My fortune was made!" (Dunn 2012).

Harvey Beaton's mother, Marie MacDonald Beaton, was her grade 4 teacher when she came to teach in Queensville and stayed with Margaret's family.

We would dance in the evenings after the homework was done when my father would get out his fiddle. This was a golden opportunity for me to learn new steps. Because my father was a fiddler, we always had lots of company and I got to see other people dance as well. After learning the basic steps it was easier to learn from people by watching. My father was able to see if I didn't have steps quite right and would tell me so. (Dunn 2012)

Margaret's father took her to local concerts, where she would pick up more steps by watching others dance. Her father often played for the dancing, and at a very early age she was asked to dance on stage herself. She feels her own style of dancing came predominantly from her father; her mother did not dance.

Figure 9.18 – Margaret Dunn, Concert Under the Stars, Antigonish Highland Games, 1971. Photo by M. Dunn, used with kind permission.

She did the concert circuit with her father to Creignish, Judique, Port Hawkesbury, Johnstown, St. Peter's, Port Hastings, Mulgrave and elsewhere. Those concerts were structured along the same lines as many are presently: piping, fiddling, dancing and Gaelic singing, or perhaps a milling frolic, a Scotch Four, and the third figure of the Square Set. At the time when Margaret was thirteen or fourteen years old, there were not as many dancers on the circuit as there were in later years. She was exposed to Gaelic, although the language was dying out. She was aware of it from the older generations around her, family and neighbours, and she picked up some.

Later, she was encouraged to start teaching step dancing alongside Angus Alex MacDonnell (later Fr. Angus) by Judge Hughie MacPherson, from St. Andrews. Margaret and Angus taught two classes per night, two nights a week, one at the legion in Antigonish and one at the school in St. Andrews. They started with about ninety students, and when Angus left for seminary, Margaret carried on teaching. Margaret remembers how Buddy MacMaster kindly recorded suitable tunes of different speeds onto a cassette for her to use in these classes. Like so many others of this generation of new teachers,

Margaret had to work out for herself how to break steps down and how best to pass them on to others. She says it was "like teaching yourself before teaching anyone else. What is it I am doing? What have I been doing for the past thirty years just as naturally as drinking water? You have to understand it yourself first before passing it on" (Dunn 2007). Margaret now lives just outside Antigonish. Her daughter Jackie is a well-known fiddler, piano player and step dancer. Jackie works as an educator in Antigonish County.

Betty (MacIvor) Matheson, Dominion

Step dancer

Betty grew up spending the summer months on the shore of the Bras d'Or Lake in Malagawatch, Inverness County, her mother's home area. There, she experienced the square dances at Marble Mountain, and her aunts and uncles came to the Gaelic *mòd* (festival), where they danced and enjoyed the music. One of her uncles was a prompter for the square sets. She recalls that step dancing was not common in the square sets in those days, and solo dancing was a very informal affair of impromptu dancing, rather than dancing on the concert stage. As an only child, her parents' love for dance music had a big influence on her. Betty's dancing experience started, however, with classes in tap, ballet and jazz in Dominion (Cape Breton County) when she was quite young. Later in life, in the early 1970s, she lived with her husband in the Boston area and was there exposed to the Irish music scene and to Cape Breton step dancing and music. She did not formally engage in Cape Breton–style step dancing until she returned home to Dominion around the time her husband passed away. She was then encouraged to join Fr. Eugene Morris's step dance classes in Sydney, alongside Margaret Gillis (North Sydney) and many others.

A lot of her learning over the years came from informally sharing steps with other dancers, such as Jean MacNeil, Harvey Beaton, Joe Rankin and many more. She has taught at St. Ann's Gaelic College in the summers for many years, in addition to her regular classes in the Sydney area. She is also a driving force in the Cape Breton Fiddlers' Association and helps encourage many of the young fiddlers of that association to step dance. To Betty, timing and a deep knowledge of the tunes are paramount to being a good dancer and more important than having lots of steps. A few steps well danced score higher than many mediocre steps, as does music played at a good, moderate speed. Betty herself never danced a set routine but went where the music took her and states that one of her favourite fiddlers over the years was the late Donald Angus Beaton.

Fr. Eugene Morris
Step dancer

Fr. Eugene Morris is originally from Colindale, but has, since 2008, been practising in Bishop Falls, Newfoundland. Fr. Eugene and his brother, fiddler Fr. Angus Morris are both highly respected as skilled and enthusiastic exponents of the dance and music tradition. Fr. Eugene only started solo dancing when he was nearly thirty years old, before which he had danced the square sets. While growing up, Angus often played the fiddle at local house parties, and Fr. Eugene danced a few steps. In time he felt he should increase his repertoire of steps and began to watch other dancers. He began teaching step dancing in the early 1970s, but having never taught formally before, he had

Figure 9.19 – Betty Matheson and Fr. Eugene Morris dancing at the Gaelic College, St. Ann's with the Cape Breton Fiddlers' Association, August 17, 2008. Photo by V. M. Faubert.

to figure out how to break down the steps into smaller components (step, hop, shuffle and so forth). He also had to figure out how to best count the steps. He ran a number of classes in the Sydney area and encouraged many other dancers to start teaching step dancing over the years. His appearance at concerts and other events is always popular with the local community. In fact, his mere presence at events these days encourages the local dancers and fiddlers, according to Andrea Beaton (March 2011).

Structural Analysis of Cape Breton Step Dance and Some Examples of Motifs

In chapter 6, I mentioned that a way to analyze the "form" of Cape Breton step dance was to establish its *structure*, the different combinations of the little movements that are combined emically in a way that is understood by the Cape Breton community, and *style*, which is the particular way those movements are performed. I will here briefly outline the structural levels that are relevant to this book.

Structural Levels

I base my outline of the structural levels on those set out by the International Council for Traditional Music (ICTM) Study Group (Giurchescu and Kröschlová 2007: 25), and as applied by ethnochoreologists such as Foley (1988, 2007, 2013) when analyzing North Kerry–style Irish step dancing, on the following vertical segmentation (decomposition) as relevant to Cape Breton step dance.

Starting with the top level: the **dance** can be divided into **parts**, which are subdivided into **phrases**, which in turn break down into **motifs**. Motifs are broken into **motif-cells**, which in turn consist of **motif-elements**. On the motif-element level, Kaeppler's term "**allo-kine**," which in terms of the emic notion of "variation of the same" but not considered as different, is also useful in relation to this dance style.

The technical description of the form-units, as outlined below, should be seen as etic (outsider) categories. In many cases, the dance community would refer to a motif or a phrase as a "step"—as an emic category. However, in some cases the etic category of motif will not correspond to the emic perception of a step, even though there is often a natural crossover between the two terms in this context. According to Giurchescu and Kröschlová (2007: 28), **motifs** are:

> "culturally grammatical sequences of movements made up of smaller structural units": Motif-cells and Motif-elements [and]

a motif is the smallest significant Form-unit having meaning for both the dancers and their society and for the dance genre/type within a given dance system. At this level, the Motif-elements are rhythmically, plastically and dynamically integrated, resulting in a choreographic pattern that may evoke in both the performer and observer a feeling of stability. It is the carrier of a choreographic idea on which higher structural levels and finally the entire dance are founded. Motifs may be repeated, modified or combined with other structural units.... Motifs are stored in the dancer's mental and kinaesthetic memory as part of his creative competence. When new variants are created, especially in the process of improvisation, the dancer relates spontaneously to pre-existent motif-models stored in his mental and kinaesthetic memory according to his dance competence. The Motif carries sufficient information about a dance idiom that its simple repetition may result in a virtual dance, recognized by people as belonging to their own tradition.

Form Units

All form-units relevant to Cape Breton step dance are described in detail by Giurchescu and Kröschlová (2007: 28-31) in their revised version of the ICTM Study Group's *Theory and Method of Dance Form Analysis*. The most significant aspects of each form-unit are (starting with the smallest components):

> **Motif-elements** – (e.g., a step, a hop or a kick) carry no meaning in themselves and form the smallest structural entity consisting of one or more "movement-impulses perceived as realized simultaneously in one-beat" (2007: 29). Even though it may be a combination of one or several kinetic elements, performed simultaneously, it cannot be further divisible into distinct units. Motif-elements carry out rhythmic and dynamic functions. Motif-elements function is only realized when combined with other motif-elements in order to build larger structural units. Only within a motif-cell, or another higher unit level, do motif-elements acquire choreographic meaning.
>
> **Allokines** – Kaeppler's term allokine, signifying a motif-element with an actual physiological difference but which is not considered different from an emic point of view, is of relevance in the

Cape Breton context. Some individuals seem to consider a hop, tap or step (named etic motif-elements) to be the same, regardless of where they are placed.

Motif-cells – (e.g., shuffle or step-shuffle) are comprised of a minimum of two, more often three, motif-elements (including pauses), which are organized rhythmically, plastically and dynamically. One strong accent is generally the focus of a motif-cell. For the most part, the motif-cell has no independent function. It must be combined with other elements or cells to form a motif. However, one-cell motifs exist where it is structurally a cell but functions as a motif (e.g., shuffle).

Motifs (e.g., backstep or the hop step) carry meaning, as outlined above, and are a combination of motif-cells and motif-elements that recur in one or several dance performances in a dance genre. They range from one-cell motifs (one-segment) to multi-cell motifs (multi-segment). The majority of Cape Breton motifs are heterogeneous multi-cell motifs. Some motifs are labelled from an emic standpoint as a step. In the Cape Breton tradition, however, very few steps have a specific name attached to them. Certain individual movement combinations are often associated with a person as a signature or characteristic step they perform/ed.

Phrases are the simplest compositional form units, identified instantly by the people of the dance tradition. A phrase is composed of a summation of motifs. In the Cape Breton tradition, certain repeat patterns of motifs create a phrase that stands at a "qualitative[ly] higher level and [give it] a well defined individuality, carrying more information on the dance Form and aesthetics" (Giurchescu and Kröschlová 2007: 30). Similarly in Cape Breton step dance, combinations of motifs forming one-bar, three-bar, four-bar and (rarely) eight-bar phrases are commonly repeated evenly on both sides. In vernacular terminology (emic), a phrase of any length would be labelled a step or a combination of steps, if referred to as anything at all.

Parts – in Cape Breton solo step dance, two tempos are generally used, strathspey and reel, and if both are danced, each tempo would form a part.

Dance – the summation, or totality, of all the "integrated structural units with their particular compositional patterns and functional interrelationships" (Giurchescu and Kröschlová 2007: 31). A supposed close relationship between the form-units and the musical structures could be investigated and analyzed by conducting this breakdown. By looking at the dance sequence as a whole, we can determine how its individuality (structure, artistic expression and so forth) can be distinguished from other dance genres (ibid).

Provided below is a modified version of Kaeppler's (2007: 53-54) comparative chart, outlining the terminology used by the International Council for Traditional Music Study Group and in linguistic theory showing the above relevant structural levels where they are analogous with Cape Breton step dance.

Language	"A dance" (ICTM)	Cape Breton step dance
Linguistic theory.	Movement theory realized in practice.	Movement realized in practice.
Phonemes	**Motif-elements**	**A step, a hop, a stamp, etc.**; have no meaning in themselves; basic units of this dance system [language].
Significant sounds of a language; have no meaning in themselves; basic units of a language.	Distinctive movements of a human movement system [language]; have no meaning in themselves; basic units of a human movement system [language].	
Morphemes	**Motif-cells**	**A shuffle, a step-kick-hop** Significant part of emic/insider notion of a step. Combined they form:
Smallest unit that has meaning in the structure of a language. Put together according to grammar to form throughout:	Distinctive units that have no independent meaning of function. (Apart from **one-cell-motifs,** which may have meaning.) Put together according to grammar to form:	

Words
Vocabulary of a language. Put together according to syntax to form a language clause, which in turn are put together to form:

Motifs
The smallest significant form-unit, having meaning for the dancers and the dance system. Put together through repetition, variation, or grouping to form:

A step
The hop step, a backstep, a jig-time shuffle. Named steps. Any significant combination of the above movements that form a meaningful step.

Sentences
Often two culturally grammatical phrases; for example, subject and predicate.

Phrases
Often two culturally grammatical groupings of motifs. The simplest compositional unit having sense for the people and which dance types are identified. Put together according to linking or grouping principles to form:

Phrases
Grouping and linking steps together.

Larger grammatical units
Such as paragraphs, chapters, etc.

Macro-structures
Culturally structural parts, such as parts put together to form:

Strathspey part
Reel part

Specific instances of spoken or literary linguistic forms
Such as a specific novel, play or speech.

Dances
Structural units are organically integrated with other patterning factors, such as music, poetry or implements. Often designated by a name.

Dances
The flow of steps performed to a string of tunes in strathspey and/or reel time, or both.

Dance Form Analysis

The central focus for dance form analysis is the motif and is thus the level at which my PhD dissertation (Melin 2012) sought to establish the core repertoire of Cape Breton step dance motifs. The few examples below were used in chapter 6 to describe the style as well as provide examples of core motifs, and they are given in Newcastle notation as well as in Labanotation (explanations for each system are available online). Note that Newcastle notation is read from the top down, while Labanotation is read from the bottom upward.

Newcastle Notation

Reel 1 – Backstep

Usually performed in combination with other backsteps or motifs.

Count	LF	RF	Modifiers		
1	step		A	:	
and		) shuffle HT		:	C, C
2		)		:	
and	hop		B	:	

Reel 2 – Toe and Toe

Described as when part of a longer motif.

Count	LF	RF	Modifiers		
1	step		A	:	
and		step		:	C
2	step		B*	:	
and		step		:	C

Reel 2 and 1 combined Toe and Toe and Backstep

Note that some dancers prefer to start with the backstep motif, followed by the toe-and-toe motif.

Count	LF	RF	Modifiers		
1	step		A	:	
and		step		:	C
2	step		B*	:	
and		step		:	C
3	step		A	:	
and		) shuffle HT		:	C, C
4		)		:	
and	hop		B	:	

Reel 3 – Hop step

Count	LF	RF	Modifiers		
1	step		A	:	
and		) shuffle HT		:	C, C
2		)		:	
and	hop		A	:	
3		tap		A	
4		tap		A	

Reel 4 – Hop-step variation

Count	LF	RF	Modifiers		
1	step		A	:	
and		) shuffle HT		:	C, C
2		)		:	
and	hop		A	:	
3		tap		A	
and	hop		A	
4		tap		A	

Strathspey

Count	LF		RF		Modifiers		
{and	tap	) lazy			RB	:	}
1	spring)				A	:	
and			tap	) lazy		:	RB
2			spring)			:	A
and	tap	) lazy			RB	:	
3	spring)				A	:	
and			catch out			:	A↑, B, C↑
4	hop				A	:	
and			catch in			:	C↑, B, A↑

Example of emic names are "1, 2, 3, kick," "shuffle, slide, step." This motif may be used on its own, or counts "and 1 and 2 and 3," as a beginning of a longer combined motif. Different endings may be applied, typical examples given below. A motif is commonly repeated four times, R, L, R, L.

Note that many dancers, when beginning this motif, often omit the very first tap on the anacrusis, thus starting the motif with a spring on count "1." However, if the motif occurs in the flow of a routine, and the previous movement allows for the use of the "tap" on the "and" count, it is commonly used.

Labanotation:

Reel 1 – Backstep　　　　*Reel 2 – Toe and Toe*　　　　*Reel 2 and 1 combined*
　　　　　　　　　　　　　　　　　　　　　　　　　　　　　Toe and Toe and Backstep

Reel 3 – Hop step　　*Reel 4 – Hop-step variation*　　*Strathspey – "1, 2, 3, kick"*

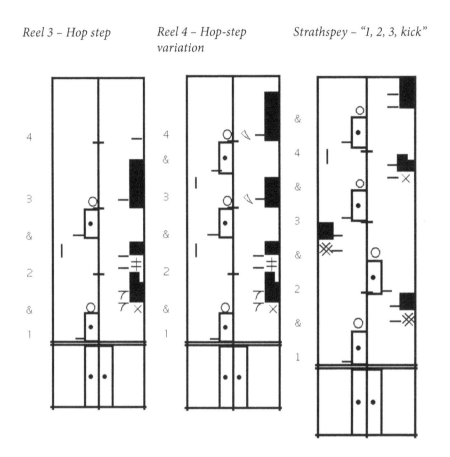

A Personal Ethnographic Reflection
on Solo Step Dancing at a Square Dance

To further illustrate the various levels of interaction between the dancer and the context where they perform, I would like to share my own experience of a dance at the hall in Brook Village. By utilizing the method of phenomenological hermeneutics as outlined by Timothy Rice (1997: 101-20)[1]—that is, studying dance, by dancing—I try to convey what goes through my mind and body when I step dance in a Cape Breton context. As is customary at most summertime square dances, there is a break after about three hours or so. The fiddler changes from jigs and reels to strathspeys and reels. The lights in the hall, which are generally dimmed for the social dancing, are brightened to allow for better viewing. The crowd rearranges so as to allow space in front of the stage for solo dancing, and the mood in the room changes to one of anticipation, even though everyone knows what is to come next. After a few bars of strathspey, the first dancer will take to the floor.

Live at the Square Dance

The dancer on the floor is finished sharing her steps with the audience. Kinnon Beaton, the fiddle player, keeps driving the reels, accompanied on the piano by his wife, Betty Lou. Who will get up next? Will anyone? Six dancers have already shared their steps with the crowd: Harvey MacKinnon, followed by an unknown female dancer with what is seen as a Sydney style, then Gerard Beaton, then one Irish dancer, Bernadette Nic Gabhann, performing in her own traditional style, then Harvey Beaton and finally Leanne Aucoin. This constitutes a fair mix of dancers from different parts of the island and beyond.

The music has been going for close to nine minutes. I am seated along the kitchen/bar side of the hall among others in attendance. Having watched these six dancers share their steps, the woman to my right encourages me: "Go on. Get up there!" So does the man on my left. A split-second reflection: I have just had local encouragement. Without it I would not get up, as I am an outsider in this community. I get up from the chair and start making my way toward the centre of the floor in front of the stage. Some people applaud the next dancer—me! Kinnon has just finished playing "High Road to Linton" and has seamlessly moved on to a version of the "St. Kilda Wedding" reel. He is coming to the end of an A phrase in the music. I can sense he has registered who is coming on to the floor. A fraction-of-a-second re-flection—he knows what type of tunes I like; will he change to any of those? The level of adrenaline in my body is rising, manifest through a nervous feeling starting in my thighs and moving upward to my stomach. Do I have a plan of what steps to do? No, not really, but I have a vague idea that a particular step will work very well to the current tune being played, but will that be the one emerging when I get into place on the floor in front of the stage?

I start dancing even before I have turned fully to face the audi-ence. The music makes me move before I have consciously decided to. Already I feel that something special is going on (for me). I have been dancing socially for about three hours at this point. I am completely warmed up and all muscles are relaxed and ready to go. All my senses are alert. I have "become one with the hall" and those around me. I straighten up. I feel the music flowing from up behind me on the stage. I can feel the adrenaline start pumping through my body thus enabling my leg muscles to give that extra bit. The level of alertness has increased gradually all through the evening and now it enables me to hear Kinnon's left foot beating out the rhythm in his characteristic way, a feature that adds to this culture's musical expression. He is creating a swing or, as the locals put it, he is really "driven'er!" My senses become more alert; I can hear every note from the piano as well, adding to the rhythm of the tune. All sounds are layered, from primary and secondary music sounds to the background noise of the crowd as they converse and laugh.

Predominantly, I hear and feel the loud music. However, I can also hear and feel my heart beating, adding to the rhythm of the moment. All scents—of the room, the heat, the dusty floor, of the attending people, of the outside air coming in through the front door—affects the performance and adds to my experience. Every decision made is decided in a fraction of a second. My leg muscles are working hard. The hips and knees feel fluid with my feet, responding to other joints' initial commands. With my mind's eye, I see Kinnon and Betty Lou playing and how they move as they do so. They do not sit still; their whole bodies work and move as they play, as I have observed on many occasions. My feet are doing their thing. I am not actively conscious that I am making any real decisions about what movements to do next, apart from occasionally when, in the middle of a tune, already in a step, a split-second flagging in my mind suggests what would be good next. This is not always what gets performed, though. The music may tell me something different. Each musician provides his or her own take or variation on a tune, which, in turn, triggers varied responses of movements that I "hear" in the music each time I dance. I do not dance many long (eight-bar) or more complex variations when sharing my steps. I stick to what I favour at that moment and I tend to do one-bar, two-bar, four-bar and occasionally three-bar combinations. I also like what I think of as older steps, which all use a lot of heel contact with the floor. Sometimes they generate a reaction from the audience in the form of applause.

The music is coming to the end of a B turn. What will come next? Kinnon is an expert in combining excellent tunes together. The first notes of the next tune ring out; it is one of my many favourite Kinnon tunes—"Judique Consolidated Grads 1991"—and it has a melody structure that I feel brings out some of the best in my dancing. The small hairs on the back of my neck stand up. That extra layer of awareness begins to kick in, as does another level of energy flow. Kinnon's speed and timing is exactly right. Not too fast, but with that fantastic drive and ability to get the timing absolutely right for the dancer, to the fraction of a second, a precision that only some of the many excellent fiddlers in the community have. Every fiddler plays a little bit differently, and even though most fiddlers in this community have the tunes and the drive, they may not necessarily always "do it for you" when you dance.

Timing, speed and mood are all part of the equation. It is very warm and humid in the hall even though it is past midnight. Two hundred or so people are there and they have all danced for about two hours, pretty much non-stop. This environment crowds you in a positive sense. In a way you feel you are part of one entity. I stop seeing the audience. I am not shutting my eyes; they just blur. It is my own being and a connection with the musicians and their music creation that exist in the first instance. I am living the moment. The music is "nourishing me," to use Melody Cameron's phrase. Time seems to slow down and I become more aware of my own being. That extra layer, the prickle of awareness, is now fully felt. I feel good all over. It is a warm, comforting feeling that comes from deep inside and spreads everywhere. Perhaps this is what Mary Janet MacDonald refers to as "a spiritual moment."

The wooden floor responds to my steps. The hall in Brook Village has a good floor; it has good give. Whether people can hear my feet is, in one respect, irrelevant as the amplified music is very loud. However, as I did with the previous dancers, and as the crowd is most likely doing with me, I sense the beats and how they are placed in relation to the music. It is more than visual or aural—it's multi-sensory. It is the feeling of experiencing or rather sensing someone else's movements and musicality. In this cocooned world of my own being interacting with the music I am not conscious of making any decisions about what movement comes next. It all flows.

Sometimes I am already executing a "good" step before I have thought of it. Why? Is it because my body or, rather, certain neurons in my brain remember and decide faster than my conscious self? Is it due to the years of learning and performing having thus embodied a substantial amount of movements that can be combined in any number of ways? Microsecond-long flashbacks flicker through my consciousness of class situations, mnemonic texts—"step, shuffle, hop, beat, shuffle"—as vocalized in these classrooms (and still with the particular voice and word pronunciation of each teacher ringing in my head), and later reinforced when seeing others from the tradition dance these steps. I also have flashbacks of other dancers, some of whom are present at this moment, in this hall, showing me, or of me observing others being shown, a movement or step. Some movement combinations are more comfortable than others, while it is still a challenge to do justice to some. The more challenging ones I have observed, but not yet internalized to a point where they flow naturally.

I have visually observed hundreds of performances by dancers over the years and seen their movement choices in relation to the music. The crucial connection between the music and how I dance is always prominent in my head, perhaps because most of my teachers instilled this connection in me as a core value in the tradition—maybe, and even more so, because the music-movement connection is what attracted me to the dance genre in the first place. These flickering flashbacks guide me, in a subconscious way rather than directly, as I dance. I have also just watched a number of local dancers make their choices, which are now stored in my short-term memory and act as a connection to my long-term memory of other performances of other dancers in the past, and will in turn be stored in my long-term memory. Furthermore, in the hours prior to this, I have been surrounded by hundreds of dancers who have made many choices of movement. It is not just that my relationship with the musicians and their music has taken over, it is also that I feel I am dancing on my terms, as "me" in this particular context—one in which I feel very comfortable and relaxed. Thus, all these impressions strengthen my belief in my ability to perform the movements well. I am experiencing the fullness of being in the present, something I experience as a warm, glowing feeling inside.

Having said this, I will also note that there is a positive sort of nervousness involved in dancing in front of a room predominantly filled with dancers who are all in the know. It is their tradition. They are the insiders. They have emic knowledge. In some respects I also dance as a sign of respect to all those who have shown me what to do, directly and indirectly. They have shared their tradition with me and now it is my turn to share my joy with them. Sometimes, but not on this occasion, their presence will suggest to me motif sequences to dance. Perhaps there is another level of respect involved here where I acknowledge their part in transmitting knowledge to me by dancing my version of their interpretation of the tradition through a particular series of movements.

At this very moment my "being" is making the decisions. Every little nuance is guided by available sensory inputs. However, despite what I said about the spontaneity and subconscious selection of movements in the moment, occasionally a conscious decision of what to do next dictates very strongly what motif or element will be executed. This is the point where I experience time as slowing down and where remembered choices of movements get filtered down to a few or only one choice that seems to be the right one at that moment. What type of ending shall this movement get—heel-toe shuffle? Or will the music and memory indicate something softer—a toe-toe shuffle—or will it demand a light "stamp" to emphasize the finality of that particular bar?

Sometimes, there is a glitch in the flow of movement. You start on something, and after a few fractions of a second it doesn't feel right. You then adapt. You change movement mid-flow or cut the sequence short and move on to something different. At other times you end up idling, perhaps dancing a series of backsteps or a series of favourite non-thinking, "in the marrow"-type movement motifs to fill the time until inspiration returns. Both conscious and subconscious decisions cooperate to get the flow of movements back on track with the music. It is that music connection that is crucial (to me). Tonight, the music triggers memories of whole sequences that combine well together and that fit with the tune played at this moment. Knowing many of the tunes helps me hear the personal variations Kinnon is playing. Understanding the character of the local repertoire's major or minor tunes is helpful too.

I am coming out of the "blur"—that particular place where time moves slower. My vision becomes clearer; the music awareness fades a little bit. Again, I recognize familiar faces around me. I am back in real time. Kinnon is in the B part of the tune and I, perhaps for the first time, make a conscious decision to dance a particular series of movements that will indicate to both musician and audience that I am done. I perform a series of backsteps, which allows me to move backward and sideways. A nod to the audience and another to the musicians, and I make my way back to my seat along the wall. The crowd applauds. It has taken less than two minutes. As I sit down, the adrenaline rush now over, heart pumping and sweat breaking out in rivers, I am aware of the people talking and laughing and applauding the next dancer—Anna MacDonald—now taking her turn on the floor. At this point the woman sitting next to me says in her Cape Breton Canadian accent, "You really enjoyed that, didn't you?"

As I begin to calm down, American dancer and choreographer Martha Graham's words come to mind: "We look at the dance to impart the sensation of living in an affirmation of life, to energize the spectator into keener awareness of the vigour, the mystery, the humour, the variety, and the wonder of life" (thinkexist.com).

These few minutes happened on the evening of Monday, August 6, 2007, at a square dance in Brook Village Parish Hall, Inverness County. The hall is owned by the parish of St. John the Baptist and is used for dances, concerts, dinners, family reunions and similar occasions. The present hall opened in 1945 and is the second hall on the site. The previous was a two-storey building with a stage and dance hall upstairs, but it burned down (Addison 2001: 37-41). The present hall is a white, one-storey wooden building with a large open area and a stage in the main room; the east-side extension has the entrance and a storage room, while the west extension houses the kitchen, washrooms and a bar area. As the hall is not insulated, most dances are held during the summer months and the regular square dances are held on Monday nights, between 9 p.m. and 1 a.m.

I sent the above reflection in an email to Mary Janet MacDonald for some feedback in 2011, and it is quite clear from her comments in return that, when she dances, she always associates the context with the person—in this case her mother—involved with her learning experience. Mary Janet also refers to her mother when teaching dance both formally and informally, I have noticed over the years. She wrote,

> no-one has *ever* written this from the mind's thoughts—you've managed to create the absolute snapshot of what happens in your mind and the physical and mental feelings that you encounter. I absolutely couldn't agree more with what you put in the attached write-up [the reflexive ethnography above]. The only thing I have to add personally—is that *every* single time I spontaneously get up to dance—Mama [Maggie Ann (Cameron) Beaton] comes back to me—her presence is there—and *I always* include a step or two that honour her memory. (2011)

Notes

Notes to Chapter 1

1. The awakened interest in Cape Breton step dancing is also reflected in Moore (1994).

2. While this investigation does not seek to ascertain where different aspects of the dance traditions originated (see for example discussions by Sheldon MacInnes 1996: 111-118), it is interesting to note that some forms of percussive step dance did exist in Scotland in the 18th and 19th centuries, as Flett and Flett (1985 [1964], 1996), for example, point out. My own research has, in addition, found further references to percussive dance accounts and legacy in Scotland. These range from often-referred-to sources such as Topham (1776) as an early example to my own research findings in Scotland since 1985. These accounts indicate that dancers there, predominantly in the Highlands but also in other parts of the country, beat out the rhythm of the dance with their feet (Melin 2006, 2014).

3. Kinaesthesia is the awareness of the position and movement of the parts of the body by means of sensory organs (proprioceptors) in the muscles and joints.

4. See http://ulir.ul.ie/handle/10344/2489.

5. Doherty (1996), Graham (2006) and Herdman (2008), among others, discuss the tune repertoire.

6. See the Instep Research Team's website for further details (www.insteprt. co.uk).

7. In phenomenological hermeneutics, the world, far from being doubted by the subjective ego, is restored to its ontological and temporal priority over the ego or subject. The world—or in our terms, the culture or the tradition—exists and the subject/ego is "thrown" into it. According to Heidegger, "being-in-the-world" is the ego's ontological condition before knowing, understanding, interpreting and explaining. What the ego/subject comes to understand and manipulate are culturally and historically constructed symbolic forms, such as language, dress, social behaviour and music. In hermeneutic jargon, the unbridgeable gulf between subject and object is mediated as the subject becomes a self through temporal arcs of understanding and experience in the world. The self, whether as a member of a culture or a student of a culture, understands the world by placing itself "in front of" cultural works. This sense of understanding a world is rather different from the notion that the outsider as subject must, through the application of "ethnoscientific" methods, get behind the work to understand another subject's (the insider's) intentions in producing the work. In the hermeneutic view, the subject, supposedly freed from prejudice by method, is replaced by the

self, who inevitably interprets and understands the world before any attempt to explain it can proceed. Understanding, in this tradition, precedes explanation rather being the product of it, as it is in the Enlightenment tradition (Rice 2008: 55-56).

8. Anklewicz (2012) recently aptly summed up "debates about the concept of tradition" (see, e.g., Bascom 1958; Eisenstadt 1973, 1974; Shils 1981; Nettl 1982). However, Hobsbawm and Ranger's (2001 [1983]) watershed publication on "invented tradition," appearing at about the same time that Handler and Linnekin (1984) published their important critique of academic understandings of tradition, has been particularly influential on subsequent academic analyses of the term. During the 1990s and into the 2000s, scholars have developed more nuanced understandings of tradition in response to these studies, while critiquing the pejorative attitude toward "invented traditions" implied by Hobsbawm and Ranger. See, for example, Finnegan (1991), Coplan (1993), Malm (1993), Glassie (2003), McDonald (1996) and Phillips and Schochet (2004: 98). Some earlier discussions on tradition further include Spalding and Woodside (1995: 249) defining tradition as a "work-in-progress": "because tradition tries to describe such a complex reality and is so commonly used by so many people in so many contexts, it may always be a work-in-progress." Also worth consulting are Atkinson (2004), Feintuch (1993), Rosenberg (1993), Handler and Linnekin (1984) and Nilsson (1997).

Notes to Chapter 2

1. For the causes for the Scottish emigration, and for detailed settlement patterns in Cape Breton, see Bumsted (1982), Divine (2011), Donovan (2002), C. Dunn (1991), Gibson (1998), Hornsby (1989, 1992), Hunter (1994, 2010), Kennedy (2002), McLean (1991), Morgan (2000, 2008, 2009), Richards (2008), Smout (1987, 1990) and Somers (1985).

2. Seumus Grannd (1998) provides further reading on Cape Breton's Gaelic language and dialects.

3. For an in-depth study of Gaelic and Gaelic culture as a whole in Nova Scotia see Dr. Michael Kennedy's seminal report (2002).

4. See also J. F. Campbell (1994a [1860], 1994b [1860]) and Carmichael (1900 [1898]).

5. For descriptions of house ceilidhs in 19th-century Scotland, see Shaw's (1992-93: 53-61) notes and bibliography.

6. "Jigging" is often equated with *port-a-beul* (with fixed texts) but sometimes refers to improvised diddling tunes for step dancing (Garrison 1985: 185) and for passing on fiddle tunes (Kennedy 2002: 194; Sparling 2000: 225-26, 2014: 41-6; Shaw 1992-93: 44).

7. Macdonald consulted Mary Janet MacDonald, for example, on the accuracy of describing dancing for these sections of the book (M. J. MacDonald 2007).

8. This chart would also be representative for a *taigh ceilidh* situation in Gaelic Scotland.

9. *Puirt-a-beul* (literally, "mouth music") is the vocal dance music of the Scottish Gaels and is discussed in detail by, for example, Sparling (2000) and Lamb (2012).

10. The two parts of the Reel are often referred to as "dancing" or "setting" when steps are performed on the spot, and "reeling" when the dancers move through the particular pattern, sometimes also referred to as the "figure" associated with a particular Reel (Flett and Flett 1985 [1964]: 156-59; Melin 2006).

11. The term "chassé" has many interpretations, depending on the dance form in question, but it generally means if travelling forward to (1) make a step forward, (2) close feet together, (3) step forward again with the leading foot. The step is repeated on alternate feet.

12. The "figure of eight" or "the reel" is a weaving pattern of four dancers passing each other by alternating passing each other by the right or the left. The point is to change positions with each other. This is described in detail by Flett and Flett (1985 [1964]: 143-47).

13. The cited solo step dances (Rhodes 1985 [1964], 1996; MacGillivray 1988) were also part of the dancing at home. When I met Margaret Gillis in Gillisdale in 2007, she vividly recalled her father teaching her and her siblings to dance various solo step dances named after the tunes to which they were danced, such as the song the "Flowers of Edinburgh," in their home. I will return to this category of dances for a closer look in chapter 3.

14. *Dwelly's Illustrated Gaelic to English Dictionary*, 1988, p. 867, reads: "*smàladh, -aidh*, Snuffing, act of snuffing a candle. *smàladaireachd*, Act of candle-snuffing. *cnap-smàlaidh*, a gathering coal, to keep the fire alive overnight."

15. See "Proprioception" by Glenna Batson and International Association for Dance Medicine and Science (IADMS) (2008) at http://www.iadms.org/?210 (accessed February 23, 2015).

16. See chapter 6 for further details.

17. For a discussion of oral/aural learning through the medium of Gaelic, see Dembling (2005), Dickson (2006), Doherty (1996), J. Dunn (1991), Gibson (1998, 2005), Graham (2006), Kennedy (2002), MacInnes (1997), Shaw (1992-93) and Sparling (2000, 2003, 2005, 2014).

18. The term "dirt" is used among Cape Breton musicians to indicate an older, grittier, quality to the music—certain grace notes, phrasings, bowings and accents that characterize a particular sound.

19. There are some good examples available online: "*S i mo ghaol-sa Màiri Bhàn*," http://www.tobarandualchais.co.uk/en/fullrecord/99829/38 and http://www.tobarandualchais.co.uk/en/fullrecord/99079/40. "*Mòrag bheag nighean Mhurchaidh an t-Saoir*," http://www.tobarandualchais. co.uk/en/fullrecord/81840/3 and http://www.tobarandualchais.co.uk/en/fullrecord/101790/4.

20. Anacrusis is the term for the note or notes preceding a downbeat, upbeat.

21. Movement on the anacrusis is used in most Irish step-dance forms but rarely in *sean-nós* dancing. In English clog and step dances there is a varied mix of the use of anacrusis and on-the-beat motifs, often within the same routine. Further research could perhaps reveal linguistic, musical and regional ties to this movement usage.

22. In Scotland, the dance is now known in Gaelic as Lusan Dhùn Eideann. The Cape Breton name suggests it to be a Gaelicized English translation of "Flowers of Edinburgh."

23. A good example of five-count tunes are those in the track "Còig Tunes" ("five" in Gaelic) on Rachel Davis's privately released *Turns* (Davis, RDCD13, compact disc. Released April 2013). The three tunes are: "Jock Broon's 70th," by the late Scottish piper Gordon Duncan, "Miracle at Glencoe Mills," by Maybelle Chisholm, and the Irish reel "Superfly," by Glaswegian Kevin O'Neill.

24. John MacLean is the youngest of five siblings and has come to cherish the previous generations of his family who held onto their music and culture since their ancestors' departure from Barra and Uist, Scotland. His mother's people came from South Uist. They were Curries, and the family oral tradition maintains that Donald Currie was a bard who left South Uist around 1815. There have always been pipers, male and female, in the Currie family, down to John. His grandfather and his great-uncle, Paddy and Alec Currie, respectively, were the last ear-trained pipers in Cape Breton.

25. Johnny "Red" Rory MacLean was a close friend of Michael Anthony MacLean, Bill Lamey, Johnny Wilmot, Angus Chisholm, Maybelle and Cameron Chisholm, Father Hugh A. MacDonald, Carl MacKenzie, Doug MacPhee, Mary Hughie MacDonald, Big Donald MacLellan and Winston Fitzgerald.

26. In relation to music learning, see Graham (2006: 108-19).

27. The clip was featured on YouTube at the time (Summer 2008) but has since been removed.

Notes to Chapter 3

1. A word of caution is in order here with respect to the accuracy of early written sources such as MacDougall (1922). There are a number of examples from the local oral histories that contradict some of the statements made or show that information was omitted or not known to MacDougall, which has been noted by John Gibson in conversation (2013). A fuller picture may be forthcoming with additional research becoming available in the future.

2. See Foley (1988 and 2013) for information on dancing masters and similar teaching contexts in County Kerry, Ireland.

3. The relationship of music and dance is, in my experience, not always emphasized in class situations in other dance forms. I have seen whole classes in both Irish and in Scottish Highland dance conducted without music being played. The class was conducted with the teacher counting out the beats (Melin 2006).

4. MacDonald appears in *One Step at a Time* (1992) and *A Family Tradition. A Cape Breton Stepdancing Instructional Video* (2002 [1999]). MacNeil appears in *Spring in Your Step: Cape Breton Stepdance Instruction* (2005).

5. The English names are from MacLeod's (1974: 13) own translation of the book.

6. It seems fairly common that, years ago, authors of dance manuals "borrowed" material from other sources without crediting them. Peacock's step names and descriptions also appear in Rudolph Radestock's (1877) *The Royal Ball-Room Guide*. Thanks go to J. Schoonover for drawing my attention to this connection.

7. Both Jennifer Schoonover (2015) and Jenny MacKenzie (2015) use *puirt-a-beul* as a means of conveying dance rhythm in their step-dance classes.

Notes to Chapter 4

1. See note 9, chapter 2, for an explanation of *puirt-a-beul*.

2. Definition according to the *Farlex Trivia Dictionary* (2012). There is also a good description of box or basket socials in Pratt (1996: 23).

Notes to Chapter 5

1. Figures are prescribed patterns of dance moves.

2. The winter of 2013-14 has seen this event reduced to a fortnightly event as a combination of bad weather and dwindling attendance made it more difficult to keep it going as a weekly for financial reasons. The weekly dances were kept going for well over twenty years till then.

Notes to Chapter 6

1. Movement systems can include any sporting activity, actions when playing a particular instrument or movements when working, to cite but three examples.

2. For further reading on the dance traditions of Newfoundland see Bennett (1989) and Harris-Walsh (2009). For Ottawa Valley see Trew (2000, 2009) and Johnson (2010). For Québec see Chartrand (1991) and Voyer (2003).

3. "Dance" in French is *danse*; in Swiss, Dutch, Norwegian and Swedish, *dans*; Spanish and Italian, *danza*; and in German, *tanz*.

4. It is worth noting that the following words all refer to dance or dancing in some way. *Ridhil*, see also *rìghil, rìghle, rìghleachan*, equals the word "Reel"; *righil* means to dance a Reel. While *rinc*, or *ring*, means to dance or hop; and *ringeach* (*ringtheach, -eiche*) is dancing; as is *ringeadh*. The word *ringeal* is a circle or sphere, and finally *ringear* means dancer. All entries in found in *Dwelly's Illustrated Gaelic to English Dictionary*, (1901 [1988]).

5. Rhodes (1985) gives the names of these dances as *Ruidhleadh Cheathrar*, *Ruidhleadh Bheag* and *Ruidhleadh Mòr*, but Ronald I. Black (1991), formerly of the Department of Celtic Studies, University of Edinburgh, explains that the noun is *ruidhle*—reel. *Ruidhleadh* can be a verbal noun meaning "reeling." *Ruidhle* is masculine, making the dance titles *Ruidhle Ceathrar, Ruidhle Beag* and *Ruidhle Mòr*.

6. Emic – an "insider" point of view.

7. Willie Francis Fraser celebrated his 100th birthday on March 5, 2015.

Notes to Chapter 7

1. The role of women in Highland society is discussed in, for example: Breitenbach (1998), Grant (1989), Gordon (1991), Heron (1794), MacArthur (1994) and Melin (2010).

2. The halling dance is an athletic Norwegian/Swedish solo dance in either 2/4 or 6/8 time, but it is also found as a couple dance accompanied by the same type of music—halling.

3. McDavid analyzes the context in which a particular priest operated and how the legend has been retold by students in masters and PhD dissertations, and as recounted by locals such as Fr. Angus Morris and in song lyrics. In some versions, the local fiddlers hide their fiddles, trick him or give him their worst "other" fiddle. The written accounts of Fr. MacDonald describe him, in summary, "as a strict disciplinarian and social advocate: he was against the consumption of alcohol; he disliked picnics; he would withhold an individual's religious services until accounts were paid to him in full; and he told his parishioners how to vote" (McDavid 2008: 125).

4. McDavid states:

Here, in Cape Breton, the fiddle stands for the "old country," for the "new country," for family, for tradition, for the working class, for hardship, for status (and lack thereof), and for counter-hegemonic power. The fiddle is key in the promotion and maintenance of traditional music and culture in general. It has been reclaimed as a status symbol, and has become iconographic cultural shorthand for "pure" or "honest" living. Fiddle music has been used to socialize, to deal with frustration without words, and to expel energy through energetic fiddling and dance. (McDavid 2008: 126)

5. The letter stated:

Therefore, as a rule, subject to more or less numerous exceptions, they who take part in such dances are guilty of grievous scandal.... There are various circumstances closely connected with balls, that are of frequent occurrence and most ruinous to purity, especially the improper intimacies between young people on the way to and from the places where the dances are held.... Those who persist in having such balls and dance in their homes ... are in a state of deadly sin.... They cannot worthily receive the Sacraments of the Church until they sincerely repent. (Quoted in LeBlanc and Sadowsky 1986: 12)

Notes to Chapter 8

1. Heather and Melanie are Clare's daughters.

2. Foot movements that are referred to as either "ankle bends" or "ankle twists" are performed, for example, by placing the working foot, with the toes or the ball of the foot touching the ground, and then pushing the heel forward or sometimes sideways, which creates an illusion that the foot or ankle is "bending."

3 Listed as Dr. Alex Kennedy (d. 1940) of Kenloch (MacGillivray 1988: 163) but as the doctor in Mabou (36).

4. Sounding the "cuts" when diddling refers to the vocal imitation of the sounds playing a "cut" on the fiddle or bagpipes. A cut is a standard feature of Cape Breton fiddling, and is "a sequence of notes of the same pitch applied by using the wrist to snap or shake the bow through the series. Cuts are ... an attempt to add a degree of complexity to simpler aspects of the melody line" (Graham 2006: 126). A cut in Scottish piping is an older term for a single grace note (a very short note). It is a way of shortening a note and is hard to describe in conventional music notation, but grace notes are frequently used in piping notation.

5. Mary Janet says that perhaps it was the "tap shoes" she had seen worn by dancers on *The Don Messer Show* that made her initially crave a pair. Maggie

Ann eventually relented and got her a pair, as "everyone" was getting them (M. J. MacDonald 2007).

6. Many Prince Edward Island step dancers still wear taps on their shoes.

7. It is clear from Harvey's comment that the Scottish connection is strong. Even though the local music style is often referred to as Scottish, as in the outdoor Scottish concert circuit, and many people referred to it as "Scotch Music" as well, this labelling is less apparent in relation to dancing. When Harvey was growing up, this type of dancing was never referred to as Scottish, although it was common knowledge that his and his community's ancestors were from Scotland, and their Scottish cultural heritage extended beyond dance to music, songs, storytelling and so forth. Colin Quigley points out that even though we are dealing with a shared percussive dance idiom across many parts of North America, it only becomes identified as a regional style (Cape Breton) or is linked to a certain identity (Scottish) "when particular conditions are ripe for it" (Quigley 2008: 37). Only in the last thirty years has identity labelling in relation to dancing become important and put into use. See Quigley (2008) for further discussion on the labelling of dance idioms.

8. http://www.feismhabu.com, accessed February 13, 2014.

9. http://www.melodyandderrickcameron.com/Home.html, accessed January 10, 2011. Acting as a good summary of a lengthy part of the interview, conducted with Derrick and Melody in July 30, 2007. More information, music and video clips are also available on their MySpace site: http://www.myspace.com/melodyandderrickcameron, accessed January 10, 2011.

10. For further information on *Up Home Tonight*, see http://www.fiddlebooks.com/uht.html, accessed February 13, 2014.

11. For more up-to-date information, see Anita's website, http://anitamacdonald.com/bio/.

Notes to Appendix 2

1. See p. 24 (chapter 1) for a discussion of phenomenological hermeneutics.

References

Primary Sources—Personal Communication

Aucoin, Leanne. 2008. Recorded interview with author. Limerick, Ireland. June 5.

Beaton, Andrea. 2009. Recorded interview with author. Limerick, Ireland. June 4.

———. 2010. Email correspondence with author. "Thoughts on Gender Issues in Cape Breton Dancing." October 2.

Beaton, Dawn. 2010..Email correspondence with author. *Thoughts on gender issues in Cape Breton dancing.* Sydney, Cape Breton Island. June 29.

Beaton, Harvey. 1994. Letter correspondence with author. Halifax, Nova Scotia. October 3.

———. 2005. Email correspondence with author. Halifax, Nova Scotia. May 4.

———. 2007. Recorded interview with author. Port Hood, Cape Breton Island. July 31.

Beaton, Sandy, Jessie Beaton and Donald Roddy MacDonald. 2008. Recorded interview with author. Mabou, Cape Breton Island. July 28.

Black, Ronald I. 1991. Letter correspondence with author. Edinburgh, Scotland. April 10.

Cameron, Melody. 2007. Recorded interview with author. West Mabou, Cape Breton Island. July 30.

———. 2010. Skype interview with author. West Mabou, Cape Breton Island. December 10.

———. 2011. Skype interview with author. West Mabou, Cape Breton Island. January 14.

Chiasson, Joël. 2009. Recorded interview with author. Sydney, Cape Breton Island. October 14.

Dòmhnallach, Goiridh. 2010. "Gaelic words for dance in Cape Breton." Email communication with author. November 10.

Dunn, Margaret (MacEachern). 2007. Recorded interview with author. Antigonish, Nova Scotia. August 11.

———. 2010. Email correspondence with author. Antigonish, Nova Scotia. December 28.

———. 2012. Email correspondence with author. Antigonish, Nova Scotia. February 29.

Dunn-MacIsaac, Jackie. 2010a. Email correspondence with author. Antigonish, Nova Scotia. June 24.

———. 2010b. Email correspondence with author. "Thoughts on Gender Issues in Cape Breton Dancing." Antigonish, Nova Scotia. June 26

———. 2010c. Email correspondence with author. Antigonish, Nova Scotia. December 17.

———. 2012a. Email correspondence with author. Antigonish, Nova Scotia. February 29.

———. 2012b. Email correspondence with author. Antigonish, Nova Scotia. March 1.

Fraser-Doyle, Maureen. 2012. Email correspondence with author. Prince Edwards Island. March 23.

Gibson, John. 2013. Personal conversation with author. Mabou, Cape Breton, October 15.

Gillis, John Robert. 2009. Personal communication with author. Gaelic College, St. Ann's, Cape Breton Island. October 11.

———. 2012. Email correspondence with author. Halifax, Nova Scotia. March 17.

Gillis, Margaret. 2007. Personal communication with author. Gillisdale, Cape Breton Island, August 10.

Graham, Glenn. (2007). Recorded interview with author. The Gaelic College, St. Ann's, Cape Breton Island. August 8.

Hall, Michael. 2009. Recorded interview with author. Judique, Cape Breton Island. October 8.

Kennedy Michael. 2010. "Gaelic names for dance steps." Facebook communication with author. Calgary, Alberta. 2 December.

Lamey, Peggy. 2008. "Comments in addition to Dance Questionnaire." Email correspondence with author. September 28.

MacDonald, Anita. 2009. Recorded interview with author. Cape Breton University, Sydney, Cape Breton Island, October 14.

MacDonald, Mary Janet. 2005. "Farquhar Mac Neil and the Barra Feis." Email correspondence with author. Port Hood, Cape Breton Island. April 18.

———. 2007. Recorded interview with author. Port Hood, Cape Breton Island. July 31.

———. 2009. Recorded interview with author. Port Hood, Cape Breton Island. October 17.

———. 2010. "Thoughts on Gender Issues in Cape Breton Dancing." Email correspondence with author. Port Hood, Cape Breton Island. June 22.

———. 2010a. "Thomas MacDonnell." Facebook communication with author. Port Hood, Cape Breton Island. November 15.

———. 2010b. Email correspondence with author. Port Hood, Cape Breton Island. December 11.

———. 2011. Email correspondence with author. Port Hood, Cape Breton Island. August 4.

MacDonald, Rodney. 2009. Recorded interview with author. Mabou, Cape Breton Island. October 13.

MacKinnon, Harvey. 2007. Recorded interview with author. Whycocomagh, Cape Breton Island. August 6.

MacInnes, Maggie. 2005. "Flora MacNeil's recollection of step dancing." Email correspondence with author. Glasgow, Scotland. 15 April.

MacKenzie, Jenny. 2015. Skype conversation with author. Mabou. Cape Breton Island. February 16.

MacLean, John. 2010. "Gender roles in Cape Breton dance." Email correspondence with author. Halifax, Nova Scotia. June 22.

———. 2012. Email correspondence with author. Halifax, Nova Scotia. February 26.

MacMaster, Buddy. 2007. Recorded interview with author. Judique, Cape Breton Island. August 7.

MacMaster, Minnie. 2009. Recorded interview with author. Troy, Cape Breton Island. October 9.

———. 2010. Email correspondence with author. Troy, Cape Breton Island. December 19.

———. 2015. Email correspondence with author. Troy, Cape Breton Island. February 22.

MacMhaoirn, Alasdair. 2014. Email correspondence with author. Rogart, Sutherland, Scotland. March 5.

MacNeil, Jean. 2007. Recorded interview with author. Sydney Mines, Cape Breton Island. August 1.

MacNeil, Lucy. 2014. Facebook communication with author. Sydney Mines, Cape Breton Island. 19 February.

MacQuarrie, Cameron, Clare MacQuarrie, Heather MacQuarrie and Melanie MacDonald. 2007. Recorded interview with author. Inverside, Inverness, Cape Breton Island. August 2.

MacQuarrie, Cheryl. 2007. Recorded interview with author. West Mabou, Cape Breton Island. August 6.

Matheson, Betty. 2009. Recorded interview with author. The Gaelic College, St. Ann's, Cape Breton Island. October 17.

McCarthy, Brandi. 2009. Recorded interview with author. Limerick, Ireland. November 2.

———. 2010. "Thoughts on Gender Issues in Cape Breton Dancing." Email correspondence with author. June 22.

McConnell, Frank. 2004. Personal communication with author. Kingussie, Scotland. November 11.

Morin, Mac. 2008. Recorded interview with author. Kilmurry Lodge Hotel, Limerick, Ireland. November 11.

———. 2010. Email correspondence with author. Troy, Cape Breton Island. December 15.

Morris, Fr. Angus. 2007. Recorded interview with author. St. Mary's, Mabou, Cape Breton Island. August 4.

Rae. Emerald. 2007. Recorded interview with author. St. Joseph du Moine, Cape Breton Island. July 25.

Rhodes, Frank. 2011. Email correspondence with author regarding dance transmission in Cape Breton in 1957. Southampton, UK. October 31.

Schoonover, Jennifer. 2015. Email correspondence with author. Boston, Massachusetts. February 15.

Tingley, Jenny. 2007. Recorded interview with author. Kempt Road, Boularderie, Cape Breton Island. August 8.

Published Sources

Adorno, Theodore. 1996 [1951]. *Minima Moralia*. New York: Verso.

Addison, Emily L. 2001. The perception and value of dance halls in Inverness County, Cape Breton. BA thesis, Trent University.

Adshead, Janet, Valerie A. Briginshaw, Pauline Hodgens and Michael R. Huxley. 1982. "A Chart of Skills and Concepts for Dance." *Journal of Aesthetic Education* 16 (3): 49-61.

Anderson, Benedict. 1991. *Imagined Communities: Reflections on the Origin and Spread of Nationalism*. London: Verson.

Anklewicz, Mike. 2012. Extending the Tradition: KlezKanada, Klezmer Tradition and Hybridity. MUSICultures, 39, 2. Available at: <http://journals.hil.unb.ca/index.php/MC/article/view/20358/23494>. Accessed 24 Apr. 2014.

Atkinson, David. 2004. "Revival: genuine or spurious?" In *Folk Song: Tradition, Revival, and Re-Creation*. Ed. I. Russell and D. Atkinson. Aberdeen: The Elphinstone Institute, University of Aberdeen.

Bascom, William. 1958. "The Main Problems of Stability and Change in Tradition." *International Folk Music Journal* 11:7-12.

Batson, Glenna and International Association for Dance Medicine and Science. 2008. Proprioception. http://www.iadms.org/?210. Accessed 23 Feb. 2015.

Bennett, Margaret. 1989. *The Last Stronghold. The Scottish Gaelic Traditions of Newfoundland, Canada's Atlantic folklore and folklife series*. St. John's, Newfoundland: Breakwater Books.

———. 1998. *Oatmeal and Catechism. Scottish Gaelic Settlers in Quebec*. Edinburgh and Montreal: John Donald Publishers Ltd. and McGill-Queen University Press.

———. 2005. From the Quebec-Hebrideans to "les Écossais-Québécois": Tracing the Evolution of a Scottish Cultural Identity in Canada's Eastern Townships. In *Transatlantic Scots*, Ed. C. Ray, 120-55. Tuscaloosa: The University of Alabama Press.

Bhabha, Hami and Paul Thompson. 1994. Between Identities. In *Migration and Identity*. Ed. R. Benmayor and A. Skotnes, 183-99. Oxford: Oxford University Press.

Blom, Lynne A. and L Tarin Chaplin. 1988. *The Moment of Movement: Dance improvisation*. London: Dance Books Ltd.

Bläsing, Bettina. 2010. The dancer's memory: Expertise and cognitive structures in dance. In *The Neurocognition of Dance: Mind, Movement and Motor Skills*. Ed. B. Bläsing, M. Puttke and T. Schack, 75-98. Hove, East Sussex (England), and New York: Psychology Press.

Boas, Franz. 1974. *The Shaping of American Anthropology, 1883-1911: A Franz Boas Reader*. New York: Basic Books.

Borggreen, Jørn. 2012 [2002]. *Right to the Helm - Cape Breton Square Dances. A collection of square sets*. 3rd ed. Jyllinge, Denmark: Jørn Borggreen.

Breitenbach, Esther, Alice Brown and Fiona Myers. 1998. "Understanding Women in Scotland." *Feminist Review* 58 (International Voices [Spring]): 44-65.

Buckland, Theresa J. 1999a. Introduction: Reflecting on Dance Ethnology. In

Dance in the Field: Theory, Methods and Issues in Dance Ethnography. 1-10. Ed. T. J. Buckland, 1-10. London: Macmillan Press.

———. 1999b. [Re]Constructing Meanings: the Dance Ethnographer as Keeper of the Truth. In *Dance in the Field: Theory, Methods and Issues in Dance Ethnography.* 196-207. Ed. T. J. Buckland, 196-207. London: Macmillan Press.

Bull (Novack), Cynthia J. C. 1997. Sense, Meaning, and Perception in Three Dance Cultures. In *Meaning in Motion: New Cultural Studies in Dance.* Ed. J. Desmond, 169-287. Durham, D.C.: Duke University Press,

Bumsted, John M. 1982. *The People's Clearance: Highland Emigration to British North America, 1770-1815.* Edinburgh and Winnipeg: Edinburgh University Press and University of Manitoba Press.

Bunting, Edward. 1840. *The Ancient Music of Ireland.* Dublin: Hodges and Smith.

Cameron, Melody and Derrick Cameron. Homepage. http://www.melodyandderrickcameron.com/Home.html. Accessed January 10, 2011).

Campbell, Donald and Raymond A. MacLean. 1974. *Beyond the Atlantic Roar — A Study of the Nova Scotia Scots, The Carleton Library No. 78.* Toronto: McClelland and Stewart Ltd.

Campbell, John Francis. 1994a [1860]. *Popular Tales of the West Highlands. Vol. I. (Vols 1-2).* Edinburgh: Birlinn Books.

———. 1994b [1860]. *Popular Tales of the West Highlands. Vol. II. (Vols. 3-4).* Edinburgh: Birlinn Books.

Caplan, Ronald. 2006. *Talking Cape Breton Music: Conversations with People Who Love and Make the Music.* Wreck Cove: Breton Books.

Carmichael, Alexander. 1900 [1898]. *Carmina Gadelica. Vol. I.* Edinburgh: Constable.

Casey, Edward. 1987. *Remembering: A Phenomenological Study.* Bloomington: Indiana University Press.

Chomsky, Noam. 1965. *Aspects of the Theory of Syntax.* Cambridge, MA: MIT Press.

Chartrand, Pierre. 1991. *La Gigue Québécoise.* Quebec: l'Association Québécoise des Loisirs Folkloriques.

Cohen, Anthony P. 1985. *The Symbolic Construction of Community.* Chichester: Ellis Horwood Ltd.

Comhairle na Gaidhlig. 2015. [Cainnt mo Mhàthar (My Mother's Language) website]. http://www.cainntmomhathar.com/speaker.php?sp=29&=e. Accessed February 27, 2015).

Coplan, David B. 1993. The Meaning of Tradition. In *Ethnomusicology and*

Modern Music History. Ed. S. Blum, P. V. Bohlman and D. M. Neuman, 35-48. Urbana: University of Illinois Press.

Crampton, Jeremy W. and Stuart Elden. 2007. *Space, knowledge and power: Foucault and geography*. London: Ashgate Publishing Ltd.

Cross, Emily S. 2010. Building a dance in the human brain: Insights from expert and novice dancers. In *The Neurocognition of Dance: Mind, Movement and Motor Skills*. Ed. B. Bläsing, M. Puttke and T. Schack, 177-202. Hove, East Sussex (England), and New York: Psychology Press.

Cruse, Holk and Malte Schilling. 2010. Getting cognitive. In *The Neurocognition of Dance: Mind, Movement and Motor Skills*. Ed. B. Bläsing, M. Puttke and T. Schack, 53-74. Hove, East Sussex (England), and New York: Psychology Press.

Csikszentmihalyi, Mihaly. 1990. *Flow: The Psychology of Optimal Experience*. New York: Harper and Row.

Csordas, Thomas, J. 1993. "Somatic Modes of Attention." *Cultural Anthropology* 8 (2): 135-56.

Davies, Charlotte Aull. 2008. Reflexive Ethnography: a guide to researching selves and others. Abingdon: Routledge.

Dembling, Jonathan. 2005. You Play It As You Would Sing It: Cape Breton Scottishness and the Means of Cultural Production. In *Transatlantic Scots*. Ed. C. R. Ray, 180-97. Tuscaloosa: University of Alabama Press.

Denzin, Norman K. 1997. *Interpretive Ethnography: Ethnographic Practices for the 21st Century*. London: Sage Publications.

Desjarlais, Robert. 1992. *Body and Emotion: The Aesthetics of Illness and Healing in the Nepal Himalayas*. Philadelphia: University of Pennsylvania Press.

Dick, Lyle. 2008. *Farmers "Making Good." The Development of Abernethy District, Saskatchewan, 1880-1920*. Calgary: University of Calgary Press.

Dick and Fitzgerald Handbook. 1878. *Dick's Quadrille Call-Book and Ball-Room Prompter*. Danbury: Behrens Publishing Company.

Dickson, Joshua. 2006. *When Piping was Strong. Tradition, Change and the Bagpipe in South Uist*. Edinburgh: John Donald Publishers.

Divine, Thomas M. 2011. *To the Ends of the Earth. Scotland's Global Diaspora 1750-2010*. London: Allen Lane.

Doherty, Elizabeth Anne. 1994. *The music of Cape Breton: an Irish perspective, Ó Riada memorial lecture 9*, Cork: The Irish Traditional Music Society, University College Cork.

———. 1996. The Paradox of the periphery: evolution of the Cape Breton fiddle tradition 1928-1995 (unpublished thesis), University of Limerick.

———. 2006. Bringing It All Back Home? Issues Surrounding Cape Breton Fiddle Music in Scotland. In *Play It Like It Is: Fiddle and Dance Studies from Around the North Atlantic.* Ed. I. Russell and M. A. Alburger, 102-109. Aberdeen: Elphinstone Institute, University of Aberdeen.

Dòmhnallach, Rob. 2012. An Cùrsa Gàidhlig. Gaelic 521 Course Notes. An Gearran: Àrd-Sgoil Chòirneil MacIlleghlas.

Donovan, Kenneth. 2002. "'After-midnight-we-danced-until-daylight': Music, song and dance in Cape Breton, 1713-1758." *Acadiensis* 32 (1), 3-28.

Dorchak, Gregory. J. 2006. Fiddling with tradition: the question of authenticity within Cape Breton fiddle music. MA thesis, Syracuse University.

———. 2010. The exported Cape Breton fiddler: a hermeneutic study of the meaning of Cape Breton fiddle music outside Cape Breton. In *Crossing Over, Fiddle and Dance Studies from around the North Atlantic 3.* Ed. I. Russell and A. K. Guigné, 250-59. Aberdeen: The Elphinstone Institute.

Dunlay, Kate. 1992. *The playing of traditional Scottish dance music: Old and New World styles and practices.* Paper presented at the Celtic languages and Celtic peoples: Proceedings of the Second North American Congress of Celtic Studies, Halifax.

———. 2002. Cape Breton Fiddle: Repertoire and Style. In *Rounder CD 7037, Traditional Fiddle Music of Cape Breton, Vol. 1 Mabou Coal Mines*, 3-7.

Dunlay, Kate and David Greenberg. 1996. *Traditional Celtic Violin Music of Cape Breton, containing Strathspeys, Reels, Jigs, etc., transcribed from the playing of some outstanding exponents of the traditional style of Highland Scottish Fiddling as cultivated in Cape Breton, Nova Scotia.* Toronto: DunGreen Music.

Dunn, Charles W. 1991. *Highland Settler. A Portrait of the Scottish Gael in Cape Breton and Eastern Nova Scotia.* Vreck Cove, Canada: Breton Books.

Dunn, Jacqueline A. 1991. *Tha blas na Gaidhlig air a h-uile fidhleir = (The sound of Gaelic is in the fiddler's music): an investigation of the possible influence the Scottish Gaelic language has had on the fiddling style of Cape Breton.* BA thesis, St. Francis Xavier University.

Eisenstadt, S. N. 1973. *Tradition, change, and modernity.* New York: Wiley.

———. 1974. *Post-traditional societies.* New York: Norton.

Emerson, Robert M., Rachel I. Fretz and Linda L. Shaw. 2011. *Writing Ethnographic Fieldnotes.* 2 ed. Chicago and London: University of Chicago Press.

Emmerson, George S. 1972. *A Social History of Scottish Dance. Ane Celestial Recreation,* Montreal and London: McGill-Queen's University Press.

———. 1995. *A Handbook of Traditional Scottish Dance,* Oakville: Galt House.

Feintuch, Burt. 1993. Musical Revival as Musical Transformation. In *Transforming Tradition: Folk Music Revivals Examined*. Ed. Neil V. Rosenberg, 183-93. Urbana: University of Illinois Press.

———. 2004. "The Conditions for Cape Breton Fiddle Music: The Social and Economic Setting of a Regional Soundscape." *Ethnomusicology*, 48 (1), 73-104.

Felföldi, László. 2001. Connections Between Dance and Dance Music: Summary of Hungarian Research, *Yearbook for Traditional Music*. 159-65.

Finnegan, Ruth. 1991. Tradition, but What Tradition, and Tradition for Whom? *Oral Tradition* 6(1): 104-24.

———. 1992. *Oral Traditions and the Verbal Arts: A Guide to Research Practices*, London: Routledge.

Flett, Joan F. and Tom M. Flett. 1953-54. "Some Hebridean Folk Dances." *Journal of the English Folk Dance and Song Society* 7 (2): 112-27, 182-84.

———. 1985 [1964]. *Traditional Dancing in Scotland*. With an appendix, "Dancing in Cape Breton Island, Nova Scotia," by F. Rhodes. London: Routledge and Keegan Paul.

———. 1996 . *Traditional step-dancing in Scotland*. With an appendix, "Step-dancing in Cape Breton Island, Nova Scotia," by F. Rhodes. Edinburgh: Scottish Cultural Press.

Foley, Catherine E. 1988. Irish Traditional Step Dance in North Kerry: A Contextual and Structural Analysis. PhD thesis. The Laban Centre for Movement and Dance at University of London's Goldsmith's College.

———. 2004. Representing Irish Step Dance Heritage: Bridging Theory and Practice. In *Dance Heritage: Crossing Academia and Physicality*. Ed. I. Björnsdóttir, 48-54. Reykjavik: Nordic Forum for Dance Research (NOFOD).

———. 2007. The creative process within Irish traditional step dance. In *Dance Structures. Perspectives on the Analysis of Human Movement*. Ed. Adrienne L. Kaeppler and Elsie I. Dunin, 277-302. Budapest: Akadémiai Kiadó.

———. 2011. "The Irish Céilí: A Site for Constructing, Experiencing, and Negotiating a Sense of Community and Identity." *Dance Research, the Journal of the Society for Dance Research* 29 (1): 43-60.

———. 2012. *Irish Traditional Step Dance in North Kerry: A Contextual and Structural Analysis*. Listowel: North Kerry Literary Trust.

———. 2013. *Step Dancing in Ireland–Culture and History*. Ashgate Publishing Ltd, Surrey, England

Foucault, Michel. 1980. *Power/Knowledge: Selected Interviews and Other Writings, 1972-1977*. New York: Pantheon Books.

Fraser, Angus. c. 1855. A Glossary. Adv 73.1.5-6: 'A Glossary of Ancient and Modern Terms and Expressions Associated with the Music, Poetry, Dancing and Oratory of the Gæil; with quotations from their poetry illustrative of their meaning and use'. By Angus Fraser c. 1855. Edinburgh: National Library of Scotland.

Gadamer, Hand-Georg. 1979. *Truth and method,* 2nd ed. London: Sheed and Ward.

Garrison, Virginia H. 1985. Traditional and non-traditional teaching and learning practices in folk music: An ethnographic field study of Cape Breton fiddling. PhD dissertation, University of Wisconsin.

Geertz, Clifford. 1973. *Interpretation of Cultures.* New York: Basic Books.

———. 1985. *Local knowledge: further essays in interpretive anthropology.* New York: Basic Books.

———. 1988. *Works and Lives. The Anthropologist as Author.* Cambridge: Polity Press.

Gibson, John. G. 1992. Màiri Alasdair Raonuil – There was no one like her. *The Clansman.* August/September. Halifax.

———. 1998. *Traditional Gaelic Bagpiping, 1745-1945.* Montreal: McGill-Queen's University Press.

———. 2005. *Old and New World Highland Bagpiping.* Edinburgh: Birlinn Ltd.

———. 2008. *Back o' the Hill - Highland Yesterday.* Edinburgh: Birlinn Ltd.

Giddens, Anthony. 2004. *Sociology.* 4 ed. Cambridge: Polity Press.

Gillis, William. 1977. Last picnic below the track marred by tragic drowning. *The Inverness Oran.* December 15.

Giurchescu, Anca and Eva Kröschlová. 2007. Theory and method of Dance Form Analysis. In *Dance Structures: Perspective on the Analysis of Human Movement.* Ed. A. L. Kaeppler and E. I. Dunin, 21-52. Budapest: Akadémiai Kiadó.

Glassie, Henry. 2003. Tradition. In *Eight Words for the Study of Expressive Culture.* Ed. B. Feintuch, 176-97. Urbana and Chicago: University of Illinois Press.

Gordon, Eleanor. 1991. *Women and the Labour Movement in Scotland 1850-1914.* Oxford: Clarendon Press.

Graham, Glenn. 2004. Cape Breton fiddle music: The making and maintenance of a tradition. MA thesis. Saint Mary's University.

———. 2006. *The Cape Breton Fiddle. Making and Maintaining Tradition.* Sydney: Cape Breton University Press.

Grannd, Seumus. 1998. "Some Influences on the Gaelic of Cape Breton." *Scottish Language* 17:119-28.

Grant, Isobel F. 1989. *Highland Folk Ways.* London: Routledge and Keegan Paul.

Guest, Ann Hutchinson. 2005. *Labanotation. The System of Analyzing and Recording Movement.* 4 ed. London: Routledge.

Guilcher, Jean-Michel. 1995 [1963]. *La Tradition Populaire de Danse En Basse-Bretagne.* Spézet/Douarnenez: Coop Breizh/Chasse-Marée-ArMen.

Hahn, Tomie. 2007. *Sensational Knowledge. Embodying Culture through Japanese Dance,* Middletown, Connecticut: Wesleyan University Press.

Handler, Richard and Jocelyn Linnekin. 1984. "Tradition, Genuine or Spurious." *Journal of American Folklore* 97 (385): 273-90.

Heidegger, Martin. 1962. *Being and time / translated [from the German] by John Macquarrie and Edward Robinson.* New York: Harper and Row.

Herdman, Jessica. 2008. The Cape Breton Fiddling Narrative: Innovation, Preservation, Dancing. MA thesis, University of British Columbia.

———. 2010. Old Style Cape Breton Fiddling: Narrative, Interstices, Dancing. In *Crossing Over, Fiddle and Dance Studies from around the North Atlantic 3.* Ed. I. Russell and A. K. Guigné, 156-75. Aberdeen: The Elphinstone Institute.

Heron, Robert. 1794. *The Hebrides.* Edinburgh: J. Paterson

Hobsbawm, Eric and Terence Ranger, eds. 2001. *The Invention of Tradition.* Cambridge: Cambridge University Press.

Hornsby, Stephen J. 1989. "Staple Trades, Subsistence Agriculture, and Nineteenth-Century Cape Breton Island." *Annals of the Association of American Geographers* 79 (3): 411-34.

———. 1992. *Nineteenth-century Cape Breton: a historical geography.* Montreal: McGill-Queen's University Press.

Hughes, David. W. 2000. "No Nonsense: The Logic and Power of Acoustic-Iconic Mnemonic Systems." *British Journal of Ethnomusicology* 9 (2): 93-120.

Hunter, James. 1994. *A Dance Called America: The Scottish Highlands, the United States and Canada.* Edinburgh: Mainstream Publishing.

———. 2010. *The Making of the Crofting Community.* Edinburgh: Birlinn Ltd.

Hymes, Dell. 1977. *Foundations in sociolinguistics: an ethnographic approach.* Philadelphia: University of Pennsylvania Press.

Inverness Oran. 2008. Old Time Box Social and Square Dance, West Lake Ainslie. [Advert]. *Inverness Oran,* July 16: 24.

———. 2015. Stepdancer Harvey MacKinnon. https://www.invernessoran. ca/entertainment/318-stepdancer-harvey-mackinnon Accessed July 29, 2015.

Instep Research Team [C. Hays, J. Jarman, A. Metherell, C. Metherell, A. Smith and E. Wilson] 2011. *Newcastle Notation: A rational system for the notation of clog and step dances*. Newcastle: Instep Research Team.

Kaeppler, Adrienne L. 1967. The Structure of Tongan Dance. PhD dissertation, University of Hawaii.

———. 1972. "Acculturation in Hawaiian Dance." *Yearbook of the International Folk Music Council* 4 (25th Anniversary Issue): 38-46.

———. 2001. "Dance and the Concept of Style." *Yearbook for Traditional Music* 33:49-63.

———. 2007. Method and theory in analyzing dance structure with an analysis of Tongan dance. In *Dance Structures: Perspective on the Analysis of Human Movement*. Ed. A. Kaeppler and E.I. Dunin, 53-102. Budapest: Akadémiai Kiadó,

Kennedy, Michael. 2002. *Gaelic Nova Scotia: An Economic, Cultural and Social Impact Study, Curatorial Report No. 97*, Halifax, Nova Scotia, Canada: Nova Scotia Museum.

Keysers Christian, E. Kohler, M. Aless, R. Umilta, L. Nanetti, L. Fogassi, V. Gallese. 2003. "Audiovisual mirror neurons and action recognition." *Experimental Brain Research* 153:628–36.

Keysers Christian, Valeria Gazzola. 2014. "Hebbian learning and predictive mirror neurons for actions, sensations and emotions." *Philosophical Transactions of the Royal Society B: Biological Sciences*, Vol. 369 (1644): 20130175.

Kissling, Werner. 1943. "The Character and Purpose of the Hebridean Black House." *The Journal of the Royal Anthropological Institute of Great Britain and Ireland* 73 (1/2): 75-100.

Kohler Evelyn, C. Keysers, M. Aless, R. Umilta, L. Fogassi, V. Gallese, G. Rizzolatti. 2002. "Hearing sounds, understanding actions: action representation in mirror neurons." *Science* 297:846–48.

Lamb, William, ed. 2012. *Keith Norman MacDonald's Puirt-à-Beul, The Vocal Dance Music of the Scottish Gaels*. Broadford: Taigh na Teud.

Lambert, Kathleen. 1985. The Spoken Web: An Ethnography of Storytelling in Rannafast, Ireland. PhD dissertation, Boston University.

LeBlanc, Barbara and Laura Sadowsky. 1986. *Inverness County Dance Project, Cape Breton, Nova Scotia*. Quebec: Centre for Canadian Folk Culture Studies.

Mac Gill-eain, Somhairle. 1985. *Ris a' Bhruthaich. The Criticism and Prose Writing of Sorley MacLean*. Stornoway: Acair Limited.

MacDonald, Allan. 1995. The relationship between pibroch and Gaelic song: its implications on the performance style of the pibroch ùrlar. M.Litt. thesis, University of Edinburgh.

———. 1998. Gaelic Music. "What is it?" *Celtic Heritage* February/March: 5: 32-33.

Macdonald, Frank. 2005. *A Forest for Calum*. Sydney, N.S.: Cape Breton University Press.

MacDonald, Mary Janet, Betty Matheson, Diane Milligan and Dolena Roach. 1994. *No Less No More - Just Four On The Floor: A Guide to Teaching Traditional Cape Breton Square Sets for Public Schools*. 4th ed. Halifax: DANS - Dance Nova Scotia.

MacDonald, Paul M. 1999. Irish Music in Cape Breton. In *The Irish in Cape Breton*. Ed. A. A. MacKenzie, 119-129. Wreck Cove: Breton Books.

MacDougall, John L. 1922. *History of Inverness County, Nova Scotia*. Privately printed.

MacEachen, Frances 1994-5. Music that will keep you alive and dancing in bed. *Am Bràighe*: Mabou: 8.

MacGillivray, Allister. 1988. *A Cape Breton Ceilidh*. Cape Breton: Sea-Cape Music Ltd.

———. 1997. *The Original - The Cape Breton Fiddler*. Marion Bridge: Sea-Cape Music Ltd.

MacGregor, John. 1828. *Historical and Descriptive Sketches of the Maritime Colonies of British America*. London: Longman, Rees, Orme, Brown, and Green.

MacInnes, Sheldon. 1996. Stepdancing: Gach taobh dhe'n Uisge (Both sides of the water). In *The Centre of the World at the Edge of a Continent*. Ed. C. Corbin and J. A. Rolls, 111-18. Sydney, Nova Scotia: University College of Cape Breton Press.

———. 1997. *A Journey in Celtic Music: Cape Breton Style*. Sydney, Nova Scotia: University College of Cape Breton Press.

MacLeod, Calum I. N. 1969. *Sgialachdan à Albainn Nuaidh (Scottish Gaelic Stories from Nova Scotia)*. Glasgow: Gairm.

———. 1974. *Stories from Nova Scotia*, Antigonish: Formac Limited.

MacNeil, Jenna. 1999. "Close to the Floor: Aggie MacLennan on traditional stepdancing." *Am Bràighe*: 15.

MacNeil, Joe Neil and John W. Shaw. 1987. *Tales until dawn: the world of a Cape Breton Gaelic story-teller*. Edinburgh: McGill-Queen's University Press and Edinburgh University Press.

Macqueen, Malcolm A. 1929. *Skye Pioneers and 'The Island'*. Winnipeg: Privately Printed.

Malm, Krister. 1993. "Music on the Move: Traditions and Mass Media." *Ethnomusicology* 37 (3): 339-52.

Manuel, Peter, ed. .2009. *Creolizing Contradance in the Caribbean*. Philadelphia: Temple University Press.

Mauss, Marcel. 1979. Body Techniques. In *Sociology and Psychology: Essays*. Ed. B. Brewster, 95-123. London: Routledge and Kegan Paul.

McDonald, Barry. 1996. "The Idea of Tradition Examined in the Light of Two Australian Musical Studies." *Yearbook for Traditional Music* 28:106-30.

McCarthy, Mary. 1999. *Passing it on: The Transmission of Music in Irish Culture*. Cork: Cork University Press.

McDavid, Jodi. 2008. "The Fiddle Burning Priest of Mabou." *Ethnologies* 30 (2): 115-36.

McEwan-Fujita, Emily. 2013. Gaelic Revitalization Efforts in Nova Scotia: Reversing Language Shift in the 21st Century. In *Celts in the Americas*. Ed. M. Newton, 160-86. Sydney, Nova Scotia: Cape Breton University Press,

McKean, Thomas 1998. "Celtic Music and the Growth of the Feis Movement in the Scottish Highlands." *Western Folklore* 57 (4): 245-59.

McLean, Marianne. 1991. *The People of Glengarry, Highlanders in Transition, 1745-1820*. Montreal: McGill-Queen's University Press.

Melin, Mats. 2005. Putting the dirt back in" - an investigation of step dancing in Scotland. MA thesis, University of Limerick.

———. 2006. Unpublished research notes on observations on dance in Scotland and Cape Breton 1985-2006. Melin personal archive, Limerick, Ireland.

———. 2010. Gendered Movements in Cape Breton step dancing. In *Proceedings of the 26th Symposium of the ICTM Study Group on Ethnochoreology 2012*, Trest, Czech Republic. Ed. E. I. Dunin, D. Stavelova, D. Gremlicova and Z. Vejvoda, 37-47. Prague: Institute of Ethnology of the Academy of Sciences of the Czech Republic.

———. 2012. Exploring the Percussive Routes and Shared Commonalities in Cape Breton Step Dancing. PhD dissertation, University of Limerick.

———. 2013a. "Step Dancing in Cape Breton and Scotland: Contrasting Contexts and Creative Processes." *MUSICultures. Special Issue: Atlantic Roots and Routes* 40 (1): 35-56.

———. 2013b. Unpublished research notes on observations on dance in Cape Breton, Scotland and Ireland 2006-2013. Melin personal archive, Limerick, Ireland.

———. 2014. The Elusive Nature of References and Recollections of Percussive Step Dance in Scotland. Unpublished.

Merriam, Alan P. 1974. "Anthropology and the Dance." *CORD New Dimensions in Dance Research: Anthropology or Dance*: 9-27.

Moore, Margaret. 1994. Cape Breton Dancing [Online title: Scottish Step Dancing] In *Scotland's Dances: A review of the 1994 Conference on the Diversity of the Scottish Traditions of Dance – October 25-26, Albert Hall, Stirling.* 17-21. Edinburgh: Scottish Arts Council. http://www.ibiblio.org/pub/academic/languages/gaelic/ssd.txt. Accessed January 31, 2015.

Morgan, Robert J. 2000. *Early Cape Breton: from founding to famine, 1784-1851: essays, talks and conversations.* Toronto: Breton Books.

———. 2008. *Rise Again!: The Story of Cape Breton Island. Book 1.* Toronto: Breton Books.

———. 2009. *Rise Again!: The Story of Cape Breton Island. From 1900 to Today, Book 2.* Toronto: Breton Books.

Morin, Mac [Hompepage]. http://www.macmorin.com/bio.htm. Accessed January 23, 2011).

Murphy, Joe. 2012. CBC News extract on Gaelic in Cape Breton. Broadcast January 31.

Ness, Sally-Ann. 1992. *Body, Movement, and Culture: Kinesthetic and Visual Symbolism in a Philippine Community.* Philadelphia: University of Pennsylvania Press.

———. 1996. Dancing in the Field: notes from memory. In *Corporealities: Dancing Knowledge. Culture and Power.* Ed. S. L. Foster, 129-54. London and New York: Routledge.

Nettl, Bruno. 1964. *Theory and Method in Ethnomusicology.* New York: The Free Press of Glencoe.

———. 1982. Types of Tradition and Transmission. In *Cross-cultural perspectives on music.* Ed. R. Falck, T. Rice and M. Kolinski, 3-19. Toronto: University of Toronto Press.

———. 2005. *The Study of Ethnomusicology: Thirty-One Issues and Concepts,* Urbana and Chicago: University of Illinois Press.

Newton, Michael S. 2009. *Warriors of the word: the world of the Scottish Highlanders.* Edinburgh: Birlinn.

Nilsson, Mats. 1997. Den Tidlösa Traditionen. In *Brottningar med begrepp.* Ed. B. Skarin-Frykman and H. Brembeck, 101-14. Gothenburg: Etnologiska Föreningen i Sverige.

Noland, Carrie and Sally Ann Ness, eds. 2008. *Migrations of Gesture,* Minneapolis and London: University of Minnesota Press.

Oldenburg, Ray. 1989. *The Great Good Place: Cafes, Coffee Shops, Community Centers, Beauty Parlors, General Stores, Bars, Hangouts, and How They Get You Through the Day.* New York: Paragon House.

———. 2000. *Celebrating the Third Place: Inspiring Stories about the "Great Good Places" at the Heart of Our Communities.* New York: Marlowe and Company.

Ong, Walter. 1967. *The Presence of the Word: Some Prolegomena for Cultural and Religious History.* New Haven: Yale University Press.

Peacock, Francis. 1805. *Sketches relative to the history and theory, but more especially to the practice and art of dancing ... Intended as hints to the young teachers of the art of dancing.* Aberdeen: J. Chalmers and Co.

Phillips, Mark Salber and Gordon Schochet, eds. 2004. *Questions of Tradition.* Toronto: University of Toronto Press.

Pike, Kenneth. 1954. *Language in Relation to a Unified Theory of Structure and Human Behaviour.* Glendale California: Summer Institute of Linguistics.

Quigley, Colin. 2008. Step Dancing in Canada: From Shared Vernacular to Regional Styles. In *Close to the Floor - Irish Dance From the Boreen to Broadway.* Ed. M. Moloney, J. A. Morrison and C. Quigley, 35-46. Madison: Macater Press.

Radcliffe-Brown, Alfred R. 1964. *The Andaman Islanders.* New York: The Free Press.

Radestock, Rudolph. 1877. The royal ball-room guide and etiquette of the drawing-room, containing the newest and most elegant dances and a short history of dancing. London: W. Walker and Sons. Available at: http://hdl.loc.gov/loc.music/musdi.140. Accessed: March 7, 2015.

Rankin, L. (1996) "Introduction to Traditional Step dancing: A quick lesson for children and adults," *Gaelic Cape Breton: 1996 Visitors Supplement,* Mabou, Cape Breton, Sandy Publishing Ltd.: 5.

Rendall, Barbara. 1996. A Sense of Family. In *The Centre of the World at the Edge of a Continent. Cultural Studies of Cape Breton Island.* Ed. C. Corbin and J. A. Rolls, 191-96. Sydney Nova Scotia: University College of Cape Breton Press.

Rhodes, Frank. 1985. Dancing in Cape Breton Island, Nova Scotia. In *Traditional Dancing in Scotland.* 267-85. J.F. Flett and T. M. Flett. London: Routledge and Keegan Paul.

———. 1996. Step-Dancing in Cape Breton Island, Nova Scotia. In *Traditional Step Dancing in Scotland.* 185-211. J. F. Flett and T. M. Flett. Edinburgh: Scottish Cultural Press.

Richards, Eric. 2008. *The Highland Clearances.* Edinburgh: Birlinn Ltd.

Rice, Timothy. 2008. Toward a Mediation of Field Methods and Field Experience in Ethnomusicology. In *Shadows in the Field: New Perspectives for Fieldwork in Ethnomusicology.* 2nd ed. Ed. G. Barz and T. J. Cooley, 42-61. New York: Oxford University Press.

Ricoeur, Paul. 1981. *Paul Ricoeur hermeneutics and the human sciences: essays on language, action and interpretation.* Trans., ed. and introduced by John B. Thompson. Cambridge: Cambridge University Press.

Rogers, Ellis. 2002. *Five Basic Quadrilles. Three French and Two Scottish Quadrilles of the early 19th century.* Orpington: Ellis Rogers.

———. 2008 [2003]. *The Quadrille,* 4 ed., Orpington: C. and E. Rogers.

Rosenberg, Neil V. 1993. Introduction. In *Transforming Tradition: Folk Music Revivals Examined.* Ed. N. V. Rosenberg, 1-25. Urbana and Chicago: University of Illinois Press.

Royce, Anya. P. 2002. *The Anthropology of Dance.* Alton, UK: Dance Books.

———. 2004. *Anthropology of the Performing Arts. Artistry, Virtuosity, and Interpretation in a Cross-Cultural Perspective.* Lanham: Altamira Press.

———. 2008. An Aesthetic of the Ordinary: Embodying Zapotec gesture, movement, and craft. Unpublished paper presented at *Annual meetings of the American Anthropological Association.* San Francisco, California, November 19-23, 2008.

Saussure, Ferdinand de. 1998 [1972]. *Course in General Linguistics, Open Court Classics.* Chicago: Open Court Publishing Co.

Schack, Thomas. 2010. Building blocks and architecture of dance. In *The Neurocognition of Dance: Mind, Movement and Motor Skills.* Ed. B. Bläsing, M. Puttke and T. Schack,11-39. Hove, East Sussex (England), and New York: Psychology Press.

Schapiro, Meyer. 1962. Style. In *Anthropology today: Selections.* Ed. S. Tax, 278-303. Chicago: The University of Chicago Press.

Shaw, John W. 1992-93. "Language, Music and Local Aesthetics. Views from Gaeldom and Beyond." *Scottish Language* 11/12: 37-61.

———. ed. 2000. *Brigh an òrain - a story in every song: the songs and tales of Lauchie MacLellan,* Montreal, London: McGill-Queen's University Press.

Shears, Barry W. 2008. *Dance to the Piper: The Highland Bagpipe in Nova Scotia.* Sydney, Nova Scotia: Cape Breton University Press.

Shils, Edward. 1981. *Tradition.* Chicago: University of Chicago Press.

Sklar, Deidre. 1991. "On Dance Ethnography." *Dance Research Journal* 23 (1): 6-10.

———. 2008. Remembering Kinesthesia: An Inquiry into Embodied Cultural Knowledge. In *Migrations of Gesture.* Ed. C. Noland and S. A. Ness, 85-111. Minneapolis: University of Minnesota Press.

Small, Christopher. 1998. *Musicking: the meanings of performing and listening, Music/culture.* Middletown: Wesleyan University Press.

Smout, Thomas C. 1987. *A Century of the Scottish People 1830-1950.* London: Fontana Press.

———. 1990. *A History of the Scottish People 1560-1830.* London: Fontana Press.

Somers, Robert. 1985 [1848]. *Letters from the Highlands on the Famine of 1846.* Melven Press.

Spalding, Susan E. and Jane H. Woodside. eds. 1995. *Communities in Motion. Dance, Community, and Tradition in America's Southeast and Beyond.* Westport: Greenwood Press.

Sparling, Heather L. 1999. "Mitigating or Marketing Culture? Promoting Mouth Music in Cape Breton, Nova Scotia." *Canadian Journal for Traditional Music/Revue de Musique Folklorique Canadienne* 27:1-9.

———. 2000. Puirt-A-Beul: An Ethnographic Study of Mouth Music in Cape Breton. MA thesis, York University.

———. 2003. "Music is Language and Language is Music: Language Attitudes and Musical Choices in Cape Breton, Nova Scotia." *Ethnologies* 25 (2): 145-71.

———. 2005. Song Genres, Cultural Capital and Social Distinctions in Gaelic Cape Breton. PhD dissertation, York University.

———. 2014. *Reeling Roosters and Dancing Ducks: Celtic Mouth Music.* Sydney, Nova Scotia: Cape Breton University Press.

Spradley, James. P. 1980. *Participant Observation,* New York: Holt, Rinehart and Winston.

Stokes, Martin. 2004. "Music and the Global Order." *Annual Review of Anthropology* 33:47-72.

Thompson, Marie. 2003. The fall and rise of the Cape Breton fiddler: 1955–1982. MA thesis, Saint Mary's University.

Thomson, Derick S., ed. 1983. *The Companion to Gaelic Scotland.* Oxford: Basil Blackwell Ltd.

Titon, Jeff Todd. 2008. Knowing Fieldwork. In *Shadows in the Field: New Perspectives for Fieldwork in Ethnomusicology.* 2nd ed. Ed. G. Barz and T. J. Cooley, 25-41. New York: Oxford University Press.

Topham, Edward. 1776. *Letters from Edinburgh written in the years 1774 and 1775,* Edinburgh (London).

Trew, Johanne. D. 2009. *Place, Culture and Community: The Irish Heritage of the Ottawa Valley.* Newcastle upon Tyne: Cambridge Scholars Publishing.

Turino, Thomas. 2008. *Music as Social Life: The Politics of Participation.* Chicago: University of Chicago Press.

Turner, Victor. 1974. *Dramas, Fields, and Metaphors: Symbolic Action in Human Society.* Ithaca: Cornell University Press.

Urry, John. 1995. *Consuming Places, International Library of Sociology,* London: Routledge.

Veblen, Kari K. 1991. Perceptions of change and stability in the transmissions of Irish traditional music: an examination of the music teacher's role/ Kari Kristin Veblen. PhD dissertation, University of Wisconsin-Madison.

Voyer, Simonne. 2003. *La Gigue, danse de pas.* Ed. GID. Quebec: Les Éditions GID.

Williams, Drid. 1991. *Ten Lectures on Theories of the Dance.* Metuchen, N.J. and London: The Scarecrow Press.

Videography

Alexander, Mike. 1985. *Down-Home with Aly Bain in North America: Cape Breton and Quebec.* UK: A Pelicula Film, Channel Four Television.

Fraser, Willie Francis. 2004. *God Bless Your Feet.* Canada: Red Liquorice Films. [n.n.]. DVD recording.

MacDonald, Mary Janet. 1992. *One Step at a Time.* Port Hood. [n.n.]. Video recording.

MacDonald, Mary Janet. 2002 [1999]. *A Family Tradition. A Cape Breton Stepdancing Instructional Video with Mary Janet MacDonald.* St George's Bay, Antigonish, Nova Scotia: SeaBright Productions / Peter Murphy. [n.n.]. DVD [video] recording.

MacNeil, Jean. 2005. *Spring in your Step - Cape Breton Stepdance Instruction from Beginner to Intermediate.* Sydney Mines: CapeBretonSteps. [n.n.]. DVD recording.

Index